NORTHERN SUNS

NORTHERN
SUNS

Edited by
David G. Hartwell & Glenn Grant

TOR®

A Tom Doherty Associates Book
New York

NORTHERN SUNS

A Tor Book
Published by Tom Doherty Associates, Inc.
175 Fifth Avenue
New York, NY 10010

Tor Books on the World Wide Web:
http://www.tor.com

Tor® is a registered trademark of Tom Doherty Associates, Inc.

ISBN 0-312-86461-2

First Edition: April 1999

Printed in the United States of America

0 9 8 7 6 5 4 3 2 1

ACKNOWLEDGMENTS

ACKNOWLEDGMENTS

David and I are indebted to the many editors and publishers in whose magazines and books these stories first appeared. In particular, we appreciate the gracious assistance of Candas Jane Dorsey and the Tesseracts imprint of the Books Collective, publishers of the *Tesseracts* series of Canadian SF anthologies. Many thanks also to Jena Snyder, Cath Jackel, and everyone in the Copper Pig Writers' Society, publishers of *On Spec* magazine.

We are also indebted to everyone who recommended stories, who supplied books and magazines, who provided addresses, who cajoled, commented, and otherwise contributed—especially (though not limited to): Mark Shainblum, John Dupuis, Jean-Louis Trudel, Yves Meynard, Peter Halasz, Allan Weiss, Wayne Malkin and Derryl Murphy (for the wonderful *Senary*), Joelle Kovach (for asking timely questions), Robert J. Sawyer, the helpful staff of the Merril Collection of the Toronto Public Library, and all the good folks at Montreal's specialty bookshop, Nebula.

For providing so many great excuses to get together, our gratitude to the organizers of the 1994 World Science Fiction Convention/Conadian in Winnipeg, ConCept/Boréal in Montreal, AdAstra in Toronto, CanCon in Ottawa, and Readercon in Worcester and Westborough, Massachusetts.

Our researches were greatly assisted by the membership of SF Canada, our national association of SF and Fantasy writers, through its e-mail listserver (thanks to Karl Shroeder) and its bilingual newsletters, *Communiqué* and *Top Secret*. For information on membership, or nonmember subscriptions to *Communiqué*, contact: SF Canada, 18030, 95A Avenue, Edmonton, AB, Canada T5T 2Z6; or look for SF Canada on the Web.

In memory of
Henry G. Hartwell (1907–1998),
who encouraged me to visit Montreal in 1959.
—David G. Hartwell

For the Montreal Commune;
forward the Revolution!
(I'll bring the root beer.)
—Glenn Grant

And in memory of Judith Merril (1923–1997),
catalyst and questioner.

CONTENTS

INTRODUCTION
ANOTHER MUSIC FROM A DIFFERENT KITCHEN

Glenn Grant

Welcome to the Canadian Invasion.

Over the past few decades, science fiction, a genre largely founded by the French and British and industrialized by Americans, has been rapidly metastasizing around the globe, becoming a true world literature. Writers all over the planet are picking up the bug, increasingly seized with the need to grapple with the future, to play with other possibilities, to transform the past and present into new and unfamiliar landscapes. From Australia to Japan, from Russia to Brazil, carriers of the science fiction contagion are taking it apart, analyzing its workings, and carefully mutating it under laboratory conditions. They cut out bits of code here and there, keep the pieces they like, and inject their own data sequences into science fiction's viral program. In their hands, SF is transformed into a vector for new cultural attitudes and fresh perspectives, a medium for previously unheard voices.

We're talking *memes,* here. As genes are the basic unit of biological evolution, memes are the basic unit of ideas, according to evolutionary biologist Richard Dawkins, who coined the term in his book *The Selfish Gene.* Just as a viral invader will induce an organism to produce more copies of the virus, a meme is an idea that infects your brain, playing off your emotional and intellectual faculties, making you want to reproduce the meme. Like I'm doing right now, exposing you to the Meta-meme, the meme about memes.

A literary genre can be considered as a whole complex of memes, a collection of ideas that have coevolved as a symbiotic colony organism. As a genre matures, its defining memes become ever more sophisticated and elaborate, calving off diverse subgenres and stylistic schools. Florid and shocking hybrids start to appear, as mad doctor-authors, hidden in their literary laboratories, conduct blasphemous experiments in generic cross-breeding and memetic engineering. Readers adopt some of these brave new subgenres, adapt slowly to others, and let the unsuccessful subspecies fade into extinction.

Memes, like all forms of life, are constantly expanding their territories. The SF meme complex has now leapt across barriers of nationality and language, infiltrated past the defenses of geography and culture. It propagates ever more rapidly as it sweeps through previously unexposed populations. Local strains flare up: Spanish SF; Hong Kong Fantasy; Congolese Magic Realism; Canadian SpecFic . . .

In the age of global media, memes carom back and forth around the planet without regard for mere imaginary boundaries. Canadian science fiction, a youthful and vibrant community of memes, has begun to radiate back into the genre's original breeding ground: more Canadian novels are appearing from American SF publishers than ever before, and more Canadian short stories are showing up in the major U.S. magazines. Canadians are picking up Hugos and Nebulas, Tiptrees and Bram Stoker awards. They're becoming downright pandemic.

Northern Suns isn't the first wave of the Canadian Invasion. This book is a companion volume to our earlier foray, *Northern Stars*, published as a hardcover by Tor Books in 1994, and as a trade paperback in 1998. Just like its predecessor, *Northern Suns* is a far-ranging cross section of the best contemporary Canadian science fiction. Again, we've defined "Canadian authors" as citizens who write here (at least part of the time), or immigrants writing in Canada, or citizens who write elsewhere but identify themselves as Canadian writers when asked.

As we'll readily admit, some of our best and brightest are abductees—er, immigrants, such as American-born authors William Gibson, Spider Robinson, and Robert Charles Wilson. But for decades we've been busily breeding up a whole army of home-grown memetic shock troops, with names like Candas Jane Dorsey, Charles de Lint, James Alan Garder, Yves Meynard, and Robert Sawyer. All of these authors and more can be found in our first volume, *Northern Stars.*

But Canada is incubating far too many good SF writers to fit into a single book. Thus, this second compendium, collecting an entirely new roster of authors, none of whom appeared in our previous anthology, including world-renowned masters as well as the most brilliant new lights on the scene. Here you'll find twenty-one great stories of cutting-edge SF, ranging from hard science fiction to visionary fantasy, from the horrific to the hilarious. Plus, an essay by John Clute, and an updated reference list of the winners of the major Canadian SF and fantasy awards. And we're still a long way from exhausting Canada's considerable pool of impressive SF writing talent.

You may well ask, what makes Canadian SF particularly Canadian?

Well, to begin with, it's written by Canadians. This observation is not quite as unnecessary as it might seem: until we start to isolate the Canadian SF strain from the U.S. and the U.K. genotypes, it's impossible to say whether there are any distinctive characteristics that unite works of Canadian SF. Until the mid-eighties, this wasn't really possible; there were too few published Canadian SF authors to form a coherent theory. Too few points on the graph to project a curve, as it were. But now that there's a substantial and rapidly growing body of work to consider, we can begin to take a stab at answering the question. (Don't expect too many unequivocal answers from me: I'd rather just present the data—these stories—and let you plot your own curves.)

Now, we're not going to identify any characteristics common to the work of *all* Canadian SF authors, just as there are no commonalities uniting all of their American or British counterparts. Anything we say is necessarily going to be a gross generalization, and rather preliminary, considering the youthfulness of the Canadian SF field. But Canadian SF *as a whole* can certainly be said to have a very different history, as compared to American and British SF, and this distinctive evolution has certainly influenced the styles of SF written here.

First of all, the modern genre of British/American SF evolved out of the commercial pulp fiction markets of the early twentieth century. By contrast, Canada has had *no* indigenous pulp-SF industry (except for a few brief, inglorious years during WWII), while the major book publishers have virtually ignored science fiction (let alone Canadian SF) as if it didn't exist. Thus, any Canadians interested in getting published as SF authors (such as A. E. Van Vogt and Phyllis Gotlieb) had to write for American markets, shaping their work to fit the expectations of American editors and American readers.

GLENN GRANT

The alternative was to write for Canadian magazines and publishers, which would be more open to specifically Canadian concerns and sensibilities. But nearly all Canadian fiction magazines are literary reviews, published mainly by university presses which only rarely touch science fiction and fantasy. Most are nonpaying markets, in some cases supported by government grants. A few literary editors in Canada have been interested in genre work, rather unusually for that field; generally speaking, their American and British equivalents would rather die than publish "sci-fi."

Being published by literary presses seems to have had an impact on the flavor, style, and form of Canadian speculative fiction produced prior to the 1980s. As a result, early Canadian-published SF was, in the main, more literary and less commercial than American or British SF. At the same time, it was often not recognized as speculative fiction, simply because it wasn't published that way. It was seen as "fabulation," "allegory," "surrealism," or something along those lines. Consider, as an extreme case, the speculative work of Margaret Atwood (such as her story, "Freeforall," here in *Northern Suns*); I have met numerous Can-Lit readers who—having been inoculated against genre writing by their university professors—refuse to believe that *The Handmaid's Tale* is a science fiction novel. Apparently, if a work scores high on the scale of literary quality, it somehow escapes from genre classification, regardless of its setting and subject matter.

The francophone SF scene in Canada has (of course) a distinct history. There have been two continuously published French-language magazines for two decades, *Solaris* (since 1974) and *imagine* . . . (since 1979). As for SF books in Quebec, most are published by specialty presses or young adult imprints. Literary influences used to be mostly one-way, with Francophones reading works by Anglos either in English or in translation. However, more Anglo Canadians are reading the Francophones than ever before, thanks to the *Tesseracts* series of SF anthologies, especially *Tesseracts*^{Q} (edited by Elisabeth Vonarburg and Jane Brierley), a book of Franco-Canadian SF translated into English. The two communities are increasingly overlapping and influencing each other.

So here's one of the major unique features of Canadian science fiction's meme-complex: we're a bilingual subculture, and hopefully this will be reflected in the work of authors on both sides of the linguistic fence. Franco-Canadian SF is influenced by French and other European SF, which is often in the mode of the "Fantastique," tending toward surrealism, allegory, and folktale, rather than in the extrapolative science fiction mode favored by Americans and Brits. Many Francophone Canadian authors seem to seek a synthesis of these two modes.

For much of the recent crossing over between linguistic cultures, we can thank a number of tireless, creative, and dedicated women. In stark contrast with the male-dominated early history of American and British SF, the Canadian scene was predominantly founded on the hard work and community-building spirit of several important women.

First, in the 1960s, Phyllis Gotlieb virtually *was* Canadian SF; no other Canadian was publishing SF as regularly, or making such a mark on the field. She remains active today, as a writer, and as poetry editor of the speculative fiction magazine, *Transversions*.

In 1968, the influential "New Wave" anthology editor Judith Merril moved from New York to Toronto, where, in the early seventies, she founded the first civic SF library in the world, the Spaced Out Library (now the Merril Collection). She began to notice some interesting commonalities between the nascent CanLit field and Science Fiction: "Sometimes it was overt SF imagery, or a certain way of thinking about the environment, a casual mixture of magic-and-realism," she wrote, in her excellent essay in the first *Tesseracts* (reprinted in *Northern Stars*). "CanLit, I was told, is about *survival* and, characteristically, the environment may become almost a character in the story! Of course! Just like SF."

In Quebec, there is Élisabeth Vonarburg, an immigrant from France. Besides being one of our better-known writers, she has edited SF anthologies and magazines in both languages, translated stories and novels, sat on the Canada Council's Quebec board, organized some of the first national SF writer's conferences, and she's a member of the Tesseracts publishing collective. Her role as a bridge-builder between the Anglo and Francophone communities has been particularly catalytic.

Out west, in Edmonton, there's Candas Jane Dorsey, one of our finest writers, and the main force behind the Tesseracts publishing collective (originally founded by Gerry Truscott as an imprint of Beach Holme). A poet, editor, publisher, and activist, Dorsey also works on building connections between our SF and literary communities. She is also on the editorial board of *On Spec*, the first national English Canadian SF magazine, where an impressive group of women have been among the prime movers.

The formative years of Canadian SF, then, have been shaped by women, every bit as much as by men, a situation unique in the world. This *must* have an effect on the fiction we produce.

In sum, we can say that Canadian SF is Canadian because of several unique historical conditions, including language, landscape, literary publishing, lack of a pulp tradition, and a lot of women.

The Canadian Invasion continues apace. Resistance is useless. You will be absorbed. But you need not be afraid. We mean you no harm. We come in peace, bearing the fruits of science-fictional lab experiments. Indeed, ours is a benevolent meme-complex, a healthy infection, designed to improve your life, transform your perceptions, awaken your mind to new vistas of possibility. The treatment is completely painless. Well, mostly.

As you read this book, you'll probably experience moments of disorientation, dislocation, and cognitive estrangement. Most test subjects report occasional periods of exhilaration, hysterical laughing jags, and rapid heartbeat, interspersed with flashes of stark terror. We're certain you'll find the experience exciting, enlightening, and ultimately rewarding.

Let's begin. . . .

FREEFORALL

Margaret Atwood

Margaret Atwood, poet, novelist, and critic, is one of the great living Canadian writers. *The Handmaid's Tale* (1985), winner of the Governor General's Award (Canada), the Los Angeles Times Prize (U.S.), and the first Arthur C. Clarke Award (U.K.) in 1986, is her one SF novel to date, a significant feminist dystopia that puts her in the company of such writers as Ursula K. Le Guin, Marge Piercy, and Joanna Russ. John Clute says of the tale of Offred the Handmaid, "Offred's liquid telling of her tale, and her ambivalent disappearance into death or liberation as the book closes, make for a novel whose context leads, liberatingly, out of nightmare into the pacific Inuit culture of the frame. *The Handmaid's Tale* soon gained a reputation as the best SF novel ever produced by a Canadian." She has often turned to the fantastic in her career: in her poetry, such as *You Are Happy* (1974), which includes a reworking of *The Odyssey* from Circe's perspective, her third novel *Lady Oracle* (1976), a parody of fairy tales and gothic romances, and in her story collections, such as *Bluebeard's Egg* (1983) and *Good Bones* (1992). She has also published an essay on the supernatural in Canadian literature in John Robert Colombo's SF anthology, *Other Canadas*.

"Freeforall" was originally published in *The Toronto Star*, and later in *Tesseracts*[2] (1987, ed. Douglas Barbour), the second in what has become the premier original anthology series of current Canadian SF (seven volumes have appeared to date) founded by Gerry Truscott and Judith Merril in 1985. It is one of two short stories in the small cluster of specifically SF works by Atwood in the 1980s. *The McClelland & Stewart World Encyclopedia* says, "In all her writing her careful craftsmanship and precision of language, which give a sense of inevitability and a resonance to her words, are recognized." It is clearly and definitively a science fiction story, and one in dialogue with her most famous novel.

Sharmayne Pia Veronica Humbolt Grey signed her full legal name on the line provided, reflecting as always that she wished her mother hadn't read so many movie magazines while pregnant, or was it comic books? Whatever they'd read in those days, while chewing gum and fixing up their pony tails and lounging around in blue jeans—blue jeans!—with their legs up over the furniture. Her mother must have thought that those names were the last word in glamour. For her first thirty years, her names had been one of Sharmayne's most cherished grudges. Over the next fifty years she'd grown used to them; fond of them even, as if they were ancient scars, familiar birthmarks. When she was younger, everyone called her Sharm. Now even her names were being eroded by time; except to old friends—not many of those left—she was mostly just First Mother.

She added the date, 14 June 2026—she still liked the idea of a June wedding, and though a lot was different now, the orange blossom had remained—and sealed the document with the Least House seal. The image on it was vestigial, an icon left over from the early days of the House. It showed two figures that looked like old-fashioned key holes, a knob topping a triangle, one big, the other smaller, two sticks for legs protruding out the bottoms. They were supposed to be a mother and child, though you wouldn't know if you weren't told, Sharmayne had always thought. She herself knew since she'd been there when they'd been cooking it up. They'd all sat around the table, in what was then the dining room but was now the First Mothers' Boardroom, drinking coffee and, in fact, beer, and laughing with excitement. They'd made up the House motto that day, too. *The Least Of These.* Too churchy, Sharmayne had thought then, but it had helped to raise money, which Lord knows they'd always needed more of, in those days. She remembered with distaste the thick plates, the strictly utilitarian bedspreads, the green garbage bags bulging with cast-off clothes, some of them none too clean, donated by women who were better off, luckier. Back then they'd taken anything they could get, and thankful for it. Now of course money was no longer a problem.

Sharmayne stood up, steadying herself against her desk, and turned toward the full-length mirror she'd had them put into her office two years ago, after the day she'd walked into General Meeting with her skirt caught up in the back and hadn't noticed until some of the young girls had started to giggle. Young girls still giggled, young boys still sniggered, that hadn't changed and probably never would. She didn't want to give them any extra excuses, however. If she was looking more than usually ridiculous she wanted to be the first to spot it.

She checked herself over, starting with the shoes. Bride of Frankenstein shoes, she called them to herself; orthopedic to the point of despair, but she was well past breaking her neck for vanity. No laces undone; too bad about the puffy ankles, but what could you expect at eighty? Blue silk skirt where it should be, long sleeves with ruffles at the knuckles, a little bow at the throat, hiding all that uncooked turkey skin, the House seal in silver, on a single string of pearls around her neck. She skimmed over her face—it was a good serviceable face, but worn out by now, of course—pushed back a few strands of hair, darned if she'd dye it like that cow First Mother Mabel, henna red at seventy-nine, and straightened up as much as she could, bent spine despite the calcium pills. Today she was a figurehead and had to look decently like one, but she was more than that. They didn't just wheel her out for special occasions: she still made some of the decisions around here, important ones for which her kind of experience was needed. She'd picked the bride, for instance.

And she'd done the deal too, though it hadn't been any pleasure and she'd had a headache for a day afterward. That old hag First Mother Corinna from Sheltering Wings drove a hard bargain, she always had. But Sharmayne was no slouch herself—in the old days, they'd always put her in charge of handling the overdraft problems with the banks—and she knew she had an ace up her sleeve, the reputation of Least House itself. She had good stock to trade with, and everyone knew it, including Corinna. Sharmayne had calculated that in a pinch, and despite her bluffing, Corinna would sacrifice a bit on the financial end to get a guaranteed pure product, and that's exactly what she'd done. No one from Least House had ended up in the Freeforall for anyway fifteen years. Sheltering Wings was good that way, too. Rumor had it they were still into turkey basters over there, but Sharmayne was no purist. She didn't give a hoot how they did it, as long as the results panned out. Though turkey basters would be hard on poor Tom, after all those First-Night Sensitivity training sessions. She'd hinted as much to Corinna during the bargaining sessions, and Corinna had spluttered and denied everything and turned a satisfying shade of red. Sharmayne started walking, which, she had to admit, was becoming more and more of a major project these days. She made her way, left

foot, cane, right foot, out the door and along the corridor, pausing to lean against the wall, which she wouldn't have done if
anyone had been watching. Here was the door to the guest suite,
for the visiting officials from other Houses; down the hall—left
foot, cane—was the door to the guest-suite nursery, still done in
late-twentieth-century Montessori. Sharmayne favored antiques;
they gave her nostalgia, an emotion she'd brusquely repressed
in mid-life but now felt free to indulge.

She leaned against the guest nursery door, looking in, remembering the glee with which they'd selected the blocks, the
little red and yellow table and chairs, at sale prices of course,
gloating over their bargains. Bargoons, they used to call them.
Funny, the way the Houses had started, back then: shoestring
operations, all of them. They'd been single houses then, in the
less affluent parts of the cities; they didn't take up three or four
blocks each, the way they did now. Homes for battered wives
they'd been originally, or shelters for abused teenage girls; a couple of them had begun as lesbian co-ops. All that idealistic fringe
self-help stuff, lumpy porridge and instant coffee. Sharmayne
still felt that one of the true luxuries of life was real coffee.

It made her cringe, thinking about how earnest and, to tell
the truth, pompous and self-righteous they'd been once, herself
included; but if it hadn't been for them, where would everyone
be now? Even the politicians, even the men in power had come
to see eventually that the House way might be the only way the
human race, or at least this part of it, could make it to the next
generation. The Houses had seen quite early on that the old hit-
or-miss courtship rituals, the old lax lip-service monogamy, just
couldn't work anymore; the price in life, or rather death, had
become too high. But most people had taken more convincing.
Sharmayne remembered the newspaper headlines, the schools
and offices closed down, whole towns and suburbs sealed off;
the forced testing, the breakdown of the health-care system, the
witch-hunts, the civil rights cases, first won, then lost again and
again as hysteria took over. Then there had been the hospital
riots, patients dragged into the streets by angry mobs, the ring-
leaders wearing asbestos fire-fighting suits, the smell of spilled
gasoline and burning flesh.

It hadn't been just one disease. One could have been dealt
with in the usual ways. It had been a whole arsenal of them, one
after another, so many that sabotage or biological warfare experiments gone out of control had been suspected, though how

could you ever prove anything like that? The new diseases had made the herpes and penicillin-resistant gonorrhea of the 1970s, the AIDS and chlamydia of the '80s, look as innocuous as a runny nose. They spread faster, they killed faster; some mutated so quickly they could not even be spotted by testing. Men or women could carry them for years, undetected, spreading them everywhere. They all had one thing in common: they were sexually transmitted. In the end, after the rubber body stockings and the Safe-T-Lips "for kissing with confidence" had been tried and had failed too often, after the virginity certificates had proven susceptible to forgery, after the Gentlemen's Chastity Society had ended in total washout, there was only one sure-fire defense against them. If you couldn't control the diseases, you had to avoid contact, any contact at all. That was when the Houses had begun to build walls and invest in barbed wire, electric fences, and broken glass. They had also begun to expel rule-breakers. "These are houses of sanctuary, and this is a state of siege," Sharmayne heard herself saying. She'd had to say it often enough, back then. "We must think of the children."

Sharmayne, wheezing a little too much for comfort, paused again on the skywalk that connected First House with Second House within the Least House compound. They could have torn down the individual houses and built some glass-and-steel monstrosity, like that Sheltering Wings carbuncle over in Park-dale, but Sharmayne preferred to have the houses look like real houses. It was more homey that way, though the nineteenth-century brick needed a lot of upkeep. The skywalk was one of her favorite vantage points. From here she could see the boys' play-ground, to the left, where the young boys were taught the rudiments of the War Games. Despite the earlier experiments with cooking classes and dolls' houses, some of them still seemed to prefer that sort of thing. To the right, separated from the boys by a high wall topped by the skywalk itself, was the girls' playground. Sharmayne remembered her own mother's stories about boys' and girls' playgrounds way back when, and how comical she'd once found them.

Down in the girls' playground, the twelve-year-olds were having a game of Life Decisions. Each team represented a House; the playground was marked out like a giant Monopoly board, with doll-house-sized houses. The game was played like Monopoly, too, though the rules had been changed to make the game fit in better with present-day reality. There were no more hotels; instead for each house on a property, you got a bride to trade with, and for each four brides a groom. Grooms were more valuable because, as everyone knew, it was harder to find un-contaminated ones. Among the Chance cards were cards representing the various diseases, and where the jail square had once been there was now a square marked Freeforall. From what Sharmayne recalled of Monopoly—and her memory was a little hazy on that score—you'd been able to get out of the jail square with a special card or several rolls of the dice. But once in the Freeforall, you were in for good.

The girls' voices floated up to Sharmayne, young, boisterous with high spirits, faint through the double glazing and her own diminished hearing. "That moldy cross-eyed earwig isn't worth any of my Grade A brides and two houses! I'll give you a Grade B and one!" "What, for that Freeforall reject? Get serious!" "Hurry up and roll before your nose falls off!" Sharmayne smiled at them, a little sadly. They had to learn the principles of bargaining somehow, but they were so innocent. They'd seen the telephoto propaganda films, of course, but it was still just pictures to them. They had no idea of what the Freeforalls were really like.

Each city now had a Freeforall of its own, or two or three, depending on how many were needed. Toronto had two: one was in a large area to the west that had once been a park, the other was to the north, in an abandoned adventure playground; abandoned since the time of the epidemics, when people habit-ually avoided large groups of strangers. Each Freeforall had its electric fences, its searchlights, its guard towers and dogs, though nobody, not even the guards, went into them. Food of a sort was dropped in daily by helicopter. In the Freeforalls, total sexual license was not only permitted but encouraged, because that way, it was thought, the inhabitants would finish each other off more quickly; although, it was rumored, you could develop an immunity, you could go into remission, you could survive for years. The babies, if there were any, were doomed. Some-times people took the fast way out and their bodies could be seen from a distance, dangling from the loops of the unused roller coaster, beside the artificial mountain that still—even in its present dilapidated state—appeared to promise some sort of frivolous and unfettered pleasure. Freedom, even; you could look at it that way.

Sharmayne shivered, thinking how swiftly she herself, the self of sixty years ago, would have been consigned to a Freeforall, had they existed then. When she'd been twenty, twenty-five, thirty, chastity had been out of style; the old nuclear family was disintegrating, everyone got divorced at least once, everyone fooled around, or so they were told. When she was twenty she'd listened to her mother's horror stories of life before the Pill— girls ruined for life, shotgun marriages, back street abortions on (how quaint!) kitchen tables—with smiles of polite disinterest. She and her friends had done more or less whatever they'd felt like at the moment, taking care, of course, to avoid anything that looked like a loser or a maniac. There had been a certain amount of talk about in-depth communicating and committed relationships, but sex was casual, not something to get warped about. In high school they'd had to study *Romeo and Juliet*, and it had seemed like something from another planet. She could still hear the boys, in the halls between classes, teasing each other in falsetto voices: "Romeo, Romeo, wherefore fart thou, Romeo?" They'd banned that play from their own House curriculum years ago. It gave the young people dangerous ideas.

Sharmayne peered down at her watch, big digits because of her eyes. She had to stop wool-gathering, or one of the others— someone bucking for First Mother—would start spreading rumors about Alzheimer's. On wedding days, now as then, lateness on the part of the groom was not appreciated. The ceremony was in an hour and a half, and she still had to collect poor Tom and his escort of Best Men and get them to the Assembly Hall. That zit Corrina would be there on the dot, with Sheltering Wings' big contribution to the future of the human race, and you could say big again. Though despite that she'd seemed a nice enough girl; though too rambunctious, as a lot of them were these days. During the interviews she'd asked a lot of pushy questions about height and eye color and other things that were none of her business. "That's the concern of the First Mothers," Sharmayne had finally told her. "We do the genetic planning around here. He's a good clean boy, he's perfect for you, that's all you need to know. Maybe a little temperamental, but just go easy with him at first and you'll do fine."

Left foot, Sharmayne recited to herself, cane, right foot, pause. It was the next hallway going across, or was it the next after that? Then there were some steps. She thought about the steps with dismay: three up, but even that was getting to be too much. She skipped over the steps in her head and went on to the Grooms' Room, where they always had the party the night before, all the married men of Least House, with the Senior Husbands in charge, getting the groom a little drunk and telling him jokes about women to defuse the terror, and staying with him all night to make sure he wouldn't run away. Not that there was anywhere to run, though one unfortunate boy had been found hiding in a laundry hamper.

Later on, much later on, when she herself was no longer alive, the diseases would be extinct, starved out; gone, like smallpox, for lack of carriers; the Freeforalls would be empty. Then maybe none of these constraints, these rules, these fears, would be necessary. Then men would be more like men again, or what she still thought of as men, though they might not remember how; wasn't it the Houses themselves that believed all social behavior was learned? Sharmayne sometimes had these disloyal thoughts; but that was just her nostalgia, a secret vice; she was getting soft in her old age.

She knew it was weakness, but nevertheless she felt sorry for the grooms, and sad about trading them away to another House; and this boy Tom was a favorite of hers. She wondered if she should tell him what a good bargain she'd made for the House on his behalf. Better not; it might give him a swelled head, and he'd need to keep his wits, and a low profile, during his time at Sheltering Wings. There'd been several husband-battering cases out of there in recent years; dismissed, of course, you couldn't disrupt the system; but still there was probably something to it. Just two children, she'd tell him, all you need is two, that's what's in the contract. After that you have a choice: you can stay at Sheltering Wings and assist in one of their businesses and work your way up to Senior Husband, it's not without perks, or you can get yourself traded to another House and try potluck that way, or you can elect the War Games. It will depend on what you feel like at the time. But do the two children first.

She wouldn't say anything about the turkey basters; it could be just a rumor, and why frighten the boy needlessly? After all, he was only sixteen. She'd pat his arm, cheer him up, tell him how good he looked, they liked that. She's a nice girl, she'd tell him, wide hips and not a germ in sight. Hardly even a pimple.

Then she'd arrange the veil, navy blue for boys, though still white for the girls, it went with the orange blossoms. Veils were obligatory these days. They covered a multitude of sins.

DIVISIONS

Eric Choi

Eric Choi was born in Hong Kong, grew up in Brampton, Ontario, and lives in Montreal, Quebec. He works at the Canadian Space Agency as an orbital dynamics engineer for Radarsat, Canada's first Earth-observation satellite and the first dedicated civilian radar-imaging satellite in the world. In 1994, he was the first winner of the Isaac Asimov and Baird Searles awards for his novelette "Dedication." His stories have appeared in *Asimov's*, *Science Fiction Age*, and in *Arrowdreams* (Nuage Editions, 1997), the first anthology of Canadian alternate history.

"Divisions" first appeared in the *Tesseracts^Q* anthology (Tesseract Books, 1997), edited by Robert J. Sawyer and Carolyn Clink. It was nominated for the 1998 Aurora Award in the category of Best Short-Form Work in English. The idea for the story, says Choi, "came from (of all places) an old exam question." This is an alternate history story about the Canadian space program in the early 1980s, and how it might have been complicated by the breakup of Canada into Francophone and Anglophone countries had the 1981 Quebec Referendum resulted in the province's separation.

Château Laurier Hotel
Ottawa
4:41 P.M., June 12, 1981

Sir John A. Macdonald stared accusingly at her as she tore the country apart.

This thought crossed Jennifer Simcoe's mind every time she looked at the painting. The railroad built under Macdonald by scores of forgotten Chinese laborers, the iron that united the nation, was just partitioned last month. She wondered what Sir John A. would have thought of the cruel twists of history that had brought her—and Canada—to this place and time.

On May 20, 1980, 39.8 percent voted No in the Québec referendum.

The official day of secession would be June 24, 1981—St. Jean Baptiste Day. In one year, all the legal and political mechanics of separation had to be worked out. The British North America Act had to be amended because it didn't have a provision for provincial secession. Other issues included the transfer of federal powers, an equitable division of federal assets and the national debt, and the formation of a new economic union.

Jennifer Simcoe was a seasoned negotiator, having secured favorable agreements with the Soviets on wheat and India on CANDU reactors. Based on her record, Minister of State Bud Olson recommended Cabinet appoint her Canada's chief negotiator in the division of national assets negotiations, dubbed the "DNA Talks" by the media.

She got the job.

Jennifer took her eyes off Macdonald's portrait and focused them across the table. The Québec team seemed to be making a rather contrived show of scrutinizing the draft DNA Treaty. Her Québec counterpart, François Beaufrère, was shaking his head while his deputy Joël Campeau thumped his finger on a paragraph.

The ninety-one-page document was the culmination of seven intense months of negotiation. The final issue, the partition of Air Canada, was settled yesterday. All that was left was for the negotiators to sign two copies of the document, which would then be passed on to their respective Cabinets for ratification.

But something was wrong. They were focusing on one section. Jennifer strained her ears, but could not make out the whispered French between them.

"Hey, François?" A voice cut in. It was Jennifer's deputy negotiator, Dan McTavish. "Are we signing today or not?"

Joël looked up. "No."

Jennifer realized he wasn't joking.

"What are you talking about?" Dan snapped.

"We wish to make a change to this section," Joël pointed, "pertaining to the assets of Telesat."

"We settled Telesat last month!" Dan exclaimed. "I thought those issues were closed."

François Beaufrère smiled. It was the type of grin Jennifer associated with used car salesmen. She hated it.

"Yes, and we still agree with those terms," he said. "However, we wish to add—"

"The Anik A1 satellite," Joël interrupted.

"*What?*" Dan shrieked.

François took a sip of water. "The current agreement deals adequately with Telesat's Earth-based assets. However, it is unfair that Québec be denied ownership of any of the Crown corporation's *space*-based assets.

"To redress this imbalance, Canada must relinquish ownership of the Anik A1 communications satellite to us."

Langevin Block
Parliament Buildings
9:52 P.M.

The now worthless pages of the draft DNA Treaty pertaining to the division of Telesat lay scattered across Jennifer's normally ordered desk. Under this agreement, Québec was to have gotten any Telesat land, buildings, teleports, and ground stations within its geographic boundaries. As for the satellites, the status quo would have been maintained until the launch of Anik C3 next year. At that time, six of the new satellite's Ku-band transponders would have been given to the new Commission de la Communication du Québec. Each transponder could carry four channels, and the CCQ—analogous to the CRTC—would then distribute them to Québec-based users.

But now Québec wanted those terms changed. François offered to give up the six transponders on Anik C3 in exchange for possession of the *entire* Anik A1 satellite.

There was a knock at the door. Jennifer looked up from the papers. "Come in."

Dan McTavish entered her office. "I saw your light on. What are you still doing here?"

"Oh, I'm just looking over the old agreement, going over some research material, preparing notes on—"

"Why?" Dan asked. "That's Kevin Debus's job. He *is* our secretary, after all."

"Well, what are *you* doing here?"

"I'm single. I'm allowed to be out late." Dan smiled. "Look, there's not much more we can do tonight. I've contacted Telesat's counsel general."

"James Doherty? The guy who advised us on the first agreement?"

"Yeah. We'll meet him in his office tomorrow." Dan handed Jennifer her jacket. "Come on, it's late. I'll walk you to your car."

Kanata, Ontario
11:08 P.M.

The porch lamp had been left on for her, but the rest of the house looked dark. At first, she thought everyone was asleep. But once inside, she saw the light on in the den. Entering the room, she found her husband Paul Tran watching the news.

An image of René Lévesque and some of his Cabinet ministers hosting an Algerian trade delegation flickered on the screen.

"Why didn't you call?" Paul asked.

"I was busy," she replied with barely concealed annoyance. As if *he* never did the same! Paul was an air traffic controller, a job that required him to work odd hours, too. Sometimes, he would be late coming home because, he claimed, he had been concentrating so hard on his shift he forgot where he parked.

"Look, you don't need to wait up for me. I've always told you that."

Paul sighed. "I left you some dinner, if you want it."

Jennifer nodded.

He left for the kitchen. Jennifer sat and watched a report on the continuing armed standoff between an Inuit band in Natashquana and the interim Québec militia.

Paul returned with dinner. Jennifer accepted the fried rice without a word and started eating. As she wolfed down the food, she thought she felt an insect tickling her neck. It took her a moment to realize it was her husband.

"Paul . . ." She shook him away. "I'm *really* tired, okay?"

He sighed and got up. "I'm going to check on Dill." Dill was their nickname for Dillon, their three-year-old son.

She turned her attention back to the TV. The latest paparazzi shots of Charles and Diana's wedding preparations were being shown. Jennifer watched this, and the rest of the newscast, alone.

Telesat Headquarters
Gloucester, Ontario
10:05 A.M., June 13, 1981

James Doherty ran his pudgy hand through his short russet hair. "Let me get this straight. Québec's willing to give up the six transponders on Anik C3 . . . to get A1?"

Jennifer nodded.

"Anik A1 . . ." Lost in thought, James stared off at a child's drawing pinned up on his bulletin board. It was a crayon rendition of a spaceship, complete with tanks, fins, windows, and astronauts tethered with ropes.

"Well, what do you think?" Dan sounded impatient.

James messed his hair again. "This whole separation thing . . . Québec's made some pretty weird demands, but this one takes the cake."

"What do you mean?" Jennifer asked.

"Well, I don't understand why they'd want to do this. Anik A1 was launched in 1972. It's already past its design lifetime. It was only supposed to last seven years, but our engineers— miracle workers, those guys—they've squeezed some extra life out of it. But A1 won't last beyond next year."

"Is there anything special about that satellite?" Jennifer asked.

James frowned. "Not that I can think of."

Dan asked, "When will Anik C3 be launched?"

"Next year, on the Shuttle. Brand new bird. Ten-year lifetime, minimum."

"So, they want to give up capacity on a new satellite for an old one that's only good for a year. Sounds like a good deal." Dan turned to his colleague. "Jennifer?"

"I was just thinking about what my parents used to say about things that seem too good to be true."

Launch Complex 17-A
Cape Canaveral Air Force Station
12:49 P.M.

Venting gases made the Delta rocket hiss and groan like a living creature. As tall as an eleven-story building, with nine boosters clustered at its base, the expendable launch vehicle was an impressive sight. It was also doomed. In a few short years, its kind will be made obsolete by the Space Shuttle. The Shuttle will be the cheap way, the safe way, and the only way to orbit.

At 12:49:01, its RS-27 main engine ignited along with six of its nine Castor IV solid rocket motors to lift the vehicle off the pad. Umbilical lines fell away as the rocket rose on a column of fire and smoke, shaking the Earth good-bye.

The Delta executed a pitch maneuver and headed out over the Atlantic. Fifty-seven seconds later, the first six solids burned out and separated from the still-climbing rocket. The remaining three were now supposed to ignite.

One did not.

The main engine gimballed its nozzle in a vain attempt to compensate for the malfunction. It wasn't enough. The Delta jerked off course, its payload shroud buckling under the aerodynamic load. Bits and pieces fell away into the slipstream as the rocket tumbled out of control. Through a wire running its length, the onboard computer sensed the break in continuity and detonated the range safety explosives.

Kanata, Ontario
11:53 A.M., June 14, 1981

"Bring the water to mommy, Dill," Paul instructed. "There's a good boy."

Jennifer looked up from her desk. "Oh, thank you." She took the glass out of his small hands and put it on her desk before picking him up. "So, whatcha gonna say now?" She pinched his cheek. "Whatcha say to mommy?"

Dillon squirmed. "I don't know."

Jennifer stroked his brush-cut brown hair. "Come on, Dill. What haven't you said to mommy today?"

He thought for a moment. "I love you, mommy."

Watching from the door, Paul chuckled. "I'll be downstairs. Lunch will be ready soon."

"Hey, wanna play with mommy? Bring Rufus. Mommy will play with Rufus and Dill, okay?" Rufus was a stuffed bear.

The phone rang. Jennifer gave Dill a hug before letting him down. The boy waddled out of the room.

"Hello?"

"Jennifer Simcoe? It's Jim Doherty calling, from Telesat."

"Yes."

"Look, I hate to bug you on a Sunday like this, but something important has come up. I'd prefer to talk about it in person. Could we meet later this afternoon?"

"Okay, I'll come right now."

A pause. "Well . . . really, there's no rush. Actually, we just got home from mass and we—"

"Look, now's not a problem for me, okay? I'll come right to your office." She hung up before he could answer.

Jennifer gathered her material and stuffed it into her briefcase. She started for the door, but then she stopped.

Dillon was standing there. With Rufus.

Jennifer sighed. "Mommy has to go now, okay?" She gave her son a quick kiss on the forehead. As an afterthought, she gave Rufus a kiss, too.

Telesat Headquarters
Gloucester, Ontario
1:06 P.M.

A security guard let Jennifer in and ushered her to a seat in the lobby. James arrived ten minutes later and informed her that Dan would be late. The pair proceeded to his office.

"Did you hear about the rocket accident yesterday?" James asked.

"No. There wasn't anything on the news."

James grumbled something. Aloud he said, "Anyway, this rocket was carrying the SBS-2 satellite, which was owned by an American company called Satellite Business Systems. This accident's put them in a real bind. All the capacity on SBS-1 is booked, and SBS-3 won't be ready until at least next year."

"What does this have to do with us?"

"Last night, representatives from SBS contacted us with an offer to lease any excess capacity we've got on our satellites."

Jennifer thought for a moment. "Excess capacity? That means—"

"Yeah," James nodded. "The only spare capacity we've got right now is on Anik A1."

"Well . . . this certainly adds a new wrinkle to the negotiations."

"I'll bet it does. But there's more." He handed her a sheet. "This is a list of the customers that had reserved transponders on SBS-2. Recognize anyone?"

Jennifer scanned the page, and her eyes widened.

Château Laurier Hotel
Ottawa
1:56 P.M., June 15, 1981

"Why have you been negotiating with Satellite Business Systems behind our backs?" Jennifer demanded.

François spread his hands. "It was a simple business transaction between our government and a private company. We thought it did not concern you."

"It *does* concern us because it directly impacts these talks!" Dan snapped. "Why did you need to lease capacity on an *American* satellite?" He paused before answering his own question. "Because you know Anik A1's only got another year, and you need to make up for the transponders you're giving up on Anik C3. Am I close?"

The Québec committee's silence told him he was.

"There's a simple solution to this," Jennifer offered.

"What is it?" Joël asked.

"Go back to the old agreement. Maintain the status quo, and when Anik C3 is launched, you get six new transponders."

François nodded. "You're right. We'll go back to the original agreement."

The Canadian team's relief was short lived.

"Provided you also relinquish ownership of Anik A1 to us," Joël added.

Dan slammed his fist on the table. "You guys want your gâteau and eat it too? No way!"

"Your terms are unacceptable." Jennifer narrowed her eyes. "Telesat stands to make a lot of money from SBS. Industry Minister Herb Gray's going to approve the deal tomorrow."

"We have a right to those profits. Québec helped finance that satellite," Joël noted. "We have a right to Anik A1."

"No," Dan said.

François said. "You won't reconsider?"

"This is it, François," Jennifer replied.

Joël passed a document across the table.

"What the hell is this?" Dan demanded.

François opened his mouth, but Joël spoke for him. "As you may know, the Anik D1 satellite is undergoing final assembly at the Spar facility in Ste-Anne-de-Bellevue. This morning, Industry Minister Rodrigue Biron filed this injunction in Québec District Court barring the delivery of Anik D1 to Telesat."

"*What?*" Dan exclaimed.

François looked pained. "I'm sorry."

Langevin Block
Parliament Buildings
6:11 P.M.

Jennifer phoned James Doherty to brief him.

"This is insane!" James sounded hysterical. "Anik D1 was just a week from being moved to the David Florida Lab for final prelaunch testing. This injunction's a low blow, Jennifer. We need to get that satellite to DFL *now*, or we won't make our launch date. NASA's booked solid. If we miss our flight, who knows when we'll fly? If we jump ship to Ariane, we'll be paying penalties through the nose. Regardless of who we go with, any delay will leave our customers without a satellite. We're stuck!"

In seeking the restraining order, lawyers representing the Québec government argued that Anik D1's traveling wave tube amplifiers, built by MITEC in Pointe Claire, employed "sensitive technologies." Under new trade regulations imposed by the PQ, Québec-based companies exporting products classified as such are supposed to get the approval of the Québec industry minister.

"What about Anik C3?" Jennifer asked. "Is it safe?"

"Yes. The C-series are built by Hughes in the U.S. But Spar is the prime contractor for the D-series." James snickered. "Buy Canadian, eh?"

"Jim, it looks like they want their hands on Anik A1 by hook or by crook. But why? Why are they so desperate for that old satellite?"

"I'm . . . I'm not sure."

"Do you have *any* ideas?"

A pause. "Yeah, maybe."

She gripped the phone tighter. "And?"

"Look, I have an idea . . . but there are some people I need to contact first. I'll get back to you as soon as I can."

**Langevin Block
Parliament Buildings
8:47 P.M.**

After eating her dinner of a Mars bar and a coffee, Jennifer pored over the research material Kevin Debus had given her. She was reading Sciarretta's *Fundamentals of Air and Space Law* when the telephone rang.

Jennifer pounced on the receiver. "Jim?"

"Uh . . . It's me, Paul."

"Oh. Hi."

"I was wondering if you were okay. Will you be much longer?"

"I don't know. I guess not."

"Well, I'll wait up for you." Paul paused. "Hey, there's a little guy who wants to talk to you."

"Hi, mommy."

Despite herself, Jennifer smiled. "Well hello, my special little man. Have you been behaving for daddy?"

"Yeah."

"Well then, how 'bout mommy brings home an ice cream from Dairy Queen for you? Wouldn't that be a nice dessert?"

Dillon squealed with delight. "Daiwy Qween!"

In the background, Jennifer heard, "Say thank you to Mommy."

"Thank you."

The next voice was Paul's. "Come home soon, okay?"

"Yeah, sure."

"Love you."

Jennifer hung up in frustration. Where the hell was James? As she pondered his whereabouts, the phone rang again.

"Hello?"

"Good evening, Ms. Simcoe."

Jennifer stiffened. "It's late, François. What do you want?"

"Meet me in the lobby of the Laurier in twenty minutes."

"Why?"

"It's important."

Her curiosity got the better of her. "Twenty minutes, then."

9:26 P.M.

François was sitting cross-legged on a couch in the lobby of the Château Laurier when Jennifer entered. He stood as she approached. "Thank you for coming."

Jennifer nodded.

He gestured at the door. "Let's take a walk."

They exited the hotel and made their way down Wellington Street. It was cool for a June evening, and Jennifer wished she had a jacket.

"It's funny," François began. "We've spoken to each other almost every day for the last seven months, yet we know so little about each other."

"I guess we didn't really make an effort."

"Well, it's never too late to start." He paused. "Is your home in Ottawa?"

"I live in Kanata."

"Then you're lucky. You see your family every night. I only see my family on weekends."

"*. . . get outta here, damn Q-Bec traitors! This is* our *country. . . .*"

Jennifer turned and saw a group of teenagers gathered at the Confederation Square war memorial. Their taunts were directed at a young couple crossing Elgin Street. The man was clutching a map.

François said, "My parents used to like vacationing outside Québec. I hated it. Once I said, '*Mais maman, nous y derrions parler leur langue.*'" He inhaled. "I remember when I was five, we went to Toronto. We went to the CNE, and I got lost in the Midway."

"That's terrible."

"I started crying, but I didn't speak English. All I could say was, '*Maman, papa, où êtes vous?*' Most people ignored me. A few pointed at me, but nobody stopped to help."

Jennifer waited for him to continue.

"Then . . . this man and woman found me. I don't remember if they were young or old. When you're a child, every adult is just a 'big person.' " He paused. "The woman knelt down and talked to me, but she spoke English and I didn't understand. The man picked me up. They took me to a place for lost children . . . but they didn't leave me. They stayed with me until my maman and papa came. The woman got a tissue from her purse to wipe my eyes, and the man . . . he even bought me ice cream."

Jennifer marveled. "You *remember* all this?"

"I remember."

They got off Wellington, entered the South Gate of Parliament Hill, and approached the Centennial Flame. Jennifer looked up. There, high atop of the Peace Tower, was the Maple Leaf. Floodlights pointed their luminous fingers upward, spotlighting the flag as it fluttered proudly in the dark heavens.

Jennifer caught her breath. "It's beautiful, isn't it?"

"Do you know what the ITU Convention is?"

The question snapped Jennifer back to reality. This was not a social walk; they were here on business.

"It's the constitution of the International Telecommunications Union," she recalled from Sciarretta's book, "the UN agency that regulates satellite communications."

"I suggest you look carefully at Article 33 of the Convention."

Jennifer was stunned. "Why are you telling me this?"

François smiled. It was the same expression she hated so much, and yet . . . she now saw it was sincere. Perhaps it always had been.

"Good night, Ms. Simcoe." He buttoned his jacket. "We should be going our separate ways now."

Kanata, Ontario
11:08 P.M.

Paul was watching the news in the den. There was a report about a possible connection between Mehmet Ali Agca, the man who shot the Pope, and the Turkish Communist Party, the TKP. He looked up as Jennifer entered the room.

Without a word, she sat beside him. Both stared at the TV for a few moments. It was Paul who broke the silence.

"I just put Dill to bed."

"Paul!" Jennifer whirled. "Why are you letting him stay up so late?"

"He was waiting for you."

"What?"

Paul balled his hands into fists. "He was waiting for *you* to bring him his ice cream from Dairy Queen! Mommy promised dessert, so Dill waited for mommy. You know how kids are! He refused to go to bed. I offered him ice cream from the fridge, but he didn't want it. Dill wanted *mommy's* ice cream. He just sat here . . . waiting. 'Mommy coming home soon,' he kept saying when I told him to go to bed. He cried a bit, but he just got too tired and fell asleep . . .

"We were waiting for *you*, Jen!"

"Don't yell at me! Why are you so upset over an ice cream?"

"It's not *about* a damned ice cream!" Paul exclaimed. "It's about *you*. It's about . . . *us*."

"You're not being reasonable! You know how important these talks are. The last seven months—"

"No!" Paul shouted. "It's not just the last seven months. It's been from day one. I was naïve, Jen. I thought you'd change after we got married. But it got worse! Why do you always make me—make Dill—seem like a big fat zero compared to your work? Why do you find it easier to negotiate a wheat deal with the Soviets than to talk—really *talk*—to your own husband? To your family?"

Jennifer bit her lip.

"This won't end after the DNA Talks. What's next? An acid rain treaty with the Americans? A fishing dispute with Japan? Work is not your whole life, dammit! Don't *we* matter?"

"I'm sorry . . ."

"We came from different worlds, Jen. Sometimes things haven't been easy. But *both* of us have to compromise to make this work!" He pointed at himself. "I don't know, but I think I've been doing *my* part."

Langevin Block
Parliament Buildings
11:52 A.M., June 16, 1981

33.2. In using frequency bands for space radio services Members shall bear in mind that radio frequencies and the geostationary satellite orbit are limited natural resources, that they must be used efficiently and economically so that countries or

> *groups of countries may have equitable access to both in con-*
> *formity with the provisions of the Radio Regulations according*
> *to their needs and the technical facilities at their disposal.*

The ITU Convention was ratified at the Málaga-Torremolinos Plenipotentiary Conference in 1973. Kevin Debus had provided Jennifer with a copy, and she spent the morning studying it. She was still unable to contact James Doherty, but another Telesat lawyer was able to give her a legal interpretation.

She began to suspect Québec wanted more than just an old satellite.

Jennifer picked up her mug. As she did so, her eyes fell upon a small photograph on her desk. The picture was taken two years ago, during a vacation to Disneyland Paul had begged her to take. In the photo, she and Paul were standing on either side of Mickey Mouse. Paul was holding Dill. The poor kid was crying because the giant rodent terrified him.

Jennifer put the coffee down and picked up the phone. She was about to call Telesat again, but suddenly she found herself dialing another number.

"Ottawa/Uplands Area Control Centre, good morning." They didn't say *"bonjour"* anymore.

"Extension 293."

"One moment, please."

Jennifer was treated to a few seconds of canned music.

"Terminal Control Unit."

"Hi, Paul."

"Jen? What's wrong?"

"Nothing's wrong . . . Uh, you're almost done for the day, right?"

"Yes."

"Dill's at the sitter?"

"Of course. Why?"

"I was wondering . . . if I could see you this afternoon."

Silence.

"Paul?"

"Jen, your negotiations are this afternoon. You've—"

"Doesn't matter."

"Why not?"

"Because . . ." Jennifer's vision began to fog, ". . . it's much too nice to work."

That was their tag line when they were dating.

"What did you want to do?" Paul said at last.

"Anything. I just want to see you."

"Well, Chris can give me a lift—"

"I'll pick you up. Okay?"

"Sure. I'll wait for you by the airside security gate."

"I love you, Paul."

"Never doubted that for a minute. See you soon." He blew her a kiss before hanging up.

Jennifer wiped her eyes before making another call.

"Dan McTavish."

"Dan, it's Jennifer. Look . . . I can't make it to the negotiations this afternoon."

"What?" He lowered his voice. "Jennifer, what's wrong. Are you sick or something?"

"No."

"Then—"

"The negotiations are off. You'd better let the Québec committee know."

"What going on?"

"I'm not going to be there. Is that clear?"

"No."

"Well . . . too bad. Just tell François, okay? See you tomorrow, Dan."

"Jen—"

She put down the receiver.

Kanata, Ontario
7:30 A.M., June 17, 1981

Jennifer woke the instant the clock radio came on. She listened briefly to Kim Carnes's "Bette Davis Eyes" before slapping the snooze button.

Paul was already awake. "Do you mind if I stare?" He was lying with his elbow propped on the pillow.

She kissed him. "How long have you been up?"

"Not long." He ran his hand across her shoulder. "You know, about yesterday. That was stupid, you know. I mean it was *really* irresponsible. Do you have any idea what you did?"

"What do you think I did?"

Paul was suddenly serious. "You put me ahead of the whole country. Two countries, I guess . . . I love you so much, Jen."

They drew each other close . . . and then the phone rang.

Paul laughed. "I was right, wasn't I? It never ends."

"Paul . . ."

He was still laughing. "You better get that, dear!"

With the greatest reluctance, Jennifer picked up the phone. "Hello?"

"Jennifer!" It was James Doherty. "Where have you been? I've been trying to reach you since—"

"Never mind," Jennifer snapped. "What's up?"

"Could we meet in my office this morning? I know why Québec's so desperate for Anik A1."

"Something to do with its orbital slot?" Jennifer asked rhetorically.

"How did you know?"

"Look, time's running out. Secession day's next Wednesday. If you've got information, we need it."

"Agreed. My office in . . . say, an hour?"

"Fine." Jennifer replaced the receiver. "Paul . . . I'm sorry, but I've got to—"

"I know."

Jennifer gave him a quick kiss before easing herself from the warm covers.

"Jen?"

She turned.

"Give 'em hell, my love."

Telesat Headquarters
Gloucester, Ontario
9:08 A.M.

"Ever heard of the Bogotá Declaration?"

Dan shook his head.

"In 1977, eight equatorial nations tried to claim sovereignty over the regions of space above their territories—up to and including geosynchronous orbit, the orbit communications satellites are stationed in. This was defeated because—"

James stopped suddenly. A trickle of blood was running down from his nose. "Aw, gee . . ." He whipped out his handkerchief to stanch the flow.

"Where was I? Oh, yeah." With his nose plugged, his voice sounded almost comical. "It was defeated because it violated

Article 2 of the 1967 Outer Space Treaty, which states that space is not subject to national claims of sovereignty. Nevertheless, these countries had made their point."

"Which is?" Jennifer prompted.

The handkerchief was soaked with blood. "The Bogotá Declaration was a protest against perceived inequities in ITU policy." James opened a book. "The crux is the last part of Article 33 of the ITU Convention. It states that the ITU shall assign slots in geosynchronous orbit 'according to their needs . . . and the *technical facilities at their disposal.*' In practical terms, this means that slots are assigned in an *a posteriori,* or first-come, first-served basis. Many developing nations consider this discriminatory because they're afraid that by the time they get comsat technology, the best slots will be gone."

"So it's about orbital slots, as I suspected," Jennifer mused. "But Jim, there's something I don't understand. I spoke with one of your colleagues, and he told me Anik A1's slot wasn't that valuable. If we lose it, we can always get another one."

"It might not be that simple anymore," James said.

"Why?" Dan asked.

"The demographics of the ITU are changing. By next year, over two-thirds of the members will be developing countries, and they're taking a page from the League of Non-Aligned Nations. The next ITU Plenipotentiary Conference will be in Nairobi in a few months. These nations will unite and vote as a bloc. They'll push *hard* to get Article 33 changed."

James produced a plain brown envelope from a drawer. "I pulled a *lot* of favors for this." He struggled to extract its contents with one hand. "I've learned that the Algerian delegation will propose replacing the last part of Article 33 with the phrase, 'taking into account the special needs of the developing countries.' "

Jennifer understood the implications. "If that goes through, we might see a massive grab by those countries to hog parts of geosynchronous orbit. The ITU can't give Québec slots because it's not yet a member, and by the time it gets membership, the changes to Article 33 might be in effect. So, Québec wants to grab one of *our* slots before it's too late."

James nodded. "If we give Québec Anik A1, the slot automatically defaults to them."

"But Anik A1's only got a year," Dan protested. "When the satellite's gone, doesn't the slot revert to us?"

"No. The ITU will allow a country to hold a slot for up to nine years before it must be reassigned."

Jennifer asked, "Jim, what are the chances of this amendment going through?"

"Better than ever, because India's now on its side. They've been sitting on the fence for years on this issue. But the ITU's just given them their slot assignments. They recently signed a contract with Arianespace to launch their Insat constellation. Since they now have what they want, they can afford to help their allies."

"Even with India's support, those changes aren't guaranteed," Dan argued.

"Nothing's guaranteed, but with India the chances look pretty good. Québec thinks so, anyway. Remember, India's one of the largest Third World shareholders in the Intelsat consortium. They've got clout." James gingerly removed the handkerchief from his nose. The bleeding had stopped.

"Jennifer, call off today's negotiations," Dan said. "We've got to confer with Cabinet."

She nodded. "Then what?"

Château Laurier Hotel
Ottawa
1:37 P.M., June 18, 1981

Jennifer, Dan, and James worked with Cabinet through the night to draft a new deal. Now, François and Joël listened attentively as Jennifer spelled out its terms.

"Anik A1 will be *leased* to Québec for the remainder of its operational life. The price: Canada will be entitled to 90 percent of the profits from the lease of transponders to Satellite Business Systems. Any Canadian traffic currently on Anik A1, and any Québec traffic on the other satellites, shall remain in place for one year. This arrangement leaves one free C-band transponder on Anik A1, which will be ceded to Québec to do with as it chooses."

These concessions were vehemently opposed by Dan and many members of Cabinet, especially Agriculture Minister Eugene Whelan. But Acting Prime Minister Allan MacEachen decided it was the only way to end the DNA Talks quickly.

Jennifer now addressed the central issue. "At end-of-life,

Anik A1 will be boosted to disposal orbit . . . and its geostation-ary slot assignment shall be *surrendered back to Canada*. Québec will then get the transponder capacity on Anik C3 as agreed upon previously."

François rubbed his chin. "Is there anything else?"

"If Québec agrees to these terms," she continued, "Canada will *support* the changes to Article 33 of the ITU Convention pro-posed by Algeria and other developing nations."

"What?" Joël asked.

"Canada will offer its support for changes to Article 33 that are beneficial to them—if *they* support changes beneficial to *us*. We will propose adding the phase, 'taking into account the ge-ographical and geopolitical situation of particular countries.' "

François rubbed his chin. "I see . . ."

"Your 'geopolitical situation' is obvious," Jennifer explained, "but with our vast Arctic, the 'geographical situation' clause is good for us. These amendments will put both of us in a better position for future ITU slot assignments."

"These poor countries have become too strong," Joël said. "We believe they will force changes to Article 33 regardless of what we industrialized nations do. Why should they accom-modate Canada?"

"Because we'll remind them that at the World Administra-tive Radio Conference four years ago, we sided with them to block the American appropriation of broadcasting services in the twelve-gigahertz band." Jennifer grinned. "They owe us."

François leaned back in his chair. "Your offer sounds good."

"Of course, it all hinges on your government lifting its in-junction against Anik D1," Dan added.

"Or else?" Joël asked.

"Or else—"

"Nothing." Jennifer cut Dan off. "Canada doesn't make threats."

François flashed his infamous smile. "Fifteen."

"Sorry?" Jennifer said.

"We want 15 percent of the profits from the SBS lease."

"Twelve. That's final."

François drummed his fingers. "Twelve it is. The other terms are also acceptable."

Joël started, *"Mais—"*

"I said, the terms are *acceptable.*" François shot his colleague a sharp glance. "Now, where do we sign?"

Jennifer and Dan couldn't contain their relief. From his perch on the wall, the framed image of Sir John A. Macdonald offered neither praise nor condemnation.

Kanata, Ontario
11:49 P.M., June 23, 1981

The final four days were hectic. After a few minor changes, the DNA Treaty was ratified. Québec lifted its injunction against Anik D1, and the satellite was trucked to the David Florida Laboratory in Ottawa for pre-launch testing. The secession of Québec was recognized by an all-party resolution in Parliament. With consultation from London, amendments to the BNA Act were passed, allowing separation to proceed.

Tonight, every Canadian TV channel—and one American network—was providing live coverage of the secession ceremonies in Québec City. Governor-General Edward Schreyer and Acting Prime Minister MacEachen delivered emotional speeches outside the National Assembly. They praised all that the French and English had accomplished together over a hundred and fourteen years, and promised that Québec and Canada would remain friends and partners despite being apart.

Dillon squirmed on Jennifer's lap. "Mommy . . ."

"What is it, dear?"

"I'm tired."

"I know, sweetie. But mommy and daddy want you to watch. This is an important day, Dill. When you grow up, you'll understand."

Paul put his arm around his wife. "Poor kid's exhausted."

"It's boring . . ." Dillon rubbed his eyes. "It's *stoopid* . . ."

The family watched René Lévesque take the podium. He declared this day the most important in Québec's history since the Plains of Abraham. When he spoke of their triumph in realizing their noblest aspiration, the audience went wild.

Jennifer pulled Paul closer.

At four minutes to midnight, the crowd fell silent as the Maple Leaf came down from the flagpole atop the National Assembly. It had been put there just for this ceremony. The camera panned the leaders. Lévesque and Schreyer stood at respectful attention, but MacEachen looked on the verge of tears.

The fleur-de-lis was rising. As it climbed the pole, the crowd began to applaud. The noise crescendoed to loud cheers when the flag reached the top at midnight.

It was now the morning of June 24, 1981. The two solitudes were realized. Québec and Canada were separate.

Dillon was fast asleep.

THE EIGHTH REGISTER

Alain Bergeron

Story translated from the French by Howard Scott

The information in this note comes almost entirely from a 1998 interview with the author in Solaris, *translated in excerpt by Jean-Louis Trudel.*

Alain Bergeron was born in 1950 in Paris, France; his family moved back to Canada soon thereafter. When he was about 16, he read and loved Tolkien, but his early forays into science fiction did not convert him. He was hooked with a vengeance at the age of 25 when he rediscovered SF in such works as Simak's *City,* Asimov's *Foundation* trilogy, some Van Vogt, and Sturgeon's *The Dreaming Jewels.* Philip K. Dick was also an influence. Bergeron launched right away into writing his first novel, *Un été de Jessica* (1978).

Despite the book's success (serialized in Quebec City's *Le Soleil* newspaper), Bergeron did not continue writing at that time. He embarked upon a Ph.D. and started a family. Coincidentally, his publisher went bankrupt just as the book went out of print. Though he would have preferred to be a working scientist, he has devoted himself to the sociology of science and science policy for the last twenty years. In his job as science and technology policy advisor to the Quebec government, his duty is to stay up to date on the latest scientific and technological discoveries, which feeds both his fiction and his new column, "The Dilettante Anchorite," in *Solaris.*

It was Élisabeth Vonarburg who dragged him back into SF, pushing him to finish his short story "Bonne Fête Univers." From there, he went on to write more stories, almost all collected in *Corps-machines et rêves d'anges* (Hull, 1997). For that collection and a young adult horror novel published under a pseudonym, Bergeron won the Grand Prix de la Science-Fiction et du Fantastique québécois, the top award in French-Canadian science fiction. His novel *Corps-machines et rêves d'anges* won the 1998 Prix Boréal for best novel. "The Eighth Register" (1993) was selected and translated to appear in *Tesseracts*[Q] (1996), the first English language anthology of French Canadian SF. It is an alternate universe story of a very different texture from, say, Eric Choi's "Divisions" or Michael Skeet's "Near Enough to Home," yet more closely tied to genre SF than Jean-Pierre April's "Rêve Canadien" and definitely has a '90s sensibility.

Memoirs of Andreas Antonikas, who occupies the Chair in Semiology at the University of Providence (Arkadia), on the subject of the ecumenical synod on historiosophy, which was held at the monastery of Mount Boreal (Galactea) in the last days of the month of March in the year one thousand, nine hundred and ninety-four of Christendom and the Empire.

Very long were the winters in that harsh land of Galactea, much longer than could be suffered by the patience of a man of breeding. April strode in, a sign for us of a feverish flowering to come. But here, on the island of Mount Boreal, a greyish sky still dropped heavy snows mixed with ice, without respite. I was told there was worse still, further north, over the thousands of miles the river Galacta stretched before plunging into the Atlas Sea. I, who had known no climate other than that of sweet and mild Arkadia, was vexed by that brutal, stubborn winter.

A young man in those days, I was just completing my studies in semiology at the University of Providence. I had learned to configure, manipulate, and decipher icons and symbols of all kinds, and I knew how to work the keyboards on most models of sign-processing organs. Such skills were much sought after. Whether it was theologians interpreting the hand of God in everything, astrologers examining the light in the depths of the heavens, or engineers drawing up plans for our engines of war, rare were the scholars who required no assistance from semiologists like me. In my case, I had the privilege of entering the service of the venerable Justin Cantarumene, one of the greatest names in modern historiosophy. And it was under these circumstances that I found myself in the monastery of Mount Boreal in the icy month of March in nineteen hundred and ninety-four.

"I am aware of the fact that you have never left our dear Arkadia," my master told me, "but this experience will be very good for you, Andreas Antonikas. The ecumenical synod to which we have been invited promises to be of prime importance for the future of historiosophy. Delegates will be coming from Britannia and Egypt, and from the great cities of the Empire, from Constantinople, Carthage, Kiev, Ravenna, Antioch, and

Parisia, from Ephesus and Trebizond, from Damascus and Novgorod. The theme of the synod is one of the most solemn possible, since it concerns the monochronism of human history. John of Thebaid has agreed to come in person to defend the doctrine, but Adam of Canterburg will also be there to denounce it. Do I need to add that we need semiologists of your caliber to prepare and operate the sign-processing organs? One of my friends, the Hegumen Theobald Zacharion, is the head of the monastery of Mount Boreal. He has promised to make his big organ available to the synod. You will see that it is one of those new machines that operate using electric fluids. Briefly, even though you have to allow almost a week to make the journey from Providence to Mount Boreal in the discomfort of those wooden carriages mounted on rails, I enjoin you, Andreas Antonikas, to make the voyage with me."

The monastery, a formidable edifice of mosaicked stone, walled in by snow, was built high on the flank of a mountain, dominating the center of the largest island in the region. Below it crowded the smoking roofs of hamlets and farms, from which the monks drew a large part of their income. All this had existed for less than sixty years.

When Iberian sailors discovered the New Continent in 1809, they had landed much further south, on the rich and sunny shores of what we now call Arkadia. It was there, too, that the Empire had chosen to establish its first colonies: Aristopolis, Syracuse, Philadelphia, Providence. All the territory lying north of the five Inland Seas, however, had only been open to settlement since the 1890s. The founding of Mount Boreal dated from 1936, when General Belgarius had ordered the erection of the monastery in thanks to the Mother of God for the victories that he had won over the pagan savages. Only seventeen other towns and villages had been established over the last century, sprinkled along the icy shores of the majestic Galacta. And all this, pompously named the Land of Galactea, in 1994 formed the youngest and the least populous of the six provinces that the Roman Empire possessed on the New Continent.

On the eve of the synod, because the snow had made most of the access routes impassable, the two main delegations had still not managed to reach us. Adam of Canterburg's paddle boat was icebound in the mouth of the river. His adversary, John of Thebaid, was held up somewhere on the seacoast, near the port of Marsila, waiting for less hostile skies in order to reboard his ornithopter. My master Justin and the organizers of the synod were desperate. It was unthinkable to open the debates in the absence of the two main leaders of contemporary historiosophy. And that evening, after supper, I had my own outburst of anger, which caused me to blaspheme in front of a few good monks.

"The devil take it!" I cried. "Is it really the end of the twentieth century, the dawn of the third millennium, when the whims of nature can still paralyze us in this way?"

The Hegumen Theobald Zacharion heard me and came over, his eyes stern, but with a slight smile on his lips.

"Calm your spirits, my son, and profit from this occasion by observing another manifestation of the hazardous nature of time. For a supporter of Master Adam of Canterburg, this cannot but be instructive."

"I am a proponent of the science of semiology," I answered. "However, without claiming to possess the skills of my Master Justin in historiosophy, it is obvious that I wish to see the triumph of Master Adam of Canterburg's side. The doctrine of the monochronism of human history defended by the Alexandrian School is already close to four centuries old."

"It is in no way invalidated by its age, my son. Do not forget that it has done very great service to Christianity by permitting it to combat the heretical threat from the renegade Hugh of Bavaria in the sixteenth century. It was the product of a troubled time that saw the devastation of some of the Western provinces of the Old Continent, Franconia and Upper Germania in particular, a time when it was believed necessary to impose on Christianity a holistic vision of history, a vision of a single long march organized since its beginnings by the Creator and ultimately directed by Him."

"But Master Theobald, could it be that you are defending monochronism!"

"God forbid. I wish only to emphasize that it is in its foundations and not by its seniority that the doctrine is weak. Even if the Alexandrian School claims to treat it as a dogma, the demonstrations upon which it is based with regard to the divine nature of time or the teleological nature of human history are quite disputable. But it does not suffice to make these shortcomings more modern. We must ask ourselves what we can propose to replace it."

"But the truth! Is that not what you are both seeking, my Master Justin and you, and Adam of Canterburg?"

Questioned little since the sixteenth century, the doctrine of the monochronism of history had come under attack over the last decade. Extremely troubling speculations on the alternative contingencies of time and the bifurcations that they might generate were circulating in certain outlying academies of the Old Continent. They arose in particular in the province of Britannia, Cornwall, and Wales. Adam of Canterburg, occupant of the Chair of Historiosophy at Oxenford, had no fear of entering into a controversy on this subject with the Scholarch of the Coptic University of Alexandria, John of Thebaid.

"Yes, yes, we also wish to reach the truth, Andreas Antonikas. But this must not prevent us from showing prudence and discernment in the days to come. The prospect of this synod is extremely annoying to the ecclesiastical authorities. Shortly before your arrival here, the Patriarch of Providence threatened your Master Justin saying he would refer the matter to the Pontiff himself. But I do not believe that he did it so. We are fortunate that an enlightened basileus recently ascended to the throne of Constantinople."

Michael XXII Philophilus, an astute scholar hardly older than I, had taken the Imperial crown the previous January, supported by a powerful party of Varangian merchants from Muscovy. He had announced his intention to reign under the sign of reasonable openness to the renewal of ideas, something which did not fail to ruffle the feathers of the Pope, His Holiness Paul VII. It was impossible to know how long this Imperial benevolence would last, but we suspected that it would be short-lived. Sooner or later, the pontifical faction would form a behind-the-scenes alliance with other parties to throw out this pretentious young Varangian who had the audacity to govern with intelligence.

"The truth is certainly the essential thing," continued the Hegumen. "But like anything it has a price. Behind the fate that this synod has in store for the monochronism of history—and do not hope for too easy a victory—there are immense interests at stake for the Empire and for the world as we have always known it."

Theobald Zacharion was looking out the window at the heavy snow falling on the shores of the river. His powerful mind seemed plunged deep in thought. I was about to withdraw when he spoke to me again.

"The unity of time, the unity of history . . . Why do we go to such lengths to combat this received idea, Andreas Antonikas?

We live in a world that seems more immovable to me every day. The Roman Empire continues to cross the ages intact. There is nothing more stable. Ever since we resisted the turmoil of the barbarian invasions of the fifth century, ever since, with the aid of the Arabs, we conquered Persia in 635, the entire Western world has lived in peace and security under the double light, divine and imperial, of Rome and Constantinople. Only China blocks our expansion. But it has been this way for over a thousand years now. Two old marble lions, the Roman Empire and the Chinese Empire, stare face to face. In the East as in the West, they are making silent, endless war, in which nothing decisive ever occurs."

"Come now, what are you saying? With all due respect, Master, it seems to me, on the contrary, that the world is always changing. In Arkadia in the south, in Galactea in the north, are we not at the outposts of a New Continent that has barely been opened up?"

"But what is there new in this? We are only perpetuating the secular order of things. With regard to this New Continent of which you speak, the Chinese are settling it from the west towards the east, while we are taking possession of it from east to west. Between the two lie vast wild and bare plains where we will meet one day. And it will be to pit ourselves against each other again."

"But finally, don't we hear that the Chinese are preparing to send one of their rockets into the heavens? And that it will go higher that any balloon has ever risen? And that they are aiming at nothing less than the Moon? And that our new Emperor, having learned this, wishes to undertake a similar project?"

"The Moon now! Do you see! It will be a race, like the others. And the Moon of the twenty-first century will become the continent on which our two empires will continue their cold war."

The Briton delegation arrived at the monastery the morning of March 26. Adam of Canterburg and his retinue had had to abandon their boat some four hundred miles to the north, downstream on the Galacta River. They had, however, been able to reach the shore near a little village called Archangel. And there, the local prefect had agreed to provide them with fast sleighs pulled by dogs. Savages served as guides for them. Exhausted, famished, sick in some cases, the delegates had finally completed their pilgrimage.

Adam of Canterburg, the recognized leader of the new historiosophy, was a man of small stature, bony, febrile, and tormented. He looked as if his face was seething under the pressure of deep emotions, and he walked with such a stoop that he appeared to be carrying the entire destiny of the human race on his shoulders.

He hardly made any fuss on his arrival, preferring to remain in the shadows and let the other members of his delegation take responsibility for the usual niceties. Jon Seymour of Glencoe took care of these very well, as did Maxentius Ingham of Sarum. As soon as he arrived, Master Adam hurried to confer, in particular, with Theobald Zacharion and Justin Cantarumene. Another personage accompanied them, but I had to wait until evening to learn who he was. My Master Justin came to find me, looking very serious, and told me that he required my services.

The man who was accompanying Master Adam was named Ramindra Thagor and hailed from Bharat, a principality on the Indian Peninsula—one of those small states that claimed to be neutral, like Abyssinia and Western Khazaria, and that, from the north to the south of the Orient, form a sort of fragile wall between the two imperial giants. Ramindra was therefore not a Roman citizen and his presence in this country posed an almost intractable problem.

"All of this is absolutely illegal," said Theobald Zacharion plaintively. "If ever the Patriarch of Galactea learned of it! And the Prefect of Mount Boreal, Marsilius Alarius! He has little love for me and would be happy to see me compromised by some scandal."

But since Ramindra had made a very long journey to come as far as Galactea, the Hegumen had to agree to accommodate him in one of the cells of the cloister. His presence was considered indispensable by the Britons, but it was essential that it be kept secret.

"This man has developed an instrument that will ensure our victory," said Master Adam, "an organ of a completely revolutionary type. Thanks to him, we will establish beyond any doubt that the doctrine of historical monochronism is a fraud. Ramindra should keep out of the debates, however. We have agreed that I alone should present our theses."

Ramindra Thagor was tall, cold, solemn, and ageless. The organ he had brought with him was of modest dimensions. It measured no more than eight cubits in width and less than four cubits in height and depth. It operated on an electric battery and had an extremely complicated control panel inside the cabinet. The gears and relays were so small that they could barely be distinguished from each other, which explained the small size of the machine. The cogwheels and circuits were made of rare metal alloys, capable of distributing the electric fluid through a very tight mesh of wires. Once operations were completed, the organ transmitted the results in the conventional manner, on an inked press over which a parchment was rolled. But it was also possible to have the result appear on a luminous panel by using a little-known process that consisted of running the electric fluid through a metal lattice covered by a sheet of light-sensitive glass.

In spite of its small size, the instrument still had the most impressive keyboard space that I had ever seen, a space that was nevertheless left empty. The device was still not finished. Its design was so new, its operation was so complex, that it could only be made usable through the extremely fine calibration of the command keys. And it was precisely this type of task that required the skills of a semiologist.

I did not do the work alone. An unexpected assistant came to me from heaven like an angel. He was a little Briton monk, a protégé of Master Adam. He was a semiologist like me, and although he appeared to be no more than fourteen years of age, his science seemed to me as advanced as my own.

"My name is Christian Lods," he said, gazing at me with his big blue eyes, "and I come from Camelot, in Cornwall."

From those first moments, it seemed obvious to me that we would become inseparable friends and that great affection would bind us to one another. I felt good in his presence, and I think the feeling was mutual. For the first time in my life, I had the delightful feeling of having found a kindred soul. The assembly of Ramindra's keyboard would, in his company, be the most agreeable of tasks.

The keys of the organ that we were to install were of reduced size, wooden blocks hardly bigger than a fingertip. Each one could have two to eight different icons, according to the register chosen. The register console itself was installed flat, widthways, just above a slightly inclined keyboard. It held no fewer than eight stop knobs.

First there were the four most common registers. The first stop controlled the normal alphabetical characters, Greek and Roman. The second governed all of the mathematical operations, including arithmetic, geometry, and pure logic. The third one controlled the functions of divinatory astrology, and the analytical reading of the celestial map. The fourth register, of course, was the entire Theologon, with all the codes required for the exegesis of the Holy Scriptures.

To these four classical registers, Ramindra had added four new ones. He explained their use to us. The fifth proved invaluable in works of hermeneutics. Using it, it was possible to reduce a text to its different levels of signification, then reconstitute it entirely in new forms. The sixth stop gave access to the languages of the Talmudic tradition and alchemy. The seventh stop opened an ecumenical translator, capable of automatically substituting the signs of one language, such as Coptic, for those of Greek or Modern Briton.

"There remains the eighth register, Master Ramindra," said Christian.

"Ah, the eighth? You will have guessed that it is, in fact, used for a new method of processing historical data. We will be testing it as soon as you have completed the installation of the keyboard."

All these new things excited me. I was delirious with joy. In my enthusiasm, I smothered the Indian with compliments.

"Few scholars know this in your Empire," he answered, not without pride, "but the very first devices of this kind were constructed around the year 1000 in India, at the time of Rajaraja Chola. And they were already based on the four thousand logical rules of the Sanskrit grammar worked out by Panini one thousand three hundred years earlier. It is still these same basic rules that provide the key to the operation of this revolutionary device that you see before you.

"From India, the invention went to China, where the mandarins made it into a hydraulic machine equipped with large clocks, for the analytical processing of their ideograms. It was then smuggled into the Roman Empire by Hungarian spies at the end of the fifteenth century. Zenon da Vinci, the famous engineer, substituted mechanical cogwheels for the hydraulic ducts and installed a keyboard analogous to those on musical instruments in order to facilitate the working of the controls. Thus was born the sign-processing organ."

The test of the eighth register finally took place on March 28 in the morning, in the presence of Adam of Canterburg, Justin Cantarumene, and Theobald Zacharion. Ramindra sat down at the keyboard, and Christian pressed the lever for the electric battery. My role was to place a roll of parchment in the inked press and connect the luminous panel on which the results would be displayed. On Ramindra himself fell the honor of pulling the stop for the eighth register. Metallic clickings and the crackling of sparks produced by the contact of the electric fluid could be heard from inside the case. This lasted for about ten minutes.

"It's taking too long!" moaned Master Adam.

"Come now, let the organ warm up," Ramindra said to him. "It has to adjust its internal structure according to the register chosen."

Finally, Ramindra turned to us, the two assistants, who were trembling with emotion in the shadows.

"We can go ahead. Suggest three dates to us, Andreas Antonikas."

"Three dates? Well, then . . . let's say 1500, 1800, and 1950."

"And you, Christian Lods. Choose three degrees of probability."

"I will say thirty to start. Then fifty . . . and end with one hundred."

Ramindra started hitting the keys of the keyboard at great speed. He entered the parameters for the current calculation of the historical probabilities, then the three dates, and finally the three chosen predictability values. The organ had in memory the key events of history in coded form, arranged in chronological order. Using this basic material, it was now possible, thanks to the eighth register, to simulate the occurrence sequences for these events on different probability values. The luminous panel began to come to life. Points appeared, then a curve took shape.

"We are still only at thirty percent," said Ramindra. "Notice the disturbances that indicate the high degree of improbability. And now, examine the consequences: Venetian mariners discover the New Continent before 1500, and, still more unbelievable, the sign-processing organ is not invented before 1800."

"Isn't that a war breaking out here, a few years before 1950?" asked Master Adam.

"A war? Yes, I think you are correct. But we would have to increase the scale in order to identify the belligerents. Let us rather move to probability fifty. Purely random: each event has as much chance of happening as of not happening."

Ramindra pressed a key to activate the second parameter. The curve now became totally chaotic.

"And now, probability one hundred. Certainty: the events of history as they have been reported to us by the chroniclers."

The line appearing before our eyes should have been perfectly straight this time, according to the doctrine of historical monochronism, which prescribed the absolute determinism of events. Nothing of the sort appeared. The curve was marked by significant irregularities, characteristic of fluctuations in certainty.

"This is extraordinary!" cried Master Justin. "You have succeeded! Look: the consistory of 1950 should never have taken place in reality. And . . . am I dreaming? The heresy of Hugh of Bavaria isn't there either. I've always thought there was something improbable about it."

Adam and Justin had just leaped into each other's arms. And Ramindra was laughing as he played on his keyboard. Theobald Zacharion shook his head but smiled. Christian looked at me, his eyes shining. We were going to win. It was certain.

"You chose dates that were too recent," Christian said to me. "The most spectacular breakdown is located in a previous time segment. Master Adam only mentioned it to me briefly. Ramindra has identified a gaping hole in the curve, somewhere at the beginning of the seventh century?"

"At the beginning of the seventh century? But what happened at the beginning of the seventh century?"

"I don't know. All that we see is a dramatic depression in the probability fabric of time, as if the facts of that period had abruptly stopped being real."

"Isn't that the kind of phenomenon the historiosophists call historical bifurcation?"

"Or an alternative time. An accidental event, completely unexpected, occurs. From that point on, our history joins a trajectory different from natural reality. But those are speculations. The eighth register should permit us to go further in reconstructing a stronger probability fabric, closer to what would have been reality."

"The seventh century—that was the time of the Emperor Heraclius, of the reconquest of the Mediterranean Basin, and of the destruction of Persia with the help of the Arabs."

"Yes . . . it was also a period of great activist spirituality.

What was the name of that holy man who saw an angel appear one day?"

"Muhammad, I believe."

"Ah, yes. Imagine for a moment that Muhammad had never existed. Let us suppose that it is the existence of that holy man that constitutes the highly improbable event we are seeking."

"I think I know what you are getting at. Continue."

"Well, if that holy man had never existed, the whole sequence of history would be very different from the one we know. Without Muhammad to rally them under the single banner of Christ, the Arabs would have remained divided, fighting one another, some for the Roman Empire, some for Persia. And it could well be that, without their aid, we would never have succeeded in conquering this rival power."

"This is very disturbing. With the Persian peril still present in the East, the Roman Empire would not have had the strength to maintain its ascendancy in the Mediterranean."

"The little barbarian kingdoms of Italy, Franconia, and Germania would have turned against us."

"Not to speak of Persia, which would finally have spilled into the Roman territories."

"And even taken Constantinople!"

"What a horrifying prospect. Can you imagine it? The Persian Empire extending its domination over the West, imposing Zoroastrianism as the universal religion . . ."

"It makes me shudder. Let's just hope that in the most probable reality, our Muhammad really existed!"

Towards the end of the afternoon of the same day, an infernal noise suddenly shook the sky over Mount Boreal. It was not thunder that was rumbling across the clouds, but a flight of wood and iron eagles that had just descended upon us, wings spread wide, their propeller blades whirling faster than the wind.

Ornithopters! There were at least ten of them dropping out of the sky together and alighting on the huge ice field that the monks had cleared as a landing area near the stables. Our adversaries were finally here. The Alexandrian delegates were arriving from Marsila, a modest seaport on the border between Arkadia and Galactea, where they had taken refuge from the snow and where, we were told later, they had been feasting for days in the local inns.

They were arriving fresh, fat, and not overly tired, just in time for the opening banquet of the synod. The huge John of Thebaid, Scholarch of the Alexandrian School, their intellectual guide, dominated them all with his size, his voice, and his intelligence. It was almost natural that he was given a place of honor at the centre of the biggest table. His flowing white tunic seemed to sparkle in the light. His supporters surrounded him, also dressed in white.

Master John's retinue was much more numerous than that of Master Adam. It was not solely made up of Copts, however. There were Syrians, Khazars, Wallachians, Bulgarians, Carthaginians, and Ephesians associated with the Alexandrian School. There were also many Macedonians, including the celebrated Manuel Anastasiac who was presenting himself as the advocate of the monochronism of history at Constantinople itself.

The banquet was a marvel. First they brought out quails' eggs in blue enamel egg cups, surrounded by fat artichokes in a white sauce spiced with nard and coriander. Then came platters of frogs, sturgeons, and sole in a sweet beer sauce, whitefish wreathed with olives pickled in brine, and semolina rolls, and other fish fried with mustard flour. After that we ate ham, kid stuffed with garlic, and duck roasted with leeks. And for those who thought they still had a little room left in their bellies, they served cheesecake with creamed honey and raisins. All washed down with dozens of tankards of rosé wine and brandy.

I was sitting beside my young and handsome friend Christian. At that time, eating and drinking together as if we had known each other for centuries, I think we both felt a wave of joy sweep over us. Indeed, I have never felt anything so intense since.

Christian told me a lot about his native city, Camelot. This name had a strange resonance for me. I had heard of it as a place filled with memories, a little like Rome, Constantinople, or Jerusalem. The Artus kings, the dynasty of the knights of Parsival, and the famous round table over which Merlin IV had sworn to resist conquest by the Normans, all those marvelous tales that had the ring of legends—I knew them well from having learned them as child. And for a sensitive, delicate creature like Christian, it had the flavor of an ancient, vanished dream, that of a great Celtic kingdom that could have been born and flourished if the Varangian armies of Vladimir the Russ had not invaded that country in the name of the Empire in the year 1066.

Alas, those delicious moments were all too brief. A delegate decided to come and sit with us. He was wearing the white tunic of the Copts and I immediately understood that he had come to scoff at us. He introduced himself: Nicolas Radomir from Muscovy, disciple of Manuel Anastasiac and faithful supporter of Master John of Thebaid. He was tall with a pointed beard, and he smiled amicably, not without a certain self-conceit. What I hated most of all was the way that this Nicolas Radomir kept his eyes fixed constantly on Christian. My young friend did not dare to reply, he was so intimidated. He kept his big blue eyes lowered, and his cheeks reddened.

Nicolas Radomir first asked about our professions, and as soon as he found out that we were semiologists, he started talking to us about Alexandrian organs, a subject about which it seemed he could go on forever. Anger swelled up inside me.

"But you'll never get anywhere as long as you're using those decrepit instruments!" I shouted.

"Wait to see the presentation of Master John of Thebaid. You will see that our techniques are not as far behind as you think. We even use the illuminated panels that you are so proud of."

"Come now, you're putting us on. It is impossible that you have made such progress."

"We have made as much progress as you, and the more we advance, the more the validity of historical monochronism is confirmed."

"That means you don't know all the registers of the organ—"

"Andreas! Be careful," said Christian suddenly with fear in his voice.

"Register?" asked Nicolas. "Have you developed a new one?"

"Yes, and it will shatter your doctrine."

"You're lying, Andreas Antonikas. Never will the Britons succeed at such a feat. No one could possibly develop a register that would respect the logic rules of Panini and at the same time contradict the doctrine of monochronism."

"Andreas, I beg of you. Don't insist."

I came close to losing control of myself and I was not very proud of it. I finally found the strength to turn my head so as not to be looking directly at that impertinent fellow. A little more and I would have betrayed Ramindra and the secret of the eighth register. Seeing that he would now be wasting his time, Nicolas got up and went over to Christian. He took his hand and held it very tightly. Christian tried to break free. I leapt up, ready to come to his defense. Nicolas let go immediately and burst out laughing.

"I hope we will see each other again, my dear young friend. Yes, I am sure that we will see each other again."

"That man is dangerous," Christian said to me once he was gone.

"No," I replied, forcing myself to sound reassuring. "He's only a little spy of no importance."

"No, he is very powerful. . . . I'm sure he's very powerful."

The synod opened in the morning of March 29. As Hegumen of the host monastery, it was Theobald Zacharion who delivered the inaugural speech. I had hoped that he would take advantage of his privilege as the first speaker to make a direct attack on the doctrine of the monochronism of history, but I was in for another disappointment. The Hegumen was diplomatic, avoiding any controversial subject. He recalled the modest but glorious origins of historiosophy. He evoked the blessed names of those who were honored as founders: Procopius of Caesarea, Leon the Deacon, and in particular Theodore Metochites and Nicephorus Gregoras, who in the thirteenth century had established the foundations of historical speculation. He just skimmed over the tragic events that had torn Christendom asunder in the sixteenth century, when the heretic Hugh of Bavaria had attempted to dispute the authority of the Church in worldly matters. He ended his speech with a comment on the need for healthy discussion among reasonable individuals. Thus Theobald Zacharion had succeeded in not showing his preferences, choosing to set himself up as arbiter, above the fray. He was not fooling anyone.

After dinner, it was John of Thebaid's turn to address the assembly. Fifty-three years old, the author of *A Treatise on Modern Hagiography,* he was regarded as the greatest historiosophist of the ecumene. His adversaries accused him of merely repeating and modernizing the thoughts of his predecessors. "All of John of Thebaid is already contained in Theodore Metochites or Nicephorus Gregoras," my Master Justin said to me. He was exaggerating. But it was well known that the eminent Scholarch of the University of Alexandria had made his whole career as an apologist for orthodoxy, a role that he carried out with the eloquence and brilliance of a superior mind.

John of Thebaid was among those most at ease in the debates. As soon as he had sat down on the rostrum, his tall silhouette dominated the hall. It even seemed to tower over the monastery organ that rose behind him, a powerful machine, both in terms of its advanced functions and its size. To his right, close to the rostrum, a great glass panel had been set up, inside which ran hundreds of electrified metal filaments. Nicolas Radomir was right, I realized with frustration; the Alexandrians were perhaps behind in their ideas, but they had been able to adapt to new technologies.

Master John's speech lasted less than sixty minutes. His words were clear, his argument irrefutable. The luminous panel displayed only convincing things: text, mathematical formulas, or diagrams. Three young assistants had been assigned to work the organ. The first one manipulated the keyboard and changed the register as required. The second one watched over the electrification of the panel, which required particular care because of the sparks that could be produced. Finally, the third one took care of the little electrogenic motor, which was enclosed in a metal case equipped with a chimney in which a sort of purified naphtha was burned.

Master John took us by the hand and guided us through his speech as if what he was saying was perfectly obvious. Near me, Theobald Zacharion tried to remain impassive, but I could see his hands trembling on his knees. Adam of Canterburg gnawed down all the nails on both hands as he listened. As for my Master Justin, the thin smile that he kept on his lips the whole time barely concealed his discomfort.

Taking advantage of the opportunity offered by Theobald Zacharion, Master John reviewed the circumstances under which the doctrine of monochronism came into being in the sixteenth century. He outlined the reasoning that was central to the doctrine and easily showed its superiority to the futile claims of the villainous Hugh of Bavaria.

"I invite you now to consider these diagrams, which we call *historicographs,* and which are, you will agree, singularly elegant. I have faith in the technological progress that permits us to illustrate with so much beauty and precision the power of the concept of historical monochronism. Could the renunciation of that vision of beauty and strength lead to anything else but wretchedness and absurdity? Should we stop believing that all phenomena are the results of their causes, in order to please certain souls who feel a need to make names for themselves? Or that the cause of an effect is itself the consequence of a previous cause? That the sequence of these causes thus forms a perfect string of inevitable events? That this inevitability is itself a manifestation of the nature of time? And that all this, on a cosmic scale, does in fact constitute a simple and obvious expression of the will of the Supreme Being?"

John of Thebaid took a long breath. His shining eyes, full of fervor, scanned the audience slowly, one last time.

"This machine should be turned off now," he said in a resounding voice, pointing to the magnificent organ that stood behind him. "Yes, it should be turned off now. For there is no need to use this artifice to achieve sound reasoning. I speak of reasoning free of the unwholesome and dangerous ambition of leaving one's name to posterity. A child could do it alone. For it would not be forbidden for the child to ask questions. Certainly, no more than an adult. The question is good; only the answer is bad. The answer found as the result of the mind drifting through waters where logic is absent is called error. And while we may charitably excuse error in a weak mind, the wilful propagation of error by men of talent must be vigorously condemned."

The tone had just become a lot more heated. Master John was no longer the scholar humbly submitting his theses to the assembly. He had been transformed into a menacing preacher anathematizing unrepentant sinners.

"The idea of a possible plurality of time is error! The idea that the order of things depends on whims of chance is error! The idea that what is happening everywhere at this very moment has not been designed, planned, and inserted into the great scheme of history at the beginning of the world by our Creator is error! Unless. . . ." (And here, John of Thebaid took a long pause on which we all hung.) "Unless one takes the error further, carried along by I don't know what aberration, to stop believing in the very existence of the Creator!"

Master John gave a slight bow. He was finished. His conclusion had been the cause of great mirth. And everyone (or almost) applauded him warmly when he stepped down from the rostrum. His supporters rushed to embrace him. Manuel Anastasiac and his disciple Nicolas Radomir ran over to kiss him. Even among the delegates who had come to follow the Briton party, several seemed prepared to review their positions. Theobald Zacharion had already left the room. Master Justin was not to be seen anywhere. As for Adam of Canterburg, he was shattered, his head buried in his hands. Christian and I took him back to his cell.

Thus ended the day of the 29th, with the triumph of Master John. No other orator wanted to follow him on the rostrum. The rebuttal of the Briton party was scheduled for the next day. I found supper infernal. I ate, my face in my plate, straining not to hear the mocking comments of the ever more numerous supporters of historical monochronism. Christian had stayed with his master. I tried to join them again after the meal, but I found it impossible to enter their quarters. Jon Seymour and Maxentius Ingham had been posted in the corridor, blocking access like eunuchs at the doors of a gynaeceum.

"Master Adam is preparing his speech for tomorrow. No one is to disturb him."

I told them that I was the disciple of Justin Cantarumene and that I had participated in other meetings previously. No use. Master Adam had given strict orders. I finally learned, though, that my Master Justin and Theobald Zacharion had been admitted to the summit meeting where, during the night, the rebuttal strategy for the next day must have been planned. I deduced that Christian was not with them. I knocked at the door of his cell. Silence.

I slept very badly that night.

On the morning of March 30, Master Adam of Canterburg came before the assembly alone, absolutely alone. No disciples accompanied him. The great organ of the monastery shone behind him with all its ornaments, but Ramindra's machine was not there. I saw neither my Master Justin nor Theobald nor Christian in the hall.

Master Adam began to speak in a trembling voice. He had neither the rhetoric nor the charisma of his adversary. During most of his speech, the organ remained silent behind him. The luminous panel, on which the almost too perfect historicographs with which Master John had sprinkled his speech the day before had been formed, remained nothing more than a sheet of dull glass, lightless and without form. It seemed that Master Adam had taken his adversary at his word when he had asked him to put himself in the sole power of the spirit to find the truth.

Master Adam spoke neither of the Creator nor of the historical destiny of man. He invoked the experience of chance, familiar to everyone. Using examples to back up his argument, he showed how our inadequate knowledge of causes was a contingency of prime importance, since it prevented us from predicting effects with any certainty. The physical world he described was very different from the one that John of Thebaid had presented the day before. It was capricious, unpredictable, chaotic. Nothing could occur in it absolutely predictably, because the most obvious relations of cause and effect could be contradicted by the appearance of an unforeseen factor.

"If I put my hand into the fireplace, chances are very strong that I will burn myself. But it is not a total certainty. Chances are not nil that one of my friends will rush in front of me to prevent me from committing this mad act. Or that a sudden rainfall will come down the chimney and put out the fire. Or else that I will trip before reaching it, knocking my head against a wall and only waking up hours later in front of cold ashes."

There was impatient shuffling in the audience and a few scoffing remarks to the effect that Master Adam had lost a lot of support the day before and he would have more and more trouble finding a friend to stop him from burning his hand.

Master Adam seemed shaken, but he continued his argument. "Certainty is an extremely variable commodity," he said, "and therefore it can only be measured proportionally. Since each event is never anything but simply probable, to various degrees, the *a posteriori* reconstitution of a determinist chain of events is illusory. Anyone who claims to go from effects to causes will never be capable of predicting effects with certainty solely through knowledge of those causes.

"If nothing of what happens, has happened, or will happen is entirely predictable, but only more or less probable, is not the normal progression of time itself marked by uncertainty? The same, therefore, is true for the unwinding thread of history."

"Oh, come now!" shouted a voice, followed by a few laughs.

"Yes, history. The great chain of events is presented to us as a predestined, perfect trajectory. It is true that if one looks back, one imagines that the events which actually occurred must be the most probable, and that it will always be so. But one thus commits a grave error in reasoning. For the improbable also occurs. Events of which the degree of certainty was very low have already occurred in history, and more will occur."

A faction of the young delegates dressed in white robes started to protest vigorously and demand proof.

"Thanks to technical advances that have recently been made to the machines that we use to put the events of history into logical order, it is now possible to analyze the coefficient of probability of each of the links in the chain and thus to bring to light important rifts in the fabric of time."

Master Adam gave a signal, and I saw Christian, from out of nowhere, step onto the rostrum two paces behind his master. He sat down at the keyboard of the great organ and started to press the keys. He seemed like an angel making music. Images started to take form on the panel. At first it was the beautiful straight line of the historicograph that Master John had shown us the day before. For anyone who put their faith in the monochronism of the Alexandrian School, that was how the route followed by human history had to appear. Soon, however, through the magic of Christian's fingers, the line became wider, and split, each segment becoming a line in itself, a jagged line, marked by peaks and valleys. For me, the most astonishing thing was that all these transformations were happening on that four-register monastery organ that I considered to be completely outdated! How had Master Adam accomplished this miracle? Had Ramindra come here the night before to transfer to this venerable monastic instrument a part of his invention? In order to avoid the risk of showing that heretical machine in public, had Master Adam chosen to produce a surprise effect on his adversary's own ground?

There were emotional shouts from in the audience, accusations of sabotage, of blasphemy, and of sorcery. There were protests and raised fists. Master Adam paled visibly. Clearly, the reaction of the delegates was not what he had hoped for.

"Look!" he pleaded. "Here, this segment! Look, instead of shouting! In the beginning of the seventh century, a drop in probability such as had never been seen occurred: the fabric of history broke down. Everything that happened inside that time segment has a coefficient of probability that is close to zero! Please just look!"

"Very well. I will agree to look," said a deep voice then, seeming immediately to drown out all the others.

Silence returned. John of Thebaid stood up slowly and came to join Master Adam on the rostrum. He went over to the organ and examined the keyboard, then asked one of his monks to open the cabinet so that he could take a look inside.

"It's all a hoax," he said finally. "All you did was modify

the logic cogwheels of this device in order to provide support for your untenable theses."

"Of course we changed the cogwheels," said Adam feverishly. "Because this archaic apparatus doesn't have all the registers required to carry out the operations properly!"

"That's just what I said. When the demonstration goes against your ideas, you accuse the apparatus of being outmoded and you meddle with the insides until it is 'modern' enough for you."

"Listen to me. Those historicographs were drawn on the basis of absolutely reliable calculations, carried out on an organ model that is much more powerful than this one. And that organ follows Panini's rules of logic as faithfully as any."

"I don't believe a word of it!"

Master Adam was trembling. Would he now find a way to talk about Ramindra's organ without mentioning Ramindra himself?

"I will do a demonstration this evening, after supper."

"I would prefer it to be immediately."

"Yes! Right away!" shouted the delegates.

Adam and John stared at each other for a moment. I realized that Christian had left the rostrum and was about to leave the conference hall. That dear soul! No doubt he was running to warn Ramindra to lie low. I tried to follow him, but a sudden movement of the crowd prevented me. When I was finally able to slip out of the hall, I left great confusion behind me. At the center of the rostrum, an altercation had just broken out between John of Thebaid and Master Adam. Around them, delegates of all tendencies hurled abuse at one another like small children in a gynaeceum.

I hurried through the corridors that led to the cloister. Christian must have been just ahead of me. Twenty paces from Ramindra's door, I saw a man in a white tunic who appeared to be running away. I ran after him; he heard me coming and turned his head and saw me. I saw him too and recognized him. It was that despicable spy, Nicolas Radomir. He started running again and disappeared towards the kitchens. I decided not to go after him. I began to feel very worried. I went back and knocked on Ramindra's door. No answer. I heard a commotion behind me. A group of delegates was approaching, arguing loudly. Could it be that John of Thebaid had finally forced Master Adam to lead him to the organ? I was overcome with panic. I tried to open the door. It was not locked. I went in.

And I screamed.

I was found a moment later, near the door of the cell, white as a ghost, my body pressed against the wall, incapable of uttering a word. Fortunately, I had been seen going in, because otherwise I could have been accused. Ramindra's cell had been ransacked. His work table, his trunks, and his bed had been turned over. But all that was only a backdrop to the more grisly scene that lay before me.

Ramindra's body was lying in the middle of the room, covered in blood. He had been stabbed in the neck. And beside him were the remains of his organ, smashed to pieces. The keys were scattered across the floor. Wires, tiny levers, and gearwheels hung loose inside the gutted cabinet.

I was taken out of the cell and someone gave me a cordial to drink. But I was only thinking of one thing: find Christian. Because if he had been seen leaving the conference hall, sooner or later someone would think to accuse him of the crime. All my efforts in the hours that followed proved in vain. Christian had disappeared. And Master Adam, who had fallen ill after these events, refused to receive anyone.

That evening, soldiers invested the monastery. Reluctantly the Hegumen had had to enlist the aid of his old enemy, the Prefect Marsilius Alarius. Following a brief investigation, the civil authorities officially recognized the fact that a foreigner had been killed in a vicious act that had also destroyed a machine belonging to the victim.

Suspicion immediately fell on the entourage of the Hegumen. My Master Justin was questioned at length, since his absence from the conference hall had been noticed that morning. He was released only on the insistence of Theobald Zacharion, who swore he had been conferring with him till the time the body was discovered. The Hegumen had a lot to explain, however, since the Prefect seemed to take a malicious pleasure in putting him in an awkward position.

Master Theobald stated that he and Justin had left Ramindra early in the forenoon, a few minutes before Adam of Canterburg began his speech. They had not seen him since. Why hadn't they gone to hear their colleague's speech? Because they already knew what he was going to say, having both participated the evening before in its preparation. Finally my Master Justin was released, but this ordeal seemed to have aged him by ten years.

Then came my turn to appear. Of course, I accused Nicolas Radomir, the man I had seen fleeing in the corridor. The Prefect took a few notes, but I heard no more about it. This confounded me. Because ultimately, the more I thought about it, the more it seemed to me that this Nicolas Radomir was the ideal suspect. He detested our ideas and he had shown excessive curiosity about our machines.

But quite obviously, embarrassing the Hegumen was Marsilius Alarius's sole objective. Instead of simply closing the case, given that the victim was after all only a foreigner, instead of arresting Nicolas Radomir, he continued his investigation. Justin Cantarumene had revealed to him that Ramindra kept the plans for his organ with him. Marsilius seized on this pretext. If his plans had disappeared, he claimed, it was because the murderer had taken them. Find those plans, and you would apprehend the guilty party. Again with a view to compromising the Hegumen, the Prefect ordered a search of all the cells.

And it was in the course of that search that Christian was found.

Or rather the person I had always called Christian. That person had hidden in Master Adam's cell and had been living cloistered there since the day of the murder, now to be found there, half dead with fear. It was there too that it was realized, when a search was made for the plans, that Christian Lods was a girl.

It turned out her name was Irene of Canterburg and that she was the adopted child of Master Adam. He had to explain that he had taken the orphan in when she was only twelve, that he had been captivated by her beauty and intelligence, and that he had wanted her to accompany him everywhere he went. Thus they had both agreed to this subterfuge. Irene passed for his disciple and Adam had, out of necessity, provided her with instruction that was far superior to what a person of her sex would normally have received. Thus, instead of marrying at sixteen and going into the gynaeceum of her husband, as do all Christian women who are not destined for the convent, Irene had since that time led the life of a man, and, what is more, that of a man of intelligence.

My dismay did not last long. The news that Christian was a girl, I realized immediately, did not change my feelings in the least. I loved a person with all my soul, and it mattered to me hardly at all whether she was a boy, a girl, or an angel. I knew that such things happened sometimes. Certain women that God had endowed with a superior mind refused their natural condition and attempted through such masquerades to taste, be it for a few days or a few months, a way of life reserved for men. Although morally indefensible, such conduct could be understood by someone with an open mind.

The scandal was enormous. It sullied not only Master Adam and the Briton party, but the monastery of Mount Boreal and historiosophy itself. Although the plans were not found on her, Irene was nevertheless arrested and charged with murder. There was no doubt, it was said in the entourage of John of Thebaid, that seeing his deception exposed, Master Adam had ordered his daughter to run and eliminate all trace of that so-called revolutionary organ, including the foreigner who had constructed it. To those who said that this story was not very credible, since a woman does not murder in this fashion, and that, in any case, Master Adam had nothing to gain from the murder of Ramindra, others answered that, precisely, Adam and his daughter wanted in this way to throw suspicion on the Alexandrian party.

I did not involve myself in these discussions. They reached my ears, I recorded them, but I did not pay any attention to them. Only one thing mattered in my eyes: the one I loved most in the world had just been arrested for murder. I made efforts to see her again, but the Prefect kept Irene in seclusion. The accused was to be taken outside the monastery, imprisoned, and tried.

The morning of April 2, I watched from the window as she emerged, her hands tied. An escort of soldiers led her to the Prefect's black coach. She no longer had on her monk's tunic, but was wearing a loose-fitting dark-colored robe. A shawl covered her head and part of her face, as befits any woman appearing in public. Before getting into the coach, she turned her head toward the window, as if she had felt my presence. I saw her blue eyes in the distance, wet with tears. She wanted perhaps to give me a sign, but she was prevented.

At that instant, I swore to save her. The Prefect had ignored my testimony, but others would perhaps listen to me. I decided to go and share my secret with my master. Justin Cantarumene listened to me absentmindedly. My revelations did not interest him. Ramindra's death had ruined his plans, the cause of new ideas in historiosophy had just gone up in smoke, perhaps for centuries, and there was no hope of reconstructing the eighth register since the plans had disappeared. So what did it matter finally whether it was Christian or Irene or Nicolas Radomir who had committed the crime? It was God's will, and there was no going back.

I did not dare to seek out Master Adam. The arrest of his daughter had finally destroyed his health. He was suffering from a fever and his condition was worsening day by day. As a last resort, I considered telling Master Theobald of my predicament. He was a man of sound judgment, I thought, a diplomat, and he would be able to tell me what to do.

Now that the guilty party had been arrested, the Prefect Marsilius Alarius had granted the delegates permission to leave. The temperature had turned a little milder, and, after the painful events of recent days, no one had any further desire to debate the monochronism of human history. Dozens of delegates had already packed their bags and started to leave. Master Theobald did not have a minute to give me, but I insisted. I rushed to his door and almost broke it down with my fist. The stern face of the Hegumen finally appeared in the doorway.

"Master, listen to me," I said breathlessly, "I know the name of the guilty one!"

"Young fool. Don't you see that it is all over?"

"But I saw him! When I came close to Ramindra's cell, he ran away."

"Who are you talking about, anyway?"

"His name is Nicolas Radomir. He's a Varangian, a disciple of Manuel Anastasiac.

"All right. Go now. And if you value your life, do not tell this to anyone."

"Wait," said the voice of a man hidden behind the door. "I would like to hear this boy."

It was Nicolas Radomir. He was sitting quite comfortably in an armchair, a cup of wine in his hand. We were not alone. Besides Theobald, there was Nicolas's tutor, Manuel Anastasiac, and Marsilius Alarius, the Prefect of Mount Boreal. All three were standing. I did not understand why. Nicolas Radomir smiled at me and invited me to sit down on the only other seat available in the cell.

"So you saw me, Andreas Antonikas, coming out of Ramindra Thagor's cell? And you said to yourself that I was the murderer?"

"Why run away, if you weren't?"

"Why run away? Yes, that is a good question. Why does one flee when one discovers a crime and is not oneself the author of that crime?"

"I—I don't know."

"You believe Irene of Canterburg to be innocent. Well, *I* saw her running away from Ramindra's cell a few moments before I went in. Why did Irene run away, do you think?"

"Because she didn't want to be questioned! She didn't want her secret to be discovered!"

"You see, an innocent person can have good reasons for fleeing from the scene of a murder. In fact, three persons saw the body that morning, and you are the only one who called attention to it."

I said nothing. If Irene had discovered the crime before him, Nicolas Radomir was obviously innocent. But why had he run away when he saw me?

"Do you still wish to have me arrested by our Prefect Marsilius Alarius?"

"I'm surprised he hasn't done so."

"My poor friend, would you wish then that he arrest your Emperor?"

I sat with my mouth open for a long minute during which he, Marsilius Alarius, and Manuel Anastasiac laughed. Only Theobald Zacharion maintained his gloomy expression. Imbecile that I was, how many times had I seen his portrait displayed everywhere, and I hadn't recognized him! And moreover, he had not even attempted to hide his identity. Everyone should have known, even as far away as China, that Nicolas Radomir was the real name of the young Varangian who had ascended the throne of Constantinople under the name of Michael XXII Philophilus!

"Historiosophy is one of my many fields of interest. Note that the ideas professed by Master Adam of Canterburg are sufficient to alarm any sovereign. All those holes that he sees in history . . . Of course, there are not very many of you who believe in these things. My tutor, the venerable Manuel Anastasiac, considers that this supposedly new tendency in historiosophy is nothing more than a fraud. He wanted me nevertheless to come and attend your synod. I was graciously invited to take a place in the Alexandrian delegation. But desiring also to show impartiality, I solicited an interview with your Master Justin Cantarumene in order to familiarize myself with your theses. I had just left him, that morning, when you saw me."

The Emperor poured another cup, looking at me amusedly.

"I do not know why I am telling you all this. It would have been quicker to have your head cut off. But what would then be said of an enlightened basileus who behaved in such a bloody manner? We have not fraternized much, you and I, since the beginning of this synod, Andreas Antonikas. I sense in you, however, a young man with a future who will be capable of being reasonable, discreet and loyal."

I bowed my head, hunched my back, and knelt.

"Oh, remain seated. I am a simple man. By the way, don't worry about our beautiful, young friend, Irene of Canterburg. She is innocent, of course. And our good Prefect will release her as soon as I tell him to. Won't you, Marsilius?"

Irene would be freed? Was it possible? All of a sudden Nicolas Radomir seemed to me to have become the incarnation of divine indulgence. I searched for the words to prove my gratitude to him.

"I doubt, however, that you will ever see her again. Nor Master Adam. That young woman was raised in error. It is not fitting to mix the education of the sexes in this way. Man and woman were created different. That difference must be assumed as their destiny. But, on the other hand, it would be a mistake to ignore her talent. Irene is a woman of resources, and I am certain that my wife, the Empress Elena, will appreciate her conversation, while for my part, I will admire the blue of her eyes. She will be the flower of the Imperial gynaeceum."

I remained on my knees, clenching my fists, hiding as best I could the hate that was tearing my heart at that moment.

"And to show you that I bear you no ill will, I have the pleasure of inviting you to witness the arrest of Ramindra Thagor's true murderer."

This time, I raised my head, so intrigued that I forgot to hide the tears that were running down my cheeks.

"You only have to reason a little, for in reality, things are very simple, are they not?" continued the Emperor, his eyes shining.

On the advice of his tutor, Manuel Anastasiac, Nicolas Radomir had chosen to speak with Justin Cantarumene rather than with the chief adversary of the Alexandrian School, Adam of Canterburg. This interview, intended to familiarize the Emperor with the new theses of historiosophy, was nevertheless supposed to take place in secret, in the strictest confidentiality. What better moment to choose than the morning when Adam of Canterburg was to present his reply to John of Thebaid? For reasons of security, it was agreed to meet in Theobald Zacharion's cell. The Hegumen therefore had invited them both in, and then withdrawn as requested.

"My interview with Justin Cantarumene was most fascinating. He spoke to me of the eighth register, of its potential, and of the much-vaunted hole that you had discovered in the fabric of history. When we left each other, Justin told me that he was going to rejoin the Hegumen and Master Adam in the conference hall. I would have done the same thing if the idea had not suddenly come to me to have a look for myself at that extraordinary organ. Take note that I had not yet heard of Ramindra. I thought I would find that cell empty. You know the rest. Irene of Canterburg, who had come to warn Ramindra of the turn of events, discovered the body and ran away. I attempted to leave too, but then you arrived, Andreas Antonikas. Hoping that you had not recognized me, I ran towards the kitchens."

"But then," I cried, "who killed Ramindra?"

"The Hegumen, of course. When he left us, Justin and me, he told us he was going to hear Master Adam. Well, no one saw him enter the conference hall that morning."

"I went outside for some air," murmured Theobald without conviction. "I had a headache and. . . ."

"Come, come, my dear Hegumen. No one saw you there either. And there were monks outside removing the snow from the steps. We checked. Didn't we check, Marsilius? The funny thing is when this poor Prefect, not knowing who I was, tried to accuse Justin. It was the testimony of Theobald that saved him. In order not to compromise his beloved Emperor in this sordid affair, our brave Hegumen had the generosity to take my place in a way, swearing that it was he who had spent the morning in the company of Justin. But by doing so, the shrewd Theobald was giving himself an alibi."

"But . . . why?" I cried. "Why kill a man who was our ally?"

"Do you want to tell him, Master Theobald? Or should I?"

Pale as the snow since he had been accused, the Hegumen remained silent, his jaw clenched shut. The Emperor, therefore, continued.

"The hole in the seventh century, Andreas Antonikas! That

abomination of a hole! By speaking with Justin Cantarumene, then later with my tutor Manuel, I understood one very important thing. One could react very differently when faced with the idea of a temporal rift almost thirteen centuries in the past. Some, such as Master Justin or Master Adam, will attempt by all means with the fervor of a proselyte to make this phenomenon known and accepted. For their part, Manuel Anastasiac and John of Thebaid gave no credence to it, and for them, it was simply a matter of denouncing and combatting the error. But there is also a third attitude that can be adopted. And that is the one chosen by our Hegumen. On the eve of the crime, as you know, Adam, Justin, and Theobald met around Ramindra's organ, where they explored the great historical depression of the seventh century. What Justin told me is truly distressing. I am delighted to be a supporter of the monochronism of history, for otherwise I would have been terrified. As Theobald Zacharion was."

"I did it for you, Michael Philophilus!" cried the Hegumen suddenly. "For you and for the Empire, and for the world as we have always known it. Because nothing of all that subsists in . . . reality! You just touched on the subject with Justin, but to open the eighth register is to open the gates of hell!"

"You see, Andreas Antonikas? That is the third attitude. Theobald Zacharion believed in those stories of temporal bifurcations. He condemned them not because he believed them false, but because, on the contrary, he was sure of their veracity. By killing Ramindra Thagor and demolishing his organ, he was only, in his eyes, exorcising evil."

"Evil! Yes, evil. . . . And it will not come back. No one in the world will know how to reconstruct an organ like that one. Ramindra is dead, and I have made sure to burn all his plans. . . ."

"Marsilius, take him away."

I never saw Irene again. The Emperor took her with him when he returned to Constantinople, as he had said he would. And if he kept his promise, she entered the Imperial gynaeceum as a companion for the young Empress Elena.

The reign of Michael Philophilus did not last twelve months. In December 1994, a little before Christmas, a sedition led by Serb merchants, military men from Western Khazaria, and without any doubt, a few influential prelates chased him from the throne and installed the dour John Gregory III in his place. And with him most of Michael Philophilus's ambitions disappeared, in particular the senseless plan to send Christians to the Moon.

I never saw Irene again, but I never forgot her. I do not know what became of her when the new basileus took power. Michael XXII met a very grim end. He who had considered himself a friend of the light had his eyes put out with a hot iron, then he was drawn and quartered in the center of the hippodrome of Constantinople. Of his wife, the very young Elena, who was then pregnant, and of her fate, no more was heard. I pray God that those women were able to find refuge in one of the convents of the Urals of the Pyrenees, which are high places of prayer and meditation.

I returned to Providence and have never left. I did not even want to return to Galactea. It would have been easy for me sometimes to cross the Atlas Sea and visit the Old Continent on the occasion of a synod or a festive occasion. I have always refused. And I never visited those ancient cities with names that ring in my ears like the stuff of legend—Carthage, Ephesus, Alexandria, Parisia, and Camelot. Nor Constantinople, flame flickering in the darkness of the world.

I am getting old now. I began getting old on the day of April 4, 1994, when I left behind me the monastery Mount Boreal and all my illusions about the goodness of the world. Adam of Canterburg passed away, his heart broken, only a few days after his return to Oxenford. I was told that the monastery of Mount Boreal was placed under military trusteeship by the Prefect Marsilius Alarius after the arrest and decapitation of the Hegumen Theobald Zacharion. Over the years, historiosophy has lost much of its interest and no one to my knowledge seeks anymore to dispute the monochronism of history.

Today I occupy the Chair of Semiology at the University of Providence. It is there that I survive, cast into the shadows. No one knows me. No one will read me before my death. My manuscripts, encrypted by my own hand, will remain carefully buried in shafts I myself dug under the vaults of my house.

I never saw Irene again, but I received something from her just before her departure, an envelope of silk paper that she perhaps could not have sent me without the benevolent collusion of the Emperor. It was not a farewell letter or even a simple note. In the envelope, she had just placed a small, ornate wooden key, such as one finds on all the keyboards of sign-processing organs.

This one, I recognized from the style and its icons, belonged to the great organ of the monastery of Mount Boreal.

The day of my departure, I returned to the now-deserted conference hall. The great organ had remained in place, and I found on the keyboard the place from which the key had come. Irene must have assisted Ramindra that fateful night when he had hastily installed a part of the eighth register. And what she had sent to me was the access key, not to the register itself (which the Prefect had had torn out and destroyed), but to something else that Ramindra had hidden that night in the belly of the machine. Had our friend sensed the Hegumen's terror? Had he believed himself threatened? I will never know, but I bless his decision to hide a copy of his plans in that place and to let Irene in on the secret.

Now, each night that God gives me, I sit down at my big keyboard and turn on the eighth register. I send through it the electric fluid that comes from the old batteries that I recharge on stormy nights. And that is enough to produce the miracle: the truth emerges from my organ and traces itself on a roll of inked parchment. Historicographs take form. I never tire of contemplating them with devotion and respect, with terror too. For their signs tell me what happened in the real world, the one with no holes, the one beside which all the others will never be anything but crude deviations.

This truth I will reveal one day to the men of my false world who still believe that time follows a long, perfect line. They will read my memoirs, but I will be far away then, on the other side of life. It will be up to them to judge me, but in particular to judge Theobald Zacharion, who was so afraid of that truth that he killed in order to smother it.

Muhammad, the holy man, did indeed exist, and he was able to rally the Arabs. But if he was visited by an angel, it was not to embrace the cause of the Roman Empire, nor that of Persia. A new form of religion was born under his reign, a religion that transformed forever the face of the real world. Constantinople ceased being a Christian city in 1453. And now, at this dawn of the twenty-first century, a new and exalted Empire unites the human race under the banner of the crescent moon.

Doing Time

Robert Boyczuk

Robert Boyczuk lives in Toronto and is a professor of computer science at Seneca College of Applied Arts and Technology. In 1993 he attended the Clarion West workshop in Seattle. Shortly after that he cofounded a no-name writing group with Brent Hayward and Nalo Hopkinson (other members of the group include Laurie Channer and Peter Watts). Boyczuk published several stories in *On Spec*—one of which, "Distant Seas," was reprinted in *On Spec: The First Five Years,* a "best-of" anthology for the magazine—and has also had pieces in *Transversions* and *Prairie Fire,* the latter, "Assassination and the New World Order," winning their speculative fiction writing contest.

"Doing Time," says Boyczuk, "was originally written during a Clarion West writing workshop. Lucius Shepard, one of the instructors for that session, passed out photocopies of two stories that made use of similar narratorial voices: William Gibson's 'New Rose Hotel' and Jayne Anne Phillips's 'Black Tickets.' Both stories took the form of the ruminations of a protagonist who had, at the opening of the piece, already been betrayed. Lucius's point was that there is nothing wrong with a writer attempting the same voice he or she has encountered in another author's work if it is appropriate to one's own story. I thought it would be an interesting challenge to write yet another story using the same kind of voice and situation, with a slightly different spin."

My cell is small, Robin, seven paces from end to end, three from side to side, and sometimes I think it too small for sanity, too narrow for any sort of clear understanding. You of all people should know what I mean, trapped in your own prison, your own desires. Not like this one, no. But a prison all the same.

Sometimes I imagine us walking together, pacing off the minutes of our sentences, in tandem, you with your small strides stretching to keep up with mine, ten seconds for each circuit, front to back, your soft voice in my ear, patient, more patient than you ever were in our time together, rhyming off the steps with me one by one. I know you are satisfied for now, and with each passing moment I can feel your smile growing inside me like a tumor. For I have done what you wanted, Robin, spoken in your place: I killed her, I killed her for you.

I hungered for you, Robin.

I remember when you first came to St. James Town, small and ginger-skinned, angry dreadlocks spilling from beneath a loose knit beret of green and gold and black. Looking for kicks, you said, in mock high school seriousness (though you were older, far older, in your nakedness), meaning drugs and sex and colorful memories, you wandering among the run-down tenements and swirling garbage like a goofy eighteen-year-old kid, another of Mick's disposable uptown friends, another clean face slumming for a thrill, stepping delicately around the dog turds in your scuffed Docs and meticulously torn jeans. He introduced us, knowing I liked your type, but not for the reasons he ever believed. He thought I was tired of Janine, poor worn-out Janine, greasy blond hair always obscuring half her tired face, shivering and shaking most of the time now when she wasn't high, wobbling down the shabby corridors of crack houses like a top about to fall over. No, I wasn't tired of her, nor she of me, but I knew she might dry up at any moment, and I didn't want to take that chance.

But you. You were young with a whole life ahead of you. A clean-cut kid. I imagined comfortable, middle-class parents for you, a lace-filled room populated with stuffed animals, and your own pink princess phone, me wanting to revel in your freshness, your naive, soap-scrubbed smell, to use you, to taste you, to consume you whole.

You said you wanted kicks.

You were shy at first, as I expected, trembling as you slipped out of your clothes though it was warm and humid, covering yourself with crossed arms, timorously, as if this were your first time. You were beautiful, untouched, a pristine sculpture, and I remember my heart, my blood, singing out, my desire rising.

Gently, hesitantly, you placed your hands on me, and I let you roam; drinking in your pleasure, the edge of your excitement, as if all this were new to you, all this unexplored, you touching me, first here, then there, cool fingers around my cock, happy to prolong your pleasure, to revel in my ache one minute more. I directed your hands, your mouth, your legs, and after a time I kissed you, long and deep and slow, rolling you onto your side then on top of you, lightly, lightly, one hand cupping your ass, the other guiding myself into you. For a moment you looked astonished, a sudden exhalation, eyes wide, shocked. Then you saw me again, lifted your legs and bent your knees, locking ankles behind my back, rocking your hips forward until our pelvises ground, bone to bone.

I began to move in a slow rhythm, knowing you were almost ready for me, for both my hungers, slipping more deeply into you, feeling the rush of your blood now, the rhythm of your heart, moving in and out of your lungs with your ragged breaths, touching the edges of your mind, spinning round your memories, ready at last for the final plunge. . . .

But I held myself. I stayed there, lingering at the boundary of your consciousness, mind jangling, catching at one of your thoughts, startled to see this wasn't your first time, that the gentle fumbling was an act only for my pleasure. I hesitated then, surprised.

And before I could begin stealing time from you, your body surged violently under mine, your mind flaring out like a lick of fire, you turning and twisting wildly beneath, a shock of energy desperate for pleasure, every nerve vibrating like a plucked string, shivering with a desire so strong I fell into your rush, your cadence, humming with your faster pace, my other need forgotten, your eyes open and fixed on mine, your small heels beating my back with the rhythm of my strokes, your lips drawn to show the too-white tips of teeth, back arched above the sheets, shuddering with the rush, 'cause you knew, you knew somehow I was experiencing it too, searing across my arms, my chest, a shuddering warmth in my loins, pouring out in staggered waves of you.

I came, I remember thinking in the shattered silence. Dear God, I came.

And then I collapsed on top of you.

Oh, you said, after a polite interval, you're heavy, pushing at my shoulder till you levered me over, spooning yourself into my side. Then you laughed, face flushed, sweat-slicked breasts against my arm.

Well, you said. That didn't take long.

What? I said, numbed, uncertain, my body trembling restlessly at this old sensation, confused, one hunger sated, the other still clamoring in anger and frustration, wanting your moments, your breath, your time. How long? I wondered. How long since I last came?

You were done, weren't you? you said, sliding your fingers lightly over the damp of my shrinking dick.

I said nothing.

You smiled sweetly, sat up, and gave my cock a peck. Don't worry, you whispered to it, pretending like you were keeping what you told it from me: There's always later, you said. Plenty of time.

Did you know, I wondered then. Did you know that I was going to steal a little piece of your life, adding it to mine? You'd have liked it Robin, the best orgasm you'd ever had, all your synapses firing, rocketing you into a state you'd never be able to equal, one that would have left you rubbery-legged and drained and bragging to your friends for months. A good exchange, a kick well worth a few weeks of your life.

I watched you sleep later, small, sharp breasts rising and falling in a steady rhythm, the trace of hip bone beneath skin, a shiny tuft of black hair. Wrapped in the smell of you and me. The smell of soap. Thinking about those moments I could have stolen from you. Might yet steal from you.

Just before midnight I grabbed my stash and slipped out. My hunger became too intense to bear. I didn't like doing it this way, so public and violent, stealing moments from an anonymous body in the street with an offer of drugs or money. But time was creeping up on me, and I knew it was somehow too late for you, had been too late the moment I met you.

Have I ever told you, Robin, it was that night, after my second feeding, in a dark, roach-infested room off Forty-eighth, I shivered, frightened you might be gone when I returned, frightened you might be there.

I have stolen lifetimes from men and women, a few weeks at a time. At the moment of orgasm, when the mind is an incoherent fiery ball, I dash in like a thief and slip out with a week, perhaps two, to add to mine.

But I never thought to ask myself what you were stealing from me.

It wasn't long before you moved in.

For me it is an indistinct time of recollection, a swirl I remember only vaguely. Comings and goings. You showing up and dragging me out to a play or movie, something new, something experimental that momentarily excited you, a different restaurant, sharp new spices, another cheap thrill, anything to try to eradicate the memory of what you insisted was a mundane life. You stayed at my place some nights, left others, until you stopped going back to your parents' place altogether.

How you loved my friends and their vials and foil packets.

I lied, told you I didn't have any money, not enough to buy that shit, but you still managed to cadge a pill here, a joint there. Sitting cross-legged on my worn little couch with your prize, puffing seriously, face falling when the effect wasn't what you craved. You falling asleep to dream of what new kicks tomorrow might bring. And I'd carry you to bed, again and again.

Robin, you needed me, I'd convinced myself, even though it was the other way around.

Do you remember how our lovemaking became more intense? Growing progressively longer, draining and exhilarating at the same time, you always wanting to push it further and higher, happy in the pool of the exhaustion afterwards, but never for long. For me it was as I had never imagined it could be. Yet painful all the same. Only part of my completion; a death half felt. Satisfaction and frustration spun together. You see, that hunger only served to fuel my other, the one I could never tell you about. A longing deferred. A desire to steal time from you, from your perfect future. My need was a burning stone lodged in my chest, so intense that after we uncoiled, always afterward, my yearning would drive me to slip out and wander the streets, careful to make sure you did not follow.

To swallow other less appetizing futures.

I knew often you lay awake as I drifted out, feeling your eyes trailing me to the door. Where did you think I was going? To see other women? It was always an understanding we had, a convenient part of our relationship. After all, you saw other men. And you never asked. Maybe you thought it wasn't cool to speak of it. Or perhaps, I reasoned, you were fearful of losing me, your latest kick.

Me your latest kick.

Did I ever tell you that you were mine?

Once a week a bus comes from the county lockups. I stare at the faces as they drift past, appraising them, their expressions cal-

culating and cagey, some desperate, some stupid. First-timers
look tired, harried, dark rings beneath their eyes, while the pros
are cool and uncaring, flashing smiles at half-remembered faces.
Then there are those trailing at the end, slack-jawed, eyes dark
and withdrawn, nervous or too stupid to be nervous, unaware
that time has already begun to slow with each step.

Once in a while, there is an innocent face. Fresh meat, I think,
and later, after they've settled, I offer them a cigarette.

We smoke in silence, leaning against a wall, and I remember
you, Robin, your lip caught between your teeth, staring at a magazine, or your tongue twisted with mine, your body tense and
waiting, and I think, my God, my God, I'm caught, I'm a captive
and I'll never be free.

It was a foolish pang of hunger.

You were supposed to be at work, breakfast shift. A job in the
diner around the corner for pocket money. Perhaps it was that
moment of weakness for which you never forgave me. Not the act
itself, which I think you understood for what it was. Three months
together, and I had been careful, to rent rooms, to haunt neighborhoods far away.

You were supposed to be at work.

I shouldn't have brought Janine back to our place. Should
never have talked her into our bed, hiding our circle of damp-
ness beneath the sheets from her. A promise of twenty dollars.
Me on top, brushing her greasy blond locks from dispassionate,
empty eyes. But I was desperate, so desperate, for her time. . . .

Had you waited for this, Robin, biding your time?

I saw you first in her mind, me sliding into her without
thinking, a reflex wrapping myself around her memories, her
moments yet to come. She must have seen you over my shoulder, leaning over us, for there you were, Janine's idea of you, a
naked woman-child with an odd expression, seeing you in a
way, as an image, I no longer could.

Then I felt you pressing against my back, distantly, for my
mind was already submerged in hers, your arms and legs covering mine like a sheath, your wetness moist on my leg, urging
me on, your mind, your thoughts there too, the three of us now
connected by our urgency, our need.

I knew this was what you wanted, more than anything else.
The ultimate kick.

I pulled too hard, pulled too fast, and she bucked beneath

me with a frenzy you had never matched, could never match, eyes white and rolling in her head, her mind wild with longing and death, spittle at the corners of her mouth, me drinking her in, taking her in monstrous gulps and passing it all to you, a conduit, not careful, not caring, but doing only what you demanded, draining her future away, in her mind until there was nothing but us, together, howling as our hunger became a single roaring beast, dragging her life out, not thinking to stop as we raged through her, only the hunger important, consuming us as it consumed her, ripping from her a deep scream, that tailed away.

She passed out, her body quivering, spasming, losing control, the stink of her coiling up around as she soiled the bed. I tried to withdraw, to pull out, but it was too late, for it was you, Robin, you who were in control, compelling us forward, drinking her lives through me as if I were a thin wire, overheating, mind blinding white and burning without remorse, until the feeling was everything, everything, and I remembered nothing more. . . .

When I woke you were gone.

A pounding on the door.

I shivered, sat up, drained and weak, in a pool of congealing blood and vomit. Could any of it have been yours? Janine was on the floor, propped next to the mattress, hands arranged neatly in her lap, half my stash tucked between her legs, needle hanging from the bruised flesh of her arm, a trickle of blood dripping from her earlobe onto the crumpled baggie. Police, a voice shouted. And you weren't there. I pressed my thumb against Janine's neck, felt nothing. Dead. Sucked dry. A husk. What had you done, Robin? How many lives did you steal from us that day?

Yet I don't grudge you any of it. Not a single minute.

Here in the prison yard I watch men measuring out their lives in small steps, grudging the moments stolen from them bit by bit. They are filled with bitter and unrepentant spirits that I swallow only reluctantly. Sitting on the edge of the bleachers, watching with a detached air the ebb and flow, the comings and goings, trying to imagine it through your eyes, seeing if I can feel the thrill for you, drawing on the parts of you left in me, as you would have wanted to, letting it wash around me, through me, without touching anything inside but you.

Why, Robin? Why didn't you take everything? Why'd you let me live?

I watch them standing in clutches, cigarettes burning down with their lives, and try to let your hunger direct me, perhaps to this one, perhaps to that one, helping me pick the life you'd have wanted.

I have every right to hate you. But I don't. Life is too long for that, and I won't be here forever. I know now that I've only been marking time, stealing bits and pieces of other lives like a petty thief, waiting for you. But when I get out, will you be waiting for me, Robin?

Will you?

THE FRAGRANCE OF ORCHIDS

Sally McBride

Sally McBride was born in 1950 in Newmarket, Ontario; grew up in Toronto ("where I took sciences at U of T for a couple of years"); and lived in Edmonton ("where I got involved in SF fandom") and Victoria, British Columbia. She moved back to Toronto late in 1997. She has taught speculative fiction writing, helped organize writers' workshops in Edmonton and Victoria, and is now involved in Toronto's Cecil Street writers group. With her husband, writer/artist Dale L. Sproule, she copublishes/edits the magazine *TransVersions*, featuring SF, fantasy, and horror work. Since its start in 1994, *TransVersions* has been nominated several times for the Aurora.

"The Fragrance of Orchids" first appeared in *Asimov's* in 1994. "I wanted to write a story about love between a human and an alien," she says, "and what that might lead to." The story won Canada's Aurora Award in 1995 for best short work in English.

November 2023; North Wells, Maine

On Monday morning, a message waited on Sarah Lightburn's answering machine. It was Seule, breathless, forgetting to say when the call was made, or if she intended to call back. Sarah, who up till now had been happy with their progress, felt a sinking in her heart.

"—I know I can handle it. Nothing will happen, we'll be working together, that's all. Clay needs me." Seule's voice was happy, excited. "His project needs me. You've helped me so much, Sarah. I really feel that I have my emotions under control, and if it turns out that I don't . . . well, I'll call you. I think of you as a friend. You know that, don't you? Please be happy for me, Sarah. Everything will be all right."

A pause, and the sound of rapid breathing. Sarah heard

Seule's claws clicking impatiently on the receiver, and thumping noises in the background.

"I have to go. The driver is taking my stuff out to the airport limo. Walter's picking me up in Washington."

Walter Farber was head of the psychiatric team assigned to the alien. He'd be happy now, thought Sarah, with his baby back in the nest. She knew that Farber resented anyone other than himself having success with Seule, and she wondered if his attitude stemmed from the past. Or did the past mean anything to a man like Farber?

"Don't worry," said Seule, unsuppressed excitement in her voice. "Thank you for everything—"

A click and she was gone.

Sarah saved the message, automatically hitting the buttons on her old machine. She'd been working with the alien for almost half a year, and they'd made it past the games, past Seule's evasions and the tricks Sarah used to counter them, and were getting to the real stuff. Contrary to her initial misgivings, she'd started to believe that their sessions might be leading somewhere.

Investigations into the similarities and very definite differences between human and animal mentation—the thought patterns forming the mind—had fascinated Sarah when she'd worked with Farber. She'd been a pink-cheeked grad student, eager as a puppy, working mainly with dogs until Farber had been tapped for the alien assignment. He hadn't taken her with him, and funding for projects such as hers had inevitably dried up without the canny grantsmanship he'd practiced. Individual animals she'd grown to understand and respect—with more than the love one gives an intelligent pet—had grown old and died, or had become too withdrawn and dangerous to work with. People hadn't liked the idea of animals who were smarter than their five-year-old children; Sarah of necessity turned her interests elsewhere. She'd gone into psychiatry, and had ended up practicing in North Wells, a medium-sized town in Maine.

Sarah spent most of her time working with clients who might most benefit from her blended background in psychiatry and nonhuman mentation, including a few of the privately owned animals still living with their human mentors. Until Seule, nonhuman had meant animal or artificial.

Sarah chewed on her lower lip and took a hard copy of Seule's message for her files. Was Seule an animal? Relations between humans and animals were sometimes very good, sometimes bad. When they were bad they were, of course, very often worse than horrid.

She queued the message for transmission to Farber later when the rates went down, and put on the morning pot of coffee.

Two weeks after Seule's breathless farewell, Sarah was on board an old government heli-jet halfway between North Wells and Washington. She was wide awake, angry and scared, and sat hunched in her seat dictating quietly into her journal. "We're flying high to avoid a snowstorm," she said. "This rustbucket is rattling and dipping like a voodoo dancer, so I'll keep this entry brief. This whole business makes me ill. It's so stupid! Can there possibly be a sane reason for what she's done? Damn, if she's going to make it as a human, she's got to learn to bear pain and rejection. Why should she be any different?"

Sarah paused, staring angrily out the tiny, triple-paned window at the indigo horizon. "Of course I don't mean that. Seule *is* different. Her problem is that though she understands it intellectually, she can't really believe it.

"I heard desperation in Farber's voice through the static on his transmission from Washington. What should I expect? He sees his life's work disappearing. And I bet the bastard'll try to blame it on me. Farber's mistake was putting too many emotional and professional eggs into one basket. My mistake? Going after Seule as a client in the first place. I was flattered even to be considered. So who wouldn't be?"

She paused. No, she thought. It was never a mistake, no matter what might happen . . . Sarah clicked off her recorder and scowled at the night.

Spring 2023; North Wells

Sarah first saw the alien when it came loping up the walk to her office for its initial session. It had an eager, dog-on-a-walk look, like a rump-heavy greyhound wearing a thick pink scarf.

Sarah unashamedly craned her neck out the window of her office, on the second floor of an old renovated mansion, the better to catch her first in-the-flesh glimpse of the creature. What had looked like a scarf around Seule's neck fluttered up to become two ragged appendages which grasped the old brass doorknob and turned it. Sarah had admitted to herself that she was nervous. This was no ordinary case. She pulled her head back inside her office.

There would be papers in it for her, perhaps a book. How many had been written already? She dumped her half-finished coffee into her washroom sink, popped a breath freshener in her mouth and ran a hand through her hair. Ready to meet the alien.

During an early session, Sarah made the mistake of handing Seule a Kleenex when they had reached an emotional crisis. It was a purely reflex action, and she felt stupid as soon as she'd done it, as though she'd been suckered somehow. Seule didn't need the tissue, having no nose to run, no tear ducts to leak, and Sarah knew that. But the alien took the token remedy, held it. It became a tradition between them, an occasion for smiles.

As the weeks went by, Sarah found that Seule knew the term "shrink," and enjoyed digging subtle meaning from the word. The alien loved words and was fluent in several languages. She loved the symbols in mathematics, and the archetypes of humanity hidden in music and paintings. Once, on entering the counselor's office, Seule had caught Sarah Lightburn, hands in pockets, squinting at a framed quotation on the wall. It was from the *I Ching*, and said:

> *And when two people understand each other*
> *in their innermost hearts,*
> *Their words are sweet and strong, like*
> *the fragrance of orchids.*

Seule came and stood beside her companionably, reading it too. Sarah suppressed a throb of anger. The quotation seemed insipid, worthless; it had nothing to do with real life. She turned her back to it, smiling brightly at Seule.

As they took their customary seats, Sarah wondered what had happened to her youthful idealism. The message she kept on her wall was vague yet hopeful, mystical yet worded simply and openly; did it have any relevance to her life now? Seule bounded in each day, eager, hopeful, seeming to fill the room with her strangeness and the queer scent of her hide. Reality was observation, deduction, counsel.

Dr. Farber's office called Sarah every week. She dared not ignore his punctilious insistence on having every session downloaded to him, realizing that she could either agree to his terms or blow the chance to work, however briefly, with Seule.

When her application as a local contact for Seule had been approved, Sarah was frankly surprised. Walter Farber's life had veered so far onto its new trajectory that she'd doubted ever meeting him again.

November 2023; Washington, D.C.

Walter and I can't avoid each other now, thought Sarah grimly. I'll be in Washington in another half an hour. The heli-jet hit a bump in the air and her stomach lurched.

In French *seule* means "alone." The astronauts who had found the alien had thought the name appropriate. The pretty creature had been doted on zealously during the long trip back to Earth from Jupiter orbit. The men were reprimanded for teaching the alien child French and English words: *lait,* for the pseudo-milk it learned to lap from a cup; hand, whisker, *bon jour,* good morning. It would have been better, they were told in stern directives from Earth, to have left its brain unsullied by human influences.

Now, eighteen years later, no back page was complete without some tidbit on The Alien.

Like an old-time movie star she passed through life in a shell of her own exclusivity, forever alone in a crowd. After years on Earth her strangeness had been diluted into triviality.

But now . . . now, she'd committed an act so outrageous, so desperate, as to vault her back into the headlines with a vengeance.

The heli-jet touched down in Washington just ahead of the snow. Sarah was taken directly to the hospital and allowed to observe Seule for a moment, then, after finding that nothing had yet been organized in the way of briefings or investigations, headed to an all-night restaurant next to the hospital. It wasn't much, but after what she'd seen she didn't feel like eating anyway. A pack of newspeople in search of coffee arrived to put in time before the first press conference. Sarah, amazed at how few people knew what was going on, sourly predicted imminent mobs of pro-and anti-aliens bopping each other with signs. As well, of course, as the ones who had claimed all along she was a hoax.

Alone in a high-backed booth, Sarah pushed her half-eaten plate of fish and chips away.

She whispered into her journal, rubbing her eyes with the back of one wrist. "She's not a hoax. It's all real; her blood and Elliot's, the violent, hopeless thing she did. Seule was unconscious when I got a glimpse of her being wheeled out of surgery. She was bandaged, slung with tubes and monitors, and looked small and very pathetic.

"Clay Elliot's body is down in Pathology, waiting for an autopsy to confirm the obvious: death by massive lacerations; that, in fact, he was torn to pieces by a creature who has spent the last half-year proclaiming her love for him."

Technically, Seule was female. People preferred to think of her that way, seeing beauty in her silver eyes and narrow black face. For her to perform an ungraceful act or to step across the boundaries of human expectation into violence was unthinkable. What would happen to her now that she'd done the unthinkable? Sarah pinched the bridge of her nose and lifted her coffee cup.

"Is Seule thankful for being saved from timeless oblivion in space? If I were Seule, I think I would rather have stayed dead."

Sarah yawned, feeling cold and tired. The ersatz coffee was weak and insipid, but she accepted a refill from the waiter. At least it was hot. "I remember the fuss that was made when Seule moved to our town," she said to her journal. "It was announced smugly that The Alien had chosen North Wells because of the excellent research facility where she would work as a member of the team decoding the ship's records. Actually she had been assigned there in an effort to keep her happy and quiet; whether she could do useful work or not was immaterial. It came out that she had developed a passion for one of the scientists studying her, a kinesiologist named Clay Elliot, and was essentially being sent out of harm's way.

"She was pining away apart from him, and needed to work it all out. Farber briefed me ahead of time, using words of one syllable in his usual dickheaded way. He warned me that she'd be reluctant to talk about it."

Sarah snorted. "So she's sent to me, the perfect person to help her get over a bad love affair. It's so stupid. I've never heard of anything so damned stupid in my life." Sarah clicked off the recorder and stuffed it in her bag.

June 2023; North Wells

Seule had come to Sarah late in spring; now it was summer, their sixth session, and hot. Sarah's office windows were open. Seule was curled on a chair, her main limbs tucked under her smooth mid-section. They were starting to be comfortable with each other. Sarah was still probing the edges of Seule's attitude of cheerful denial of any real problem.

Seule was silvery-rose in color, her dense silky coat more like napped fabric than fur. The mouth in her long, thin head bore an alarming set of teeth revealed when her narrow black lips drew back in a smile or a laugh. She had a human propensity to laugh, a human appreciation for the absurd.

"People ask if I mind being monitored," said Seule. "I don't. It's necessary." They were talking about freedom; what the word meant when used in the context of Seule's life. "I must be a tempting target."

"Unfortunately, yes," affirmed Sarah, keeping her expression bland. Her long legs were crossed ankle over knee, manlike, and her short brown hair was tucked behind her ears.

She wondered at first if the government had wired her office when Seule had started her sessions, but knew that it didn't make a bit of difference. Of course they had wired it. The bodyguards in her reception area, the eye that hovered outside the building to gain a clear view through her window were all deemed necessary by someone. The eye followed Seule everywhere, and rumor spread that it had the capability of defensive fire. It had not yet been put to the test.

During the last year, Seule had been allowed to travel, to visit private homes, to live relatively unsupervised. Social conventions on how to treat the alien were being formulated ad hoc; so far Seule remained unharmed.

Sarah had read the multi-volume case history Dr. Farber sent her, skipping over the charts and bio-chemical analyses of Seule's flesh and excretions, snorting at the extrapolations as to her kind's origin. Guesses, Sarah had thought. They're only giving her a loose leash now because they can't think of any more tests to run. It's damned pathetic, really.

"Walter Farber has been with you all along, hasn't he?"

Seule's limbs shifted, a silky whisper against the chair's fabric. Absently she poked holes in her unused Kleenex with one of the soft, fingerlike projections on her neck.

"Yes, he has. I remember being bounced on his knee, and the expression he wore when I jumped to his shoulder and then to the top of a filing cabinet. He never got used to that sort of thing. I think he wanted me to be more like a human child. Perhaps he still does."

Seule's silver eyes slid past Sarah's. She seemed bored; they'd gone over this before. She leaned forward. "Do you know, he kept my dog until I could find a place here and get him sent out. Would you like to see Amie's picture?"

Seule rummaged in the leather pouch she wore slung around her hind quarters. Seule had mentioned Amie before, with great affection, and Sarah had always found it oddly poignant that the alien had a pet. She accepted the photo-vid Seule passed to her: the alien and her dog, pausing for a moment in a romp, then bounding away in unison. The dog was some kind of wolfhound and looked like a primitive, masculine version of Seule. Sarah could tell by the way the dog moved that he was a true dog, not enhanced, and she felt a small pang. It was hard to look at animals and not see instead the pseudo-human personalities laid on top like icing on a perfectly good cake. Though she missed some of her old doggy friends, Sarah was glad that no more enhancement was being done. Dealing with Seule was another order of magnitude entirely. The two, terrestrial dog and space-faring alien, leapt in Sarah's hand until she passed the photo back.

"He's a beautiful animal."

Only one stasis pod in the alien ship had been intact, in what must have been a creche area: it contained the baby Seule. The others held only the dead: thirty thousand years dead, according to analysis of the exterior of their ship and the deterioration of components within. All of her family, and most likely all of her race, were extinct.

"Let's talk about Clay," said Sarah quietly. "If it's all right with you."

Seule's ears drooped immediately, and she curled herself more tightly in the chair.

"Yes. Let's." Her eyes were unreadable, though Sarah had noticed how the moods telegraphed by Seule's lips and ears were easily understood, as one would read joy, or eagerness, or disappointment in a dog's face.

"Have you sent a letter to him, as I suggested last week?"

Seule's ears drew back against the rounded crown of her skull. Her fringe of fingers was completely still for once.

"I can't. What if he doesn't answer?"

"What if he does? Tell me how you'd feel if he answered."

Seule looked away. She replied slowly, choosing words which caught harshly between her pointed teeth. "He won't. I really hope he doesn't, you know. I'm afraid I might abandon all my self-respect and run to him."

"It's been almost six months, Seule . . ."

"What does time have to do with it? And who else may I love but a human? Human is what I am, though I don't look it. What if my kind mates for life? What if I never get over him?"

"It takes time, I know. Believe me. . . ."

Seule's powerful hind legs propelled her off the chair. She bounded to the window, stared out at maple trees dressed in new green. "I look into a mirror and see this alien thing. But I don't *feel* alien. You humans say I'm lovely, you say I'm exotic, unique. Well, you're right, damn you all. I'm the only one of me, and it hurts."

November 2023; Washington DC

"It's now four in the morning," said Sarah tiredly into her recorder. "I'm back at the hospital. Washington never goes to sleep completely, certainly a big hospital never slows down. They had to clear a floor for her, which no one here seems happy about, but she'll be whisked off to Houston as soon as she's able to be moved." She had to raise her voice over the babble of talk, clacking footsteps, and cell phones beeping.

"Apparently Seule's guardian eye, confused by the fact that Seule was the attacker, didn't try any fancy shooting. It screamed for help and hovered, recording, till someone came. Fortunately, for Seule anyway, that wasn't long. It all happened so fast . . . it was very painful to watch."

Sarah was still shaken. There were few civilians among the tight-lipped men and women in uniforms at the briefing. The videotape was fish-eye distorted, and the sound buzzed and squalled.

Seule and Clayton Elliot were working alone in a mock-up of the alien craft's interior, observing the varied responses of an environmental panel. They were talking quietly, the eye only picking up the odd innocuous phrase. Clayton, a dark, angular man with the weedy look of a student, leaned across his station and took Seule's left forefoot in his hand, forcefully directing it to a spot on the panel. In slow motion replay, Sarah watched his expression. He looked peevish, impatient.

Seule's forefoot, claws sheathed, slid up Clayton's arm and around his neck, pulling him toward her. He drew back. It was obvious that her strength exceeded his. His muscles tensed, his face showed repulsion. Worse, it showed boredom, irritation. When Sarah saw this look, she knew instinctively what would happen next.

Clayton pushed Seule away. Seule clasped him more firmly; he struggled, swore. She began to whine, a high keening. Sarah was familiar with the look of Seule, but this sound was utterly alien. Its meaning was universal. The next few seconds were full of action, too fast to follow well even in slow motion. Clayton struck at her and she raked him with her hind legs, as a cat would a rabbit, still clutching him with her clawed forelegs. She was licking his face as he screamed. Her neck-fingers grasped and stroked his face, his neck, his eyes and mouth.

Hands and bodies intruded suddenly, the eye pulled back, wobbled, and recorded five or six people trying to separate them. Upon being removed from contact with Clayton's body, Seule collapsed and began to slash at her own limbs with her teeth. Someone pulled her head back, two men held her limbs. Crashing noises, shouts, the spurting of blood. It had been, literally, a shambles.

Sarah rubbed her eyes, replaying the scene in her mind, and fought down an intense longing for her own bed in North Wells. She forced herself to sit straight in her orange plastic chair and take a deep breath. The taped scene intruded mercilessly past the blank taupe walls of the visitor's lounge, where she'd gone to hide from the uproar after the briefing.

Her face brightened momentarily. "At least I got a chance to talk to Jim Wright," she told her recorder. "I recognized him as we entered the briefing room, and figured that of course he'd be here—where else at a time like this? When I was twenty, a junior at Colorado State, I fell madly in love with Jim (didn't we all?); big, handsome, holding the alien baby in his arms. The man who entered the derelict ship and came back with a real E.T. He's still handsome, still a figure of romance, and I got a bit light-headed sitting next to him. Me and my bump of hero-worship. We talked about Seule, and I figured out the kind of man Jim is."

Sarah smiled bleakly. Jim Wright had taken the viewing harder than anyone else, though unlike some others he hadn't turned away. White-faced and flag-pole straight, he'd watched every second of the carnage.

"There's a certain kind of parent who brings their child to me for diagnosis. The kid is ostracized, friendless; usually ugly, often intelligent and artistic. A complete misfit. Everyone except the parent knows the poor kid is a hopeless case; the parent, however, loves this child with a complete, stubborn devotion. The parent never gives up on the idea that someday everything will come out right for the ugly duckling. Jim Wright is that sort of parent. As far as I know he has no children of his own. Only Seule. I wonder if she knows how much he loves her?"

Sarah stopped to blow her nose. She pulled a mirror out of her capacious bag and dabbed haphazardly at her eyes while the recorder paused, waiting for her voice.

"He's left to try calling Yves Giguere, another crew member who is now high up in the European Space Agency, and who might want to be here. None of the others has made it yet, but Jim keeps trying to collect them all by the bedside. I'll tuck this away now, and try again to see her."

Sarah, clad in baggy blue track pants and an unflattering sweater, a huge, crammed bag slung over one shoulder, tangled with the security guard outside Seule's room once again. Before she could make headway, she was waylaid by Dr. Walter Farber. She'd seen him at the briefing and had slipped away before it became necessary to speak to him.

Farber stopped her outside the door, gripping her elbow. "Sarah Lightburn. What are you doing here?"

Sarah frowned at him sullenly. "What's your problem? Everyone in God's creation is here."

Farber relaxed his grip and gave her a sour look. "Hello to you too. Glad you could make it, Sarah. I really am. I'm hoping you'll contribute some ideas."

Sarah jerked her arm free. "Seule and I made progress, whatever you may think. Don't blame me for what went on after she left me."

"And don't you be defensive. I think you're more prickly now than when we were in Colorado."

"I'm amazed you remember," said Sarah tightly. "It's been a while. And prickles are a form of self-defense."

"Are we going to start in on all that now?" He clamped his teeth together and stared down at her, then stuffed his hands in his pockets and abruptly turned away. When he turned back his face wore a look of apology. "Look. I was twenty years older than you then; I still am. I liked you, Sarah. You were one of my favorites, one of the really good ones. Grad students like you don't come along all the time. I didn't mean anything more."

"Then why—" Sarah stopped, controlled her voice. *What am I doing? Why can't I let it go?* "Why did you let me think I was special to you?"

"You *were* special!"

"You know what I mean. Did you kiss me because my work bolstered up yours? Which did you like better, the curve of my graph or the curve of my breast?"

"Damn." Farber's voice was soft. He ran a hand across his mouth. "Sarah, what do you want me to say? You knew the score, or I thought you did. Beryl was on assignment in China, you were a beautiful girl—"

"Jesus." Sarah shook her head. "You were everything I wanted to be." She paused, biting her lip. "You could so easily have taken me on the assignment with Seule. Why didn't you?"

"You want the truth? It was because, damn it, I needed a clear head for the work. Beryl understood that, and she was out of the country most of the time anyway—truth, remember? We'd battled it out. But you . . . you, I couldn't afford to have around."

"It was my work too!"

"Don't kid yourself, Sarah. I had to make decisions I didn't like, but I believe it was worth it. Personalities could not enter the situation."

Sarah sneered. "Personality was everything, can't you see that?"

Seule's door swung open and a woman bedecked with government insignia put her head out. "Will you two be quiet, please! The alien is awake in here, and she can hear you."

Sarah flushed red. She stepped forward. "I have access to the alien, and I'd like to see her now. If it's all right." Sarah bit her lip hard, and kept her chin up.

"Let me check your badge." The woman ran a sensor across Sarah's clip-on ID. "Yeah, okay." She eyed Farber, who abruptly turned and stalked off down the corridor.

Inside, Sarah noticed Seule's smell. She remembered finding it unpleasant the first few times Seule came to her office; now it seemed almost to soak into her. It was unlike anything else on Earth, but it gave her the feeling of slipping into a sweater borrowed from a friend. The olfactory image was wiped out by the sight of Seule strapped onto her bed.

She couldn't turn her head; it was restrained, as were her four main limbs. Only the soft, relatively feeble appendages on her neck were free to move; they fluttered and waved as if blown by a wind. When Seule felt Sarah's eyes on her, the motion stopped and the tendrils fell to lie across her high, arched chest. Sarah moved closer and attempted a smile, but found it too painful an exercise.

"Oh, Seule," she said, gently touching one forelimb on an area not covered by bandages. The animals Sarah had mostly dealt with had been those dosed with intelligence-enhancing drugs. Some had responded to touch, most hadn't. Heightened mentation seemed also to sharpen the sense of individuality; the animals—dogs, apes, cetaceans—were often intractable.

Seule drew her lips back behind the muzzle clamped around her jaws in what Sarah at first thought was a smile of welcome. Feeling a perverse satisfaction in the intimacy she, and not Farber, had been granted, Sarah bent over the softly lit bed.

Seule snarled, a sound like a direct assault. Sarah flinched back in a primal response that was in a split second replaced with anger. Just as quickly, the anger was veneered in professional detachment, but it was still there.

Seule was neither animal nor human. She must remember that."What's she on?" Sarah asked, addressing the woman who let her in. The reply listed dosages of various drugs being pumped into Seule, which Sarah recognized as standard antibiotics and mild sedatives.

"Okay. Thanks."

Sarah turned to Seule, wary this time and careful to keep her hands in a nonthreatening attitude.

"Seule, do you know why you're here? Do you know what happened?"

For answer there was a high wailing whine that issued from Seule's throat; very doglike, distressing to Sarah's ears. It went on and on; finally Sarah nudged the bed, moving it enough to make Seule's eyes flick to the side and register her.

Seule's black lips moved behind the plastic muzzle, and she

spoke. Her whisper was soft, spiritless; the keening whine still echoed in Sarah's ears. "He was with me and he was not with me. He was my friend and he was my enemy. He was with me." She strained her limbs against the straps. "He was not with me."

"You were working with Clay and his team. Everything was going well. Seule, whatever happened, for whatever reason, it's over now."

If this were a human friend or sister who'd suffered a trauma, thought Sarah, I'd know what to do. Hugs, understanding words; more hugs. The comfort of warm primate skin against skin. But I don't understand her. She isn't one of us. Sarah found that her arms were tightly crossed over her breasts. Self-consciously she let them relax to her sides.

"He wouldn't touch me," whispered Seule. "We were alone in the lab. He was so beautiful, so soft . . . I, I thought . . . I held him, he resisted."

"He died."

"He wouldn't touch me. None of you will *touch* me!"

Christ, thought Sarah. She ripped his guts out and almost tore his head from his body. Is that love to her? Thwarted love, frustrated desire; a death sentence to the one Seule chooses?

"I'll touch you, Seule. I, I'm your friend, you know." Tentatively Sarah forced her hand up, stroked Seule's forelimb lying strapped on the white sheet. Seule turned her head away slightly and closed her eyes.

Suddenly Sarah felt an almost irresistible urge to flee the room. The alien's life-blood pulsed under the tips of her fingers, life hot with urges. Sarah had imagined only in her darkest, most private moments. She snatched her hand away, stood panting in a flush of heat that burned her face. Thankful that the room was dimly lit, she tried to gather her thoughts. But before she could speak, Seule sighed and shifted her limbs minutely, all that was allowed by the restraints.

"All these years on your planet. I thought it was my home, I thought I was one of you. I listened to Walter Farber and tried to please him, I made friends with the people in Houston. And the men who discovered me—" Here she paused, and her black tongue tried to lick some moisture onto her lips. "Those men. They call me, send me letters and presents. I suppose I'm a mascot, a special toy to them . . ."

Sarah caught her breath. "Jim Wright is here. He's hanging around trying to get in to see you."

Seule turned her dry, glittering eyes on Sarah. "Don't let him in," she whispered. "I couldn't stand it."

Strangely, it was the lack of tears that disturbed Sarah the most. It had always disturbed her. No need for her, no need for her damned Kleenex. Seule's appearance disturbed her, Seule's intelligent doglike way of moving and sitting and listening, her un-earth smell. Her hot silvery body.

And not a tear for the lonely horror of her life.

"I have to go." Sarah backed away from the bed, turned, pushed through the door to the white-lit corridor. Farber was nowhere to be seen.

She ran for the elevator. During the interminable wait for its arrival, Sarah saw Jim Wright, fast asleep in the visitors' lounge, his head nodding, his knees up. She looked away, pushed the call button again and again.

Down, alone thank God, down and out the nearest door to the cold night air. The freshness of melting snow piled beside the walkways was like a balm on her nerves; she headed for a bench and slumped down on it, shivering, yet hot with the feel of Seule still in her fingers.

Sarah bent over and clutched her stomach, squeezing her eyes shut. She breathed slowly and deeply, pulling in the moist freezing air which smelled of nothing, not even the damp soil; no scent of alien flesh in her nostrils. She dug her fingers hard into her abdomen.

Oh, God, she wondered darkly, have I really gone so long without a lover? She gasped a little at the pain inside her, under the skin and muscle; it was like the bitter distillation of anger and denial. Poison.

Cautiously she straightened on the hard, slatted bench, very glad she wasn't crying, because she might not be able to stop. That primal longing—how terribly *intense* it was . . . could it be that she had once felt it for Walter? She had forgotten how powerful it was, how lonely and terrible. . . .

"No," she whispered aloud, her breath puffing in the cold. "Walter was a different sort of pain . . . a betrayal, and what I just felt, up there with Seule. . . ." She stopped, confused. What *had* she felt? It had been electric, visceral; unexpected and overwhelmingly demanding. Its dregs had been vinegar. She shook her head, trying to think.

There was a shout from the corner of the building, and she turned to see six or seven newspeople, armed with cameras and lights, bearing down on her. Rising in dismay she looked in vain for an escape and was surrounded.

"Are you a nurse? A doctor? Where is the alien—where is Seule?"

"How bad are her injuries? Will she die?"

One of them checked a fax sheet of photos and called out her name.

"Leave me alone," cried Sarah. "I don't know anything."

"You're Sarah Lightburn, the alien's psychiatrist—"

"I am nothing of the sort! I only counseled her, briefly—" A mistake. The newsies moved in closer and Sarah was forced to push her way past them. One of them caught her by the arm and shouted into her face. "Will the alien be destroyed now? She's a killer."

Sarah stopped, mouth open. "Destroyed? Don't be a fool—"

"Yes," screamed someone from the back of the growing crowd. "She killed one human, she'll kill more!"

"What if there are more aliens coming?"

Sarah, appalled, felt incongruous laughter well up. More of them! Seule would appreciate the irony of that.

"Is it true that Clay Elliot was her lover?"

"Leave me alone!" Sarah bolted for the door. Two security men, attracted by the noise, let her through and closed the thick reinforced glass doors against the reporters.

"Oh, journal, I'm so tired. And this coffee is awful. It *must* be almost morning by now."

Sarah looked up at the TV suspended in a corner of the hospital cafeteria. It confirmed her predictions: mobs of Seule denouncers harassing Seule supporters. By now the whole world knew what had happened. "I'm here at the center," whispered Sarah, "and I'm not sure I know anything at all."

Slumping in the chair, she rubbed her eyes. "*Why?* Why did she kill him?" Blinking, she looked up and stared at nothing. "Will we ever really know why she does anything? By now, her life among us may have rendered her incapable of rational behavior, or even whatever instinctive behavior is proper for her race.

"And I really thought I was getting somewhere. Damn . . ."

Sarah sipped her coffee, winced.

"And why did I run away from her? Was it the feel of her flesh on mine?" She felt her face heat with confusion, with shame. "What happened up there, anyway? I, I . . . journal, I find myself having a hard time talking about this."

Sarah Lightburn stared morosely into her cup, wondering if she was losing her mind. She watched her hands place the cup neatly in front of her as the apex of a chevron pattern of plastic knife, fork, spoon, and stir-stick. The cafeteria was growing crowded and noisy with talk and the clatter of dishes as the day shift arrived.

"I can't deal with this right now," she told the journal. She clicked it shut and stowed it in her bag.

Sarah left the cafeteria and headed for the elevators, wondering what kind of man Clayton Elliot had been. She stabbed at the elevator button. Had Elliot treated Seule like an intelligent pet, perhaps expected her to get the coffee? Of was he kind, thoughtful—just a nice guy who simply couldn't find it within his heart to love someone who looked like a dog?

The elevator door opened and she shuffled tiredly on, not noticing until too late that the only other occupant was Farber.

He stood his ground, smiled remotely as she reached across him to push the button. The door closed. Farber put his thumb on the stop button.

"I don't want you to go up to Seule's room just now, Ms. Lightburn," said Farber in a flat voice.

Sarah refrained from pointing out that she had intended only to get to the main floor and out. She withdrew her arm, hauled her heavy bag higher on her shoulder.

"Fine. We'll park right here while you tell me where I *should* go." Sarah wished her voice matched her feelings. She hated the way it went high and girlish in a confrontation. Typical female, Sarah sneered at herself. "I'd like to know why you've chosen to blame me. What about Elliot? Is anyone looking into his actions? What kind of background checks did you do on him?"

"That's not what I want to talk about, and besides, it's immaterial. You encouraged her to remain in contact with him. She went off with stars in her eyes, looking for romance." Farber took his thumb off the button and the elevator started upward, called from somewhere above.

"And what's wrong with romance?" Sarah snapped. "What was wrong with that dumb shit Elliot? She loved him. Do you know anything about love, *Doctor* Farber?"

"Sarah, please. This is neither the time nor the place—"

The elevator stopped and the doors slid open onto the sixth floor. Farber, tight-lipped, motioned for Sarah to exit ahead of him; she did, and when he started down the corridor she followed.

"I don't really give a damn anymore," she said. "There was a time when you were my hero, right up there with the astronauts, but not anymore. I've wised up."

Farber reached a door, keyed it open and stood to one side. "Well?" he said. "Shall we continue in private, or do you prefer to rant out here?"

Sarah stalked in and threw her bag on the floor beside a table surrounded by straight-backed chairs. It was some sort of meeting room, windowless and stale.

Farber yanked out a chair and dropped into it. He bent over and rubbed his temples. After a moment Sarah sat too. It seemed stupid and childish to keep standing. Hadn't she grown up? Wasn't it impossible for this man to make her do foolish things anymore?

Farber looked up, steepling his hands under his chin. It was a mannerism Sarah remembered from long ago. "I did try to keep track of you after I left," he said. "Not all my time was spent with Seule. You distinguished yourself at Colorado, did a couple of years with Arthur Kemp before he went to work for Biostym. Then you disappeared for a while. Let's see . . . I next saw you in Edmonton, at a lecture. You were at the back."

Sarah kept her eyes on the tips of his fingers, unable to speak.

"Believe it or not, it pleased me to see you again, though you left with someone and it didn't seem the right time to renew old acquaintances. I thought that soon I'd meet you at a conference, laugh over old times. You'd be married, I'd have Beryl with me, we'd have drinks. Something." He looked down again. Sarah could barely keep her eyes on him, her urge to run was so strong.

"Why did you resist my counseling Seule?"

"I didn't. When your name came across my desk I thought about what might happen, but then I realized that it might be a good idea to have you on board. I'm still not sure if it is, all things considered. Perhaps I was trying to make up for the past. I do know that there's obviously a lot still to learn about Seule."

He sighed deeply, running his fingers over his lips. "When she was just a baby, I'd visit her quarters every day, and every day she'd come leaping at me out of nowhere. I always caught her. It was a game we played, until she got too big. I had to remind her over and over to keep her claws in, to be gentle, to take it easy on us humans."

He looked exhausted. He looked like an old man coming to understand that the best part of his life was ending.

In her mind's eye, Sarah saw Farber as he'd been when he landed the plum assignment. Suave, dark-haired, grinning wolf-ishly, he had abandoned everything to make Seule his own. He'd been with her from then on, in every newscast, at every conference and study. It's all getting away from him now, she thought. We get old, the children grow up and leave. This one has been a heart-breaker, but then, the special ones always are.

Sarah looked at her watch. Eight o'clock in the morning, and she felt as though sleep did not exist anymore, at least on this world. Almost time for the news conference. What an ordeal that was going to be—she was thankful she wouldn't have to be there. She hoped Farber could handle it.

He looked up at her finally. His eyes were unreadable. The eyes show nothing, Sarah told herself—it's the lips, the brows, the tiny muscle-pulls that tell the story. Animals can show their emotions if they're smart enough, if they have anything inside to show . . . Farber tipped his chair back and crossed his ankle over his knee in a way Sarah instantly recognized.

She felt her thoughts realign themselves. Had it really been Walter Farber she wanted? Or did she want what he had, what he *was*? Seule had seduced him away, and all Sarah's tears and anger and wanting had never gotten him back. . . . *Stupid woman*, she jeered at herself. *Daddy loved her more than me!*

And if he'd taken me along to work with Seule, how long would I have been content to be in their exceptionally thick shadows?

Sarah had a sudden merciless vision of herself, an imitation of him, hands steepled and legs crossed in just his way, sagely nodding at a distraught client. She jammed her hands between her knees and almost laughed out loud. Hadn't that been a sort of apology she'd heard a while back? Something about making up for the past?

Sarah leaned forward and stood, stretching her shoulders and running her fingers through her hair. She grinned suddenly. "It doesn't matter now. I'm okay. Truce, all right?"

Farber stood too, looking at her uncertainly. He turned for

the door, then stopped and looked back at her, clearing his throat. "Within the next few days you'll be getting a request to come to Houston. I'd like you to do some very careful thinking before you make a decision."

Sarah, completely surprised and not knowing what to say, said nothing.

"There's a lot of work to be done," Farber continued. "I'm not sure if we can treat this whole episode as an advance or a setback in our knowledge of Seule. Whatever the verdict, she's going to be locked away for a while. No way around it, I'm afraid. It's hoped you'll have something to contribute."

Farber straightened his tie briskly, seeming to come fully awake by the sheer power of will. "They're broadcasting soon from the directors' boardroom," he said. "I'd better get myself up there." He squinted at her speculatively. "My office will be in touch with you."

He turned and put his hand on the doorknob, then looked back at her as if he was going to say something else, but did not. He left, letting the door remain open behind him.

"Did you really want Clayton Elliot for your lover?" asked Sarah softly, into the gently beeping, monitor-lit dimness of Seule's hospital room. There was a different military nurse on duty now, a man who kept his eyes on her carefully. Sarah ignored him.

"Or did you want him to love you? There's a difference, you know. It has to do with possession. It gets mistaken for love so often. . . ." She stepped closer to the bed.

Seule's eyes seemed brighter now. The look in them of lost despair had retreated a bit, and she turned her head to follow as Sarah moved up beside her.

"I was so jealous of you." Sarah's voice was soft; all the anger had left her. "You didn't know Walter and I had once been lovers, did you? When you came along, he just wasn't interested in me anymore. He had found something so absolutely lovely and new that he had to let everything else go." She gazed at Seule almost kindly, feeling light as a husk from which a spoiled seed has been shaken.

"I'll never love Walter again, or even really like him, but I can admire him for what he's done with you. That's good enough."

The alien moved slightly on the bed under her restraints, and her soft pink tendrils undulated across her chest.

"Clayton Elliot wanted you to be a piece of experimental equipment conforming to his thesis. Walter Farber wanted you to be his brilliant, beautiful little girl. And I wanted to use you to get next to him, to show him . . . to show that I mattered."

"Sarah," croaked Seule, barely audible.

Sarah backed up a little. She wasn't ready to risk touching Seule again, not yet.

"Sarah." The alien's eyes were on her, those dark-silver, tearless eyes, and Sarah almost stopped breathing. "Please. I'm sorry, I'm sorry I let you feel what I was feeling. I'm . . . so tired of being human, but I don't know how to be anything *else*."

Sarah bit her lip, backing off still farther. She retreated to the window and drew aside the drapes to let in the brightening day. "They're asking me to come to Houston," she said, around a lump in her throat. "Walter wants me, he thinks I can be useful." She swallowed carefully and turned back to the bed. "How . . . how about you? Do you want me there?"

Sarah forced herself to look unflinchingly at Seule.

The alien reached toward Sarah with her neck-tendrils, something she had never done before; she had never touched Sarah unless Sarah initiated it. In fact the alien had deftly avoided contact during their sessions.

A moment of self-doubt, of struggle against the urge to flee, and Sarah stepped forward, bracing herself for whatever might flood into her.

Almost, she didn't feel the first moment of touch, Seule's tendrils were so light and soft and tentative. Like a baby's fingers—warm, slightly sticky, full of innocent life—they gently explored the lengths of Sarah's fingers, probed between them into the soft webs of flesh, slid across the hard nail surfaces. It was, to Sarah, so intensely sensual that she could only watch. The blood pounding in her ears made it impossible to move or react.

Yes, she thought, this is it—that moment, that fragrance sweet and strong; this is what it means.

And under the sweetness was a bitter taste, and behind the new light the shadow of a permanent darkness that could never pass; Sarah knew it. There were no miracles to offer, only friendship to ease the path.

"Yes, please come with me," whispered Seule.

THE SAGES OF CASSIOPEIA

Scott Mackay

Scott Mackay's first novel was the thriller, *A Friend in Barcelona*, 1991, and his second was SF, *Outpost*, 1998. He began to publish short stories in the SF field in 1994 and has since been selling steadily to the American genre magazines. "The Sages of Cassiopeia" first appeared in *The Magazine of Fantasy & Science Fiction*.

Mackay says the story evolved when he learned that the great Danish astronomer, Tycho Brahe, had a stillborn twin brother: "This dead twin brother occupied Brahe's thoughts on numerous occasions, and appeared in his writings often." Shades of Philip K. Dick, who was obsessed with his dead twin sister! The story is one of that breed of science fiction stories set in the fictional historical past, but with an individual signature. On the one hand, it is reminiscent of Sturgeon's famous "The Martian and the Moron," and on the other of Daniel Keyes's "Flowers for Algernon." Although alternate history stories are currently fashionable, Mackay's gives us a fictional explanation for how history proceeded as it really did.

On a clear cold November night in 1572, near the town of Knudstrup in Denmark, Tycho Brahe, one of the last great naked-eye astronomers, stood on the west tower of his uncle's abbey, Herritzvad, gazing up at the sky. He took his eye away from his sextant and glanced at his brother Magnus. Magnus swept the stone floor, his mongoloid eyes staring at the dying embers in the grate, his breath frosting over in the frigid air.

"Magnus," called Tycho. "I've discovered a new star. Come see for yourself. It outshines Venus."

Magnus didn't look up. His idiot brother continued to sweep the same spot of stone floor, his red hair shaggy over his flattened skull, his eyes good-natured but dull. *If only he would do something useful, like build the fire, fetch some warm spiced wine, or empty the chamber pot. I have studied at Copenhagen,*

Leipzig, Rostock, and Augsburg, have given lectures by royal command to King Frederick and his court. And I ask myself, can this unfortunate dunce be my sibling?

Tycho turned back to his sextant and looked up at the newly luminous object shining brightly among the murkier stars of Cassiopeia. How far is this new star away from the Earth? Is it part of the great cogwheel of planets that rolls around the Earth, or is it perched somewhere between the moon and the sun? Tycho lifted his quill and made a notation. Position unchanged. How to explain this phenomenon? Was it something that might confirm his own careful notion of the universe, that the sun revolved around the earth, that the planets revolved around the sun, that together the sun and the planets rolled like a big wheel through the sky with Earth as its hub?

Behind him, Magnus stopped sweeping. Tycho put his quill down and turned around.

Magnus leaned the broom against the wall and lumbered over to the fire. He lifted the iron poker and stirred the embers, showing unexpected initiative, took a few small pieces of firewood and piled them in an intricate cat's cradle. Tycho dropped his quill and took a few steps forward, forgetting about the new star. Was this his brother, the same unfortunate soul he had to feed and clothe every morning, the same dullard who had never spoken an intelligible word in his life, and who didn't have the manual dexterity to fit his own cod-piece? Was this Magnus, building this well-designed and thoughtful palace of wood?

Magnus leaned forward and blew on the embers, coaxing the flames. Was it a miracle? Magnus stirred the embers again, turning them the way a baker folds currants into a pudding, his fingers, for the first time ever, nimble and careful. The fire sprang up, licked the fresh wood, then cracked and popped. The light of the fire played over Magnus's freckled face, danced in his mongoloid eyes, rippled through his carrot orange hair. Was this God's fair hand at work, a divine intervention turning a fool into a sage?

Tycho put his hand on his brother's shoulder. Magnus looked up at Tycho, and in the idiot's eyes the mist of stupidity lifted, and a brother's recognition, love, and devotion took their rightful place. Tycho leaned forward.

"Magnus?" he said.

Magnus got up, straightened his shoulders, stood to his full height, and walked, not lumbered, to the sextant. With unexpected delicacy he put his eye to the instrument. Tycho stood back, his blood running lightly through his body, tickling his heart with anticipation. The idiot worked his lips back and forth. Then he looked at Tycho, his eyes bright with discovery.

"Venus?" said Magnus.

His brother's first word; so fitting it should be the name of earth's sister planet. Tears came to Tycho's eyes. This was a miracle. Nothing like this had ever happened in Knudstrup before.

"No, Magnus," he said. "Not Venus. A new star in the Cassiopeia constellation. But you will learn, dear brother. You will learn everything I know."

Tycho sat on the hard uncomfortable chair across from Bishop Anders, feeling out of place in these holy chambers, uneasy, as if the mounted stag's head above the large and never-extinguished fire watched him. Despite the bright day and unseasonable warmth, the shutters remained closed. The bishop wore his heaviest black robe. Tycho was here to show the old man his latest astronomical notes. The bishop was an important man, the king's envoy in this province of Scania, and if Tycho could please the king through Bishop Anders, his work would continue unhindered, and with royal sanction.

The bishop pushed the sheets aside, his brow knitting. He got up, ambled over to the fire, and stirred the embers with the poker. The fire danced from the ashes, casting unruly shadows on the rafters. So prudent to please the court, and more importantly, the Church, even after the Reformation, especially because he was a Lutheran in Catholic territory. But what, exactly, pleased Bishop Anders? Bishop Anders preached frugality and sacrifice from the pulpit, yet lived like a prince and allowed the brothers of the order to eat red meat every day. How was one to reconcile the stag's head mounted on the wall with the figure of Christ on the Crucifix next to the window? Truly a puzzling man, an unpredictable and unpleasant man, a man who had always envied the house of Brahe. The bishop turned from the fire.

"Circles and numbers and endless observations," said Bishop Anders. "A truly meticulous account of Our Lord's universe." He walked to the table and shuffled through the sheets. "But this here," he said, pointing, "where you mention Kopernik of Cracow. Why must you do that? Everyone knows he was damned as a heretical fool. His work is no better than the scrawl of a madman."

"Your Holiness, I mention Kopernik because of the discrepancies he discovered in Ptolemy's system. Certainly he was misguided to claim the sun resides at the center of the universe, but perhaps you haven't fully understood my final calculations," said Tycho. "You'll see that I've explained Kopernik's inconsistencies while keeping Earth in its true and proper place."

"I don't care about your calculations, Lord Brahe," said the bishop. "I care about your soul. And I sometimes fear the way of science leads directly to the Devil. Is it not better to behold and worship God's miracles? Everything you need to know is written here." The bishop tapped the thick Bible on the table. "Let us not question God's wisdom in putting the Earth in the center of the universe. Let us not question this new star in the sky, for there was once a star over Bethlehem with the same benign radiance. Let us not question how your brother has gained reason or how the widow Huitfeldt's Peder has been touched with intelligence. These are miracles, Lord Brahe, and to pursue them with scientific study shows ill judgment and a temperament hardly attuned to the truer course of prayer."

The Brahe brothers walked through the village of Knudstrup, Tycho on his mare, Magnus leading the horse by a rope. As they neared the canal, the village bullies emerged from behind the embankment and pelted Magnus with mud and cow dung, laughing, shrieking with cruel glee.

"Be gone with you, wretched curs," cried Tycho, drawing his sword.

Much to Tycho's surprise, Magnus darted away from the horse. The boys stood there with terror in their eyes. Magnus grabbed two of the biggest, dragged them kicking and screaming to the embankment wall, and, using his ox-like strength, pitched them into the canal. The others scattered like wheat chaff in the wind while the two wet culprits sputtered for breath and pulled themselves up onto the muddy bank. Magnus turned to Tycho.

"A chilly immersion for these ne'er-do-well knaves," he said, laughing. "For all the cripples they've stoned and all the idiots they've scoffed."

"Dear brother, are you truly Magnus?"

"Of Herritzvad Abbey, the simple sibling of the great Tycho. My beloved Tyge, who knows the secret clockwork of the stars."

"Yes, but not as simple as before. The Holy Father has blessed me, Magnus. I've found a new star, and I've found a new brother."

They walked past the village common, where the grass had turned brown and the hoar-frost bearded the brambles in the far thicket. Magnus strode along beside the horse, a new man, refashioned into the brother Tycho had never had, his eyes quick, full of purpose, his face rosy in the morning cold. Off to see the widow Huitfeldt, because she, too, had been blessed by this miracle. Tycho had to see it for himself, had to know that the widow Huitfeldt's idiot son Peder had been touched by the same hand of reason. Tycho had to see it because if the light of intelligence had finally come to Peder Huitfeldt, then Tycho could embrace, without secret doubt, the miraculous transformation of his brother.

"Then it is not Venus, Tyge?" asked Magnus.

And yet was this intelligence, to pick up the strain of a conversation days old, with no proper reference, to dive right in and expect the listener to follow?

"No, Magnus, not Venus. Venus roams across the sky and this new star is fixed. What we see each night in the constellation of Cassiopeia is not only a new star, but a new kind of star."

"But why doesn't this star move like Venus, Mars, or Jupiter? Why must it be shackled to the sky like a prisoner, and not free to roam like its brothers and sisters?"

"Magnus, I believe this new star must make its home in the celestial globe, beyond the endless round of the sun, the moon, and the planets, and that it is affixed to this globe like all the other stars."

"Brother Tyge, perhaps this new star is not a star at all, perhaps it floats just beyond the ether and watches us. Perhaps this silver smudge in the heavens may be the Holy Creator's eye."

Tycho smiled. The light of intelligence may have touched his brother Magnus, but in many ways he was still a child, naive and precocious, eager to jump to swift conclusions in order to avoid careful study and observation. Yet even the most farfetched speculations couldn't be dismissed at this early stage; if the Holy Maker's hand could so change his brother, why couldn't His eye hover just above the ether? Had there ever been an object like this before? The solar eclipse of 1560, which so inspired his interest in astronomy, now seemed commonplace. The conjunction of Saturn and Jupiter in 1563, which had determined the nature of his life's work, was of no significance when compared to this strangest and most brilliant of celestial objects. Only rigorous measurement would ensure an explanation.

"Brother Magnus, your devotion is strong and deep, but let us not allow our religious fervor to overrule a more reasonable approach. We shall wait and see. The star shall make itself known."

"But Tyge, believe me when I tell you, this is not a star. It is an eye. And it watches us, even when we sleep in our beds."

"We shall see, Magnus, we shall see."

They passed the tanner's, the cart-wright's, and the silk weaver's, and soon came to the widow Huitfeldt's thatched roof cottage at the edge of the village. Peder stood outside with a large staff in his hand, gazing at the sun, and the moment Tycho saw him, he knew it was true, that the imbecile's torpor had been lifted by the same divine hand that had so graced his brother, and that Peder now observed the world with keen quick eyes. As Peder heard their horse approach, he turned from the sunrise, and when he saw Tycho, sank to one knee and doffed his hat, in homage to the astronomer's noble rank.

"Rise, Peder," called Tycho. "I see with my own eyes the change God has wrought in you. The bishop tells me you have been blessed with the full use of your faculties, and that you have been conducting experiments on the movements of the sun."

Peder and Magnus acknowledged each other with a silent nod, as if they belonged to a guild of freemasons, or some such other secret society; joined by this common miracle, they were brothers in their new-found intelligence. How strange to see the folds of Cathay lidding their eyes, yet the mist of the fool wiped clear.

"I have measured here with my staff the angle at which the sun's light falls upon the Earth," said Peder, talking not to Tycho but to Magnus. "See here with these strokes in the ground the way the angle widens from yonder plane tree as the sun daily retreats south. Witness the leaves of yonder tree; they lie on the grass, yellow and brown, and as brittle as eggshell. The nights are long, the days short, and the wind blows cold from the north-west. I sense a change of season."

"Your observations are correct, Peder. Winter is only weeks away," explained Tycho.

"But can the seasons be so short?" asked Peder, again addressing Magnus. "What of the wheat in the field? Will it have time to ripen? Surely we shall starve."

They were like children, discovering the world for the first time, visitors from the realm of idiocy, observing the Earth without reference, unable to connect the pieces in any meaningful way, drawing false conclusions from reasonable conjecture.

"Have no fear, Peder," said Tycho. "Perhaps in less fortunate kingdoms the subjects may starve. But here in Denmark we've always made sufficient provision for winter."

"Perhaps it is the tilt," said Magnus.

"Aye, Magnus," said Peder. "I suspect this orb spins a-kilter on its axis."

"Aye, Peder," said Magnus, "but what of Ptolemy?"

"Now, see here," said Tycho, interrupting. "You haven't read the thirteen books of Ptolemy's *Almagest*, have you, so please desist." Talking of astronomy, his voice took on an imperious tone. "The Earth doesn't spin. The Earth sits motionless in the center of the universe. It does not tilt. Claudius Ptolemy was at least right about that."

The two simpletons gazed at each other. Neither of you understands me, thought Tycho. As much as he loved his brother, as much as his brother shared his same profound interest in astronomy, he couldn't expect Magnus to immediately comprehend the complex workings of the universe in the few months since the appearance of the new star.

In late May, Tycho and Magnus, ever in the pursuit of scientific curiosity, traveled to the asylum at Skokloster. The carriage bounced over the road, hitting potholes and ruts carved by the rain. Four mounted squires in chain mail, armed with battle swords for the protection of Tycho and his brother, shared coarse jests and oaths as they rode their chargers on either side of the carriage. Tycho found it insufferable. Yet this noise, this bone-shaking ride didn't distract his brother—a great tome lay open upon his lap, the revered Ptolemy's *Almagest*. As they crossed the bridge over the River Skern, and the drab stone walls and towers of Skokloster came into view, Magnus turned the last page and put the heavy book aside. He looked up at Tycho, lifted his knuckle to his mouth, and nibbled, as if he were preoccupied with a great worry.

"You are right, Tyge, his system is faulted. Why does he worship the perfect circle as if it were a deity? He wears the

Aristotelian cosmology like a shackle, clings to it like a wet-nurse, feeds upon its milk of false assumptions, and postulates the most unlikely machinery of epicycle, deferent, and equant. The universe must be far simpler than this."

"And how do you propose the planets move, Magnus? In perfect squares?"

"You tease me, brother. But you must see this weakness: if my thumb is long, I will make a bigger glove; if my planet strays, I will make a larger epicycle, or perhaps shrink my deferent; if the wayward path continues, I will happily explain all with my equant. I have forty wheels, and I can fit my forty wheels to anything I see. No, Tyge, I fear Ptolemy was less interested in a single ultimate truth than in reconciling the suspect Aristotelian cosmology with the things he saw."

"Your raw intelligence needs to be tempered by wisdom and experience, Magnus," said Tycho. "You must understand that compromise, especially when it comes to scientific inquiry, is always the most reasonable approach. No doubt the intricacies of Ptolemy's system at times seem labored. Kopernik of Cracow, on the other hand, has nothing but heretical speculation and only twenty-seven of the most inexact observations. The answer lies somewhere in between. I am at present drafting my own system, a compromise between old and new, the best and most reason-able course."

"As you say, brother. But let us watch the way the eye in the sky watches," he said, gesturing out the carriage window at the new star, which now burned even during the daylight hours. "Then we shall know the truth."

"Magnus, it's not an eye. Why do you insist on that?"

"Tyge, it's an eye, and it watches us."

Such are the notions of fools. But he had a tender heart for his brother, and gladly tolerated the occasional nonsense that came out of his mouth.

The carriage came to a stop in front of the asylum. The door-keeper let them through. And Tycho saw that all the rumors were true, that wit, sense, and logic had come to these inmates of Skokloster, that the benign radiance of Cassiopeia's star had set them free of their delusions and nightmares.

Skokloster's turnkey no longer bothered with leg-irons or any of the other customary restraints used to safeguard the public from the unpredictable antics of madmen. The inmates wandered freely, conversed in small groups, their words scholarly and gen-

tle, as if this weren't the madmen's pen but the quadrangle at the
university in Rostock. Some sat at tables; quills scribbling, making
notes, puzzling through calculations, recording observations,
while a group of others gazed at the new star as if, like Magnus,
they understood its exact nature. A few others, huddled in their
rags atop the archway leading to the stable, dropped object after
object—first a rooster's head, then an apple core, then a rusted
cannon ball—into the small alley below, recording on a slate tab-
let the speed and manner with which each one fell.

So it was true of Skokloster as well. And everywhere in Denmark it was the same. Fools and madmen waking up for the first
time in their lives. All displayed the same observational zeal and
scientific curiosity, just like Magnus. But if you were to ask any
of them about the new star, they all had the same answer. That
it watched Earth. That it wasn't a star but an eye.

A year later, in June of 1574, the new star no longer shone so
brightly. Tycho and Magnus sat at a groaning board up in the
abbey's west tower enjoying a midnight repast of wild thrush
stuffed with sage and bread crumbs, figs with salami, and warm
beer sweetened with honey. Magnus, no longer dressed in coarse
woolens but in the stylish finery befitting a young lord, studied
Tycho's latest notes. You will learn, brother Magnus. You will
learn everything I know—and so it had come to pass. Magnus
collected the sheets, straightened them, put them on the table,
and looked up at Tycho.

"Tyge . . ." he said. He faltered. "Tyge, you are my brother
and I love you. I'm glad we've spent these eighteen months together. You have taught me much." Magnus pushed his plate
away, as if he were no longer hungry, as if what he were trying
to tell Tycho caused him a great deal of distress. "Your observational genius I will never doubt. You understand the worth of
measurement such as no scientist ever has. But science is more
than just measurement, Tyge. You should not so quickly dismiss
Kopernik's idea. The Polish monk is right. The Earth roams. Why
shouldn't it roam? Why must it cling to the center of the universe
the way you cling to the old Aristotelian cosmology?"

Tycho felt the blood spreading through his face. "The Earth
doesn't move," he said. "The Earth is like the hub of the miller's
wheel, silent, still, and majestic."

"But what about the way Mars has behaved over the last
few weeks?"

Tycho looked at his brother, his eyes growing wide. "Yes, a most interesting backtracking. And you can see here in the final pages of this draft just how I've accounted for these rogue movements of the red planet."

"You've built a castle of Ptolemaic mathematics to explain something a child should understand. Let old Sol act as a maypole. Let Earth roam like its Jovian brothers and sisters."

"A child's explanation can never map the complexities of the universe, Magnus. This hurried work of Kopernik's is pretty, and has a geometric appeal, but unfortunately is insupportable, even with my current observations."

"But what of Mars? Not even your accommodating system can account for this curious retrograde we see nightly. Come. Let us look again. The air is mild. It is a fine night for the play of planets."

They left the table and climbed the few steps to the turret. The air smelled of lilac, an owl hooted somewhere off in the wood, and the starry heavens arched above them in a moonless night. Two sextants, one clamped in the position of Casseopeia's new star, one unclamped and ready to follow the movements of the planets, stood against the parapet.

"Tyge, you have done all the work," said Magnus. "You have made hundreds upon hundreds of your own personal observations with the finest instruments yet available. I love you, Tyge. I will never forget the time I've spent with you. And when I go I will always remember you."

"Brother, you utter the words of a fool. What is this leave-taking you speak of? We will be together. Always. I know we will."

"Tyge, listen to me. The eye in the sky grows dim and I haven't much time. Must the world remember the noble Brahe of Knudstrup as the man who could see only with his eyes and not with his mind? Your system has many ponderous incongruities. The geometric center of your universe is badly placed. Your planets swirl and strut like a band of drunkards, careen and spin like acrobats, all to support the dim notion that the Earth is at the center of the universe. I love you, Tyge, you have been the best of brothers, so please . . . please, listen to me."

"Are you again losing your reason, brother Magnus?"

Magnus put his eye to the second sextant. He turned to Tycho and rested his hand on his brother's shoulder.

"Remember your brother as you see him now," said Magnus. "Remember what I tell you. The sun resides in the center of the universe. Earth revolves around the sun, along with the planets, moves not in a circular orbit, but in an ellipse, rotates once a day, and provides the geometric center for only the moon's orbit. All the idiots of Casseopeia agree on this. Please. Take another look at the red planet and you will see that I speak the truth. It is with a brother's love I wish for you a more proper understanding. Aristotle is dead. Ptolemy is dead. But if you just take another look at Mars, Tycho Brahe will live forever."

"Why do you stand like that, Magnus, with your shoulders showing the stoop of the simpleton? And why has your face gone so pale?"

"Please, Tyge, one more look at ancient Ares, and you will see his movements can only be explained by the Polish monk's configurations."

They gazed at each other. Tycho had never seen Magnus so desperate. He looked like a man about to face the gibbet. What could he do but humor his beloved brother?

He put his eye to the sextant and discovered that since last night's observation, Mars had moved in retrograde several degrees of an arc. Tycho adjusted the sextant and clamped it. The warrior planet shone like a red ember in the midnight sky, brightly and more persistently than ever. Tycho began to see that this newly observed luminosity had to have a reason, that this brightness worked hand in hand with the backward tracking, smoothly and simply, not with the swirl and strut of a drunkard, but with the even-kiltered grace of a ship on settled waters. This rogue movement couldn't be explained with the tangled mathematics of Ptolemy, but maybe, after all, with the childlike precepts of the Polish monk. How simple it now seemed. How beautiful and exalted. At last he saw it, not only with his eyes, but with his mind. The holy clockwork of the heavens as it really was, not as a castle of far-fetched calculations.

But then he heard a broom behind him, and in that same instant, the light of the new star finally went out. He turned around and saw his brother sweeping the same bit of stone floor over and over again, the spark of reason gone from his mongoloid eyes. Gone, all gone in an instant, his beloved brother, again banished to his tormented life of nightmares and delusions, his body again twisted out of shape. "Magnus?" said Tycho, taking a few steps forward. "Magnus, where have you gone? Please, dear Magnus, come hither. Do not leave me."

But Magnus stood there and swept, gazing at the dull dark spot where the star of Cassiopeia so recently shone. Then calmly, deliberately, he urinated in his silk hosiery.

The bishop's palace loomed dark against the moonlight, its towers jagged and imposing, the crenellations of its battlements like teeth. Here, on this stony and barren approach near the sea, the wind never stopped and nothing but a few patches of yellow grass clung to the sparse topsoil. Tycho, as always, looked up at the sky. Magnus led his horse toward the palace gates. His brother should have stayed at Herritzvad Abbey. Storm clouds moved in from the north and he and Magnus would get drenched coming home. But there was nothing the simpleton liked better than to lead the horse by the rope, and a little rain would never harm him.

Magnus stopped the horse outside the gate. Tycho dismounted, knowing full well why the bishop had sent for him in the middle of the night: his revised system, amended to include many of the principles Magnus had clarified, had met with displeasure at the court.

He pounded at the door with the large iron knocker. One of the brothers of the order, wearing a black skullcap, let them in. Magnus led the horse to a pile of hay just inside the palace walls and stood in the dark, obedient and silent, ill-at-ease, while the horse ate. Tycho followed the brother into the large hall, where the finest tapestries from Persia hung on the walls and smoky torches cast fitful shadows over the rough floor. He followed the brother down the passage to the bishop's chambers. The brother gave him one last look, as if he were an object of curiosity and pity, then pushed the heavy oak door open.

The bishop stood in front of the fire with his back to Tycho, his black robe darker than the surrounding gloom. Something fluttered up in the rafters. Outside, the wind, gaining strength, moaned over the rocks and through the turrets, and a few large drops fell against the shutters.

"I have prayed for you, Lord Brahe," said the bishop, keeping his back to the astronomer, his voice grave. "I have asked the Divine Creator to forgive you your trespass and blasphemy, and to bless you with His holy guidance. I have asked Him to lead you to a better understanding of His true design." The bishop turned around. He advanced to the table and lifted a sheaf of papers. "I cannot permit this," he said. "You haven't evaluated the evidence as a true scientist should. Would a true scientist allow the sun to reside at the center of the universe? I fear you must undertake a serious revision, Lord Brahe, if you are to align your work with the principles of the Holy Maker."

With his method and observations called into doubt by the bishop's unswerving views, Tycho at last understood the breadth and darkness of the gulf that stood between them; but he must try and bridge that chasm, to make the bishop understand that there was indeed a place for empirical measurement in science.

"Your Holiness," he said, as calmly as he could, "I believe you'll see by my latest calculations, especially those describing the motions of the warrior planet, that the discrepancies so shrewdly detailed in Kopernik's *De revolutionibus* can only be explained by—"

"We are not here to discuss your explanations and calculations, Lord Brahe," said the bishop, raising his hand. "Kopernik made a better canon than he did a scientist, and his heretical notions are of no value or relevance. We are now concerned with your soul."

The bishop dropped the sheaf of paper on the table, his skin stretched like parchment over his bony face as he held the astronomer's gaze. Out in the passage, Tycho heard doleful plainsong emanate from the palace chapel, the brothers joining in a lugubrious chant, praising their Almighty God with a dark and unvarying melody.

"Your Holiness, all my hundreds of observations support Kopernik's heliocentric theory."

"Do not talk to me of heliocentricity," said the bishop. "Let us concern ourselves with your salvation, Lord Brahe. Let us concern ourselves with your Uncle Steen's estate here in Knudstrup and how by royal order, Herritzvad Abbey could be confiscated, just as it was once so easily confiscated from the Benedictine monks. Let us concern ourselves with your mother Beate and her position as Mistress of the Robes to Queen Sophia, and how she could be so easily dismissed if her son were to persist in this blasphemy."

The bishop turned away from Tycho, walked over to the fire, and stirred the embers until the flames leapt up the flue, the wood cracking and popping like the breaking of bones. The confiscation of Herritzvad Abbey from the Benedictine monks still rankled the old bishop, even though it had happened many years ago. Tycho felt like striking the bishop against the back of his head with the flat of his sword, but he kept his weapon sheathed, and stiffened his resolve.

"I will not be coerced," he said, his voice quiet but firm.

Bishop Anders turned from the fire, his eyes as grim as death. "Lord Brahe, this is not coercion, this is guidance," he said, approaching the table. "We can't have you gainsaying the age-old doctrines of the Church." He lifted the hot poker toward Tycho's face and held it a few inches from the astronomer's right eye. "I won't have the power and prestige of my diocese undercut by a mischievous Lutheran who thinks he understands the heavens better than I do."

"And you have the king's blessing in this?"

"I have the king's blessing in everything," he said, lowering the poker. "Heliocentricity! And the Earth to roam like a common vagabond? These are the notions of a madman." The bishop leaned forward, pinning him with his rheumy blue eyes. "And do you know what we do with madmen, Lord Brahe? We put them in leg-irons and lock them in the darkest cell at Skokloster where they never see the stars again."

Tycho found his brother Magnus standing in the rain next to his horse in exactly the same spot, as if he were unaware of the downpour. Tycho trudged across the yard, numbed by the injustice, struggling to think of a way out; but if he insisted on telling the truth, such as Magnus had revealed it, he would never see the stars again. The bishop was unpredictable and unpleasant; he was also diabolical. If Tycho told the truth he would bring ruin to his uncle and mother. And he couldn't do that, even if as a result his work suffered.

Magnus looked sodden and miserable; but, oh, how Tycho loved him. He took off his cape and swung it around the simpleton's shoulders.

"You ride, Magnus," he said. "I'll lead."

He slapped the saddle and gestured. Magnus's eyes lit up. He liked riding the horse even more than he enjoyed leading it.

They set off from the bishop's palace into the midnight storm. Tycho looked up at the sky; no moon, no stars, no planets, a typical view from the darkest cell at Skokloster asylum. He glanced over his shoulder at Magnus. Coerced. Yet as he looked at his brother, he now had the glimmering of an idea, the half-formed notion of a way out. His step lightened as he marveled at the simplicity of his idea, so simple even a fool could think of it.

He didn't have to tell the truth. All he had to do was *show* the truth. He would make thousands upon thousands of observations, designed and manufacture the finest and most accurate astronomical instruments, find a place far away from the court, far away from this diocese, an island, perhaps, where the ether was clear and the stars beautiful and wondrous, and continue his work undisturbed. So many observations that those who could see with their eyes as well as their minds would come to one inescapable conclusion. He didn't have to tell them. His observations would speak for themselves. His observations wouldn't lie, the way Bishop Anders lied. He would watch and watch, and his brother's season of intelligence would not be wasted, nor the sages of Cassiopeia forgotten. Those who saw with their eyes as well as their minds would understand that Brahe of Knudstrup knew the truth, the heretical, immutable, exalted truth: that the Earth roamed with its sister and brother planets like a vagabond and that the sun resided at the center of the universe in all its shining glory.

He turned to Magnus, a smile coming to his face. "I am an eye, brother Magnus," he said. "And I watch." He looked up at the stormy sky. "I watch."

DOMESTIC SLASH AND THRUST

Jan Lars Jensen

Jan Lars Jensen grew up in Yarrow, British Columbia, and currently lives in the nearby city of Chilliwack. He graduated from the University of Victoria creative writing program in 1993 and currently works for the Fraser Valley Regional Library system mostly as a librarian. His stories have appeared in *On Spec*, the Tesseracts anthology series, *Interzone*, *Aboriginal SF*, and *The Magazine of Fantasy & Science Fiction*. In 1998 "The Strip Mall Selects for Evolution" won first prize in an SF writing contest sponsored by *Prairie Fire*, a Canadian literary magazine. Jensen's first novel, *Shiva 3000*, will be published by Harcourt Brace in 1999.

"Domestic Slash and Thrust," a science fiction story about industrial design, engineering, and marketing, qualifies as a horror story as well. It first appeared in *Tesseracts 5* (1996). Jensen tells us that the inspiration for the story "came from the realization that everyday appliances are becoming increasingly sophisticated, while comprehension of how they work diminishes in their users. On the other hand, there's a small group of people responsible for designing these items and making them work, and they develop a knowledge so specialized it's difficult for them to relate to people outside their own field. I imagined a gulf developing between these groups, a breakdown in their ability to relate as human beings. Around the same time, I heard someone on TV talking about an electric carving knife that had caused unexpected injuries among users, and it seemed a perfect middle point—please forgive the pun."

1011. *Subject carves holiday turkey with Brunhaus Electric Carving Knife, grabs blade, severs muscles in the palm; suffers blood loss, distressed tissue, infection from bacteria transferred from meat.*

1012. *Subject attempts "precision cut" with Brunhaus knife, cuts off distal phalanx of thumb. Subject's aunt faints at the sight of thumb on plate.*

1013. Subject attempts to open milk carton using Brunhaus knife, also cuts open left wrist. Severed radial artery, blood loss, shock.
1014. Subject asks friend to "pass" the Brunhaus knife . . .

For reasons of privacy, the name of the individual in every case had been substituted with the term "subject." Lausanne knew this, but when scrolling through the list she nonetheless thought of the subject as being one distinct person who had suffered *all* the wounds involving the Brunhaus Electric Carving Knife, yet continued to use it and inflict further damage on himself, his friends, his relatives, his pets. Clumsiness, ineptitude, drowsiness, drunkenness, failure to read the manual. Failure to turn off the knife, failure to avoid hard objects, failure to avoid his fingers. Blood, tissue, bone. By now, she thought, the subject would keep a good ten meters between himself and the knife. Or throw it in the trash.

But no. He kept returning to it, in some composite of a hundred thousand homes he crept into the kitchen and knelt before the cupboard, checking that no one watched as he reached inside with a hand that still smelled of disinfectant until his fingers closed over the treble-clef handle of the Brunhaus Electric.

What makes you such a masochist? she wanted to ask him.

Lausanne pushed away from the desk, chair gliding silently back. "I need a vacation," she said. "White beaches and steel drums . . ." But she couldn't afford more time away from the case studies than a cup of camomile tea would require.

The staff room looked like a show room. Dishwasher and clothes dryer, bread baker and cappucino maker; they all sat in gleaming rows like concept cars at an auto show, configurations of ivory plastic and bright stainless steel so aggressively *new* that their exact function sometimes eluded Lausanne. Their alienness, however, was curtailed by prominent flourishes of Brunhaus design.

Clashing with the swirled lines and smooth finials this afternoon was someone she'd never before seen. Crew cut, bushy eyebrows, and terrible glasses with thick black frames—like a concession to safety in a woodshop. He busily dispensed ice cubes from the front of the fridge. A large mound sat in the receptacle tray and he transferred the cubes one by one to the microwave nearby. Lausanne watched as he stacked them inside in precise, measured rows.

"I've given up on ordinary consumers," she announced.

He said nothing, didn't look away from the ice cubes.

"Did you hear me?"

No response.

"Hello . . . ?" She prodded him with her foot. His eyes flickered her way.

"You all right?" she said.

"You're taking me out."

"Out?"

She didn't know what he meant but decided to focus on making tea. Normally she nuked a cup of water in the microwave. A little digging revealed that Brunhaus had provided an ovoid of ivory plastic called a Tea-maker, so new the plastic still smelled, and she pretended to concentrate on its instructions as she continued observing the oddball. When he'd filled the microwave to capacity he gently closed its door and pressed a button on the front display. Maximum heat, the microwave said, and followed with an appropriate hum.

"Sorry," he said. "I'm not used to this."

"Not used to what?"

"This."

"Talking?"

He nodded.

Lausanne shuddered, realizing he must be from Programming. "Why aren't you in your own staff room?"

"Remodeling. Guys in blue coveralls, sawdust, power tools."

"Oh."

"I wasn't being rude before. You were taking me out."

"What do you mean, out?"

"In our staff room we avoid talking to one another. It's courtesy. Programming, you see—" he paddled his hands in a way that didn't clarify what he was saying. "We get into it," he said. "We get into the code. If we divert our attention from programming, well, we slip up. Bugs. Logic errors. Extra work."

She raised her eyebrows and took a chair. Fine. "I guess that's why we have separate staff rooms in the first place."

"I wasn't being rude." He stood and closed his eyes. *"I've given up on ordinary consumers."*

She complimented his recall.

"What caused this crisis?" he said. "What do you do?"

"Product Safety in Design. Supposedly I'm re-imagining the Brunhaus Electric Carving Knife without the tendency to slice off thumbs. I have a database of thousands of cases where people cut themselves, their friends, their relatives, et cetera, with our knife. No amount of exclamation marks in the safety manual can persuade them to use it properly."

"So you've come back to the product."

"I come back to how people use the product. The problem is I can't get a handle on the average user. I can't predict how he thinks. When I try to assimilate my case studies I form an image of him as a reckless idiot."

"Oh, oh, oh," he said, and made swimming, paddling motions with his hands. "Same in software design. Any application where the user might not also be a programmer. We live under the tyranny of the everyday user. Trying to create a buffer between the actual program and his or her most ignorant impulses; simplifying complex routines into a string of questions that can be answered with one word. *O.K.? O.K.? O.K.?*"

Lausanne digested this.

"We're idiot-proofing the world," the programmer said enthusiastically. "Retooling everyday items, matching them to the incompetence of their users."

"That may be true of software," she said. "But in Design we're trying to enhance those everyday items. With safety features, with aesthetic qualities."

The programmer said, "I don't believe you," and returned to his microwave full of ice. Lausanne tried to guess what would happen inside. Sublimation? Would steam blow the little door off its plastic hinges? Would boiling water pour to the floor and scald his feet? But reality wasn't so just. The makers of the microwave, it seemed, had anticipated this scenario.

ITEM(S) PLACED IN OVEN INAPPROPRIATE FOR MICROWAVE COOKING, it said, and shut down automatically.

"The idiot lives to see another day!" The programmer gave a laugh like live static. When Lausanne didn't join him he regained composure and introduced himself. "Willis," he said. "Advanced Simulations. We're actually working on something that could matter to you. An ergonomic modeling system. We have a beta-version up and running if you'd like to come have a look."

"Thanks all the same but I'm under deadline."

"Sure. Who isn't? I'm only offering because it might answer some of your questions about everyday users."

She reconsidered. On his suggestion she dug around the staff room for one of the old models of electric carving knife and brought it along as they walked the cool ivory hallways. The elevator had been reprogrammed to stop at a floor previously only a number to her, 55. Despite the continuing Brunhaus aesthetic she had the sense of crossing into another country, a silent crowd saying nothing to one another, feverishly manipulating screen-based text and imagery.

They reached a door with a security sensor shaped like the Brunhaus B. For some reason they were required to remove shoes and socks before proceeding. Barefoot, they crossed into a dark, narrow space with few distinguishing features. The walls seemed glossy brown, and Lausanne thought she felt patterns against her soles, like a finely engraved picture, but examining the floor she saw only the burnished sepia.

"So where's the computer?"

"We're standing in it," he said. "Part of it."

She looked around with new attention to detail. A table in the room's center extended continuously from the floor, she noticed; it wasn't a distinct piece of furniture.

"Beta-version," Willis said, and another person appeared.

Or not a person. A photonic representation of an adult male, naked but devoid of sex organs and distinguishing marks. Much like the boyfriend to a plastic doll Lausanne had undressed and examined in her childhood. A shimmering, continuously reconfiguring quality made the figure seem like a visitation.

"We're working late this evening," it said mildly.

"What is it?" Lausanne asked Willis. "Some kind of AI?"

"An ergonomic modeling system. Graphic representation of human kinetics. Don't be fooled by the interface, there's no great intelligence behind it. The real strength is adaptability: the model is full of great algorithms describing body mechanics."

"I warn you not to put complete faith in my behavior," the luminescent figure said politely. "I am only a beta-version."

"This is a real sneak peek," Willis told her. "Management doesn't want anyone outside of Programming to see this yet."

"What is that?" the beta-version asked, indicating the carving knife on the table. It reached over and "grabbed" the handle. The actual knife remained where it lay but the beta-version lifted away a ghostly simulacrum, part of his projection, which it turned at different angles. The beta-version thumbed the ON/OFF switch but the action on the projected blade was wrong: rotary, where it should have been in-and-out.

"Here," said Lausanne, and switched on the real knife for

the simulation to model. She held it to a lens in the wall. The projection corrected itself until one knife mirrored the other.

"I'd like some time here alone," she said.

"I thought you'd approve," Willis laughed.

"I'm serious. Would anyone care if I used the beta-version for a while?"

He checked the watch decalled onto his wrist. "Morning shift starts at four A.M., then everyone starts logging on, the projection becomes maddeningly slow . . ."

"Three hours will do," she said, or meant to say; her focus has zeroed upon the beta-version, and the distinction between thoughts and statements became as peripheral as Willis walking backward and quietly letting himself out of the room.

It was the way the projection had first picked up the knife: startling. How many times had she tried to visualize a stranger's initial grasp of the appliance? Never, she knew, with the clarity realized by the beta-version. Now, upon instruction, she could observe a naive reaction to the knife. She examined raw human impulses toward its design. Three hours was nothing; she only realized her time was up when the projection took a full minute to dice an imaginary apple.

"Okay," she yawned. "I'm done."

The room blinked to darkness and she felt her way to the door. She was exhausted, but knew the time had been worth a week of conventional approach to user behavior. While wearily lacing her shoes she spotted Willis punching away at a workstation.

"You haven't left?" she said.

"I have a bed here. A cot."

"What about home?"

He shrugged. "I have no other cots."

"I'm impressed with the beta-version," she said. "Heads will spin in Design."

He nodded, without pride.

"But for me the need already exists. I mean, three hours was great, but listen, I've got this huge database of case studies with the knife. Couldn't we patch in this wealth of data? Would you be up to that? Or does Internal Security make you nervous?"

He smirked. "A little nervous. But I'm always up for a good hack. What's your workstation number?"

She told him. He didn't ask for passwords.

"I'll see what I can do," he said, "but don't get your hopes up."

"Understood," she said, and went upstairs to see if she could get her deadline pushed back a week or two.

The first time she saw it, she gasped. Willis had left a plastic glove at her workstation which she brought down to floor 55. The security door was locked but when she put on the glove it accepted her handprint, allowing her inside the sepia chamber. And that was when she made the noise of surprise, seeing the beta-version standing there, its body tapered by a thousand wounds. Conceptual wounds: the flesh appeared sheared off, with a precision suitable for a geometry model. Both eyes were scooped away and the nose was absent. Parallel slashes made the torso appear gilled, and although the projection lacked enough fingers to logically do so it held a Brunhaus Electric Carving Knife in the stub of one hand.

"I'm sorry if my appearance startles you," the beta-version said, and smoothed away the wounds.

"Not at all."

The inspiration from average users was apparent; the beta-version could not move the knife without plunging it into an arm, a wrist, a hand. When allowed to cycle freely through its database the projection seemed to perform a *kata*, with each swing finding a new way to pass the shimmering blade through its shimmering body. She recognized the wounds the beta-version inflicted on itself from her readings but the qualitative difference was huge: the intermediate moments, the body mechanics, the position in which the beta-version held the knife when it placed a nonexistent milk carton between its legs and proceeded to saw open one spout, then two . . .

"From now on," she said at one point during that session, "I'm going to have to call you 'subject'."

"Subject," it said, and nodded, and lopped off its thumb.

As her major deadline approached, Lausanne traded sleep for extra hours in the building. She kept working at her station, late every night, hoping for word from Willis that it was safe to sneak downstairs and steal more time with the subject. *The subject.* Her weary sessions reinforced this appellation. Willingly it obliged her instructions to repeat the same wound upon itself. Over and over, at different speeds, at different angles, from another point of view. *Gladly* the subject obliged, it sometimes seemed, or was that just her spinning head? It was often dizzying. She stood in a room with the average user, at last, and every interaction sent the Brunhaus blade through its body. It was late in the evening— or late in the afternoon, she had lost track of the day—when their relationship changed fundamentally.

"Number four forty-six is my favorite."

She spun about. "Excuse me?"

"Number four forty-six. My favorite wound. *You* know. Downward slash through the right ventricle?" He demonstrated, closing his eyes with pleasure as he dragged the blade across his chest. "That's the spot . . ."

"Willis?!" She spun toward the lens in the wall. "Is this some kind of joke?!"

"No joke," said the subject, getting closer. "I just wanted to tell you what I enjoy. Because you don't seem to know."

"What are you—"

"I hate to see you wasting time with safety issues. Why not give me what I really want? A product that rewards my hand for holding it. Something that says, 'You made a wise spending decision,' the moment I make contact." It raised the Brunhaus knife. "Something like this."

"But the wounds . . ."

"The wounds," it said, and laughed. Then it turned the knife onto her, jabbing her beneath the neck. Lausanne thought she could feel the tip of the blade as he traced over her skin, making a variation of the Brunhaus B.

$

"That doesn't feel so bad, does it?"

She blinked at the red phosphenes of "blood" trickling down from the symbol, then looked into the grinning veil of his face. "Blood money? You think I'm making blood money?"

"I think you should find out what the average user *really* wants."

She shook her head, shook it with her whole body, and when she opened her eyes again the beta-version stood opposite her, dimmed down, a power-saving measure that occurred whenever it hadn't been commanded for five minutes or more.

Lausanne burst from the sepia chamber.

The pale persons attached to the workstations ignored her storming through level 55, one or two leaning back to stare after she bumped against their ergonomic chairs. Were they in on that joke? How many lines of code had they contributed? She managed to contain her anger until she got to the stack of cots where Willis lay staring at a wall—but he didn't burst out laughing or even smirk as she approached.

"Why are you looking at me like that?"

"No reason," Lausanne said evenly.

"Shouldn't you be working on your design?" he said. "Shouldn't you be in there with the beta-version?"

"I need a change of scenery," she said. "I thought maybe you'd go for a walk with me."

As they left the building she stole occasional glances at him, but he was inscrutable. If Willis had programmed those comments into the beta-version his behavior didn't give him away. Maybe he'd open up a little if she took him out of his element.

Soon they distanced themselves from the building with its ubiquitous conceits of design. At one point, a spiral pattern in the pavement opened the sidewalk into a plaza, but local denizens had thwarted this lone flourish in the cityscape by holding a tag sale, the vendors sitting on the ground, encircled by old possessions. Loose pages of printed matter had become pasted to the ground with rain; a dollar each, even though their text bled over the pavement. The vendors raised their heads as Willis and Lausanne splashed through the plaza but not, it seemed, with raised hopes for a sale. They looked spent inside their tents and see-through rain gear.

Willis said, "Why would you want to come out there?"

"What's the matter? Don't you like it outside?"

"I don't leave the building much."

"No, you don't look like you get a lot of sun."

"This is sun?" He turned her way, rain drizzling over his hood.

"We're too far removed from the real world," she said quickly. "We spend so much time holed up inside. Good to get out once in a while."

He said nothing to this, just kept glancing around at their surroundings. They walked through a series of arches supporting an overhead road, and there were shanties attached to their sides, people staring out from cardboard nests.

"Maybe I *should* let the hoi polloi design this knife," Lausanne said. "I guess that's what you were implying before, when you said we were idiot-proofing the world."

But all he said now was that they should probably turn around. Lausanne led him on. They waded through a blue puddle, residue of oil making color like a peacock's neck. "How do I know what they want?" she said. "How do I sink to their level?"

"How—"

The question went unanswered. Walking around an ancient building of brick and mortar they looked up to an outcrop of roof, where a police ornithopter sat perched like a gargoyle. Its wings were folded against the fuselage, and a door hung open to reveal empty cockpit. Xenon lights strobed blue and red but there were no cops around, nobody at all. The area was dead. When Lausanne and Willis continued walking, the ornithopter spoke to them. Its synthetic voice warned, "Stay back—there is a crisis situation in the vicinity."

"We better go," Willis sputtered, and tugged her sleeve. But he didn't know the best retreat. They made a few wrong turns and emerged on a wide boulevard with broken pallets and bundled cardboard sitting in the street. No traffic.

She said, "How do we connect with the average user?"

"How do we . . . Christ, I don't know."

He continued glancing around nervously.

And then froze, staring straight ahead.

"What's that?"

She looked where he was pointing. A long box—it looked like a cardboard casket from some tropical border conflict—lay partially in the street. Willis squinted at the text printed on one side, as if that would explain whatever he'd seen. "Contains one . . ."

Lausanne kept thinking design. "A safety message they can't resist . . ."

"There!" said Willis. "You see it move?"

The box came to a rest.

They both stood and stared. Slowly the box rose onto its end. A knife pushed through the flaps, followed by a soot-smeared, half-naked vagrant, one eye showing through the mask of hair over his face. Lausanne could see teeth, too, and realized he was smiling, or something. But her focus rested on the knife: not the elegant lines of any Brunhaus product but some butcher's throwaway, browned by corrosion and chipped along its edge.

"Run!" said Willis, pulling Lausanne.

She stood her ground. "I know my statistics," she said. "He'll cut himself before he gets halfway here."

"Stow that bullshit, he looks deranged—"

She stayed. "He'll slice his own throat."

The man staggered about, slashing little arcs through the air before him. Willis ran down the street, stopped when Lausanne didn't follow. "What are you doing?"

"Just what you said. Experiencing the average user."

"When did I ever say that?!"

"The beta-version," she replied. "Your nasty joke this afternoon. *Give me what I really want.* Well this is the average user, this is what it's like outside. Weren't you saying I should make a knife that caters to this kind of world?"

"I don't know what you're talking about!"

Three other figures hustled into view. Police. They wore black body armor with cylinders of gas that fed into ARWEN guns. At the sight of the vagrant they formed a three-point position and raised their weapons. Willis said something more just as they were hit with an acoustic weapon: the ornithopter had taken off and moved overhead, beating its wings and pummeling them with a downwash of sound, a noise like jet engine friction. It penetrated the fissures of Lausanne's skull but she remained standing, as did the vagrant, still swinging his knife as he walked toward her.

"GET DOWN!" a cop shouted.

Willis yelled too, something like "Get out of the fucking way," and when she still remained standing he leapt into her, as shots ripped through the blanket of sound, thwops of black rubber plugs walloping the vagrant and the concrete, thick ricochets, and the target went down, folding onto his knife.

Unintended targets, too. "This is it," Lausanne said as she and Willis fell over the wet ground. ARWEN wads bounced around them, and even now the designer in her kept seeing that blade, and those guns, the molded grips and their squared black barrels.

. . . Consider the fabulous weight of the new Brunhaus Carving Knife.

To hold it in one's hand is not simply to hold a household appliance, but a tool, which must be treated with respect. Added to this sensation is the sound the knife makes when activated, another conceit of the designer—a buzzing like a

sawmill in miniature—a constant reminder to the user that
this machine is all about the business of cutting . . .
                                    —*Design Edge Monthly*

The executive said, "You seem like the sort of person who can keep a secret."

"Sure," said Lausanne.

They stood in his office, looking into several testing booths. An enormous flatscreen divided the wall into a grid of six different views. In each, a test subject carved a roast beef into smaller and smaller segments, using a prototype of the knife Lausanne had designed. All this cutting might have been going on a few doors away, or in another building, or another time zone. Lausanne didn't know or care, but the executive—Marcus Philo, VP Domestic Design—seemed excited to take her into the testing process, as if they were on safari.

"Someday we'll be rid of them," he said.

"The test subjects?"

He nodded happily.

"How?"

"Brunhaus has a major piece of software in the works. An ergonomic modeling system. We'll be able to address safety issues without consulting real people."

"Sounds too good to be true," she said, with fake enthusiasm.

"Sad that it wasn't ready in time for your knife."

She gave him a weak smile.

"But you didn't need any help." He crossed to his desk and picked up one of the prototypes, stroking its bullpup handle. "I can't keep my hands off!" he exclaimed, and yes, his expression lit up the moment he made contact; the knife seemed to deliver direct physical pleasure.

"What a job you've done! I assume you read the glowing review in *Design Monthly*?"

"Yes."

"I love the handle. What made you decide to model it after the grip of a gun? It's brilliant; it instantly conveys the care that must be taken with the knife; powerfully conveys a sense of unleashed potential."

She thought of Willis lying in a generic white bed, surrounded by dull, utilitarian machines of beige and lime green. Brunhaus would pay to keep them glowing and beeping by his bedside for as long as the odds favored full recovery. The blow from the ARWEN gun had fractured his skull, put him in a coma, and nothing had *conveyed a sense of power* for Lausanne like that moment in the street. She watched the executive with grim detachment as he fondled the knife it had yielded.

"You'll never get rid of the live bodies," she said.

"Why not?"

She walked over, placed her hands on the knife, on his hands. "Feedback," she said, and nodded toward the people disassembling beef onscreen, one of them holding up a bloody palm. "They design our products, not us, not simulations."

He looked at her. "Well, whatever the case. You've demonstrated rare insight into what delights our target consumer; the test subjects can't get enough of your knife.

"We'd like to expand that vision within Brunhaus," he continued. "In practical terms it would mean a management level position overseeing design. You'd take charge of next year's domestic line."

Lausanne was only vaguely aware this was a job offer, and that she was still gripping the knife, his hands, watching the grid of screens, where all the test subjects had become generic as the beta-version, tapered and shiny, all of them raising palms to the cameras and coming up with blood, *$, $, $*, one after another, and Lausanne was smiling as she realized these wounds were a small price to pay for luxury.

HALO

Karl Schroeder

Karl Schroeder was born in Brandon, Manitoba, and moved to Toronto in 1986 to pursue his writing career. His family is part of a Mennonite community that has lived in southern Manitoba for over one hundred years. Schroeder is the second science fiction writer to come out of this small community—the first was A. E. van Vogt. His father was the first television technician in Manitoba (quite a distinction at the time) and his mother published two romance novels. "I grew up with those books on the bookshelf—I always considered it perfectly natural to see 'Schroeder' on a book cover," he says.

Schroeder has been active in Toronto SF circles, serving for several years as the president of SF Canada, maintaining the SF Canada listserver, and winning an Aurora Award for short fiction (for "The Toy Mill," in collaboration with David Nickle). He has also published a novel with Nickle that developed out of the story. His first solo novel, *Ventus*, will soon be published by Tor.

"Halo," says Schroeder, "is an attempt to be both 'hard SF' and character-driven fiction; to introduce a new kind of interstellar civilization and a new kind of interstellar travel; and to take the most marginal and hostile environment for life, and make it perfectly believable that people would choose to live there." It is interesting to compare it to Atwood's "Freeforall." "Halo" first appeared in *Tesseracts 5*. Schroeder is one of the few contemporary Canadian SF writers of the younger generations who uses distant future settings or writes hard SF, one of the mainstays of American SF.

Elise Cantrell was awakened by the sound of her children trying to manage their own breakfast. Bright daylight streamed in through the windows. She threw on a robe and ran for the kitchen. "No, no, let me!"

Judy appeared about to microwave something, and the oven was set on high.

"Aw, Mom, did you forget?" Alex, who was a cherub but had the loudest scream in the universe, pouted at her from the table. Looked like he'd gotten his breakfast together just fine. Suspicious, that, but she refused to inspect his work.

"Yeah, I forgot the time change. My prospectors are still on the twenty-four-hour clock, you know."

"Why?" Alex flapped his spoon in the cereal bowl.

"They're on another world, remember? Only Dew has a thirty-hour day, and only since they put the sun up. You remember before the sun, don't you?" Alex stared at her as though she were insane. It had only been a year and a half.

Elise sighed. Just then the door announced a visitor. "Daddy!" shrieked Judy as she ran out of the room. Elise found her in the foyer clinging to the leg of her father. Nasim Clearwater grinned at her over their daughter's flyaway hair.

"You're a mess," he said by way of greeting.

"Thanks. Look, they're not ready. Give me a few minutes."

"No problem. Left a bit early, thought you might forget the time change."

She glared at him and stalked back to the kitchen.

As she cleaned up and Nasim dressed the kids, Elise looked out over the landscape of Dew. It was daylight, yes, a pale drawn glow dropping through cloud veils to sketch hills and plains of ice. Two years ago this window had shown no view, just the occasional star. Elise had grown up in that velvet darkness, and it was so strange now to have awakening signaled by such a vivid and total change. Her children would grow up to the rhythm of true day and night, the first such generation here on Dew. They would think differently. Already, this morning, they did.

"Hello," Nasim said in her ear. Startled, Elise said, "What?" a bit too loudly.

"We're off." The kids stood behind him, dubiously inspecting the snaps of their survival suits. Today was a breach drill; Nasim would ensure they took it seriously. Elise gave him a peck on the cheek.

"You want them back late, right? Got a date?"

"No," she said, "of course not." Nasim wanted to hear that she was being independent, but she wouldn't give him the satisfaction.

Nasim half-smiled. "Well, maybe I'll see you after, then."

"Sure."

He nodded but said nothing further. As the kids screamed

their goodbyes at full volume she tried to puzzle out what he'd meant. See her? To chat, to talk, maybe more?

Not more. She had to accept that. As the door closed she plunked herself angrily down on the couch, and drew her headset over her eyes.

VR was cheap for her. She didn't need full immersion, just vision and sound, and sometimes the use of her hands. Her prospectors were too specialized to have human traits, and they operated in weightlessness so she didn't need to walk. The headset was expensive enough without such additions. And the simplicity of the set-up allowed her to work from home.

The fifteen robot prospectors Elise controlled ranged throughout the halo worlds of Crucible. Crucible itself was fifty times the mass of Jupiter, a "brown dwarf" star—too small to be a sun but radiating in the high infrared and trailing a retinue of planets. Crucible sailed alone through the spaces between the true stars. Elise had been born and raised here on Dew, Crucible's frozen fifth planet. From the camera on the first of her prospectors, she could see the new kilometers-long metal cylinder that her children had learned to call the *sun*. Its electric light shone only on Dew, leaving Crucible and the other planets in darkness. The artificial light made Dew gleam like a solitary blue-white jewel on the perfect black of space.

She turned her helmeted head, and out in space her prospector turned its camera. Faint Dew-light reflected from a round spot on Crucible. She hadn't seen that before. She recorded the sight; the kids would like it, even if they didn't quite understand it.

This first prospector craft perched astride a chunk of ice about five kilometers long. The little ice-flinder orbited Crucible with about a billion others. Her machine oversaw some dumb mining equipment that was chewing stolidly through the thing in search of metal.

There were no problems here. She flipped her view to the next machine, whose headlamps obligingly lit to show her a wall of stone. Hmm. She'd been right the night before when she ordered it to check an ice ravine on Castle, the fourth planet. There was real stone down here, which meant metals. She wondered what it would feel like, and reached out. After a delay the metal hands of her prospector touched the stone. She didn't feel anything; the prospector was not equipped to transmit the sensation back. Sometimes she longed to be able to fully experience the places her machines visited.

She sent a call to the Mining Registrar to follow up on her find, and went on to the next prospector. This one orbited farthest out, and there was a time-lag of several minutes between every command she gave, and its execution. Normally she just checked it quickly and moved on. Today, for some reason, it had a warning flag in its message queue.

Transmission intercepted.—Oh, it had overheard some dialogue between two ships or something. That was surprising, considering how far away from the normal orbits the prospector was. "Read it to me," she said, and went on to Prospector Four.

She'd forgotten about the message and was admiring a long view of Dew's horizon from the vantage of her fourth prospector, when a resonant male voice spoke in her ear:

"Mayday, mayday—anyone at Dew, please receive. My name is Hammond, and I'm speaking from the interstellar cycler *Chinook*. The date is the sixth of May, 2418. Relativistic shift is .500435—we're at half lightspeed.

"Listen: *Chinook* has been taken over by Naturite forces out of Leviathan. They are using the cycler as a weapon. You must know by now that the halo world Tiara, at Obsidian, has gone silent—it's our fault, *Chinook* has destroyed them. Dew is our next stop, and they fully intend to do the same thing there. They want to 'purify' the halo worlds so only their people settle here.

"They're keeping communications silence. I've had to go outside to take manual control of a message laser in order to send this mayday.

"You must place mines in near-pass space ahead of the cycler, to destroy it. We have limited maneuvering ability, so we couldn't possibly avoid the mines.

"Anyone receiving this message, please relay it to your authorities immediately. *Chinook* is a genocide ship. You are in danger.

"Please do not reply to *Chinook* on normal channels. They will not negotiate. Reply to my group on this frequency, not the standard cycler wavelengths."

Elise didn't know how to react. She almost laughed—what a ridiculous message, full of bluster and emergency words. But she'd heard that Obsidian had gone mysteriously silent, and no one knew why. "Origin of this message?" she asked. As she waited, she replayed it. It was highly melodramatic, just the sort of wording somebody would use for a prank. She was sure she would be told the message had come from Dew itself—maybe even sent by Nasim or one of his friends.

The coordinates flashed before her eyes. Elise did a quick calculation to visualize the direction. Not from Dew. Not from any of Crucible's worlds. The message had come from deep space, out somewhere beyond the last of Crucible's trailing satellites.

The only things out there were stars, halo worlds—and the cyclers, Elise thought. She lifted off the headset. The beginnings of fear fluttered in her belly.

Elise took the message to a cousin of hers who was a policeman. He showed her into his office, smiling warmly. They didn't often get together since they'd grown up, and he wanted to talk family.

She shook her head. "I've got something strange for you, Sal. One of my machines picked this up last night." And she played the message for him, expecting reassuring laughter and a good explanation.

Half an hour later they were being ushered into the suite of the police chief, who sat at a U-shaped table with her aides, frowning. When she entered, she heard the words of the message playing quietly from the desk speakers of two of the aides, who looked very serious.

"You will tell no one about this," said the chief. She was a thin, strong woman with blazing eyes. "We have to confirm it first." Elise hesitated, then nodded.

Cousin Sal cleared his throat. "Ma'am? You think this message could be genuine, then?"

The chief frowned at him, then said, "It may be true. This may be why Tiara went off the air." The sudden silence of Tiara, a halo world half a light-year from Elise's home, had been the subject of a media frenzy a year earlier. Rumors of disaster circulated, but there were no facts to go on, other than that Tiara's message lasers, which normally broadcast news from there, had gone out. It was no longer news, and Elise had heard nothing about it for months. "We checked the coordinates you reported and they show this message *did* come from the *Chinook*. *Chinook* did its course correction around Obsidian right about the time Tiara stopped broadcasting."

Elise couldn't believe what she was hearing. "But what could they have done?"

The chief tapped at her desk with long fingers. "You're an orbital engineer, Cantrell. You probably know better than I. The *Chinook's* traveling at half lightspeed, so anything it dropped on an intercept course with Obsidian's planets would hit like a bomb. Even the smallest item—a pen or card."

Elise nodded reluctantly. Aside from message lasers, the Interstellar Cyclers were the only means of contact with other stars and halo worlds. Cyclers came by Crucible every few months, but they steered well away from its planets. They only came close enough to use gravity to assist their course change to the next halo world. Freight and passengers were dropped off and picked up via laser sail; the cyclers themselves were huge, far too massive to stop and start at will. Their kinetic energy was incalculable, so the interstellar community monitored them as closely as possible. They spent years in transit between the stars, however, and it took weeks or months for laser messages to reach them. News about cyclers was always out of date before it even arrived.

"We have to confirm this before we do anything," the chief said. "We have the frequency and coordinates to reply. We'll take it from here."

Elise had to ask. "Why did only I intercept the message?"

"It wasn't aimed very well, maybe. He didn't know exactly where his target was. Only your prospector was within the beam. Just luck."

"When is the *Chinook* due to pass us?" Sal asked.

"A month and a half," said the tight-faced aide. "It should be about three light-weeks out; the date on this message would tend to confirm that."

"So any reply will come right about the time they pass us," Sal said. "How can we get a confirmation in time to do anything?"

They looked at one another blankly. Elise did some quick calculations in her head. "Four messages exchanged before they're a day away," she said. "If each party waits for the other's reply. Four on each side."

"But we have to act well before that," said another aide.

"How?" asked a third.

Elise didn't need to listen to the explanation. They could mine the space in front of the cycler. Turn it into energy, and

hopefully any missiles too. Kill the thousand-or-so people on
board it to save Dew.

"I've done my duty," she said. "Can I go away?"

The chief waved her away. A babble of arguing voices followed Elise and Sal out the door.

Sal offered to walk her home, but Elise declined. She took old
familiar ways through the corridors of the city, ways she had
grown up with. Today, though, her usual route from the core of
the city was blocked by work crews. They were replacing opaque
ceiling panels with glass to let in the new daylight. The bright
light completely changed the character of the place, washing out
familiar colors. It reminded her that there were giant forces in
the sky, uncontrollable by her. She retreated, from the glow, and
drifted through a maze of alternate routes like a somber ghost,
not meeting the eyes of the people she passed.

The parkways were packed, mostly with children. Some
were there with a single parent, others with both. Elise watched
the couples enviously. Having children was supposed to have
made her and Nasim closer. It hadn't worked out that way.

Lately, he had shown signs of wanting her again. Take it
slow, she had told herself. Give him time.

They might not have time.

The same harsh sunlight the work crews had been admitting
waited when she got home. It made the jumble of toys on the
living room floor seem tiny and fragile. Elise sat under the new
window for a while, trying to ignore it, but finally hunted
through her closets until she found some old blankets, and covered the glass.

Nasim offered to stay for dinner that night. This made her feel
rushed and off-balance. The kids wanted to stay up for it, but
he had a late appointment. Putting them to bed was arduous.
She got dinner going late, and by then all her planned small talk
had evaporated. Talking about the kids was easy enough—but
to do that was to take the easy way out, and she had wanted
this evening to be different. Worst was that she didn't want to
tell him about the message, because if he thought she was upset
he might withdraw, as he had in the past.

The dinner candles stood between them like chessmen. Elise
grew more and more miserable. Nasim obviously had no idea
what was wrong, but she'd promised not to talk about the crisis.

So she came up with a series of lame explanations, for the blanket over the window and for her mood, none of which he seemed to buy.

Things sort of petered out after that.

She had so hoped things would click with Nasim tonight. Exhausted at the end of it all, Elise tumbled into her own bed alone and dejected.

Sleep wouldn't come. This whole situation had her questioning everything, because it knotted together survival and love, and her own seeming inability to do anything about either. As she thrashed about under the covers, she kept imagining a distant, invisible dart, the cycler, falling from infinity at her.

Finally she got up and went to her office. She would write it out. That had worked wonderfully before. She sat under the VR headset and called up the mailer. Hammond's message was still there, flagged with its vector and frequency. She gave the *reply* command.

"Dear Mr. Hammond:

"I got your message. You intended it for some important person, but I got it instead. I've got a daughter and son—I didn't want to hear that they might be killed. And what am I supposed to do about it? I told the police. So what?

"Please tell me this is a joke. I can't sleep now, all I can think about is Tiara, and what must have happened there.

"I feel . . . I told the police, but that doesn't seem like *enough*, it's as if you called *me*, for help, put the weight of the whole world on my shoulders—and what am I supposed to do about it?" It became easier the more she spoke. Elise poured out the litany of small irritations and big fears that were plaguing her. When she was done, she did feel better.

Send? inquired the mailer.

Oh, God, of course not.

Something landed in her lap, knocking the wind out of her. The headset toppled off her head. "Mommy. Mommy!"

"Yes yes, sweetie, what is it?"

Judy plunked forward onto Elise's breast. "Did you forget the time again, Mommy?"

Elise relaxed. She was being silly. "Maybe a little, honey. What are you doing awake?"

"I don't know."

"Let's both go to bed. You can sleep with me, okay?" Judy nodded.

She stood up, holding Judy. The inside of the VR headset still glowed, so she picked it up to turn it off.

Remembering what she'd been doing, she put it on.

Mail sent, the mailer was flashing.

"Oh, my, *God!*"

"Ow, Mommy."

"Wait a sec, Judy. Mommy has something to do." She put Judy down and fumbled with the headset. Judy began to whine.

She picked *reply* again and said quickly, "Mr. Hammond, please disregard the last message. It wasn't intended for you. The mailer got screwed up. I'm sorry if I said anything to upset you, I know you're in a far worse position than I am and you're doing a very brave thing by getting in touch with us. I'm sure it'll all work out. I . . ." She couldn't think of anything more. "Please excuse me, Mr. Hammond."

Send? "Yes!"

She took Judy to bed. Her daughter fell asleep promptly, but Elise was now wide awake.

She heard nothing from the government during the next while. Because she knew they might not tell her what was happening, she commanded her outermost prospector to devote half its time to scanning for messages from *Chinook*. For weeks, there weren't any.

Elise went on with things. She dressed and fed the kids; let them cry into her shirt when they got too tired or banged their knees; walked them out to meet Nasim every now and then. She had evening coffee with her friends, and even saw a new play that had opened in a renovated reactor room in the basement of the city. Other than that, she mostly worked.

In the weeks after the message's arrival, Elise found a renewal of the comforting solitude her prospectors gave her. For hours at a time, she could be millions of kilometers away, watching ice crystals dance in her headlamps, or seeing stars she could never view from her window. Being so far away literally give her a new perspective on home; she could see Dew in all its fragile smallness, and understood that the bustle of family and friends served to keep the loneliness of the halo worlds at bay. She appreciated people more for that, but also loved being the first to visit ice galleries and frozen cataracts on distant moons.

Now she wondered if she would be able to watch Dew's destruction from her prospectors. That made no sense—she would be dead in that case. The sense of actually *being* out in space was so strong though that she had fantasies of finding the golden thread cut, of existing bodiless and alone forever in the cameras of the prospectors, from which she would gaze down longingly on the ruins of her world.

A month after the first message, a second came. Elise's prospector intercepted it—nobody else except the police would have, because it was at Hammond's special frequency. The kids were tearing about in the next room. Their laughter formed an odd backdrop to the bitter voice that sounded in her ears.

"This is Mark Hammond on the *Chinook*. I will send you all the confirming information I can. There is a video record of the incident at Tiara, and I will try to send it along. It is very difficult. There are only a few of us from the original passengers and crew left. I have to rely on the arrogance of Leviathan's troops, if they encrypt their database I will be unable to send anything. If they catch me, I will be thrown out an airlock.

"I'll tell you what happened. I boarded at Mirjam, four years ago. I was bound for Tiara, to the music academy there. Leviathan was our next stop, and we picked up no freight, but several hundred people who turned out to be soldiers. There were about a thousand people on *Chinook* at that point. The soldiers captured the command center and then they decided who they needed and who was expendable. They killed more than half of us. I was saved because I can sing. I'm part of the entertainment." Hammond's voice expressed loathing. He had a very nice voice, baritone and resonant. She could hear the unhappiness in it.

"It's been two and a half years now, under their heel. We're sick of it.

"A few weeks ago they started preparing to strike your world. That's when we decided. You must destroy *Chinook*. I am going to send you our exact course, and that of the missiles. You must mine space in front of us. Otherwise you'll end up like Tiara."

The kids had their survival class that afternoon. Normally Elise was glad to hand them over to Nasim or, lately, their instructor—but this time she took them. She felt just a little better standing with some other parents in the powdery, sandlike snow outside the city watching the space-suited figures of her children go through the drill. They joined a small group in puzzling over a Global Positioning Unit, and successfuly found the way to the beacon that was their target for today. She felt immensely proud of them, and chatted freely with the other parents. It was the first time in weeks that she'd felt like she was doing something worthwhile.

Being outside in daylight was so strange—after their kids, that was the main topic of conversation among the adults. All remembered their own classes, taken under the permanent night they had grown up with. Now they excitedly pointed out the different and wonderful colors of the stones and ices, reminiscent of pictures of Earth's Antarctica.

It was strange, too, to see the city as something other than a vast dark pyramid. Elise studied it after the kids were done and they'd started back. The city looked solid, a single structure built of concrete that appeared pearly under the mauve clouds. Its flat facades were dotted with windows, and more were being installed. She and the kids tried to find theirs, but it was an unfamiliar exercise and they soon quit.

A big sign had been erected over the city airlock: HELP BUILD A SUNNY FUTURE, it said. Beside it was a thermometer-graph intended to show how close the government was to funding the next stage of Dew's terraforming. Only a small part of this was filled in, and the paint on that looked a bit old. Nonetheless, several people made contributions at the booth inside, and she was tempted herself—being outdoors did make you think.

They were all tired when they got home, and the kids voluntarily went to nap. Feeling almost happy, Elise looked out her window for a while, then kicked her way through the debris of toys to the office.

A new message was waiting already.

"This is for the woman who heard my first message. I'm not sending it on the new frequency, but I'm aiming it the way I did the first one. This is just for you, whoever you are."

Elise sat down quickly . . .

Hammond laughed, maybe a little nervously. His voice was so rich, his laugh seemed to fill her whole head. "That was quite a letter you sent. I'm not sure I believe you about having a 'mailer accident.' But if it was an accident, I'm glad it happened.

"Yours is the first voice I've heard in years from outside this whole thing. You have to understand, with the way we're treated and . . . and isolation and all, we nearly don't remember what it was like before. To have a life, I mean. To have kids, and worries like that. There're no kids here anymore. They killed them with their parents.

"A lot of people have given up. They don't remember why they should care. Most of us are like that now. Even me and the others who're trying to do something . . . well, we're doing it out of hate, not because we're trying to save anything.

"But you reminded me that there are things out there to save. Just hearing your voice, knowing that you and Dew are real, has helped.

"So I decided . . . I'm going to play your message—the first one, actually—to a couple of the people who've given up. Remind them there's a world out there. That they still have responsibilities.

"Thank you again. Can you tell me your name? I wish we could have met, someday." That was all.

Somehow, his request made her feel defensive. It was good he didn't know her name; it was a kind of safety. At the same time she wanted to tell him, as if he deserved it somehow. Finally, after sitting indecisively for long minutes, she threw down the headset and stalked out of the room.

Nasim called the next day. Elise was happy to hear from him, also a bit surprised. She had been afraid he thought she'd been acting cold lately, but he invited her for lunch in one of the city's better bistros. She foisted the kids off on her mother, and dressed up. It was worth it. They had a good time.

When she tried to set a date to get together again, he demured. She was left chewing over his mixed messages as she walked home.

Oh, who knew, really? Life was just too complicated right now. When she got home, there was another message from Hammond, this one intended for the authorities. She reviewed it, but afterward regretted doing so. It showed the destruction of Tiara.

On the video, pressure-suited figures unhooked some of *Chinook*'s hair-thin Lorentz Force cables, and jetted them away from the cycler. The cables seemed infinitely long, and could weigh many hundreds of tones.

The next picture was a long-distance, blue-shifted image of Obsidian's only inhabited world, Tiara. For about a minute, Elise watched it waver, a speckled dot. Then lines of savage white light crisscrossed its face suddenly as the wires hit.

That was all. Hammond's voice recited strings of numbers next, which she translated into velocities and trajectories. The message ended without further comment.

She was supposed to have discharged her responsibility by alerting the authorities, but after thinking about it practically all night, she had decided there was one more thing she could do. "Mr. Hammond," she began, "This is Elise Cantrell. I'm the one who got your first message. I've seen the video you sent. I'm sure it'll be enough to convince our government to do something. Hitting Dew is going to be hard, and now that we know where they're coming from we should be able to stop the missiles. I'm sure if the government thanks you, they'll do so in some stodgy manner, like giving you some medal or building a statue. But I want to thank you myself. For my kids. You may not have known just who you were risking your life for. Well, it was for Judy and Alex. I'm sending you a couple of pictures of them. Show them around. Maybe they'll convince more people to help you.

"I don't want us to blow up *Chinook*. That would mean you would die, and you're much too good a person for that. You don't deserve it. Show the pictures around. I don't know—if you can convince enough people, maybe you can take control back. There must be a way. You're a very clever man, Mr. Hammond. I'm sure you'll be able to find a way. For . . . well, for me, maybe." She laughed, then cleared her throat. "Here's the pictures." She keyed in several of her favorites, Judy walking at age one, Alex standing on the dresser holding a towel up, an optimistic parachute.

She took off the headset, and lay back feeling deeply tired, but content. It wasn't rational, but she felt she had done something heroic, maybe for the first time in her life.

Elise was probably the only person who wasn't surprised when the sun went out. There had been rumors floating about for several days that the government was commandeering supplies and ships, but nobody knew for what. She did. She was fixing dinner when the light changed. The kids ran over to see what was happening.

"Why'd it stop?" howled Alex. "I want it back!"

"They'll bring it back in a couple of days," she told him. "They're just doing maintenance. Maybe they'll change the color or something." That got his attention. For the next while he and

Judy talked about what color the new sun should be. They settled on blue.

The next morning she got a call from Sal. "We're doing it, Elise, and we need your help."

She'd seen this coming. "You want to take my prospectors."

"No no, not *take* them, just use them. You know them best. I convinced the department heads that you should be the one to pilot them. We need to blockade the missiles the *Chinook*'s sending."

"That's all?"

"What do you mean, that's all? What else would there be?"

She shook her head. "Nothing. Okay. I'll do it. Should I log on now?"

"Yeah. You'll get a direct link to your supervisor. His name's Oliver. You'll like him."

She didn't like Oliver, but could see how Sal might. He was tough and uncompromising, and curt to the point of being surly. Nice enough when he thought to be, but that was rare. He ordered Elise to take four of her inner-system prospectors off their jobs to maneuver ice for the blockade.

The next several days were the busiest she'd ever had with the prospectors. She had to call Nasim to come and look after the kids, which he did quite invisibly. All Elise's attention was needed in the orbital transfers. Her machines gathered huge blocks of orbiting ice, holding them like ambitious insects, and trawled slowly into the proper orbit. During tired pauses, she stared down at the brown cloud-tops of Crucible, thunderheads the size of planets, eddies a continent could get lost in. They wanted hundreds of ice mountains moved to intercept the missiles. The sun was out because it was being converted into a fearsome laser lance. This would be used on the ice mountains before the missiles flew by; the expanding clouds of gas should cover enough area to intercept the missiles.

She was going to lose a prospector or two in the conflagration, but to complain about that now seemed petty.

Chinook was drawing close, and the time lag between messages became shorter. As she was starting her orbital corrections on a last chunk of ice, a new message came in from Hammond. For her, again.

In case this was going to get her all wrought up, she finished setting the vectors before she opened the message. This time it came in video format.

Mark Hammond was a lean-faced man with dark skin and an unruly shock of black hair. Two blue-green earrings hung from his ears. He looked old, but that was only because of the lines around his mouth, crow's-feet at his eyes. But he smiled now.

"Thanks for the pictures, Elise. You can call me Mark. I'm glad your people are able to defend themselves. The news must be going out to all the halo worlds now—nobody's going to trade with Leviathan now! Total *isolation*. They deserve it. Thank you. None of this could've happened if you hadn't been there."

He rubbed his jaw. "Your support's meant a lot to me in the past few days, Elise. I loved the pictures, they were like a breath of new air. Yeah, I did show them around. It worked, too; we've got a lot of people on our side. Who knows, maybe we'll be able to kick the murderers out of here, like you say. We wouldn't even have considered trying, if not for you."

He grimaced, looked down quickly. "Sounds stupid. But you say stupid things in situations like this. Your help has meant a lot to me. I hope you're evacuated to somewhere safe. And I've been wracking my brains trying to think of something I could do for you, equal to the pictures you sent.

"It's not much, but I'm sending you a bunch of my recordings. Some of these songs are mine, some are traditionals from Mirjam. But it's all my voice. I hope you like them. I'll never get the chance for the real training I needed at Tiara. This'll have to do." Looking suddenly shy, he said, " 'Bye."

Elise saved the songs in an accessible format and transferred them to her sound system. She stepped out of the office, walked without speaking past Nasim and the kids, and turned the sound way up. Hammond's voice poured out clear and strong, and she sat facing the wall, and just listened for the remainder of the day.

Oliver called her the next morning with new orders. "You're the only person who's got anything like a ship near the *Chinook*'s flight path. Prospector Six." That was the one that had picked up Hammond's first message. "We're sending some missiles we put together, but they're low-mass, so they might not penetrate the *Chinook*'s forward shields."

"You want me to destroy the *Chinook*." She was not surprised. Only very disappointed that fate had worked things this way.

"Yeah," Oliver said. "Those shits can't be allowed to get

away. Your prospector masses ten thousand tonnes, more than enough to stop it dead. I've put the vectors in your database. This is top priority. Get on it." He hung up.

She was damned if she would get on it. Elise well knew her responsibility to Dew, but destroying *Chinook* wouldn't save her world. That all hinged on the missiles, which must have already been sent. But just so the police couldn't prove that she'd disobeyed orders, she entered the vectors to intercept *Chinook*, but included a tiny error that would guarantee a miss. The enormity of what she was doing—the government would call this treason—made her feel sick to her stomach. Finally she summoned her courage and called Hammond.

"They want me to kill you." Elise stood in front of her computer, allowing it to record her in video. She owed him that, at least. "I can't do it. I'm sorry, but I can't. I'm not an executioner, and you've done nothing wrong. Of all of us, you're the one who least deserves to die! It's not fair. Mark, you're going to have to take back the *Chinook*. You said you had more people on your side. I'm going to give you the time to do it. It's a couple of years to your next stop. Take back the ship, then you can get off there. You can still have your life, Mark! Come back here. You'll be a hero."

She tried to smile bravely, but it cracked into a grimace. "Please, Mark. I'm sure the government's alerted all the other halo worlds now. They'll be ready. *Chinook* won't be able to catch anybody else by surprise. So there's no reason to kill you.

"I'm giving you the chance you deserve, Mark. I hope you make the best of it."

She sent that message, only realizing afterwards that she hadn't thanked him for the gift of his music. But she was afraid to say anything more.

The city was evacuated the next day. It started in the early hours, as the police closed off all the levels of the city then began sweeping, waking people from their beds and moving the bewildered crowds to trains and aircraft. Elise was packed and ready. Judy slept in her arms, and Alex clutched her belt and knuckled his eyes as they walked among shouting people. The media were now revealing the nature of the crisis, but it was far too late for organized protest. The crowds were herded methodically; the police must have been drilling for this for weeks.

She wished Sal had told her exactly when it was going to

happen. It meant she hadn't been able to hook up with Nasim, whose apartment was on another level. He was probably still asleep, even while she and the kids were packed on a train, and she watched through the angle of the window as the station receded.

Sometime the next morning they stopped, and some of the passengers were off-loaded. Food was eventually brought, and then they continued on. Elise was asleep leaning against the wall when they finally unloaded her car.

All the cities of Dew had emergency barracks. She had no idea what city they had come to at first, having missed the station signs. She didn't care. The kids needed looking after, and she was bone tired.

Not too tired, though, to know that the hours were counting quickly down to zero. She couldn't stand being cut off, she had to know Hammond's reply to her message, but there were no terminals in the barracks. She had to know he was all right.

She finally managed to convince some women to look after Judy and Alex, and set off to find a way out. There were several policemen loitering around the massive metal doors that separated the barracks from the city, and they weren't letting anyone pass.

She walked briskly around the perimeter of the barracks, thinking. Barracks like this were usually at ground level, and were supposed to have more than one entrance, in case one was blocked by earthquake or fire. There must be some outside exit, and it might not be guarded.

Deep at the back where she hadn't been yet, she found her airlock, unguarded. Its lockers were packed with survival suits; none of the refugees would be going outside, especially not here on unknown ground. There was no good reason for them to leave the barracks, because going outside would not get them home. But she needed a terminal.

She suited up, and went through the airlock. Nobody saw her. Elise stepped out onto the surface of Dew, where she had never been except during survival drills. A thin wind was blowing, catching and worrying at drifts of carbon-dioxide snow. Torn clouds revealed stars high above the glowing walls of the city. This place, wherever it was, had thousands of windows; she supposed all the cities did now. They would have a good view of whatever happened in the sky today.

After walking for a good ten minutes, she came to another

airlock. This one was big, with vehicles rolling in and out. She stepped in after one, and found herself in a warehouse. Simple as that.

From there she took the elevator up sixteen levels to an arcade lined with glass. Here finally were VR terminals, and she gratefully collapsed at one, and logged into her account.

There were two messages waiting. Hammond, it had to be. She called up the first one.

"You're gonna thank me for this, you really are," said Oliver. He looked smug. "I checked in on your work—hey, just doing my job. You did a great job on moving the ice, but you totally screwed up your trajectory on Prospector Six. Just a little error, but it added up quick. Would have missed *Chinook* completely if I hadn't corrected it. Guess I saved your ass, huh?" He mocked-saluted, and grinned. "Didn't tell anybody. I won't, either. You can thank me later." Still smug, he rung off.

"Oh no. No, no no," she whispered. Trembling, she played the second message.

Hammond appeared, looking drawn and sad. His backdrop was a metal bulkhead; his breath frosted when he breathed. "Hello, Elise," he said. His voice was low, and tired. "Thank you for caring so much about me. But your plan will never work.

"You're not here. Lucky thing. But if you were, you'd see how hopeless it is. There's a handful of us prisoners, kept alive for amusement and because we can do some things they can't. They never thought we'd have a reason to go outside, that's the only reason I was able to get out to take over the message laser. And it's only because of their bragging that we got the video and data we did.

"They have a right to be confident, with us. We can't do anything, we're locked away from their part of the ship. And you see, when they realize you've mined space near Dew, they'll know someone gave them away. We knew that would happen when we decided to do this. Either way I'm dead, you see; either you kill me, or they do. I'd prefer you did it, it'll be so much faster."

He looked down pensively for a moment. "Do me the favor," he said at last. "You'll carry no blame for it, no guilt. Destroy *Chinook*. The worlds really aren't safe until you do. These people are fanatics, they never expected to get home alive. If they think their missiles won't get through, they'll aim the ship itself at the next world. Which will be much harder to stop.

"I love you for your optimism, and your plans. I wish it could have gone the way you said. But this really is goodbye."

Finally he smiled, looking directly at her. "Too bad we didn't have the time. I could have loved you, I think. Thank you, though. The caring you showed me is enough." He vanished.

Message end, said the mailer. *Reply?*

She stared at that last word for a long time. She signaled *yes*.

"Thank you for your music, Mark," she said. She sent that. Then she closed her programs, and took off the headset.

The end, when it came, took the form of a brilliant line of light scored across the sky. Elise watched from the glass wall of the arcade, where she sat on a long couch with a bunch of other silent people. The landscape lit to the horizon, brighter than Dew's artificial sun had ever shone. The false day faded slowly.

There was no ground shock. No sound. Dew had been spared.

The crowd dispersed, talking animatedly. For them, the adventure had been over before they had time to really believe in the threat. Elise watched them through her tears almost fondly. She was too tired to move.

Alone, she gazed up at the stars. Only a faint pale streak remained now. In a moment she would return to her children, but first she had to let this emotion fill her completely, wash down from her face through her arms and body, like Hammond's music. She wasn't used to how acceptance felt. She hoped it would become more familiar to her.

Elise stood and walked alone to the elevator, and did not look back at the sky.

A HABIT OF WASTE

Nalo Hopkinson

Nalo Hopkinson is a black Canadian writer who won the Warner Aspect First Novel Contest in 1997; her novel, *Brown Girl in the Ring*, was published in 1998 as a result. She is an original voice in fiction who has emerged from the Canadian SF community in the late 1990s. Hopkinson was born in Jamaica in 1960 to a Guyanese father and Jamaican mother; she lived in Jamaica, Guyana, and Trinidad up to age sixteen, with a stint in Connecticut while her father was a student in a graduate theater program at Yale. "By the time I was twelve, my mother had given me her adult library card, and I discovered the science fiction section of the public library on Tom Redcam Drive in Kingston, Jamaica." Hopkinson came to Toronto at sixteen, entered university at seventeen, and graduated in 1982 with a B.A. in Russian and French. Currently she lives in Toronto, and works part-time as an arts administrator.

"I started writing in 1993, when I wanted to enter an SF writing course taught by Judy Merril. The course never had enough registration to run, but Judy got a bunch of us together and taught us how to form our own writing workshop. We're still going." In 1994 her short story "Midnight Robber" tied for second place in the Short Prose Competition for unpublished writers, sponsored by the Writers' Union of Canada, and was subsequently published in Toronto's "Exile" Magazine. In 1995 Hopkinson attended Clarion East and made her first and third short story sales with two fantasy stories she wrote at Clarion. (Ellen Datlow and Terri Windling took "Riding the Red" and "Precious" for two volumes of their "fairy tale" series.) "The six unfinished pages of prose I had submitted to Judy Merril to get into her writing course became the novel *Brown Girl in the Ring*.

"'A Habit of Waste' was my first attempt at a science fictional short story," Hopkinson says. "I wanted to explore internalized racism and body shame. The main character in the story isn't able to break through those twinned self-hatreds until she has a chance to view her own handsome black body from the outside, inhabited by someone else who treats it with love and respect. The title is a line from one of my father's poems which speaks in part about the self-hatred that colonialism left in its wake, and about how some of the scholars of Daddy's day thought social issues were too lowbrow to be the subjects of poetry. I can imagine what they would have thought of science fiction."

"A Habit of Waste" was published in 1995 by *Fireweed*, a Toronto feminist journal. The story falls comfortably into the category of the fantastic, Caribbean division, but is substantially outside genre SF traditions, providing an energetic and original literary blend, for which SF is the richer.

> *These are the latitudes of the ex-colonised,*
> *of degradation still unmollified,*
> *imported managers, styles in art,*
> *second-hand subsistence of the spirit,*
> *the habit of waste,*
> *mayhem committed on the personality,*
> *and everywhere the wrecked or scuttled mind.*
>
> *Scholars, more brilliant than I could hope to be, advised that*
> *if I valued poetry, I should*
> *eschew all sociology.*
>
> —*Slade Hopkinson, from "The Madwoman of Papine:*
> *Two cartoons with captions."*

I was nodding off on the streetcar home from work when I saw the woman getting on. She was wearing the body I used to have! The shock woke me right up: it was my original; the body I had replaced two years before: same full, tarty-looking lips; same fat thighs, rubbing together with every step; same outsize ass; same narrow torso that seemed grafted onto a lower body a good three sizes bigger, as though God had glued left-over parts together.

On my pay, I'd had to save for five years before I could afford the switch. When I ordered the catalogue from Medi-Perfiction, I pored over it for a month, drooling at the different options: arrow-slim "Cindies" had long, long legs ("supermodel quality"). "Indiras" came with creamy brown skin, falls of straight, dark hair, and curvaceous bodies ("exotic grace"). I finally chose one of the "Dianas" with their lithe muscles and small, firm breasts ("boyish beauty"). They downloaded me into her as soon as I could get the time off work. I was back on the job in four days, although my fine muscle control was still a little shaky.

And now, here was someone wearing my old cast-off. She must have been in a bad accident: too bad for the body to be salvaged. If she couldn't afford cloning, the doctors would have just downloaded her brain into any donated discard. Mine, for instance. Poor thing, I thought. I wonder how she's handling that chafing problem. It used to drive me mad in the summer.

I watched her put her ticket in the box. The driver gave her a melting smile. What did he see to grin at?

I studied my former body carefully as it made its way down the center of the streetcar. I hated what she'd done to the hair— let it go natural, for Christ's sake, sectioned it off, and coiled black thread tightly around each section, with a puff of hair on the end of every stalk. Man, I hated that back-to-Africa nostalgia shit. She looked like a Doctor Seuss character. There's no excuse for that nappy-headed nonsense. She had a lot of nerve, too, wrapping that behind in a flower print sarong mini-skirt. Sort of like making your ass into a billboard. When it was my body, I always covered its butt in long skirts or loose pants. Her skirt was so short that I could see the edges of the bike shorts peeking out below it. Well, it's one way to deal with the chafing. Strange, though; on her, the little peek of black shorts looked stylish and sexy all at once. Far from looking graceless, her high, round bottom twitched confidently with each step, giving her a proud sexiness that I had never had. Her upper body was sheathed in a white sleeveless T-shirt. White! Such a plain color. To tell the truth, though, the clingy material emphasized her tiny waist, and the white looked really good against her dark skin. Had my old skin always had that glow to it? Such firm, strong arms . . .

All the seats on the streetcar were taken. Good. I let the bitch stand. I hoped my fallen arches were giving her hell.

Home at last, I stripped off and headed straight for the mirror.

The boyish body was still slim, thighs still thin, tiny-perfect apple breasts still perky. I presented my behind to the mirror. A little flabby, perhaps? I wasn't sure. I turned around again, got up close to the mirror so that I could inspect my face. Did my skin have that glow that my old body's had? And weren't those the beginning of crow's feet around my eyes? Shit. White people aged so quickly. I spent the evening sprawled on the sofa, watching reruns and eating pork and beans straight from the can.

· · ·

That Friday afternoon at work, Old Man Morris came in for the usual. I stacked his order on the counter between us and keyed the contents into the computer. It bleeped at me: "This selection does not meet the customer's dietary requirements." As if I didn't know that. I tried to talk him into beefing up the carbs and beta-carotene. "All right, then," I said heartily, "what else will you have today? Some of that creamed corn? We just got a big batch of tins in. I bet you'd like some of that, eh?" I always sounded so artificial, but I couldn't help it. The food bank customers made me uncomfortable. Not Eleanor, though. She was so at ease in the job, cheerful, dispensing cans of tuna with an easy goodwill. She always chattered away to the clients, knew them all by name.

"No thanks, dear," Mr. Morris replied with his polite smile. "I never could stomach the tinned vegetables. When I can, I eat them fresh, you know?"

"Yeah, Cynthia," Eleanor teased, "you know that Mr. Morris hates canned veggies. Too much like baby food, eh, Mr. Morris?"

Always the same cute banter between those two. He'd flattened out his Caribbean accent for the benefit of us two white girls. I couldn't place which island he was from. I sighed and overrode the computer's objections. Eleanor and Old Man Morris grinned at each other while I packed up his weekend ration. Fresh; right. When could a poor old man ever afford the fresh stuff? I couldn't imagine what his diet was like. He always asked us for the same things: soup mix, powdered milk, and cans of beans. We tried to give him his nutritional quota, but he politely refused offers of creamed corn or canned tuna. I was sure he was always constipated. His problem, though.

I bet my parents could tell me where in the Caribbean he was from.

Give them any inkling that someone's from "back home," and they'd be on him like a dirty shirt, badgering him with questions: Which island you from? How long you been here in Canada? You have family here? When last you go back home?

Old Man Morris signed for his order and left. One of the volunteers would deliver it later that evening. I watched him walk away. He looked to be in his sixties, but he was probably younger; hard life wears a person down. Tallish, with a brown, wrinkled face and tightly curled salt-and-pepper hair, he had a strong, upright walk for someone in his circumstances. Even in summer, I had never seen him without that old tweed jacket, its pockets stuffed to bursting with God knew what type of scavenge; cigarette butts, I supposed, and pop cans he would return for the deposit money. At least he was clean.

I went down to shipping to check on a big donation of food we'd received from a nearby supermarket. Someone was sure to have made a mistake sorting the cans. Someone always did.

My parents had been beside themselves when they found out I'd switched bodies. I guess it wasn't very diplomatic of me, showing up without warning on their suburban doorstep, this white woman with her flippy blond hair, claiming to be their daughter. I'd made sure my new body would have the same vocal range as the old one, so when Mom and Dad heard my voice coming out of a stranger's body, they flipped. Didn't even want to let me in the door, at first. Made me pass my new ID and the doctor's certificate through the letter slot.

"Mom, give me a break," I yelled. "I told you last year that I was thinking about doing this!"

"But Cyn-Cyn, that ain't even look like you!" My mother's voice was close to a shriek. Her next words were for my dad:

"What the child want to go and do this kind of stupidness for? Nothing ain't wrong with the way she look!" A giggled response from my father, "True, she behind had a way to remain in a room long after she leave, but she get that from you, sweetheart, and you know how much I love that behind!"

I'd had enough. "So, are the two of you going to let me in, or what?" I hated it when they carried on like that. And I really wished they'd drop the Banana Boat accents. They'd come to Canada five years before I was even born, for Christ's sake, and I was now 28.

They did finally open the door, and after that they just had to get used to the new me. I wondered if I should start saving for another switch. It's a rich people's thing. I couldn't afford to keep doing it. Shit.

"What's the matter with you?" Eleanor asked after I'd chewed out one of the volunteers for some little mistake. "You've been cranky for days now."

"Sorry. I know I've been bitchy. I've been really down, you know? No real reason. I just don't feel like myself."

"Yeah. Well." Eleanor was used to my moodiness. "I guess it is Thanksgiving weekend. People always get a little edgy around the holidays. Maybe you need a change. Tell you what; why don't you deliver Old Man Morris's ration, make sure he's okay for the weekend?"

"Morris? You want me to go to where he lives?" I couldn't imagine anything less appealing. "Where is that, anyway? In a park, or something?"

Eleanor frowned at that. "So, even if he does, so what? I wish you'd take more interest in the people who come here. Some of them do have homes, all right? You know what it's like, trying to live on a government pension nowadays."

She strode over to the terminal at her desk, punched in Mr. Morris's name, handed me the printout. "Just go over to this address, and take him his ration. Chat with him a little bit. This might be a lonely weekend for him. And keep the car till Tuesday. We won't be needing it."

Mr. Morris lived on the creepy side of Sherbourne. I had to slow the car down to dodge the first wave of drunken suits lurching out of the strip club, on their boozy way home after the usual Friday afternoon three-hour liquid lunch. I stared at the story-high poster that covered one outside wall of the strip club. I hoped to God they'd used a fisheye lens on that babe's boobs. Those couldn't be natural.

Shit. Shouldn't have slowed down. One of the prostitutes on the corner began to twitch her way over to the car, bending low so she could see inside, giving me a flash of her tits into the bargain: "Hey, darlin', you wanna go out? I can swing lezzie." I floored it out of there.

Searching for the street helped to keep my mind off some of the more theatrical sights of Cabbagetown West on a Friday evening. I didn't know that the police could conduct a full strip search over the hood of a car, right out in the open.

The next street was Old Man Morris's. Tenement row houses slumped along one side of the short street, marked by sagging roofs and knocked-out steps. There were rotting piles of garbage piled in front of many of the houses. I thought I could hear the files buzzing from where I was. The smell was like clotted carrion. A few people hung out on dilapidated porches, just staring. Two guys hunched into denim jackets stopped talking as I drove by. A dirty, greasy-haired kid was riding a bicycle up and down the sidewalk, dodging the garbage. The bike was too small for him and it had no seat.

Mr. Morris lived in an ancient apartment building on the

other side of the street. I had to double-park in front. I hauled the dolly out of the trunk, and loaded Mr. Morris's boxes onto it. I activated the car's screamer alarm, and headed into the building, praying that no weirdness would go down on the street before I could make it inside.

Thank God, he answered the buzzer right away. "Mr. Morris? It's Cynthia; from the food bank?" The party that was going on in the lobby was only a few gropes away from becoming an orgy. The threesome writhing on the couch ignored me. Two women, one man. I hoped that he was on some very special drugs tonight. I stepped over a pungent yellow liquid that was beetling its way down one leg of the bench, creeping through the cracks in the tile floor. I hoped it was just booze. I took the elevator up to the sixth floor.

The dingy, musty corridor walls were dark grey, peeling in places to reveal a bilious pink underneath. It was probably a blessing there was so much dirt ground into the balding carpet. What I could glimpse of the original design made me queasy. Someone was frying Spam for dinner ("canned horse's cock," my Dad called it). I found Mr. Morris's door and knocked. Inside, I could hear the sound of locks turning, and the curt "quack" of an alarm being deactivated. Mr. Morris opened the door to let me in.

"Come in quick, child," he said, wiping his hands on a kitchen towel. "I can't let the pot boil over. Siddown on the settee and rest yourself. Why you come today? Don't Jake does deliver my goods?"

Standing in the entranceway, I took a quick glance around the little apartment. It was dark in there. The only light was from the kitchen, and from four candles stuck in pop bottles on the living room windowsill. The living room held one small, rump-sprung couch, two aluminum chairs, and a tiny card table. The gaudy flower-print cloth that barely covered the table was faded from years of being ironed. I was surprised; the place was spotless, if a little shabby.

"Eleanor sent Jake home early today, Mr. Morris. Holiday treat." I wheeled the dolly into the living room and perched on the edge of the love seat.

He chuckled. "That young lady is so thoughtful, oui? It ain't have plenty people like her anymore."

Settee. Oui. In his own home, he spoke in a more natural accent.

"You from Trinidad, Mr. Morris?"

His face crinkled into an astonished grin. "Yes, doux-doux. How you know that?"

"That's where my parents are from. They talk just like you."

"You is from Trinidad?" he asked delightedly. "I know that Trini people come in all colors, but with that accent, I did take you for a Canadian, born and bred."

I hated explaining this, but I guess I'd asked for it, letting him know something about my life. "I was born here, but my parents are Black. So was I, but I've had a body switch."

A bemused expression came over his face. "For true? I hear about people doin' this thing, but I don't think I ever meet anybody who make the switch. You mean to tell me, you change from a Black woman body into this one? Lord, the things you young people does do for fashion, eh?"

I stood up and plastered a smile on my face. "Well, you've got your weekend ration, Mr. Morris; just wanted to be sure you wouldn't go hungry on Thanksgiving, okay?"

He looked pensively at the freeze-dried turkey dinner and the cans of creamed corn (I'd made sure to put them in his ration this time). "Thanks, doux-doux. True I ain't go be hungry, but I don't like to eat alone. My wife pass away ten years now, but you know, I does still miss she sometimes. You goin' by you Mummy and Daddy for Thanksgiving?"

The question caught me off guard. "Yes, I'm going to see them on Sunday."

"But you not doing anything tonight? You want to have a early Thanksgiving with a ol' man from back home? I making a nice, nice dinner," he pleaded.

I'm not from "back home," I almost said, but the hope on his face was more than I could stand. Eleanor would stay and keep the old man company, if it were her. I sat back down.

Mr. Morris's grin was incandescent. "You going to stay? All right, doux-doux. Dinner almost finish, you hear? Just pile up the ration out of the way for me." He bustled back into the kitchen. I could hear humming, pots and pans clattering, water running.

I packed the food up against one wall, a running argument playing in my head the whole time. Why was I doing this? I'd driven our jacker-bait excuse for a company car through the most dangerous part of town, just begging for a baseball bat through the window, and all to have dinner with an old bum. What would he serve anyway? Peanut butter and crackers? I

knew the shit that man ate—I'd given it to him myself, every
Friday at the food bank! And what if he pulled some kind of
sleazy, toothless come-on? The police would say I asked for it!

A wonderful smell began to waft from the kitchen. Some
kind of roasting meat, with spices. Whatever Mr. Morris was
cooking, he couldn't have done it on food bank rations.

"You need a hand, Mr. Morris?"

"Not in here, darling. Just sit yourself down at the table, and
I go bring dinner out. I was going to freeze all the extra, but
now I have a guest to share it with."

When he brought out the main course, arms straining under
the weight of the platter, my mouth fell open. And that was just
the beginning. He loaded the table with plate after plate of food:
roasted chicken with a giblet stuffing; rich, creamy gravy; tossed
salad with exotic greens; huge mounds of mashed potatoes;
some kind of fruit preserve. He refused to answer my questions.
"I go tell you all about it after, doux-doux. Now is time to eat."

It certainly was. I was so busy trying to figure out if he could
have turned food bank rations into this feast, that I forgot all
about calories and daily allowable grams of fat; I just ate. After
the meal, though, my curiosity kicked in again.

"So, Mr. Morris, tell me the truth; you snowing the food
bank? Making some money on the side?" I grinned at him. He
wouldn't be the first one to run a scam like that, working for
cash so that he could still claim welfare.

"No, doux-doux." He gave me a mischievous smile. "I see
how it look that way to you, but this meal cost me next to nothing. You just have to know where to shop, that is all. You see
this fancy salad? You know what this is?" He pointed to a few
frilly purple leaves that were all that remained of the salad.

"Yeah. Flowering kale. Rich people's cabbage."

Mr. Morris laughed. "Yes, but I bet you see it somewhere
else, besides the grocery store."

I frowned, trying to think what he meant. He went on: "You
know the Dominion Bank? The big one at Bathurst and Queen?"
I nodded, still mystified. His smile got even broader. "You ever
look at the plants they use to decorate the front?"

I almost spat the salad out. "Ornamental cabbage? We're
eating ornamental cabbage that you stole from the front of a
building?"

His rich laugh filled the tiny room. "Not 'ornamental cabbage,' darlin'—'flowering kale.' And I figure, I ain't really

stealin' it; I recyclin' it! They does pull it all up and throw it away when the weather turn cold. All that food. It does taste nice on a Sunday morning, fry-up with a piece of saltfish and some small-leaf thyme. I does grow the herbs—them on the windowsill, in the sun."

Salted cod and cabbage. Flavored with french thyme and hot pepper. My mother made that on Sunday mornings too, with big fried dumplings on the side and huge mugs of cocoa. Not the cocoa powder from the tin, either; she bought the raw chocolate in chestnut-sized lumps from the Jamaican store, and grated it into boiling water, with cinnamon and condensed milk. Sitting in Mr. Morris's living room, even with the remains of dinner on the table, I could almost smell that pure chocolate aroma. Full of fat, too. I didn't let my Mom serve it to me anymore when I visited. I'd spent too much money on my tight little butt.

Still, I didn't believe what Old Man Morris was telling me. "So, you mean to say that you just . . . take stuff? From off the street? What about the chicken?"

He laughed. "Chicken? Doux-doux, you ever see chicken with four drumstick? That is a wild rabbit I catch meself and bring home."

"Are you crazy? Do you know what's in wild food? What kind of diseases it might carry? Why didn't you tell me what we were eating?" But he was so pleased with himself, he didn't seem to notice how upset I was.

"Nah, nah, don't worry 'bout diseases, darlin'! I been eatin' like this for five-six years now, and I healthy like hog. De doctor say he never see a seventy-four-year-old man in such good shape."

He's seventy-four! He does look pretty damned good for such an old man. I'm still not convinced, though: "Mr. Morris, this is nuts; you can't just go around helping yourself to leaves off the trees, and people's ornamental plants, and killing things and eating them! Besides, how do you catch a wild rabbit?"

"Well, that is the sweet part." He jumped up from his chair, started rummaging around in the pockets of his old tweed jacket that was hanging in the hallway. He came back to the table, clutching a fistful of small rocks and brandishing a thick, Y-shaped twig with a loose rubber strap attached. So that's what he kept in those pockets—whatever it was.

"This is a slingshot. When I was a small boy back home, I

was aces with one of these!" He stretched the rubber strap tight with one hand, aimed the slingshot at one of his potted plants, and pretended to let off a shot. "Plai! Like so. Me and the boys—them used to practice shooting at all kind of ol' tin can and thing, but I was the best. One time, I catch a coral snake in me mother kitchen, and I send one boulderstone straight through it eye with me first shot!" He chuckled. "The stone break the window too, but me mother was only too glad that I kill the poison snake. Well, doux-doux, I does take me slingshot down into the ravine, and sometimes I get lucky, and catch something."

I was horrified. "You mean, you used that thing to kill a rabbit? And we just ate it?"

Mr. Morris's face finally got serious. He sat back down at the table. "You mus' understan', Cynthia; I is a poor man. Me and my Rita, we work hard when we come to this country, and we manage to buy this little apartment, but when the last depression hit we, I get lay off at the car plant. After that, I couldn't find no work again; I was already past fifty years old. We get by on Rita nurse work until she retire, and then hard times catch we ass. My Rita was a wonderful woman, girl; she could take a half pound of mince beef and two potatoes and make a meal that have you feelin' like you never taste food before. She used to tell me, 'Never mind, Johnny; so long as I have a little meat to put in this cook pot, we not goin' to starve.'

"Then them find out that Rita have cancer. She only live a few months after that, getting weaker till she waste away and gone. Lord, child; I thought my heart woulda break. I did wish to dead too. That first year after Rita pass away, I couldn't tell you how I get by; I don't even remember all of it. I let the place get dirty, dirty, and I was eatin' any ol' caca from the corner store, not even self goin' to the grocery. When I get the letter from the government, telling me that them cuttin' off Rita pension, I didn't know what to do. My one little pension wasn't goin' to support me. I put on me coat, and went outside, headin' for the train tracks to throw myself down, oui? Is must be God did make me walk through the park."

"What happened?"

"I see a ol' woman sittin' on a bench, wearing a tear-up coat and two different one-side boots. She was feedin' stale bread to the pigeons, and smiling at them. That ol' lady with she rip-up clothes could still find something to make she happy.

"I went back home, and things start to look up a little bit

from then. But pride nearly make me starve before I find meself inside the food bank to beg some bread."

"It's not begging, Mr. Morris," I interrupted.

"I know, doux-doux, but in my place, I sure you woulda feel the same way. And too besides, even though I was eatin' steady from the food bank, I wasn't eatin' good, you know? You can't live all you days on tunafish and tin peas!"

I felt myself blushing. Two years in this body, and I still wasn't used to how easily blushes showed on its pale cheeks. "So, what gave you the idea to start foraging like this?"

"I was eatin' lunch one day; cheese spread and crackers and pop. One paipsy, tasteless lunch, you see? And I start thinkin' about how I never woulda go hungry back home as a small boy, how even if I wasn't home to eat me mother food, it always had some kinda fruit tree or something round the place. I start to remember Julie-mango, how it sweet, and chataigne and peewah that me mother would boil up in a big pot a' salt water, and how my father always had he little kitchen garden, growin' dasheen leaf and pigeon peas and yam and thing. And I say to meself, "but eh-eh, Johnny, ain't this country have plants and trees and fruit and thing too? The squirrels—them always looking fat and happy; they mus' be eatin' something; and the Indian people themself too; they must be did eat something else besides corn before the white people come and take over the place!

"That same day, I find my ass in the library, and I tell them I want to find out about plants that you could eat. Them sit me down with all kinda book and computer, and I come to find out it have plenty to eat, right here in this city, growing wild by the roadside. Some of these books even had recipes in them, doux-doux!

"So I drag out all of Rita frying pan and cook spoon from the kitchen cupboard, and I teach meself to feed meself, yes!" He chuckles again. "Now, I does eat fresh mulberries in the summer. I does dig up chicory root to take the bitterness from my coffee. I even make rowanberry jam. All these things all around we for free, and people still starving, oui? You have to learn to make use of what you have.

"But I still think the slingshot was a master stroke, though. Nobody ain't expect a ol' Black man to be hunting with a slingshot down in the ravine!"

• • •

I was still chuckling as I left Mr. Morris's building later that evening. He'd loaded me down with a container full of stuffed rabbit and a bottle of crabapple preserves. I deactivated the screamer alarm on the car, and I was just about to open the door when I felt a hand sliding down the back of my thigh.

"Yesss, stay just like that. Ain't that pretty? We'll get to that later. Where's your money, sweetheart? In this purse here?" The press of a smelly body pinned me over the hood. I tried to turn my head, to scream, but he clamped a filthy hand across my face. I couldn't breathe. The bottle of preserves crashed to the ground. Broken glass sprayed my calf.

"Shit! What'd you do that for? Stupid bitch!"

His hand tightened over my face. I couldn't breathe! In fury and terror, I bit down hard, felt my teeth meet in the flesh of his palm. He swore, yanked his hand away, slammed a hard fist against my ear. Things started to go black, and I almost fell. I hung onto the car door, dragged myself to my feet, scrambled out of his reach. I didn't dare turn away to run. I backed away, screaming, "Get away from me! Get away!" He kept coming, and he was big and muscular, and angry. Suddenly, he jerked, yelled, slapped one hand to his shoulder. "What the fuck . . . ?" I could see wetness seeping through the shoulder of his grimy sweatshirt. Blood? He yelled again, clapped a hand to his knee. This time, I had seen the missile whiz through the air to strike him. Yes! I crouched down to give Mr. Morris clear shot. My teeth were bared in a fighter's grin. The mugger was still limping toward me, howling with rage. The next stone glanced by his head, leaving a deep gash on his temple. Behind him, I heard the sound of breaking glass as the stone crashed through the car window. He'd had enough. He ran, holding his injured leg.

Standing in the middle of the street, I looked up to Mr. Morris's sixth-floor window. He was on the balcony, waving frantically at me. In the dark, I could just see the "Y" of the slingshot in his hand. He shouted, "Go and stand in the entranceway, girl! I comin' down!" He disappeared inside, and I headed back towards the building. By the time I got there, I was weak-kneed and shaky; reaction was setting in, and my head was spinning from the blow I took. I didn't think I'd ever get the taste of that man's flesh out of my mouth. I leaned against the inside door, waiting for Mr. Morris. It wasn't long before he came bustling out of the elevator, let me inside, and sat me down on the couch in the lobby, fussing the whole time.

"Jesus Christ, child! Is a good thing I decide to watch from the balcony to make sure you reach the car safe! Lawd, look at what happen to you, eh? Just because you had the kindness to spen' a little time with a ol' man like me! I sorry, girl; I sorry can't done!"

"It's okay, Mr. Morris; it's not your fault. I'm all right. I'm just glad that you were watching." I was getting a little hysterical. "I come to rescue you with my food bank freeze-dried turkey dinner, and you end up rescuing me instead! I have to ask you, though, Mr. Morris; how come every time you rescue a lady, you end up breaking her windows?"

That Sunday, I drove over to my parents' place for Thanksgiving dinner. I was wearing a beret, cocked at a chic angle over the cauliflower ear that the mugger had given me. No sense panicking Mom and Dad. I had gone to the emergency hospital on Friday night, and they disinfected and bandaged me. I was all right; in fact, I was so happy, I felt giddy. So nice to know that there wouldn't be photos of my dead body on the covers of the tabloids that week.

As I pulled up in the car, I could see my parents sitting in the living room. I went inside.

"Mom! Dad! Happy Thanksgiving!" I gave my mother a kiss, smiled at my dad.

"Cynthia, child," he said, "I glad you reach; I could start making the gravy now."

"Marvin, don't be so stupidee," my mother scolded. "You know she won't eat no gravy; she mindin' she figure!"

"It's okay, Mom; it's Thanksgiving, and I'm going to eat everything you put on my plate. If I get too fat, I'm just going to have to start walking to work. You've got to work with what you've got, after all." She looked surprised, but didn't say anything.

I poked around in the kitchen, like I always did. Dad stood at the stove, stirring the gravy. There was another saucepan on the stove, with the remains of that morning's cocoa in it. It smelled wonderful. I reached around my father to turn on the burner under the cocoa. He frowned at me.

"Is cocoa-tea, Cyn-Cyn. You don't drink that no more."

"I just want to finish what's left in the pot, Dad. I mean, you don't want it to go to waste, do you?"

THINGS INVISIBLE TO SEE

W. P. Kinsella

W. P. Kinsella was born in 1932. He was educated at the University of Victoria and the University of Iowa, Iowa Writer's Workshop, and was recently a professor at the University of Calgary. He is a major contemporary writer, the author of *Shoeless Joe* (1982), made into the movie "Field of Dreams" (1989); *The Iowa Baseball Confederacy* (1986), *Red Wolf, Red Wolf* (1987), other novels, and many short stories, some of them collected in *Dance Me Outside* (1977) and made into a movie in 1994, *Scars* (1978), *Born Indian* (1981), *The Mocassin Telegraph* (1983), *The Thrill of the Grass* (1984), *The Fencepost Chronicles* (1986), and *The Dixon Cornbelt League* (1992). Kinsella says that he always thought of himself as a writer, though he wrote more than fifty stories before getting published. "I was read to a lot as a child. I don't recall anything that influenced me until Ray Bradbury's *The Illustrated Man*. I was raised in unusual circumstances, on a farm in an isolated area of Alberta, Canada. I was an only child, the nearest neighbors were miles away, the nearest neighbors with children were, I don't know where, because I never saw any children while I was growing up. When I was ten we moved to Edmonton, Alberta, and I've been suffering from culture shock ever since.

"What struck me about *The Illustrated Man* and later *The Martian Chronicles* and *The Golden Apples of the Sun* was the inspired imagination. I had no role models. There were no talented Canadian fiction writers for me to look up to; we didn't study any fiction in high school. I read Ray Bradbury and said, 'If he can do it so can I.' Later Richard Brautigan was an influence. If I could own only one book it might well be *In Watermelon Sugar*, by Brautigan."

"Things Invisible to See" is a charming little piece from *On Spec*.

On a Saturday morning I reported to the waterfront for two days of work that had been advertised by a two-line newspaper ad: Intelligent person for weekend work. Pier 64, Sat. 8:00 A.M.

Most of those who applied were stevedore types, built like

walking oil barrels. A man in a business suit walked down the line of us, exchanged a couple of words with those of us who appeared capable of replying verbally to a question, and chose me.

"It's a simple job," the man said. He stared at me, nodding, indicating by the vertical bobbing of his head that he considered me capable of doing a simple job. A freighter was docked at Pier 64, and over a hundred Japanese automobiles were being driven off the *Maegashira Maru* by a hatchet-faced boy with a sullen look, a sunken chest and brushcut hair. These were some of the first Japanese cars to arrive in North America. The sullen-faced boy created three rows on the parking lot. After he parked each car he opened all the doors, the trunk and hood, then walked sullenly back aboard the *Maegashira Maru* to take another vehicle for a short spin.

The cars were of identical make and model, only the colors were slightly different but not much; they were all street colors, shades of beige, of tan, concrete-gray, several benign blues ranging from bruise to twilight. The cars, wide open as they were, had a nakedness about them, a vulnerability, like half-dressed people waiting in line for medical treatment.

I was supplied with a vacuum cleaner, which was connected to electrical power by an apparently endless succession of extension cords, some black, some orange, some white, that stretched off toward the dock like knotted snakes.

"You vacuum out each car," the man in the suit went on. "Very carefully. You vacuum the engine, the interior front and back, the trunk." He might have been part oriental, Hawaiian possible. He was taller than average, with blue-black hair and orangish skin. His ill-fitting suit was as colorless as the cars he was supervising.

"But the cars are new," I said. They all looked showroom clean. "They don't look dirty," I added, sticking my head inside one, smelling the delicious odors of newness.

"You'd be surprised," said the man. "Just do your job. You can take up to ten minutes per car. I want you finished by Sunday evening. Work overtime if you have to, but be thorough. You must understand that there are some things invisible to see. Most men don't understand that, they get careless, skip a trunk or back seat because it appears clean. I chose you because you look like you have an imagination. Imagine muddy footprints and cracker crumbs everywhere and you'll get along fine."

I was calculating the hourly rate over two eight-hour days plus a little overtime. I'd be able to pay Mrs. Kryzanowski the rent, perhaps afford some takeout Kentucky Fried Chicken.

"You empty the vacuum bag after every seventh car," the man continued. He was smoking a slim cigar. "Here's a supply of vacuum bags." He handed me a package that must have contained fifty, all folded cleverly together like Kleenex. "You deposit the full ones in that incinerator over there," and he pointed to the far corner of the chainlink-enclosed lot, where the incinerator sat, a smoke-stained hulk of blackness that looked like armor for a rhinoceros.

I didn't say anything, but it seemed to me that the residue from all one hundred-plus cars would be lucky to fill even one bag. Looking serious, the man repeated his last instruction in such a manner that I decided to humor him.

I set to work. It *was* an easy job. I vacuumed the shiny unused engines, the floormats which held only slight traces of dust, the back seats and trunks which couldn't even offer up a tuft of lint. After the seventh car I dutifully opened the vacuum cleaner and extracted the bag, which, to my surprise, appeared to be full. I carried it to the incinerator, where a banked fire burned, and deposited it. The flames hissed and flapped, a few tendrils of ash drifted off from the smokestack.

It was after the twenty-first car that I made my mistake. I carried the vacuum bag to the incinerator. Curious as to what actually filled it, I took my pocket knife and slit the bag lengthways, intent only on having a glance at what gave the receptacle weight.

It was as if I had unleashed a confetti storm. I tried to close the long narrow wound with my hands, but failed miserably. What I unleashed were thousands of *words*. Many were so tiny they might have been cut from the fine print of a newspaper column. The paper was gossamer light, thousands of very small fragments drifted on the breeze, while I chased after them like a cat leaping for butterflies. I had set the bag down, intent on capturing as many as I could. When I next looked in its direction I saw more thousands of words were rising like gnats from the gash in the bag.

I raced frantically about the lot, capturing only a few, while the remainder floated away on an inland breeze. I was more concerned about losing the job than in what I might be unleashing on North America. Knowing that because of my curiosity I had betrayed a trust, I snuck off home, never put in for the three hours work I had already done. Most of the words I captured were strange to me, though many have become second nature to Americans over the past twenty-five years: *Mazda, Toyota, Datsun, Mitsubishi, Suzuki, teriyaki, sushi, tekkamaki, gyoza, oshidashi, haiku,* were just a sampling.

When I got back to the castle, when I removed my shirt in preparation to shower, I discovered in among my chest hairs, skulking like a large louse, the seven-syllable middle line of a haiku: Mist lies soft as a blanket.

When I turned my socks inside out, the word *sashimi* scuttled across the carpet. I stomped after it as if it were a cockroach but, like a cockroach, it eluded me.

THE DUMMY WARD

David Nickle

David Nickle was born in Newmarket, Ontario, studied journalism at Ryerson Polytechnical Institute in Toronto, and works as a city hall reporter for a chain of Toronto community newspapers. Like Sally McBride, he belongs to the Cecil Street Writers Group. He has been published in each of the *Northern Frights* anthologies, *Tesseracts*, *On Spec*, and *TransVersions*. Most of what he writes could be classified as horror fiction. In 1993, Karl Schroeder and Nickle won the Aurora Award for English-language short fiction for the humorous Christmas fantasy "The Toy Mill," which has since been expanded into *The Claus Effect* (Tesseract Books, 1997). Another collaboration, "Rat Food"—written with Edo van Belkom—won the Bram Stoker Award of the Horror Writers of America for Short Fiction, in 1998.

"'The Dummy Ward' had an odd genesis," says Nickle. "I was driving one day listening to the radio, when I heard an introduction to a song by the Crash Test Dummies, and I got to wondering just why—aside from the fact it sounded good—the band had picked that name. I began to develop a theory: crash test dummies are the simulacre that we send ahead of us into the worst places we can imagine, to experience the worst kinds of mishaps we can imagine, so that we don't have to go there ourselves. Maybe the band was trying to extend the metaphor from simple physical danger to emotional and psychic mishap as well. I never got a chance to ask them, but the notion stuck in my head, and 'The Dummy Ward' followed." It is an SF horror story—Canadian SF is often blended with fantasy or horror, and it is characteristic of Canadian SF writers to blur genre boundaries in general.

Different smells, thought Dennis as the speckling cleared. There was a hint of ozone where the antiseptic should have been; intermingled with that, another sharp tang—like copper, an old penny on the tongue. And where was the stink? There was not a trace of the diaper-pail stink he'd been getting used to over the past two weeks of his stay at the General Ford North-Eastern Regional Trauma Centre.

He was in another long ward—a dim, still corridor of drawn yellow curtains, it was nothing like the trauma ward where he'd spent the lion's share of his stay. In the distance, Dennis could hear the buzzing snore of machinery that matched and amplified the capillary-drone behind his eyes. There was a chair beside the door, an old, vinyl visitor's rocking chair. Dennis lowered himself into it, and his vision speckled threateningly as he did so. But it did not darken, and in the end Dennis returned to himself.

"Who's there?"

The voice was tinny, as though it came from an intercom. But when Dennis looked, he didn't see a speaker anywhere nearby. Dennis cleared his throat.

"I'm sorry. I seem to have—" What? Blacked out? Wandered off? Dennis was suddenly embarrassed. "I'm Dennis Robertson," he finally managed. "I'm not really supposed to be here."

"Dennis Robertson." The voice seemed to be coming from behind the curtain opposite Dennis. Through the distortion, Dennis couldn't tell whether it was a man or a woman. "I used to be good with names, but since the crash. I have to repeat introductions back before they stick. Dennis Robertson, right?"

"Right."

"Well I'm Tom Grey. I'm not supposed to be here, either."

Dennis got up and stepped over to the drawn curtain. If there was an intercom in there, he decided he would call a nurse, get back to his ward. But what was a patient's voice doing coming out of a bedside intercom?

Tom Grey continued: "The doctors here are saying my spine's broken, and I'm not going to walk again. I think that's a lot of crap."

The curtain rattled on its runners as Dennis pulled it aside.

"Of course, maybe I'm just in denial. What do you think, Dennis?"

Dennis had no answer. He stood frozen in place, gaping.

"Denial, or old-fashioned stubbornness?"

Jesus. Dennis couldn't make the word.

Tom Grey was a simulacrum of a man. Pink latex skin stretched like a stocking-mask over the ridges and seams of his plastic face and he wore a toupee of silver-grey hair on the dome of his skull. His mouth moved up and down mechanically, like a ventriloquist dummy's. The most credible aspects of his visage were his eyes, which were a light hazel and convincingly shot with blood.

Tom Grey lifted his arm and Dennis watched, fascinated, as he flexed his fingers. Dennis thought he could hear tiny clicks—carbon-fiber knuckles cracking arthritically as the joints bent and straightened again.

"See?" said Tom Grey. "Strong as an ox. You should see the guy two beds down—he can't do anything but blink."

"That's—" Dennis felt a wave of dizziness and stepped back to the rocking chair. He sat down hard. "That's too bad."

Tom Grey's realistic eyes swiveled to look at the ceiling. "Tell me about it. He's got three kids, one who's going to college next year. His wife comes in everyday and she tells me this. Who knows what they'll do, now he's"—he glanced back at Dennis, and his voice dropped to a staticky hiss of a whisper—"a vegetable?"

He'd seen things like Tom Grey before.

Dennis was working the phones at the tele-dealership that day. The dealership was pushing its mail-order service, and the pitch was emphasizing GF's comprehensive warranty-insurance package. Dennis and the dozen or so other reps who'd pulled pit duty watched the pitch on a big wall-monitor. Dennis was paying more attention than usual—he'd just bought the Taurus, his first GF product since joining the company, and he had lately found himself seeking affirmation for the decision. The warranty-insurance package was shaping up to be very affirmative indeed.

About fifteen minutes into the show, the host announced a special segment. He stepped off to one side as the curtains behind the half-dozen showroom cars began to part. The lights in the showroom dimmed, the host stepped out of view, and new lights lit up the glassed-in space behind.

It was a concrete-walled corridor, running parallel to the glass wall, that extended beyond the showroom in one direction and ended in a scarred cinder block terminus near the spot where the host stood.

The view cut to a remote shot of the same or a similar corridor. At its end, a burgundy GF Lance idled, waiting its turn like a bull in an abattoir.

Without warning, the unseen driver threw it into gear. The Lance lurched forward and out of the frame.

Seven point three seconds later (this according to the running digital time display at the bottom of the screen) the Lance hit the terminus in the showroom. Although it was moving at sixty-seven point one-ought-three kph when it struck (another superimposed readout confirmed this number), there were no flames. The front end accordioned even as the rear tires left the concrete floor and the car's windshields cracked and buckled. A hubcap popped off the front wheel and flew toward the showroom audience, leaving a scuff-mark where it struck the thick glass between them.

Even through the headset, the noise of the crash stabbed at Dennis's ears.

As he lowered his hands, Dennis could make out what he was sure were screams. Not from the showroom audience—they sat in a shocked silence—but inside the car itself, screams and weeping noises, muffled by the enormous airbag which had plastered against the fragmented safety glass. Something was moving under the airbag.

"In the last century," said the host, "the old automobile manufacturers began an ambitious safety testing program on all their vehicles. Those were the days when shoulder-straps and safety glass were as far as anyone was willing to go with passenger protection."

As he spoke, a yellow-jumpsuited GF team poured into the chamber and surrounded the wreckage of the Lance.

Two of them hefted an enormous set of metal cutters and set to work on the driver's side door.

"They were sending their customers into the most terrible, most horrific circumstances," the host continued. "They were sending you—people just like you!—to places they'd never been themselves, places they'd only imagined. So Ford, General Motors, and other major automobile manufacturers, decided to visit some of those places. They used dummies—crash-test dummies—to learn more about what happened to the human body in a crash. They wanted to make sure that anything that might happen to a driver of one of their cars would happen to a crash-test dummy first.

"In those days, that was enough."

The Lance door came away with a shriek. The crew with the cutters stepped back, while two medics pushed the sagging airbag out of the way. A third and fourth medic were maneuvering a stretcher through the car's detritus as the camera started to zoom in on the jagged-edged doorway.

"In those days, of course, four-fifths of all drivers could afford to carry some form of medical insurance. Major insurance carriers still issued collision policies. Motorists knew there was at least one hospital in their city that had a well-equipped trauma unit. When they were out of the hospital, drivers could count on a whole array of outpatient services, from counseling and physiotherapy sessions to home care programs to get them back on their feet."

Something like a hand appeared around the edge of the air bag, and one of the medics took hold of it. "You're going to be all right, sir. Take it easy," she said.

"General Ford owners know they can't count on any of those things today," said the host. "And because of that, General Ford knows that it's no longer enough to just make the safest cars on the road. Now, automobile safety is just the beginning of our responsibilities to our customers. The time-honored 'crash test' is just the beginning of our safety research program. Using new holographic artificial-intelligence processors and the most sophisticated animatronics technology in the world, we can now take our testers through every phase of the trauma—from the moment of the crash through the stay at a General Ford-registered trauma center, to the day the General Ford owner gets behind the wheel of her own brand new Scorpio and puts all the nastiness behind her."

The air bag slid away, and the trauma team moved their patient onto the stretcher. The thing arched its shoulders and opened its ventriloquist-dummy mouth so wide it clicked.

"I can't feel my legs!" it screamed. "Oh Jesus fucking Mary, I'm paralyzed!"

Mercifully, the camera cut away from the dummy and returned to the host, who now was sitting in the driver's seat of a gleaming new Mustang convertible, his arm slung confidently over the back of the seat.

"We know what happens to the human body in a crash. Now, armed with the latest in predictive technology and the most sophisticated diagnostic techniques, engineers at the General Ford Group are learning just what happens to the human being."

Before the host could say anything more, the phones started

ringing. Dennis had little time to watch the rest of the infomercial, but he closed few sales that day nonetheless.

Tom Grey stared at Dennis as the reality of his predicament settled in: In his blackout, he had wandered farther afield than ever
before. He was wasn't in a dummy ward.

Dennis had always imagined that General Ford's testing facilities would be quite distant from their actual trauma centers—
if for no other reason than to avoid exactly the kind of situation
Dennis found himself in now. GF programmed their AI crash-
test dummies with simulacrum-personalities to match their features, and designed blind spots in their programming such that
the AIs remained convinced they were really people—GF drivers
who had hit an icy patch on the highway or jumped a red light
or smashed into a guardrail. Dennis understood that when they
saw other dummies, the images they saw were simply those of
other unlucky GF drivers, bloodied and bandaged. When they
looked at their carbon-fiber, latex-and-metal hands, they saw
flesh, bone, fingernails. GF must have been confident indeed in
the strength of their illusion to have dropped their robotic guinea
pigs in the middle of a working trauma center.

"You got a girlfriend?" asked Tom Grey suddenly.

"Uh, yeah. As a matter of fact, I do." He hesitated only an
instant before adding: "Mr. Grey."

"Call me Tom."

Dennis smiled. Play along, he thought. Play along, just to be
safe.

"Okay, Tom."

"Now tell me about her."

"Well . . ." Dennis thought about Shelly, conjured a mental
picture. "Her name's Shelly Wolkerski."

"Polish," offered Tom Grey helpfully. "You may not be able
to tell by looking at me, but I'm Polish too."

"Is that so?"

"On my mother's side." The latex around Tom Grey's mouth
pulled up at the corners, into a strangely convincing smile. "So
how's she taking it? Shelly, I mean."

"She's all right, I guess," said Dennis. In fact, he hadn't seen
much of Shelly during the entire two weeks of his stay. It was
a ninety-minute drive to the trauma center from her condo, and
Shelly had been pulling a lot of overtime these past few months.

The dummy nodded sympathetically. "Got you pretty hard on the head, didn't it?"

"It shows?"

"Takes one to know one, I guess." Tom Grey's laughter came jagged. "You're taking your time remembering things. It's a good sign something's not right."

"It could have been worse," said Dennis quietly.

"You got that right. A guy was through here Tuesday, he had a bandage on his head, and he couldn't stop swearing. He was screaming these words, these terrible words, at anybody he saw, like he was a crazy on the street. He was a young one, just like you."

Just like Dennis. The idea sent a shiver up Dennis's arms, but there was a certain comfort to knowledge as well: as the infomercial told him, GF was going there first.

Dennis sat forward in his chair. "How long have you been here, Tom?"

"Six weeks," replied Tom Grey. "And three days."

Dennis couldn't help relating Tom Grey now to the dummy in the infomercial, as the trauma team pulled it from a demolished Lance at the end of a showroom crash tunnel. Arching its back, screaming about its useless legs: panicking.

Tom Grey, with his easy banter, his pleasantly innocuous interrogations, seemed quite distant from that image: as distant, Dennis supposed, as anyone would be six weeks and three days following the accident that crippled them. General Ford had made one hell of a simulation in Tom Grey, there was no denying it.

The dummy's voice lowered confidentially. "I tell you, Dennis, it's been a bloody eternity in here. You can't know."

"I've just been here two weeks," Dennis admitted.

"I hope they let you out soon," said Tom Grey. "You're up and walking, that's one thing in your favor. But listen, you look like you could do with some rest. Do you want me to call the nurse?"

Dennis opened his mouth to answer, reconsidered, and shook his head.

"There's no rush," he said. "I'm fine."

The crash had shut him down.

The instant of the impact was lost to Dennis. Prior was a

blur of activity: the Taurus starting into its spin as Dennis massaged the brake and worked the steering wheel—shadows cast from the stationary lights above waltzing across his tightened knuckles in ever-more frenetic circles—the approaching guardrail from the front—now from the side—the back—and finally—cessation.

It was as though a fissure had opened then and Dennis's life lay on either side, cleaved in two. The elephant-scream rending of the jaws on his car door marked the fissure's nearest edge.

Dennis's arms came up, pushed the billowing fabric of the air bag away from his face. Cold January air flooded into his lungs, even as he felt his seat shift underneath him, the world spin. He groped wildly, searching for purchase in the whirling wreck of the Taurus.

From the darkness above, a hand found his. He gripped it, the hand squeezed back, and the Earth steadied a moment in its off-kilter spin.

"It's all right, Mr. Robertson. Take it easy. You're going to be all right."

She wore a yellow GF Trauma Team coverall. Her short-cropped hair impaled the snowflakes as they fell. In the distance, he could hear the unattended cries of another victim, an import owner no doubt, waiting for the Salvation Army meat truck.

Dennis had no words for his rescuer, and when it came time for the team to move him, he did nothing to impede them.

"What happened to you?" asked Dennis. "How did you come to be here?"

Tom Grey's gaze fell away from Dennis. It landed on his angular hands, and he studied them awhile.

"I was trying to merge from the Lawrence on-ramp," he finally said. "Northbound. But it was busy, and it looked like I was going to get pinned at the merging point. So I took a chance."

Of course, nothing of the sort had happened. Engineers had strapped the dummy in a test car, set its foot against the gas pedal, and put it on a course at the end of which stood an implacable cinder block wall.

To the dummy, the test course was the Don Valley Parkway's Lawrence Avenue on-ramp, northbound. There was no wall; just fifty yards of merging lane, a thick wall of traffic on the left, guardrail to the right. Tom Grey's perception was that he existed in this unhappy circumstance because of his own hubris; he had stupidly decided to take a chance.

In fact, Dennis reflected, Tom Grey had never stood a chance. The wall was ever before him, invisible.

"I don't remember much for a while after that," said the dummy. "They pumped me up with a lot of drugs. They tell me I was forced off the highway by a semi, and my car flipped over on its roof when it hit the curb. You remember much about your crash?"

"No," said Dennis. "Not much at all."

"Do you remember a light?"

Dennis thought about it, shook his head.

"Me neither," said Tom Grey quickly. "I only bring it up because I hear that some people do see lights. A near-death experience, it's called. I guess neither of us rated; we weren't near-enough dead."

"It felt pretty near to me," said Dennis.

"Close but not touching." Tom Grey had adopted a gently chiding tone. "Don't forget that, Dennis. You're going to be out of here in no time."

Dennis smiled. "Thanks," he said.

"Don't mention it." Tom Grey coughed. He glanced over at his empty night-table then, and swore.

"What is it?" Dennis asked.

"Ah, nothing. The goddamn nurse took my water jug away. All this talking has left me parched. Well, nothing for it but to call." He reached for the intercom button at his side.

Dennis felt a sudden panic, and when he spoke it was nearly a shout: "Wait!"

The dummy's hand froze, and he looked at Dennis with questions in his eyes.

"Don't bother the nurse," said Dennis, struggling to find calm for his voice. "I'll go find you some water."

"You're sure?"

"Really," said Dennis. His legs trembled as they took his weight. "It's no trouble."

Before Tom Grey could object again, Dennis turned away from him and started down the length of the ward. He thought about his Shelly—Shelly Wolkerski, twenty-seven years old. Polish, like Tom Grey's mother—tried to picture her face. It wasn't easy, but eventually Dennis drew her forth, like a card from a conjurer's sleeve.

. . .

Dennis's first experience of the Trauma Centre was through the clearing house of its massive Intensive Care Unit. It was a cavernous space with a cathedral ceiling, reminding Dennis of the old rail terminal near the lake. The beds and attendant machinery were scattered haphazardly around a central nursing station and cold January light filtering through high, vaguely Catholic windows. It cast shadows of IV stands and curtain-rails on the broken patients and the grim-faced ICU nurses.

Everyone went through ICU at the General Ford Trauma Centre and Dennis spent fully sixteen hours there before they found him a proper bed. It was a morality play of sharply skewed punishment and diabolical injuries, of which Dennis could only recall fragments. The man whose legs had been stripped of their flesh when he foolishly stepped out of the driver's side of his stalled mini-van at the side of a highway, into the path of a skidding pickup; the broken-backed woman whose face was sliced by glass (Dennis heard someone call her a "Liability case"—GF was issuing an immediate recall on one of its products as a result of her accident); a tiny Asian girl, not more than six years old, who seemed unharmed except that she did not awaken or even stir in her sleep the entire time that Dennis was there; and countless men and women on backboards, black metal halos bolted to their skulls in five places to keep their shattered spines from twisting into even worse configurations. Even in the early, fragmented stages of his stay, Dennis could tell that his own simple injuries didn't compare.

Still, before moving him to the ward-room, the ICU manager made sure Dennis was visited by two yellow-smocked members of GF's Post-Trauma Counseling Team. They introduced themselves as Helen and Peter, and told him that they were there to make sure Dennis was as comfortable as possible throughout his recovery at the Trauma Centre. Did he have any questions before they got started? Helen asked helpfully.

Are you doctors? was the first question that came to Dennis's mind, and Peter told him no, they weren't. Did they know how Dennis's car was? Totaled, said Helen, a complete write-off. But she and Peter weren't there to sell him a new car. They'd both been over Dennis' charts, continued Peter, and were happy to inform him that he was a good candidate for full and speedy recovery. But they wanted to make sure, said Helen, that Dennis's mind healed as well as his body. Is that part of my warranty package? Dennis had asked, intending it as a feeble sort of joke. But Helen and Peter took the question quite seriously.

Absolutely, they both said, nearly in unison. You're going to come out of this as good as new.

When they moved Dennis to his semiprivate room later that night, the blackouts had already begun.

The doctors at the Trauma Center were very concerned about the blackouts; if they persisted, it might mean that Dennis would be legally barred from driving a General Ford product or any other motor vehicle, possibly for the rest of his life. The thought gave Dennis a vague chill as well; just how was he supposed to sell GF products down at the tele-dealership if he couldn't drive one?

Simon, who worked in GF's accounting division and shared Dennis's room for the first week, was the one who explained his predicament to him best. When the Taurus slammed into the guardrail, Dennis's brain had actually shifted inside his skull. The force of the impact pulled one side clear of the brain pan, even as it compressed the opposite side hard against the un-yielding bone. And then the damaged cerebellum sloshed back into place, its delicate structure scrambled in ways that even GF's sophisticated neuromedical technology couldn't repair. If Dennis's brain were to fully heal, Simon had told him levelly, it would have to do the job itself.

The machine noises oscillated wildly as Dennis moved through the dummy ward. They might have been from a dummy oper-ating theater. Dennis imagined it as a cavernous service bay, where the GF surgical technicians used every instrument at hand to complete their indelicate procedures: oxy-acetylene torches, band-saws, drill-presses, soldering irons, and rivet-guns. They'd need them, thought Dennis—an ordinary scalpel would make little impression on Tom Grey's unyielding flesh.

But there was no sign of an operating theater anywhere along the corridor of the ward. The stretch of curtained beds seemed to go on endlessly, identical cubes of yellow vinyl that trembled in the breeze of Dennis's passing.

He stopped only once, frozen like a rabbit in a hawk's shadow, as a torrent of obscenities grew from behind one of the curtains.

The voice was female in the digitized manner that Tom

Grey's voice could have been a man's, and the words it snarled and spat were terrible. Dennis was certain the commotion would draw a nurse, and he wondered briefly where he would hide if one were to come.

The panic that had brushed at Dennis with Tom Grey solidified then. A nurse would return him to his own ward, to the inclusive care of the GF Trauma Regional Trauma Centre. And then he'd be no better off than Tom Grey, or the poor woman-machine that cursed from her scrambled brains behind the curtain. Dennis would once more be reduced to a project for the GF medical techs, cut off from his own resources.

If your brains are going to heal, they'll have to do the job themselves.

The obscenities finally abated, and as they lessened Dennis was overcome with another certainty. The dummy behind the curtain didn't simulate a woman at all, but was an imperfect simulacrum of Dennis Robertson. If he pulled the curtain aside, that was what he'd see—Dennis Robertson in plastics, whose holographic brain remembered a job at the tele-dealership and a friendship with Shelly and a GF Taurus only a little more vividly than Dennis did himself. The certainty was preposterous, Dennis knew that; but he wouldn't test it by drawing aside the curtain.

Heart pounding, Dennis continued down the corridor. It wasn't long before he came upon an empty station. Hands shaking, Dennis found a plastic jug and filled it from a tap. It mustn't have been used in some time, this tap, the way the water shrieked as it filled the pipes.

Dennis returned with the water jug to find that Tom Grey had drifted off to sleep. With the rubber eyelid flaps pulled down over his eyes and his clicking fingers motionless at his sides, the simulation of humanity was laid bare. Dennis set the water jug down on Tom Grey's night table and looked at him. He wondered if the dummy's simulated dreams were anything like his own.

It didn't occur to Dennis that Tom Grey might not be asleep at all until he heard the urgency in the flat-soled footsteps that clattered from the far end of the ward.

Dennis leaned closer to Tom Grey's face, studied it for any sign of activity in the simulation. He lifted Tom Grey's hand— the device was such a cunning piece of puppetry that Dennis couldn't believe the GF engineers would have left out something as easy as a pulse. There was a lot you could learn from a pulse, thought Dennis. It ought to be there.

But there was no pulse, and Tom Grey's face was placid.

Catching his breath, Dennis set the hand down at Tom Grey's side. He slipped behind the yellow curtain to the next bed, and waited there silently until the nursing team arrived.

"All right, let's review." It was a woman's voice, rasping a little with age and cigarettes. "The patient was listed stable at the last inspection, 1854 hours."

"There was nothing out of the ordinary, Dr. Corbett. If anything, he seemed a little livelier than he had at yesterday's inspection." This voice was male, and didn't sound as though it belonged to someone who was much older than Dennis.

" 'Livelier.' Would you care to quantify that observation, Lorne?" asked Dr. Corbett.

"It—I mean he—he was making jokes," replied Lorne. "He was barely talking to anyone the day before."

"We'd been charting a clinical depression curve," said a third voice, female. "If he had gone on that way another day, we would have moved him onto a Prozac simulation and—"

Dr. Corbett interrupted. "We're getting off-track, Louise. The patient was listed as stable, and Lorne had noted an improvement in mood tangential to a previously noted depression curve. Anything to add, either of you?" Neither spoke, and after a moment Dr. Corbett continued.

"Sometimes in the real wards, we lose a patient, just as suddenly as"—she paused, rustled paper—"Tom Grey here shut down. A burst aneurysm between shifts is all it can take. The older ones are particularly vulnerable, and I see here that Mr. Grey was configured as a sixty-three-year-old male; the possibility of such an event is built into his program."

Dennis peeked around the edge of the curtain and saw that Dr. Corbett was taking a small notebook computer from under the bottom of a clipboard. She set it down on the backboard and took a pair of connecting cables from her yellow smock. After another moment of fiddling, the computer was connected to a socket in the side of Tom Grey's skull. Squinting, Dennis could make out cutaway anatomy drawings flash by on the computer's tiny screen.

"And an aneurysm it was," said Dr. Corbett finally, a note of satisfaction creeping into her voice. "It looks as though our

Mr. Grey had a history of strokes—this was his third. And what have we here?" Dr. Corbett's voice seemed to fall an octave. "Lorne, why didn't you think to prescribe a decoagulant after this"—she tapped the screen with her pen—"showed up on the blood inspection Thursday?"

"I—" Lorne hesitated.

"That was a rhetorical question," said Dr. Corbett. "I can tell you why you didn't think, Lorne. You and Louise were treating Mr. Grey in terms of the injuries he had sustained in his motor vehicle accident. You fulfilled his Trauma-Plus Warranty to the letter. But you forgot that Tom Grey was an old man, whose body may have been betraying him in ways that had nothing to do with the trauma of his accident."

"That's not entirely true, Dr. Corbett." It was Louise. "He was on a prescription, and if you'll look, that wasn't interrupted throughout—"

Dr. Corbett yanked the cables from Tom Grey's head and the computer screen flashed white. "And who," she snapped, "do you think the Widow Grey would sue? The walk-in clinic that wrote out her dead husband's prescription two years ago and hasn't been in touch with him since? Or GF, who was looking after Mr. Grey when he died and had a clear legal responsibility as attending physician? This isn't some dealership service bay, Louise. This is a hospital, we're what passes for physicians these days, and our responsibility extends a little bit farther than making sure we're using the right engine oil."

Dennis could see Louise draw her breath to reply, but she appeared to think better and stood silent, fists rammed into the pockets of her lab coat.

"There's nothing more we can do here," said Dr. Corbett. "Lorne, call downstairs and tell them to send someone from the morgue. Maybe we can use this for some loss-counseling simulation with the others tomorrow—it's not often they have to deal with the shutdown of one of their fellows. I want to see a program drawn up before the end of your shift, Louise."

"Right away, Dr. Corbett," said Louise and turned away. Lorne started to follow.

"People," said Dr. Corbett, and they stopped. "This is only a dry run. An experiment. Nobody's dead. But remember how you feel about it."

The doctor turned to leave just as Dennis felt the ground under his feet slide, the familiar speckling come before his eyes.

"What—" Dr. Corbett started, but before she finished Dennis was tumbling forward and his senses had shut down completely.

The world was black and Dennis's limbs grew numb, but his awareness remained intact. His body and his mind, he realized, had become discrete objects.

And here, he thought with a little wonder, is the fissure, the space between his life before the crash, and his life now. The space he traversed unconscious every time he blacked out.

Was there a light? Tom Grey had asked. Dennis was sorry the dummy hadn't asked it later, because Dennis had an answer now. There is no light here—only the perfect blackness of the fissure.

Tom Grey, or the dummy that contained him, would become another when it emerged on the far side. It would suffer new agonies, played on a mind fresh from trauma and unhardened by experience.

The final tingle of sensation vanished from Dennis's awareness, and he drifted alone in the black spaces. Who would Tom Grey become? he wondered, and thought of his day in the ICU: man with his legs flayed to the bone; woman on a backboard, face cut too deeply; sleeping child who never stirred.

It's better here, thought Dennis. A better place by far.

Of course, the GF R&D teams wouldn't let Tom Grey stay in the fissure for long before saddling him with the burden of recovery once more. He would awaken, smashed against a wall that was an on-ramp or a dirt road or the grille of a semi, and the dummy's healing would begin once more.

Dennis took comfort in the knowledge that he would not be joining Tom Grey on the other side. If the cinder-block wall loomed before him, it grew no closer in the safety of the fissure, the deepening void of his new coma.

NEAR ENOUGH TO HOME

Michael Skeet

Michael Skeet was born in Calgary, Alberta, and lived in Edmonton before moving to Toronto. He has been a working writer for more than twenty years—in public radio and journalism, and now as a corporate and technical communications specialist, and in the Canadian SF community. It was he who named the Aurora Awards, having played an active part in the defining of the award structure as it currently exists. In a 1988 editorial in his newsletter *MLR* he called for the creation of a writers' organization for Canadian authors of speculative fiction; a year later SFCanada was organized in Edmonton; and Skeet served as its founding vice-president. He has in addition worked as an editor for Tesseract books; in 1993 he and his coeditor (Lorna Toolis, to whom he is married) won an Aurora for their work editing the anthology *Tesseracts 4*. He and Toolis (who is head of the Merril Collection, the world-renowned Toronto SF library) have coauthored a number of nonfiction articles on SF-related subjects. He began writing fiction in the mid-eighties, and has had short stories published in a variety of anthologies, including *Tesseracts, Northern Frights*, and *Arrowdreams*. In 1992 his story "Breaking Ball" was cowinner of the Aurora for best Canadian SF short story in English.

An amateur student of history, Skeet claims always to have been fascinated by alternate history SF, though "Near Enough to Home" is his first story in this subgenre. "Near Enough to Home," Skeet says, "was intended to be an ironic commentary on Canada's continuing insistence on defining itself in terms of its relationship to its southern neighbor. Though its protagonist is Canadian and its background suggests a vastly different North America with Canada as its dominant factor, the story takes place in the sundered United States of an alternate-history Civil War, and every character but the protagonist is American." The story is also not without relevance to the continued politics of separation in contemporary Canada.

Perhaps the most striking thing about Canada is that it is not part of the United States.

—*J. Bartlet Brebner*

Sanderson stumbled forward through a universe of misery. His lungs ached as he struggled to keep them filled, his mouth blocked by the gag his captors had stuffed there; wind-blown Kentucky rain stung his eyes, and with his hands bound behind him he could not wipe them clear; his feet chafed and bled where the cheap, ill-fitting American boots cut them. It wasn't enough that these Federal prisoners had cold-cocked him and dragged him along as a hostage to aid their escape; they'd stolen his boots, too—and them just broken in to where they were comfortable—and replaced them with shoddy atrocities that were almost worse than being barefoot. *Don't give up*, he told himself. *If you give these men a reason, they'll kill you, and then you'll never find Scott.*

"Keep moving, you redcoat bastard." A hand thumped him between the shoulder blades, driving him forward until he stumbled. A branch slapped him in the face; blinded by the rain and the moonless night, he felt his way forward, fighting to keep his balance, until he was sure it was bush and not a tree trunk he was about to step into. Then he fell forward, thrashing and kicking out as he did. Thin branches scratched his face, but the pain was worth it so long as his captors didn't figure out what he was doing.

Night was giving way to dawn when Sanderson went into the bushes next. Again he was pushed, and this time the man who pushed him clipped him on the side of the head before shoving him sideways. When Sanderson came to his senses, it was to hear the tail end of a scream for mercy, and the sickening crunch that ended it.

He struggled to his feet, working at the rope that bound his wrists in an effort to keep the rain from shrinking it. As he struggled upward, thorny branches whipped across his face, drawing blood. One of the thorns caught a tip of the gag; when he drew his head back, the gag stayed behind.

Emerging from the bush, Sanderson saw the Federal soldiers who'd captured him gathered in a loose semicircle around a mule that stood patiently in the middle of a muddy road. He didn't know Kentucky very well, but he knew his captors were moving north, to get away from the Confederate army; that made it likely this was the road between Bardwell and Wickliffe. Two bodies in Confederate white lay in the mud; heavy stones beside the shattered skulls made eloquently clear to Sanderson the source of the sound he'd just heard. None of the Federals even looked at the bodies now; they were talking amongst themselves and pointing at something behind the mule.

The sergeant who was the ringleader was pointing, too—with the heavy old Colt he'd taken from Sanderson along with his boots. The man thumbed back the Colt's hammer. *Not with my gun*, Sanderson thought; *not yet*. He struggled with the rope that bound him. A five-shot Currie stingy-pistol was tucked into a special holster in the small of his back; the Federals, being content with the obvious, had stopped searching him when they removed the Colt. If he could get his hands free, they'd regret their carelessness.

"We can use the mule, I guess," the sergeant said. "Since we already got us a hostage who can walk, I don't see much use for you, though." He aimed the pistol; Sanderson gave up on getting his hands free and rushed forward. "Nothing personal, colonel," the sergeant said, and then Sanderson hit him from behind and to the side. The two men splashed into the mud.

The others were on Sanderson before he could do anything else; not that he'd had any plan beyond disrupting the murder long enough to give the other man a chance to escape. When the Federals had stopped beating on him, though, Sanderson saw that he'd made a critical error in his original assumption: Escape had never been a possibility for the man he'd tried to save.

The colonel the sergeant had been speaking to was lying on a crude sort of travois, a blanket suspended between poles thrust under the horse's harness. A bandaged stump on the end of his left leg where the foot should have been explained the sergeant's remark about a hostage who could walk. Sanderson was astonished to see that the colonel wore a Federal uniform. Why would these men want to kill one of their own officers?

"Damn," the sergeant said as he got to his feet. "I ought to kill you for that, Englishman. Pity we need you to get across the river."

"I told you before," Sanderson said, "I'm not—" The last word exploded from him as the sergeant kicked into his ribs with enough force to knock him over sideways.

As he fought to get air into his agonized lungs, Sanderson

heard the sergeant mutter, "Goddamned barrel's full of mud," and shove the Colt back into its holster. "Guess we'll have to do him like we done the others."

"If what you want is to get across the river to home, I'm worth more to you alive than I am dead."

Sanderson looked up. The colonel had struggled upright, in order to be able to look the sergeant in the eye. The colonel's face was pale and sweating; no doubt he'd got a fever from the amputation. Even if he'd been healthy, though, this colonel would have been one of the more ugly men Sanderson had ever seen. Tall and impossibly thin, he looked more like a corpse than many dead men. His face was long and angular, and so raw-edged and bony it looked as though it had been carved with an axe. Huge ears gave him a look that suggested to Sanderson a sort of elongated gorilla. The man's eyes were dark and sunken, and though there was something almost mesmerizing about them, Sanderson attributed that to the fever-gleam.

"I'm a fair man," the sergeant said with a smile that gave the lie to his words. "I'll give you a chance to explain yourself."

"I'm being paroled. The Confederates are letting me go home, instead of sending me to a prison." The colonel's voice was pitched high for such a tall man. "I guess they don't consider me a threat anymore." He looked down at the bandaged stump. "You"—the colonel paused just long enough that Sanderson, at least, was aware of the irony—". . . gentlemen . . . want to get across the river. I assume that you would be interested in the boat that's waiting for me."

"Waiting for you where?"

"Ah," said the colonel. "That's what you'll keep me alive to find out."

"You're a Canadian?" the colonel asked. They had stopped for a rest in a small clearing in the woods somewhere northeast of Wickliffe. After introducing himself, the colonel had thanked Sanderson quietly for his attempt at intervention; while the words and voice were pitched low, Sanderson felt the power behind them nevertheless.

"I'm from St. Louis, yes," Sanderson said. He worked at his bonds, but in spite of his efforts the cord had shrunk in the rain, and all he was getting for his efforts was bloody wrists. They'd bound the colonel, too—more to keep him from helping me, Sanderson guessed, than because they think he's really a threat. "I believe you're the first man I've met since crossing the river who hasn't called me an Englishman. Thank you for that."

"You'll have to forgive my countrymen their ignorance," the colonel said. The rain had stopped a while back, but the woods were still soaked; the colonel's uniform was so wet the blue wool looked almost black. "Canada is a relatively new concept to us, and by and large my countrymen are slow to adapt to new concepts that they consider an inconvenience. Besides, until forty-eight you *were* Englishmen, at least legally."

"Do you have any idea why these men are doing this?" Sanderson asked. "Surely they'd have been exchanged soon."

"That assumes they were taken on the field of battle," the colonel said dryly.

"You mean they might be deserters? But they were in a Confederate prison enclosure when they took me." Sanderson flushed with embarrassment at the memory.

"Their presence in a prisoner camp is no guarantee that they actually took part in the fighting at Bardwell," the colonel said. "The situation has been somewhat chaotic this week." That was an understatement, Sanderson knew. The Federal army had been destroyed at Bardwell, and he'd heard that only a few thousand had made it back across the Ohio River into Illinois and Indiana. If the Confederates invaded Illinois or captured Washington— and either looked possible now—there was a good chance the war would be over before 1852 gave way to 1853.

"Might I inquire just what you were doing in that prisoner camp? Our escorts here"—the colonel nodded sarcastically at their guards—"called you a redcoat. You're not in uniform, though, so you're not a Canadian military observer. In that duster you might be any farmer. You're not a spy, are you?"

"No, sir. I'm with the Northwest Mounted Police."

"So how did they know to call you a redcoat?"

"I had a pass, signed by the Confederate military attaché in St. Louis. I'm here looking for a fugitive who'd joined your army under a false name."

"You show an admirable determination," the colonel said. "This fugitive must have done something particularly horrible."

Scott had left their mother in tears, but Sanderson didn't feel like sharing that fact with the colonel, so he simply nodded. "I'm anxious to get him back," he said.

"I see," the colonel said, and smiled. "Is he a murderer? Or is it some more political crime?"

"I'm not at liberty to talk about that," Sanderson said, after what he knew was too long a pause. He saw the colonel's appraising glance, and was grateful when one of the deserters appeared to kick him to his feet.

"What do you think of our chances, constable?" The question was pitched quietly enough that Sanderson nearly didn't hear it over the rustling of the foliage.

"Not good, I'm afraid," he said. He twisted himself around in the hope that by talking back at the colonel he could avoid being overheard by the deserters. They had turned him into a draft animal, crudely harnessing the stretcher to his shoulders so that he could drag the colonel while their captors took turns riding the mule. "Your chances are better than mine, though. If they're hoping to use me to get them past any Confederate patrols, my usefulness ends as soon as they get to the river. You probably gain in value the closer they get to Ohio or Indiana or wherever it is they decide to go."

"A cruel assessment, but probably accurate." The colonel laughed bitterly. "That makes me wonder something, though. Not to pry, but Canada and Britain *are* allied with the Confederate States now. So why would you have been in a prisoner camp without an escort? I'm assuming that you were captured because you were alone."

"I was." Sanderson shook his head.

"So why would your confederate allies value you as a hostage, but not value you enough to ensure your safety before you were taken?"

The brush to his left rattled and shook as some surprised animal fled from their approach. "I guess that was my fault, colonel. I'd hoped to speak with General Lee about my fugitive, but apparently the general has been recalled to Virginia. The rewards of success, I suppose." The colonel grimaced, though whether it was from pain or embarrassment, Sanderson couldn't tell. "I spent a whole night waiting to talk with someone, and when I finally did the man was less than polite. Some captain named Stewart, who made it clear enough that he didn't like me or anyone else from the other side of the Mississippi, treaty or no. He told me he couldn't spare anyone to help me search. So I went off on my own. Not the best of ideas, I guess."

"I've met Captain Stewart," the colonel said. "He was polite enough to me. I gather he was with the commissioners who negotiated the treaty with your government and the English last year. I don't think he likes the English very much."

"It's a damned curious war," Sanderson said. "I'm supposed to think of those slave-owners as allies, and I just can't. But I can't say as I like the English much either. Or you folks, come to that. Nobody asked me what I thought about any of this." His eyes stung as sweat trickled into them; he desperately wanted to wipe his forehead, but had to settle for brushing his face against leafy branches as he dodged around trees.

"Politics is what makes it curious," the colonel said. "If the Confederate States are victorious, then Canada becomes the dominant country on this continent. Neither the C.S.A. nor the U.S. would be able to challenge Canada's westward expansion unaided. Texas is already in debt to Britain, and California will probably follow. And I suspect that an independent Confederate States wouldn't be as independent as they'd like. They'll be junior partners to Canada and Britain. Unfortunately, our southern brothers aren't interested in listening to my theories right now. We'll all be learning bitter lessons before long, is my guess."

Sanderson wondered about the lessons Scott had learned. If he'd lived long enough to learn anything, that is. He shook his head; that wasn't the way his thoughts should be moving. He had to keep himself ready should the opportunity for escape arise.

The Ohio River—the liquid border between Kentucky and Illinois—flowed muddily past their vantage point; the river was bloated with rain, and its confluence with the equally swollen Mississippi had a look of lazy evil about it that Sanderson, who'd grown up on the bigger river, had learned at an early age to mistrust.

Sanderson and the colonel lay in a hollow at the edge of a bluff overlooking the river, two of their captors watching them while the other four struggled to get the stolen boat into the water.

"You know what's ironic?" the colonel asked. He didn't wait for a response. "If it hadn't been for the British taking Louisiana, we might none of us be here right now. If we'd been allowed to expand westward, we'd have had enough new territory to worry about that we wouldn't have had time to fight over slavery or states' rights. We might have avoided this war. For a while longer, anyway."

The colonel rolled over to look at Sanderson. "Are you all right, constable? I trust I'm not boring you."

Sanderson closed his eyes and took a deep breath. He'd run out of time; it had to be now.

"Colonel," he said slowly. "Could I ask you a favor?"

"I'm not in much of a position to do much at the moment," the colonel said. "But in so far as it's within my power, I'd be honored to help you. You saved my life this morning. What can I do for you?"

"If I don't come out of this alive, colonel, would you see what you can do about finding that soldier I told you about?"

"The fugitive you're tracking? Constable, I'm no policeman."

Sanderson sighed. "He's not really a fugitive, sir. He's my younger brother."

"I suspected as much." The colonel's face crumpled into a tiny, satisfied smile. "No doubt your Confederate allies were prepared to accept your story at face value because you had the proper papers. But I had to wonder why you were so reluctant to tell me what this man had done. The only conclusion I could draw was that he hadn't done anything. Actually, constable, I congratulate you for not compounding the original lie. That's what trips most people up. They start with one lie, then find they have to keep lying to keep the first lie from being found out. The lies get bigger, and before they know it they're the governor or the president."

Sanderson laughed. "You're a very observant man, colonel."

"I was a lawyer before all this began," the colonel said. "And a momentarily successful liar myself, since I spent a couple of years in Washington. Noticing things about people has proved helpful to me. Do you want to tell me what happened between you and your brother?"

"It really wasn't between us," Sanderson said. "Scott and I weren't what you'd call close. I'm eight years older than he is. No, the trouble was between my mother and her father. Scott ended up listening to grandfather."

"Now you've got me interested," the colonel said. Sanderson noticed that their guards had edged closer as well, though they were taking elaborate pains to appear to be watching their companions with the boat. "How does a father-daughter dispute drive a young man into the middle of our civil war?"

"It's a long story," Sanderson said. "Truly. It goes back fifty years, to when Grandpa was a young man. He was from Virginia, you know. Says he met Washington once. Canada might be a federated kingdom now, but when Grandpa talks about his country, he still means Virginia."

"People are born in the strangest places," the colonel said. "I was born in Kentucky myself. If my father hadn't been so restless, I might have ended up wearing white and fighting for John Calhoun, Davey Crockett, and Dixie's Land."

Sanderson looked at their guards. They were exchanging glances of amusement that suggested they might be susceptible to further distraction. Raising his voice a little, he said, "Grandpa moved to Louisiana when he was sixteen and set himself up as a trader in St. Louis. Married a half-Indian daughter of a French trader." In the guise of settling into a more comfortable position, Sanderson located a stone and began to carefully work his bound wrists against it. "But when Bonaparte died back in oh-two and the British got Louisiana, Grandpa refused to take the loyalty oath. He even got himself put in prison in 1810 at the beginning of Jefferson's War."

"Interesting that you should call it that," the colonel said. "That's an American term. Don't the British call it the War of 1810?"

"Like I said, my grandpa still thinks of himself as American," Sanderson said. He could feel the friction of rope against stone, and hoped that the fibers were beginning to break down. "Right up until Confederation, he truly believed that America was going to take Louisiana back. When I joined the police and put on the red uniform, he stopped speaking to me. And, my mother tells me, he started filling Scott's head with all sorts of stories about the greatness of America and the treacherousness of the English. He hates the English—and just like the sergeant down there, he seems pretty generous in terms of who he thinks of as English. His neighbors despise him. They burn him in effigy every First of July, I'm told."

"I've heard stories about what happened to American sympathizers in Louisiana after Jefferson's war," the colonel said. "Pardon me if I'm being rude, but I find yours a strange country. I can't think of any other modern state that was founded the way yours was, on the negation of a principle."

"That principle being republicanism?" Sanderson shook his head. "Some of us are equally opposed to monarchy, colonel."

"And so you don't know what you are so much as you know what you aren't—you're not English and you're not American."

"I know what I am, colonel." Sanderson shook his head again, trying to clear his thoughts. "I'm tired and I'm wet and as far as I'm concerned the whole lot of you can blow yourselves to perdition if you'll just leave me out of it."

The colonel's reply was cut short by the return of the sergeant. He had cleaned the Colt, Sanderson saw. "Time to go, boys," he said.

You can say this much for being tied up, Sanderson thought: *At least I didn't have to haul that thing down to the river.* The boat was a big, ugly, flat-bottomed thing that must have weighed nearly a thousand pounds. It didn't look like something that should be used on a river in flood.

Across the Ohio and downstream a little were the ramshackle docks and warehouses of Cairo, the Illinois town from which the Federals had launched their futile attempt at keeping western Kentucky in the Union. Further west, and rendered invisible by the low cloud and haze that persisted though the rain had stopped, was Thompson, on the Canadian side of the Mississippi just south of its confluence with the Ohio. Sanderson thought again about his chances for getting back there. They hadn't improved, he decided. In fact, they were probably worse, since his captors could easily decide to turn him over to the Federal authorities across the Ohio. With no one to vouch for his mission, he'd be all too easily condemned as a spy. *And me not a single step closer to finding Scott.*

"I suppose this is where we say good-bye," the sergeant said to him. For one brief moment Sanderson hoped he was going to be released. But as soon as he thought it, he knew the hope was misplaced. The deserters had decided they didn't need him any more, that's all.

"I see you've decided to let him go," the colonel said. He'd been seated on a large rock while the deserters tried to maneuver the boat alongside in such a way that he wouldn't have to be carried far.

"And what makes you think that?" the sergeant asked. He drew the massive Colt from its holster.

"You still need me if you're to avoid punishment once we're across the river," the colonel said. "And I'm not crossing without this man."

"With a mind like that it's no wonder we're losing," the sergeant said, to tired laughter from the others. "What makes you think we're going back to Illinois? I'm thinking we'll just cross all the way over, to that fine Canadian frontier we've all heard so much about. Arkansas is near enough to home for my tastes." The sergeant sneered at Sanderson. "By rights it should've been ours anyway, if you English hadn't stolen it from us."

"I don't recall the Louisiana Territory being yours to claim," Sanderson said. "As I've read it, it was the French and Spanish the British took it from."

"Should have been ours. If that bastard Jefferson had've been quicker with his wits when Bonaparte died, we'd have drove you English right off this continent." The sergeant cocked the pistol.

Sanderson knew he should be calm, should be agreeing with this idiot, anything to keep the man occupied, to keep him from getting angrier. But Sanderson didn't care anymore. *If I'm going to die*, he decided, *I'm going down fighting*. "It seems to me," he said, flexing his wrists behind him, "that you Americans already tried that once. Nelson and Wellington whipped you forty years ago, and I haven't seen anything in you to make me think we should be worried now."

"It seems to me," the sergeant said, "that I've put up with your damned smug superiority long enough."

"Don't do something you'll regret," the colonel said from his rock. He tried but failed to stand up. "If you're determined to go to Canada, you still need this man. Don't go making a mistake when you're so close to getting what you want."

"What I want is not to hear anything more from you," the sergeant said. He spat derisively. "Don't think I don't know you, colonel. I know you, all right. I made the mistake of voting for you six years ago. This," he said to Sanderson, "is one of the political geniuses who got us into this mess that you're so superior about. Went to Congress talking about preserving the Union, and what did he do? Voted against annexing Texas. Voted to condemn the men who tried to filibuster Cuba into the Union. We couldn't get him out of Washington fast enough. And now he's pleading for your life? You picked a poor lawyer, Englishman."

I'm tired of you, Sanderson thought. He said nothing, though. Instead, he forced his wrists apart with all the strength in him. After a second's hesitation, the frayed cord snapped. Sanderson thrust his right hand through the vent in the back of his duster and into the holster under his shirt. He drew the Currie.

"You son of a bitch," the sergeant said. As Sanderson aimed at his belly, the sergeant smiled crookedly. "Go to hell," he said, and pulled the trigger.

The Colt exploded like the First of July.

The sergeant stared, shocked into silence, at the bloody wreckage of his hand. He was still staring, still silent, when a musket ball spattered his brains across the stones at the river's edge.

Sanderson jumped backward as the sergeant's body toppled and fell. *What the hell happened? I didn't pull the trigger.*

"Drop the weapon, sir."

Sanderson looked up. At the top of the bank a confederate soldier reloaded a smoking musket. Beside the soldier, a white-clad officer pointed at Sanderson.

"Captain Stewart," Sanderson said. "It's about time."

"Might I ask why you've taken my pistol?" Sanderson hadn't protested at first, but now that the surviving deserters had been chained together and were being marched up the bank he was becoming worried.

"I can't think it would be prudent," said Captain Stewart, "to re-arm a spy after only just apprehending him."

"A spy?" Without wanting to, Sanderson began to laugh. He shook and spasmed for an embarrassingly long time, and when he was able to lift his head it was to find the white-clad captain glaring death at him. "My apologies, captain," he gasped. "It must be nerves; I haven't slept for several days now." When Stewart's expression didn't change, Sanderson returned the glare. "What in the world possessed you to think I was a spy?"

"You went to the prison encampment without my permission, sir, and the next thing I knew, a half-dozen prisoners—and yourself—had gone missing. It was our good fortune that you were so clumsy. You left a trail a blind man could follow."

"Of course I did! I fell into bushes so many times I was convinced those idiots would figure out what I was about. Look at my face, damn it!" Sanderson leaned forward so that Stewart couldn't fail to notice the cross-hatch of cuts and lacerations. "I'm cut so many times I look like a truant's bottom," he spat. "And you think you found me because I was clumsy!"

"Fine words, sir," Stewart began.

"They're also true," the colonel said. Stewart raised his hands as if to protest, but the colonel silenced him with a look. "This man was treated abominably by his captors, and risked his life to save mine. Rather than arresting him, you should be offering your best hospitality; I'm not without friends in Illinois and other places."

"I'm aware of that," Stewart said. Sulking, he handed Sanderson his pistol, then told two other men to prepare to row the colonel across the river.

Sanderson crouched down to retrieve his boots. "Thank you," he said, turning to face the colonel as Stewart stomped away. "I owe you one."

"We're even, then," the colonel said. "I hope some day to thank you properly for saving my life. You showed fine courage standing up to that homicidal idiot . . ." The colonel's voice died away, and Sanderson looked up from the sergeant's body, from which he was in the process of removing the holster.

The colonel was eyeing him carefully, the way one might an unfamiliar snake. "The gun was yours?" he asked. After a moment's silence he said, "You knew. You were expecting that gun to burst."

Sanderson flushed, and got to his feet. "If there had been a way to let you know, colonel, I would have."

"What I don't understand," the colonel said, "is precisely *how* you knew." His eyebrows lifted suddenly. "Unless you had prepared it that way. Good God."

"I once saw a man lose his hand firing one of those," Sanderson said, pointing at the smashed pistol, which was still smoking. "That was a Walker Colt; they were made for the Texas army, which turned out not to like them that much. Oh, they had their good points. I've never encountered a pistol that packed as much powder in a single charge as the Walker. But the tolerances were awfully loose. Every ninety rounds or so, firing one chamber would set off all the caps and the whole thing would explode. So I got to thinking as how that might come in handy should I ever find myself in a situation just like this one. I made the cylinder a bit more loose than it already was, primed the back of the frame, and then made sure it was loaded with clay balls coated with just enough lead to keep them from crumbling until they were fired. You'll have noticed that I keep my real gun in a less obvious place." He patted his back.

The colonel whistled long and low. "You are a—wait a minute." The eyebrows dropped and the colonel's eyes darkened. "When you dove at that man back on the road, you knew he couldn't have killed me. So you were just trying to preserve your secret for a little while longer."

Sanderson shook his head. "I couldn't say that, colonel. I wanted to keep him from finding out about the gun, that's true. But I was also trying to prevent him from killing you. I honestly couldn't say which was foremost in my mind."

"Yet another case of you not knowing yourself," the colonel said. "At a hazard to everyone around you. You people *are* a menace."

"You know, colonel," Sanderson said with a grin, "I think I'm beginning to like this not knowing myself. It can't be a bad thing to keep folks wondering.

"Besides, you people have been sure of who you are for nearly four-score years, and look at where it's got you."

The colonel's face lost all of its animation, and for the first time since Stewart's arrival Sanderson was ashamed. "I'm sorry, colonel. That was uncalled for."

"Don't chastise yourself," the colonel said slowly: "I was just indulging in a spot of self-pity. You came a little too close to home, I guess." He looked down at the empty space where his foot should have been. "I look at myself today and I see a failed soldier. You'll have gathered that I failed as a politician too. I suddenly find myself wondering what it is that I'll do with myself when I get across the river."

"There's more than one river you can cross, you know," Sanderson said. "Whatever's happened to you so far, you're a clever man. I'm told there's a new country building to the west, if you cared to share your abilities with us." He extended a hand.

The colonel shook it, firmly. "Thank you for your kind offer," he said. "But something tells me I shouldn't give up on this old country too quickly. Let me go home and see if I can't do something for her yet." He hobbled slowly to the boat, and suffered the white-clad enemy to hand him in.

"Good luck, constable," the colonel said as the Confederate oarsmen pushed the boat away from the bank. "I hope you eventually find your brother."

"I intend to. I'll keep looking in Kentucky for now," Sanderson said. "As long as Captain Stewart doesn't arrest me again. If you come across him in Illinois, will you write me care of headquarters in St. Louis?"

"Count on it," the colonel said as the oars bit into the river.

As the colonel waved farewell, Sanderson said, "If you decide that your future involves politics, colonel, might I suggest you keep the beard? It softens your face, you know. Makes you look as if you know yourself a little bit less than you do."

The colonel laughed at that. The laughter echoed off the water and the shore. It continued to tickle Sanderson's ears as he climbed up the bank and mounted a borrowed horse to resume his search.

FARM WIFE

Nancy Kilpatrick

Nancy Kilpatrick was born in Philadelphia, resided in San Francisco and Chicago, and eventually moved to Canada where she has now spent more than half her life, much of that time in Toronto, with a year each in Vancouver and Montreal. She moved back to Montreal two years ago "because the flavor of the city suits [her] gothic temperament." Her work generally falls into the catagories of fantasy, dark fantasy, horror, and erotic horror—although she has written several mystery stories, and in 1992 won the Arthur Ellis Award for best short story.

Kilpatrick has published thirteen novels, the most recent *Reborn* (Pumpkin Books), the third book in her vampire world, and *Dracul*, a novelization of the stage musical by that name, for Mainstage Productions. She has published more than one hundred short stories, four issues of a comic book, four collections of short fiction, and has cowritten a bilingual play, humorously political, produced at the Fringe Festival in Toronto. Kilpatrick has also edited six anthologies, the latest, *In the Shadow of the Gargoyle*, for Ace/Berkley. She writes under her own name and under the *nom de plume* Amarantha Knight.

"Farm Wife"—originally published by Don Hutchison in *Northern Frights*—is set on the farm ten miles outside Napanee, Ontario, where Kilpatrick lived for one year. "The characters are a composite of many of the people in that area—practical, down-to-earth types who automatically deal with whatever life sends their way because that's the nature of farmers." This horrific story was nominated for the Aurora Award in 1992.

Noma stationed herself at the back porch and propped the screen door open with her left foot. The sun hadn't set but one hour ago and already the Napanee sky was the color of ashes from the woodburner. Out past the pale tripod fencing and across the dying rye fields she saw Bert shuffling, Dog by his side. The sickness drained him. And left him hungry. Hungry all the time. Lord knows she fed that man a baker's dozen meals a day, but it was never enough. The more he ate, the thinner he got. Wasted. Just this morning she noticed he barely cast a shadow.

A mosquito trying to sneak into the house paused on her meaty upper arm. Yard was swarming with the last of 'em. She watched the bloodsucker poke its snout into a pore. "Want blood, you'll get blood," she promised. Her skin began to itch bad but she made herself wait. Easy now. Ball the fist and knot the shoulder, like her daddy had showed her. Noma's work-developed muscles tensed. She believed she could feel the strong blood forced up that chute.

The sucker went rigid.

Swelled to triple size.

Probably didn't even think about getting away.

She flicked the bloody corpse into the coming night and scratched her wound.

Noma shut the screen door but continued watching Bert make his way slowly toward the house. Sure is a stubborn man, she thought. Had been the forty-odd years she'd known him. Her daddy'd warned her, said it ran in Bert's family, but she wouldn't listen. When Bert first come down with the sickness she tried getting him over to the hospital. But he didn't trust city-trained doctors, didn't trust doctors at all, especially since his sister. Noma couldn't blame him, though. Seeing Ruby lying like milkweed fluff on those crisp sheets, color of white flour and brittle as dead leaves, eyes shot with blood and sunk back into her head, breath rank, gums shrunk up from the teeth like that . . . God, what a waste.

The doctors claimed it was some fancy kind of anemia. Gave her stuff but it didn't make the slightest bit of difference that Noma could see. Bert did the right thing in bringing her home. Ruby stayed upstairs in the room next to them, fading day by day, withering to less than nothing, just like Bert was now, until one morning when Noma took up eggs and bacon and found that Ruby had departed. "Best that way," Bert said. Noma had to agree.

And now it's him, she thought. As he reached the vegetable garden, even in the poor light she could see his bones pressuring the skin to set them free. His face wasn't more than a skull, with hardly any flesh for that pale hide to stretch across, and just a tuft of red on top. He lifted an arm and waved—she knew how hard that was for him.

As Bert reached the porch, Noma stepped out, ready to give him a hand up the steps, but he shrugged her off. You old curmudgeon, she thought. Even now, when he can use it most, he won't take no help. Well, that's just like a farmer, isn't it.

By the time she'd latched the screen door and closed and locked the inside one, he was at the refrigerator, dragging out the apple pie she'd baked this afternoon. He got a dessert plate from the cupboard and placed a hearty slice of pie on it. That slice went right back into the refrigerator. Out came the cheddar, and pure cream she'd whipped. He plunked himself down in front of the bulk of the pie, helped himself to a wedge of cheese the size of Idaho and scooped seven or eight kitchen spoons of milk fat onto the whole mess. She figured by eating so much, he fooled himself he wasn't sick.

"Cuppa coffee?" she asked.

He grunted and nodded but didn't pause.

Noma plugged in the kettle, but before the water got a chance to boil the pie tin was empty and he was back for that abandoned slice.

She measured freeze-dried coffee into two mugs—one twice the size of the other—and glanced out the window while she poured water over it. Gonna be cool tonight—October tended to be like that. Leaves on the willow been gone over a week; branches swayed in the breeze like a woman's hair. Might be a harvest moon come up, if the sky stayed clear. Low on the horizon. And full. She checked the calendar. Nope. Full moon tomorrow night. Be plenty to do come sunrise.

When Bert finished the pie he leaned his skinny self back in the chair and belched loud, then patted his stomach, or what used to be a stomach but had become so bloated he looked like he swallowed a whole watermelon. "Waste not want not," he said, and she agreed. She handed him his coffee and he took it to the living room. She heard the television; sounded like a sports show.

About eleven Noma put Dog out and they went upstairs. Bert tossed and turned, keeping her awake for a time, but she must have dozed off because she woke when she heard the stairs creak as he stumbled down. The refrigerator door opened and closed. Opened and closed again. Then the back door. The screen door slammed. She turned onto her side and pulled the feather pillow over her ear and went back to sleep.

Noma got up with the sun. Down in the kitchen she cleared the mess Bert had left. She opened the back door to let Dog in and fed him the scraps. The sky was packed with clouds the color of cow's brains, the air snappy. *Farmers' Almanac* promised frost tonight.

When breakfast was out of the way and she'd fed the chickens and pigs and milked the cows and turned them out to pasture, Noma harvested as much of the Swiss chard from the garden as she could—two and a half bushel baskets worth. She washed and blanched the iron-rich greens then stuffed them in airtight plastic bags that she sealed for the freezer. Bert hated chard, hated vegetables on principle, he said, but Noma couldn't get enough.

There was bed making, washing to do, some mending, lunch to get ready and eat, vacuuming, and a call to the feed store to see if that new corn and soya mix for the pigs was in yet. It wasn't.

Around four Noma began supper. Hadn't seen Bert all day. Didn't expect to. Still, she cooked up a mess of chard, and a ton of beef stew, the way she'd made a big lunch and breakfast, just in case.

Around six the cows came back. She locked them up in the barn and on her way to the house looked across the rye. The fields had faded to the color of dry bone. No sign of Bert. Not surprising. Still.

Noma watched that show with the fat woman but it wasn't very funny this week. She crawled into bed early, not quite tenthirty. She'd done all she could, all anybody could, but sleep wasn't about to help her out tonight.

The eaves creaked. The wind picked up and howled the way it can. The house her daddy left her was old but solid. Noma grew up here, married here, had her kids, buried her folks. Through every season, lean and plenty—she was used to the sounds.

But when Dog howled at the moon, well; Bert always looked after Dog. She went to the window at the back and was about to warn the mutt to settle himself or else but stopped. Dog wasn't making a peep now. He stood quivering, scruffy tail between his legs, ears back, about to bolt. And staring at Bert.

A cloud lifted from the bloated moon and Bert turned his face up. The sickness was all over him. Eyes flecked with red like the blood that spurts from a leghorn when you chop the head off. He'd turned into a skeleton and what flesh he had left the moon showed was a kind of whitewashed blue. "Noma," was all he said. He grinned at her and she saw that his gums had receded; his teeth reminded her of the sharp teeth on the combine. But the worst of all was his shadow. It was gone.

"Ain't letting you in," she told him firmly.

His eyes got hard and fiery red like sumach fruit. He stepped up onto the porch, out of her sight. She heard him rattling the back door. "Noma," he called again, so pathetic it got to her.

Despite her better judgment, she went down to the kitchen and opened just the inside, keeping the screen door between them.

"Best you be off," she told him. He cocked his head to one side—that always softened her up. The yellow kitchen light gave him some color. "Noma," he whispered, like they were in bed together.

She shook her head but opened the screen door.

He was on her in a second, pitchfork teeth tearing into her throat. Noma'd always been a big strong woman, but he was stronger—she'd discovered that early in their marriage. This was more so. He stank like the compost heap and his skin rivaled the frosty air. It was plain enough, he was starving, she was supper.

He held her against the kitchen table. She felt the iron-blood being drawn from her like milk from a cow. Wasn't but one thing to be done, what her daddy had taught her.

Noma worked slow, tensing the muscles up from her legs, through her privates and stomach, her arms, chest and back. When that was done she eased up a second. One final overall squeeze did the trick.

Bert looked like he'd been slammed by a bale of hay. Blood gushed from his mouth, nose, and ears. His eyes popped wide. He swelled fast, the way the skin does when you're frying up chicken. A funny sound, kind of a cross between her name and a goose hissing, started to rise out of him but didn't get much of a chance.

Noma shook for a while but figured there wasn't much point to that. The clock over the stove read two-thirty. She glanced out

the window. Frost had taken the last of the chard. The waste of
it troubled her.

The walls and ceiling were splattered, the floor slime. She
cleaned up what she could of the gory mess, then opened the
door. Dog bounded in, happy to gobble the scraps.

Noma dabbed alcohol on her neck and checked the clock
again. Time to get herself to bed. Sunrise wasn't far off. Tomorrow there'd be plenty to do. Always is for a farm wife.

BEYOND THE BARRIERS

Charles Montpetit

Translated from the French by the author

Charles Montpetit, born and raised in Montreal, has been involved in the publishing business ever since he was 13. Amongst other distinctions, his books have won the Actuelle-jeunesse Award (*Moi ou la planète*), the Signet d'or Prize (*Copie carbone*), and the Governor General's Award (*Temps mort*). His anthology *The First Time*, a six-volume series of true stories for adolescents about first sexual experiences, has also garnered a White Raven from Munich's International Youth Library, and made both the New York Public Library's and the American Library Association's honor lists. He is a cartoonist and stage performer as well, touring throughout Canada.

This story was originally published in the special SF issue of *Prairie Fire* (published to celebrate the World Speculative Fiction Convention in Canada in 1994), and later won the Canadian Broadcasting Corporation's Morningside radio drama competition, for which it was adapted. "'Beyond the Barriers' is, quite simply, based on the way many Montrealers already talk, including me," says Montpetit. It is so close to contemporary in setting that the author revises it for each appearance, so the text here is in part original. SF, in this particular case, stands for speculative fiction, not science fiction.

From *The Nature of Things*, 13 September 1984:
UNDERWATER SHOT: BLUE WHALES MIGRATING TO THE NORTH POLE.
"Every animal on Earth communicates with its fellow creatures. Whether it chants, gropes, or grumbles, it must always be able to make its needs and desires known to others."
AFRICAN VELDT: A WOUNDED LION KEEPS HYENAS AT BAY.
"But what of the ones who have nothing in common? How do they make themselves understood if they do not share the

same vocabulary? Can different beings cohabitate in peace if they cannot transcend the language barrier?"

U.N. CONFERENCE ROOM: DIPLOMATS HURL EPITHETS AT EACH OTHER.

"Tonight, we'll take a look at bilingualism. The way it works, its effects on society, and the brand new crisis it has brought on our doorstep."

CUE TITLE SEQUENCE.

From Dr. Lamoureux's interview with Michelle Lambert-Clemens's parents, 10 July 1987:

Dorothy Clemens: I know it's an awful thing to say after twenty years of marriage, but . . . if it means that our baby would have been all right, I'd have called it quits without a second thought.

Réginald Lambert: On l'savait-tu, nous autres, que c'était dangereux? On s'aimait, c'est tout, on pensait pas que ça ferait une miette de différence!

Dorothy Clemens: Mind you, it's not as if we blame ourselves. We're no fools, we've read up on Darwin and stuff. The scientific link just doesn't exist.

Réginald Lambert: Ça pourrait être une coïncidence, c'est sûr.

Dorothy Clemens: Yes. Yes, it very well could be.

From the files of Dr. Ulrich Weishaupt, 28 January 1988:

ORTHOPHONIC ERGOTHERAPY—M. LAMBERT-CLEMENS

No sign of cerebrovascular damage, contusions, or hematomas. Blood circulation to the brain optimal. Nervous system and sensory inputs functioning at peak efficiency. Motor skills (lingual, facial, gestural) unimpaired.

Suggest psychological evaluation, but so far, no reason to suspect an early trauma.

From a taped interview with Michelle Lambert-Clemens, Holycross Care Center, 2 March 1989:

Michelle Lambert-Clemens: It's all so frustrant! C'est comme si my brain bypassed une étape quand je parle, so I don't even stop pour sélectionner one of the tongues que j'ai apprises when I grew up. C'est même pas un reflex, it's totally random!

Therapist: Are you at all conscious of your predicament?

Michelle Lambert-Clemens: Hey, as far as ce qui me con-

cerne, I don't even realize que j'ai un problem. I know exactly
ce que je veux dire all the time, mais on dirait que la switch
controlling mon choix de mots is constantly flipped du français
à l'anglais. It feels as if I spoke avec des phrases unilingues, but
if I pay attention au visage de mes partenaires, I can almost see
à quel point they start having difficulties à me comprendre.
Uh . . . Am I making sense?

From *Tanzsprache und Orientierung der Bienen*, 1965 (abstract):
Bees are known to have developed complex dance languages, which vary from one species to the next; since the species do not mix, this usually doesn't cause any confusion.
However, Nobel Prize-winner Karl von Frisch recently managed to interbreed Austrian and Italian bees, which are similar
enough even though they use different "dialects." As he discovered, many of the Austro-Italian hybrids inherited the physical
appearance of the Italian bees, but "spoke Austrian"—a situation
that generates endless confusion in their dealings with Italian
hive-mates.

From CBC's *Lunchbreak*, 22 April 1997:
Host Leanne Connelly: . . . and later on, of course, we'll
open up the lines for your calls. But first, let's try to clear up
this language thing: joining me in the studio is Dr. Camille
Somers, head of the Linguistics Department at McGill University
and the very person who coined the term "Babel Syndrome," as
the dysfunction is now known in most scientific circles. Dr.
Somers, welcome.
Dr. Somers: Hello.
L. C.: Dr. Somers, can language abilities be inherited or not?
Dr. Somers: Ah, tough question. To a certain extent, yes:
most animals discover their communication skills as their body
develops, sort of like breathing, really. As Chomsky used to say,
the fundamental aspects of language are determined by our biological endowment, *not* by learning or training . . .
L. C.: He used to work with chimps, I believe. Is their speech
similar to our own?
Dr. Somers: Mmm . . . not exactly. The chimps' voice boxes
are too different, but they can express themselves in ways which
are comparable, within limits. For instance, we've trained them
to use plastic shapes, you know, a star to represent an apple, a
cube as a symbol of giving, etc. They catch on pretty fast, and

soon enough, they learn to form sentences like *you give apple me*, and like that.

L. C.: Wait a minute. You're talking about in-lab lessons, not heredity.

Dr. Somers: True, but the *idea* of language, the matrix if you wish, that basic principle is transmitted through the genes.

L. C.: So . . . when we're talking about bilingual couples . . .

Dr. Somers: Just a moment now, we musn't confuse cause and effect. We tried to reproduce the Lambert-Clemens case in our laboratories, by teaching different languages to separate chimp clans, and then encouraging males and females from each group to breed together. But we didn't get any significant results.

L. C.: Oh.

Dr. Somers: Indeed. However, we obviously couldn't keep the *mating* couples from sharing the two languages, and the more bilingual they became, the more we came across interesting cases, which we would never have spotted if it hadn't been for the controlled atmosphere of the experiment.

L. C.: What happened?

From *Nova*, 6 May 1999:

A COMPUTER IS SWITCHED ON, AND THE CROSS-SECTION OF A BRAIN APPEARS IN VIVID COLORS UNDER THE WORD *NORMAL*. AN OUTSTRETCHED HAND TAPS ON THE SCREEN NEXT TO A DARK SPOT.

"There, next to Wernicke's Area. This is where the brain decides to switch from one language to another. Right now, the patient is at rest, and the region is inactive. However . . ."

PAN TO A BAY WINDOW, BEYOND WHICH A VOLUNTEER IS BEING SCANNED IN AN EEG MACHINE.

". . . the subject will now start counting from one to ten. He's been instructed to start using a different language midway, and we'll be able to see the neuronal changes as they happen."

THE TECHNICIAN PRESSES THE BUTTON OF AN INTERCOM.

"Arturo? You can start now."

A TINNY VOICE IS HEARD OVER A LOUDSPEAKER. WITH EACH WORD, BRIGHT WAVES OF COLOR FLOW ACROSS THE VIDEO DISPLAY.

"Uno . . . dos . . . tres . . . cuatro . . . cinco . . ."

A BRIEF DASH OF YELLOW LIGHTS UP THE DARK AREA.

". . . six . . . seven . . . eight . . . nine . . ."

THE TECHNICIAN TURNS TO THE CAMERA.

"The yellow flash you just saw represents the effort we make whenever we decide to use a different language. Think of it as a bicycle derailleur: its sole use is to log onto a new vocabulary, and then the rest of the brain resumes its train of thought.

"Now, let's compare this with the brain of an advanced year-one Babel Syndrome victim. The only difference is—*this* patient was specifically asked to stick to a single language. And yet . . ."

ANOTHER CROSS-SECTION APPEARS ON THE SCREEN, UNDER THE HEADING *A1BS*. AS A NEW VOICE IS HEARD, A MULTITUDE OF FLASHES LIGHT UP THE DISPLAY AT IRREGULAR INTERVALS.

"Pazekw deux trois kaié:ri five nguedôz tôbawôz eight tióhton oié:ri' onze twelve nsônkaw iawônkaw . . ."

THE TECHNICIAN SWITCHES OFF THE MACHINE.

"You see? It's like a loose connection that sparks random bursts of current, whether they're required or not. Nasty biological incidents like this are not uncommon—thousands of them occur every day in our bodies. But they're usually eliminated just as fast, while this particular modification seems to be permanently ingrained, and possibly contagious. This poor guy, for instance, used to be the top translator for two of our First Nations. Now that he hardly controls his own speech patterns, not only can't he make himself understood, but natives avoid him like the plague. For people like him, the Babel Syndrome is an absolute tragedy."

From "From Bible to Babel" by Elena Limon, Executive Director of the Esperanto Promotional Association, *Maclean's*, 7 February 2002:

Of course, the Babel Syndrome wouldn't cause any problem if we'd already adopted a single world language, but that is neither here nor there. While people might think that this situation is a boon for our Association, Esperanto is in fact under the exact same threat as any other means of communication on Earth. If everyone starts speaking in tongues, the resulting noise is a hopeless jumble, not an organized mode of expression relying on a universal grammar and a simplified vocabulary. It may be a step in the right direction, but it's far from an elegant solution.

From a street interview, *Pulse News*, 18 October 2002:

"Nah, it can't be that bad. You mix anything with English, it still comes out English."

From "Emergency Measures Decreed in Chile," *Associated Press*, 1 June 2003:

SANTIAGO—As of 10:30 this morning, police officers have started rounding up Babel victims in government-sponsored Treatment Centers, where their contacts with the rest of the community will be kept to a minimum. [. . .] Official spokespersons have repeatedly stated that trained physicians are administering "reeducation courses" to counter the effects of the Syndrome, but the rumors circulating among the population are more reminiscent of Second World War concentration camps than actual clinics in charge of dispensing a therapy.

From the Babel Relief press conference, 13 January 2004:

Rei Nakamura, coordinator, Eastern Affairs: In many countries, we're already past the point of no return. Whether they exhibit any symptoms or not, bilingual couples are often separated by force—all that's required is an anonymous denunciation. Schoolchildren who fail to demonstrate an adequate grasp of the official language are taken away during recess. Interpreters, foreign correspondents, and embassy personnel are constantly harassed. Needless to say, international trade relations are becoming somewhat strained.

On average, it is said that the Syndrome affects about 0.1 percent of the Asian population, but this figure may be deceptively low. Not only are there few places that keep formal statistics on the issue, but the victims themselves tend to deny their own condition. This, by the way, is precisely why the epidemic has grown unchecked over the last few years: most people consider their lapses of language as benign, and they resent any implication that they are "sick" or in need of serious care.

From *the fifth estate*, 29 November 2004:

ANGLO-GERMANO-ITALIAN VICTIM:

"Forget it. Ich habe ganz fallen lassen l'idea di comunicare with anyone; most people gehen mit mir um als wäre ich del pianeta Marte, und ich muss von nun an schreiben tutte le cose that I have to say damit Sie es begreifen."

SUBTITLES FOR GERMAN DIALOGUE (WHERE APPROPRIATE):

I'VE COMPLETELY ABANDONED / TREAT ME AS IF I CAME / AND I MUST WRITE / TO GET MY POINT ACROSS

SUBTITLES FOR ITALIAN DIALOGUE (WHERE APPROPRIATE):

THE VERY IDEA OF COMMUNICATING / FROM THE PLANET MARS / EVERYTHING.

· · ·

From a Health and Welfare leaflet distributed to all Canadian citizens, February 2005:

If you know someone whose speech constantly shifts from one language to another, or if you are such a person yourself, you must remember the following principles.

1. STAY CALM. The Babel Syndrome cannot be transmitted through mere contact, nor can it be contracted through the consumption of ethnic food. Birth and genetic engineering are the only means through which the Syndrome can be passed on to a new generation.

2. WATCH YOUR LANGUAGE. A certain amount of bilingualism is to be expected in any conversation with a person of the opposite tongue. This situation is normal. Count how many times you or your partner have strayed from your respective languages; simple awareness of the issue often reduces the frequency of Babel-type mishaps. If the number of lapses is below the National Average, your problem is probably not irreversible.

3. CONSULT YOUR LINGUIST. If the symptoms persist, language specialists can help you adapt to your new condition. Trust them; all Babel-related information will remain confidential.

If you follow these rules, you and yours have no reason to worry. Remember: the Babel Syndrome is not a disease, it is a genetic phenomenon. It shouldn't reflect on anyone's lifestyle, beliefs, or orientation. As of yet, no one can place a value judgment on this unusual predicament.

From a *Morningside II* interview with Michelle Lambert-Clemens's parents, 11 March 2006:

Host Jon Strobotsniak: Do you still hope for your daughter's return to normalcy?

Dorothy Clemens: Of course. She's been in therapy for more than eight years, now, and I'm told she'll make real progress if we all stick to sign language for a while.

Réginald Lambert: J'ai même acheté un de ces fameux jeux de cubes dont on parle tant. Paraît que ça donne de bons résultats avec les SyBatiques.

J. S.: Words to live by. Au nom de toute l'équipe, I wish you the very best.

CUE MÚSICA-THÈME, CUT TO UPPEHÅLL PUBLICITARIO.

BUGTOWN

Ursula Pflug

Ursula Pflug was born in Tunis, Tunisia, grew up in Toronto, traveled widely, attended the University of Toronto and the Ontario College of Art. She and her partner, the interactive sculptor Doug Back, and their two children recently moved into a house in the tiny Ontario village of Norwood. Pflug has worked as a graphic designer and technician, an editorial illustrator, an art columnist for Toronto's *Now* magazine, a scriptwriting workshop instructor, and on a Hawaiian chicken farm, among other things. Pflug has published over two dozen stories in three countries, in both literary and genre publications. She was a contributing editor at the now defunct *Peterborough Review* which she "fantasizes about resuscitating as a slipstream anthology, including a Web version with hypertext fiction." She has had SF narratives produced for stage and film. A winner of the Rose Secrest prize for short literary SF for her unpublished story, "Python," Pflug has also been the recipient of numerous Ontario Arts Council and Canada Council grants in support of her writing.

"Bugtown," first published in *TransVersions*, is a sequel to "Version City," which appeared in Derryl Murphy's anthology *Senary* (1992). They are set in a surrealistic, dark, near-future Canada among the desperate or depressed survivors of everyday (and some absurd and miraculous) disasters that have changed civilization in major ways. "The prequel was written one hot summer when I lived in an almost entirely empty sublet loft on Spadina, in Toronto's Chinatown. The ideas in both stories date from a time when I believed the end of the world might be fun, and whichever of the many possible forms it might take would almost certainly come in my lifetime. This might still be the case. There's a little of Jayne in me, or at least, Jayne's job, as I worked for several years as a printer/designer/darkroom technician." This story is literary speculative fiction of a different sort than the Charles Montpetit story, sort of hip, *noir*, William Gibsonian.

The Bugtown nexus is a warehouse in the middle of a six block radius of evacuated Chinatown territory, full of shoestring insecticide operations and street vendors. Many of the Chinese left with the evacuation; Lee stayed, and some of his family and friends. It is my friend Jayne who asked me to describe them this way, more truthfully.

"Why?" I say. "Everyone trashes the Chinese."

"I know. I do it too. It's the stress. But you know it isn't really true, and there are, in any case, very few Chinese left to trash."

"It's just another way of dividing us."

"I know. But I'm afraid, too."

"Afraid of what?"

"Of Lee."

"Me too. And afraid of Bugtown. But why are we more afraid of Lee than of Max?"

"*Je ne sais pas.* But if we go, maybe we'll find out."

A lot of the buildings aren't on city plumbing anymore and raw sewage runs down the streets, just a little worse than on our side of Spadina. Walking down those streets in the middle of the night you feel like you're in the Third World; no, on another planet altogether. Mostly I can't afford to be too thin-skinned, but Bugtown always makes my head spin. Why do they call it that? Ask Max; he named it himself, the night his little shop in the shadow of the Toshiba light board under the Gardiner exploded, and his face turned purple. Yeah, same accident.

In school we used to call him Blue Max. Not anymore. The beginning and end of it all. Some people would have run when a thing like that happened, but not ol' Max. He could've got a job at the Procter and Gamble labs, a new face, a house and a wife and a debit card, but he decided to stay down here with us, our only public servant.

The city sends a big load of Roach Motels and Black Flag and boric acid and maybe even female roach pheromones on a really lucky month, but their shit don't do shit on our bugs. Maybe they're hoping if they leave us alone down here with ineffectual powders we'll come up with something on our own. Something they can swipe for themselves, take the credit, natch. Like everything they take of ours. Our music, our art, our clothes. We're like a little experiment for them, I think on the mornings when conspiracy theory looms large as the new cockroaches. Why they let us stay? An experiment in adaptation.

Give people the most adverse living conditions possible, see what they come up with.

Mostly we come up with a life. I'd take the conviviality of the monthly neighborhood dances, or the bike repair shop that doubles as a repertory cinema, any day over being locked in a box up there, staring at Superchannel, or whatever shit they've got spewing out of the box these days.

Max, one of their best and brightest, decided to stay. With us. He said it was the explosion that made him see things differently. He said it turned his head around. I'm beginning to think he meant it literally. I'm beginning to wonder what that explosion of wine-colored powder made him see.

Like I said, Max is our public servant. He took it upon himself to help us remedy the situation, having been in chemistry with me at McGill. Max, unlike me, drank like a fish even back then.

I miss him sometimes. I don't go over there much, because of what you hear. The newskids: teenagers who sell powders, working under Lee, doing street sales in the bars and cafes. Sleeptalker, one of them, a friend of mine. Found dead in an alleyway last month—murder or suicide; no one's talking, least not yet.

A good kid; we talked often and went drinking a few times together, uncovering one another's secrets early in the whisky mornings. He had a fireworks concession. Made his own, too; measuring out saltpeter and magnesium on his sales table right on Spadina. You'd think nobody'd have time for luxuries like fireworks down here on the fringes of Chinatown, but it's more like the opposite. We make lots of art. And we dance. You know what they said about Damocles.

I miss Max's blue eyes, talking about the future. He was the big idealist. What if he is, still?

Well, I've seen the future, Max, and it crawls. Like tropical breeds, bigger. Some talk of a new strain, from the radiation. You hear these things. Is it true or urban legend?—who knows; they'd be the last to tell us. Max is a chemist, not a biologist, but he does keep a lot of bugs over there, in little aquariums, feeds them different colored powders. They're beautiful, those powders, of every imaginable hue, and once every month or so a new one winds up on the street. The newskids who sell say it doubles as a drug, paint it on their skin, wait for it to come on, dance when it does. Never seen anything like those dances. People say, sometimes, at the end, they start fires and climb into them. Sometimes at the end there are dead; not just the burnt corpses, so lacking in dignity, but worse still, arteries slashed open with razor blades. Skin so young desecrated; I only saw it once, now I don't look anymore, let others gather round staring when the ambulance circles.

What makes them do it? Or is it done to them? Not looking, I have no proof, no evidence, unlike the tiny greasy footprints on my kitchen counter, mornings I didn't scrub out the night's chicken pan.

Procter and Gamble canceled Max's job offer when they found out the explosion made him crazy. It gave him visions of the chemical chains for better powders, he said. Powders that worked. These things happen, he said, citing the famous case of the benzene ring. Maybe his idealism just changed, like his face, into something unrecognizable. Blue Max, newly Max Maroon, set up his new shop in an abandoned building on Huron Street, started mixing up batches. People don't go around there much; they say the air is so full of dust when Max is in production you get wired just walking down the street.

It was Tuesday night, I was out of powder; the street showed no sign of any sellers and so I was on my way to Max's shop, Jayne in tow. She wouldn't go there alone, she'd said. Didn't know Max like I did.

Tanya the newsgirl was sitting on a bench outside Max's building. You could tell they were working on Blue again, because in the glow of the sodium lamps blue dust was swirling out of the open windows, covering everything. Tanya sat with her eyes closed, her lips parted, a fine blue coating covering her skin, her clothing, every inch of her. Max in full production. Why didn't he let her in, I wondered? Not that she needed to go in. She had all she wanted here. Crazy Max must be more strung out than anyone. Maybe he knew she was wired by now, and he wouldn't let her deal anymore,'cause there wasn't any profit in it for him. It meant she might be about to explode.

Except that Max doesn't deal, Lee does. Public sentiment runs hot and cold against Lee; people blame him for the news-kids' deaths but they continue to buy from him because Max's powders are the best, the only ones that really work. I don't like the racist comments I hear about Lee, even when I hear them coming out of my own mouth, but the truth is down here everybody gets called names: for their race, their gender, whatever they happen to be selling. Like the school yard: if you come home with anything less than a bloody nose you figure you're still ahead of the game.

I ran a finger through the dust on Tanya's nose. She didn't even blink. "Is she alive?" Jayne asked, in that sardonic way she has. We rang the intercom and someone buzzed us in.

In the hall leading to Max's shop a Chinese woman had a little booth selling last week's Orange. Cut rate: it probably had only had a few days left in it. Jayne paused, but I wanted the good stuff.

"Wait," Jayne said. "She's selling books, too."

"Books?"

She was, too. Laid out on the table beside the little twist-tied baggies of Orange were poetry chapbooks, a xeroxed copy of Kafka's "Metamorphosis" and several copies of a story collection, entitled "Cockroach Culture."

"Art out of life," Jayne said, picking one up. "It seems so real."

"Your posters are like that, too," I said, complimenting her on them as I could never stop myself from doing. Jayne designed and printed posters for community dances; she ran an old offset in her loft. She had an orphaned laser printer too that still ran but said she preferred the Gestetner; the print quality was warmer, like vinyl sound. She had an uncanny eye for color; I used to wonder where she got it, even worry; I knew she'd used more than once.

"Thanks," she said. "They're Cockroach Culture, too. Here's to it; I like it better than the old one. Maybe if I have any money left I'll get it on the way out. It's not too expensive."

"Printed on recycled stock."

"Homemade recycled stock at that; only affordable paper still extant. I know; it's my business."

"Speaking of business. . . ."

We abandoned our browsing to visit Max. No one came to our knocking and the shop door was locked.

On the way back down the hall Jayne said, "You want to hear my secret fantasy?"

"I don't know. Don't you think you want to keep it to yourself?"

"I'll tell you. I'd be Max's girlfriend, lover, whatever. I could be strung out forever. I'd never run out. I could stay here like a pig in shit. Max is the big time, isn't he?"

"Jayne, you scare me. If you got strung out you'd end up on the beach, cutting up your arms at some bonfire party."

"That's never been proven. Hey, looks like I get to buy my anthology after all."

We each bought a baggy of Orange from the vendor and Jayne bought the book, too. "You buzzed us in?" she asked.

The woman pointed at the buttons on the wall behind her. "I do door for Max."

"Oh, and he has an intercom in his room too and you tell him who it is?"

"Yes."

"He must trust you a real lot."

"I'm Lee's sister."

"That explains it then," Jayne said wryly. "By the way, you know there's a newsgirl sitting on the street bench? Only she isn't doing much selling."

The woman sighed and shook her head. "Tanya. I've been telling her for days to go home, get some sleep."

On the way down the stairs Jayne read to me:

"It is the disfigured face that heals us, the monster who kills our monsters for us, those we have created. Lee. I never told the truth about him, never told the truth about Chinatown. We look down on those who carry our pain for us, who wear the face we hide from the world. We have always done this."

"Strong stuff."

"It's true, isn't it?"

Too true, I thought. Like me when I don't think about the butcher at the abattoir, every time I take a bite of meat. Just so: we also don't think of razors and bonfires every time we buy powder that works. Max knows this too; it's why Lee sells for him, wholesaling to kids. To hide our own part in the newskids' pain we prefer to make racist remarks. But it's not because Lee is Chinese, but because of what he does, that we owe him. It is this debt which is too painful to acknowledge. Not acknowledging it, Jayne and I parted ways to our separate apartments to kill bugs, each of us quite alone.

• • •

Predictably, the Orange lasted all of two days. Once again, I walk
those brown steps, his steps. Up, up, up: looking for Jayne who
hasn't answered her phone in two days; not looking for Tanya,
'cause I know where she is. She's the known quantity, the one I
can't retrieve. It's Jayne who stands on the border, has stepped
across it once or twice, always come back. So far.

At the beginning I used to work with Max: factory help,
powder production. And then I got tired. Tired of the sleepless
nights, the beer, the coffee, the endless low-paid drudgery up
and down those dusty stairs of my Chinatown youth. It was only
two years ago but somehow it always feels I left my youth behind, there, with that job. When the kids started to get hurt I
quit, figuring it was the least I could do.

But I still bought powders.

Max is crazy like they all say to let those kids slash themselves, or have it done, as some say, when they get too greedy,
but nobody else is doing anything about the bugs. For the salvation we will not attempt ourselves there is always a price.

Carry a flashlight up the stairs, in case of one of the frequent
power outages. Look for my face in Max's own. Dream a new
game.

Green. Green of trees, not of powders. Sleeptalker, listener.
I dreamed of him last night. He spoke to me, saying, "Don't kill
them, let them live." When I woke I said, in answer, "It's easy
to be a Buddhist when you're not talking about foot-longs, and
I don't mean hot dogs."

Not foot-long yet. But who knows what tomorrow will
bring?

In my dream he wore ratty jeans and long, thin brown hair,
just like in real life, just like in old photographs of us when we
were in high school. Nobody listened to us then when we said
the apocalypse was near and it looks like we were right.

Who is it we in turn aren't listening to now? Not forty yet,
I still have a chance to do something. Some small thing. Save
one life.

Tanya. I can mark the time by her colors; the layers of powder
nicked away on her cheek where a candy wrapper or a dry leaf
has blown against her immobile face.

I looked at her for a moment and went on, to the twenty-
four-hour Mr. Submarine on Spadina. I bought a large assorted

which I somehow knew, don't know how, was the kind she liked. And a large bottle of Evian, although I'm sure she would have preferred Pepsi. I tried to give it to her but her hands remained clasped in her lap and so I set it down on the bench beside her. A shadow of a smile.

Rich blue and green layered in the folds of her clothing, iridescent peacock colors. Judging by the layers of color she hadn't been home for a bath in-between, had sat here all week.

The green a pale green; a Day-Glow with white in it. I'm starting to sound like Jayne, like colors matter. Just as colors. I'd bought extra and stopped by her place on my way home. She was printing; the new posters were blue and orange, colors lush and familiar.

"I hope you feel good cutting those poor kids' arms and legs to ribbons," I said. "So when's the dance?"

"Saturday. You have such a perspective, Jack. So hip, so new, so now. It hasn't been proven. Maybe doing that is just what they do, nothing to do with the powders. How come we aren't doing it, is what I want to know? Not many reasons not to. The way I figure it, the whole ship is gonna be sunk any time now. So we might as well have fun. Cockroach Culture: the last people's culture. It gives a whole new meaning to the words 'save the last dance for me.' "

"Are the colors what I think they are?"

"Yes, as you probably guessed I'm using bug powders. Can't get hide nor hair of printer's ink anymore, and I thought I'd give it a try. The last couple of days of a powder run are never any good anyway, so everyone's got these little twist-tie baggies of colors lying around; happy to unload 'em to me for a song. Cheaper than printer's ink, in fact." She pushed the hair out of her face.

"So that's where you've been the last couple of days, is shopping for colors."

"Not that it's any of your business. Also I'm feeling very ecologically correct as they're water-based. The colors might fade but who cares: this world will be gone by then."

"But at least you'll have left a slightly cleaner water table behind for the use of the survivors."

"Exclusively animal and vegetable."

"One would hope."

"No kidding, Jack."

Watching a really proficient woman work always gets my gonads going so after a while I asked her if she wanted to go out for a few beers when she was done.

"Sure," she said, "but it's Tanya you should be asking out."

"Why?"

"She loves you."

"How d'you know?"

"She told me."

"Well, I like Tanya, Jayne, but she's trouble. She's an addict and you just have fantasies."

"Not for long."

"What are you waiting for?"

"Waiting to know."

"Know what?"

"Tell you sometime, later, not now."

While Jayne washed up and looked for her windbreaker I went and stood at the window. It was so dusty it was almost impossible to see out, but on the ledge stood three printed cards, side by side. Picture divided from caption by a thin dotted line: sun, sky, grass. Things we don't see much of around here. They were beautiful and the fact of their existence, the only decor in Jayne's completely functional shop and living space seemed to speak of a longing and vulnerability I never otherwise saw her betray. I felt like I'd uncovered a secret, although it wasn't anything she'd tried to hide. I turned the cards over; on the back was the English word for each picture, and beside it the Chinese ideogram. They were teaching cards, and yet the purpose she had put them to was quite different.

I could have razzed her about it, but didn't; no one wants their shrines desecrated, especially when they only have such thin lonely ones. Let her show me that side of herself when she was ready, if ever.

We went to the last Chinese grocery and bought homemade beer from under the counter, brown-bagged it Montreal-style, wandering the alleyways. There were stars. It was very romantic.

"Hey Jack," she said, "I'll read to you out of this story collection. It's really awesome."

"Oh, right. That again. So read on: the last bit gave me enough to think about for a week."

"I have a new friend now; someone like Jayne, someone like Tanya. A friendship that makes me feel able to complete these

stories I abandoned so many years ago for another kind of life. His name is Jack.

"We will squander our youth in the dark nights of the city, counting stars, like Max and I did that one night. Like holes in space, he said, space itself like the front of the little fifties bar in the booze can we went to: a sheet of metal with holes drilled in it, letting in tiny points of light like starlight from the light bulb behind it.

"The heavens a vast sheet of metal with drilled holes; if we ripped it away we'd find huge fluorescent tubes, or quartz halogen. Anyway a light too bright; it would make everything look white. This is why the holes are so tiny; it's only a small amount of light we can stand. Surely we need a new metaphor for the sky; it's about time we stopped talking about diamonds scattered on black velvet.

"There is a fable about loving too much, but I can't quite remember what it is. My first thought is Narcissus, looking into a still pond surrounded by green-stemmed white flowers, delicate and strong.

"And yet was that a story about love or self-obsession? Is that what I'm doing here, writing like this? Perhaps it is a story that needs to be written.

"Up up the dark wooden stairs to the sooty loft apartment where he worked. At a table red candles in old pewter sticks and an open chemistry book.

"Out his back window I looked out at the few mature hardwoods and felt communion with them, more intensely than I do in the country. Because of the contrast; because there are less of them. Because I haven't been to the country in years. I wonder if it's still there?"

Jayne shut the book, put it in the back pocket of her jeans, looked at me, ironic and meaningful.

"He was writing about us," I said, "if the author's a he."

"What else is there to write about?" Jayne asked.

"Let's go home." I wanted to go to her place but huffily figured I wouldn't suggest it; she'd upset me with her talk of fantasizing about Max, her nonsense about Tanya loving me. Was it possible?

On our way we passed her, still sitting under the light. The sandwich I was glad to see was half eaten and neatly wrapped in several layers on the bench beside her, where the bugs couldn't get at it.

Gutter bugs, in summer.

Saturday afternoon. Every day I've brought Tanya a sandwich and water, but only today have I needed to go up the stairs. Max in his visor, working; Lee sitting at the table, smoking, reading a Chinese newspaper I'll never be able to understand, not in my whole life. Unless I ask him. Like Jayne's shop, too, the surface of the table littered with full ashtrays, empty styrofoam cups, looped brown rings of coffee. Yellow dust coating everything: the lab, the countertops, the empty take-out food containers. I put my money on the table.

"Don't you guys feel bad?" I asked.

"Feel bad about what, Jack?" Max asked in that convivial way I was always so fond of in college. The way it could brighten a day.

Lee looked up from his paper, smiled hello.

"About the newskids, about Sleeptalker?"

"You don't buy from them anymore, Jack," Max said, "How come? You've come straight to the factory every time this month. You better have a good reason; we don't let everyone in here, you know. It's only 'cause we're old pals."

Lee swung his legs, looking decidedly collegiate and unsinister. Not saying anything.

"It's cheaper," I lied.

"True, true."

Not saying: because I can't look at their hands anymore. Because I stay away from abattoirs. Because I was afraid of both of you.

Because people died.

Lee got up and went to a shelf, handed me a newly bagged package of Yellow. "It's the first one with a name, not just a number," he said.

"What's it called?"

"Perilous Yellow," he said, as though that was very funny. I wondered how fast I could leave.

"About the other question," Max said.

I was already at the door, wishing I hadn't opened my mouth. "Yeah?"

"There's an answer to that question, but this isn't the day you get it."

I turned back, hesitantly. "When is?"

"The day you stop buying for good."

I left, my boots resounding on the dusty stairs. I could hear them laughing behind me.

The ventilator open as always and yellow dust swirling out, glowing like a cloud of gnats under the streetlight. She sat there, waiting for the Yellow to coat her eyelids, enter her bloodstream through the skin. Like yellow eye-shadow.

I heard stapling and turned; Jayne was on the corner of Spadina, putting up her new posters. The stapling sounded angry.

"Jayne, hi."

"I didn't think much at the time, (bang) Jack, but you really got me mad. Who (bang) are you (bang) to talk about what I do? You support the deaths as much as I do, (bang) by supporting the industry. You could just let them live."

"That's what he said."

"Who?"

"Sleeptalker."

"Now you're dreaming about him. That's a beginning, I suppose."

"What do you mean?"

"Listen, I'll read. The book's by Sleeptalker, as you so obviously didn't notice. It's the details that count, Jack, the details. The details will save you."

"I didn't want to check the author's name at the time. I liked the anonymity of someone writing about me, someone I didn't know. But ever since then I've been wondering. I'd walk the street and everyone I saw, I'd wonder. I thought one day I'd find out, one day I'd talk to them about their stories, the ones I'm in."

"Too late. He's dead."

"Speaking still in dreams."

"And in stories he left behind."

"I wonder if he knew he'd die? If he wrote it to leave behind a part of himself?"

"Isn't that why anyone writes?"

"I wonder what he knew, that they killed him for?"

"Max, or Lee, or neither? Maybe he killed himself."

"I don't know."

"You should think about it. Listen, though. There's a bit about Chinatown. I haven't read it yet." Jayne took the book out of her pocket and opened it. I sat on the curb beside her and read over her shoulder. She turned the rough brown pages, always politely asking first to see if I was ready.

Before the evacuation when there were more of them, more of us, more people, aside from the young ones who were our friends and made us ginger tea when we had colds, the Chinese were inscrutable as the old cliche goes; divided from us by language and culture, seemingly having no interest in getting to know us better or else just busy with their lives. They said hello when we came into their restaurants, taking great pleasure as always in their food: mu shew pork and garlic egg-plant.

I miss them, now that they're gone, miss the stores I loved, the toys, especially the mechanical metal chicken laying eggs, and the picture cards. The strangeness of an alphabet we could never hope to learn, it's form more like painting, like pictures than like words; this seemed to intimate something we did not have and by nearness would hope to absorb through osmosis. Also the imagery, not drawn in a traditional Chinese style at all: moons and dogs and flowers, sun, grass, sky, window; the western-style graphics were simple and beautiful and clear and while ostensibly to teach Chinese children or adults for that matter, English, to us they had another purpose. We took them home and shuffled them like oracles, laid them out in neat rows on shelves or windowsills: sun, sky, window; their images resonating with one another. Echo, palpation, vibration: they would assume a delphic aspect; like tarot cards from another planet we would hope to soak up some of the mystery of a different culture and learn about them and also as always, hoping to learn in the mirror of another something about ourselves.

As we sat reading the bugs came and began trying to eat the sweat from our sneakers; we moved up the block, to sit protected at Tanya's feet. I noticed someone had been there before us; at her feet lay a bunch of plastic paper-white narcissi, now turned into yellow daffodils, even the stems, the leaves.

Jayne said, "I didn't know anyone else did that."

"What?"

"The picture cards, as a tarot deck. I thought I was the only one."

"He knew so much about us," I said.

"He was one of us," she said, "how could he not?"

"Who will tell our stories now?"

"Will we stop killing them?" Jayne asked.

"I don't know. We have to see first."

"See what?"

"What happens to Tanya."

"It's all a circle, don't you see?"

"We're not immune."

"What does it matter—if he killed himself, if he was murdered. Either way it could happen to us. Don't you feel like suiciding, living as we do?"

"No sign of razor marks on Tanya's arms yet. Good-bye Tanya, I'll be by tomorrow." I kissed her on the forehead. Jayne snickered.

We walked. Jayne said, "I never believed the colors were so bad. I believed, secretly, the way you believe things when you're a child, that they were a doorway. The powders would show you a different way to live. It was the contrast that made them suicidal. Coming down they'd see this," she pointed at the sluggish contents of someone's toilet rising from a storm sewer, "and the pain of it, compared to the beauty they'd experienced, was what made them do it."

Jayne in her scraggly brown hair and dirty ink-stained coveralls made me so hot I barely heard what she said but I knew that was unfair and tried hard to concentrate.

"Why does Sleeptalker tell us not to kill them?" I asked, knowing it was important.

"Because it's not our work."

I realized she was leading me toward the dance hall, in the old temple on Cecil.

We went in, while Jayne read:

"I dreamed we moved to the islands in the harbor. I saw a houseboat whose top was made of a camper/trailer and something else beneath the sleeper overhang; a small greenhouse perhaps. A young woman in iridescent blue and purple clothes steered the boat down the lagoon, and suddenly I realized it was Tanya."

At the dance Max was there, and Lee. All our friends; most of the newskids. No Sleeptalker. No Tanya.

I watched how Max and Lee stayed separate, giving the lie

to the camaraderie I'd witnessed in the factory. I watched how in their glances people honored one and hated another, and thought: but doesn't everyone know they are one and the same?

Can't they see?

Jayne and I stayed away from the gossip and the rumors, dancing only with one another, resting on the stage to read from Sleeptalker's book. It was as though we had new eyes. I looked out the window at the full moon and worried.

It rained sporadically throughout the night. I worried about Tanya, thought often I should go back and get her, save the one life. But then Jayne was stroking my hair and whispering sweet nothings. As she said, there's no proof. Am I responsible for another's life, even one who seeks her own undoing? I guess a part of me wanted to see. But I still felt bad.

We had a fun night. Jayne's right: Cockroach Culture is better than the one that went before. Except for the cockroaches. The fires. The razor blades. The deaths; among them, rumored or real, one true one, one I called friend.

But that's not much, really, is it? Compared to everything else, I mean.

After the dance, in the bits of sleep arranged like small still ponds in our first sweet night of lovemaking, I dreamed of Sleeptalker again.

His story was in the dream too, and the picture of Tanya it had conjured in my mind. And Sleeptalker spoke again, over my shoulder as I read his words.

This is the woman to ask about how to live.

It's always after a dance they do it, people say; always after it rains, after a full moon, after a new color hits the streets.

We'd had all four.

It was very early morning when I got up, to go to Chinatown, alone.

Tanya wasn't on her bench.

On a hunch I took the ferry to the island. I went to Snake Island first, I don't know why. Maybe because I used to go there when I was young, camp and party with my friends all night long.

On a path I found a bunch of plastic flowers, tied in string, rain washed and white again. I continued walking until I came to a campsite in a clearing. Tanya sat, drying her sneakers on two sticks over a fire. The fire worried me, but she looked quite sane. I tried for the jocular approach.

"You're safe around fires now?"

"Always have been, Jack. It was your fear that prevented you from seeing me."

"These yours?" I offered her the flowers.

"Oh, thanks, I thought I'd lost those."

"Jayne said it was a circle. Sleeptalker's stories, Max, Lee, the bugs. Does he talk in your dreams, too?"

"He talks to me all the time, not just in my dreams. You can do it too; you just have to listen."

"I guess. You know, he gave me a homemade Roman candle once. We set it off together, four in the morning, middle of Spadina."

"I know."

"You do?"

"Yeah. And you said: ''Sleeptalker, you're the only one I know who can make the stars bloom.'' ''

"I said that?"

"He told me. He loved you, Jack. A better line than you usually come up with. Like something he might've said. Or written. So why you here, Jack?"

"To bring you your sandwich."

She smiled and took it, went back to toasting her shoes. I noticed she'd finally bathed, and only a few glints of color remained in her blond hair.

"It'll taste better than those."

She smiled, reluctantly examined the sandwich. "There's meat in it."

"Yes."

She took a bite. "We can never be blame-free, no matter how much we do. But we still have to leave."

"To come here?"

"Leave in our heads. Leaving physically is good, too. I won't be able to stay; I was just getting sick of raw sewage. The boat isn't finished yet; we all take time off newsing to come down here and work on it. Sleeptalker says that as long as we kill the bugs we're doing their work. The people who made it this way. Who made the bugs grow, with their poisons. It's not because of the powders that teenagers kill themselves, but because of the world. Why are any of us still alive? Those kids' deaths are just a way to make us feel guilty, immobilize us. The powders are the only thing we have. Too bad it's also a way for them to get us to clean up their mess."

"So?"

"So that's the fable about the people who love too much."

"What?" I took a bite of her sandwich, thinking it really was time to be a vegetarian again. Although it tasted good.

"Us. We clean up after them, with our thoughts, with our guilt, with our powders, even our deaths, our deaths most of all. Loving even them, forgiving even them. They'll make us do it forever. Too much love."

"So what should we do?"

"One thing at a time." She led me to a clearing in the trees. Sleeptalker hadn't seen a place like this, for years before he died.

Through the stands of birch I saw a houseboat, parked in the lagoon. It was built entirely out of junk, had a container garden and a satellite dish on the roof.

"Not only that," she said.

"Not only?"

"There's no bugs. We shouldn't kill them, because they're alive like we are, but we shouldn't have to live with them either."

"Then what should we do?"

"Exodus."

"Where to?"

"We'll think of it along the way. We'll build it along the way. We have his stories now to show us the way."

"Sometimes I think I'm going crazy."

Tanya laughed, reaching as though across dream space to stroke my cheek with fingers that felt unusually warm. "Does it matter? How can dreams be any less reliable a guide than anything else? Than them? Desire or so-called reality; which will you choose?"

"Why couldn't they just do it quietly, jump in front of a subway or something, like a normal person?" Fires and razor blades made me more than squeamish.

"When's the last time you saw a subway, Jack?"

"True. But even still."

"Even still if you're going out why not go out burning?"

"I'd never thought of it that way." She was the first person I'd heard speak with any kind of inner authority for years. It was compelling, but I worried; perhaps all crazy people did that. And yet we heard the same voice, dreamed the same dreams. It filled a longing so old I'd no longer known I'd once had it. Till she'd reminded me: beautiful, scary Tanya. "I really do think I love you, Tanya." I did, too. It was almost frightening; she was so weird.

"It's about fuckin' time."

She hugged me and a little color passed from her hair to mine. I waited in vain for the buzz but it was hard to tell, what with standing in a sun-dappled glade with a beautiful, if possibly demented, woman, a vision of the future parked in the lagoon.

"Actually," she said, licking my lip, "the powders don't do anything."

"Now what?" I sounded so smart this morning but Tanya didn't seem to mind.

"It's a metaphor."

"Oh, of course."

"It's the last story. You'll understand when you read it."

"Maybe they work on other people, just not on you."

"Not on me, not on Sleeptalker. You're getting warmer, Jack."

I raised my hands up to touch my face, to wonder at skin that had been cold, it seemed, for years. She was right.

THE HISTORY OF PHOTOGRAPHY

Derryl Murphy

Derryl Murphy, born in Nova Scotia in 1963, was raised (and lives) in Edmonton, Alberta. He has worked as a naturalist, daily newspaper photographer, camera salesman, commercial photographer, and government photo clerk. Currently he is writing, shooting for seven stock photo agencies around the world, and "topping that up with a part-time job." His first brush with SF as a (near) pro came when he edited and published an impressive anthology of original Canadian SF, *Senary: The Journal of Fantastic Literature,* in the early 1990s. It was announced as the first of a serial, but no further volumes appeared. His fiction appeared in *Tesseracts 4* and his second published story, "Body Solar" (*On Spec,* Winter 93), was nominated for the Aurora Award in 1994, as was his SF review column for the *Edmonton Journal.* He has since been published in *TransVersions* #5, *On Spec, Tesseracts 6, Time Machines: The Best Time Travel Stories Ever Written,* and in *Arrowdreams.*

"The History of Photography" is another selection from the special SF issue of *Prairie Fire.* It is a nostalgic, and at the same time ironic, look at a near-future disaster scenario in a peculiarly gentle and engaging tone and style. "This story came about the day after Ansel Adams died, when I was still rather... unformed as a writer. I sat down and wrote a maudlin piece about a photographer who uses the last film on Earth, then steps off a building out of anguish. Overwrought, overdone, it resembles 'The History of Photography' only as a *camera obscura* resembles a large format camera. The resolution of view was not yet there. Thankfully, Skeet and Toolis turned down [for *Tesseracts*] yet another generation of the story, giving me the chance to go back at it one more time, which is when I latched onto the aperture-numbers-as-chapters motif, and more importantly when I discovered the joys of subtlety."

1

There are many people who think that the camera is a relatively new device in mankind's long list of inventions. They're wrong. While photography itself is fairly new, the camera as a concept is an old and venerable idea.

Some nomads in the Middle East and Northern Africa probably understood the concept. Imagine sitting in a dark tent in the middle of a hot and sunny day, with a tiny hole in the fabric on one wall of the tent. The hole would act a bit like a lens, casting a faint inverted image on the inside of the opposite wall of their tent.

We in the West, however, have our caucasiocentric point of view. So to us the camera obscura was a revelation from around the time of the Renaissance.

The idea behind the device was understood in Europe as early as the year 1435, and by 1525 people were using it as an aid for portraiture. Paintings and drawings of course, not yet photography.

For those who don't know what the camera obscura is, think of a basic automatic single lens reflex (SLR) camera. If you understand that without the prism the image would be upside down and backwards, then you already have a good grasp.

Now imagine, instead of a complex electronic machine all you have is a box. At one end of the box in the exact center of its face, rather than a lens you have a pinhole. Light that shines through the pinhole is turned upside down and backwards, shining an inverted image on the opposite end.

Take this simple box and add to it a knowledge of optics. A lens in place of the pinhole, and a piece of ground glass at the opposite end. Put a piece of tracing paper on the ground glass and begin to draw. A recipe for a near-flawless portrait or landscape.

There were other tools as well, but it was primarily the camera obscura that paved the way for photography.

1.4

The morning is cool, a slight breeze blowing through the trees, rustling leaves and waving small branches. Dew sits heavy on the grass, waiting for the first glint of the sun's rays to light up in crystalline brilliance.

I set down my pack, leaning it against a rock beside the stream that passes by. For a moment my exhausted breathing and the rush of blood in my head block out the sound of both the water and the breeze. But as I rest, sitting on the same rock, my own personal noises begin to fade and nature's take over.

I sit and listen, eyes closed, letting the sound form wave after wave that flow over me. I remember as a child, the first time that it struck me that Thornton W. Burgess was right, and that brooks really do babble. A delightful surprise, and one that continues to please me.

But eventually my time of meditation comes to an end. My watch has beeped; a half hour to get things set up.

First I undo the straps on the side of my pack, releasing my tripod. It's a Gitzo, forty-five years old and far better than any of that fibrecore or aluminum crap that is your only choice today. Sturdy but lightweight, when compacted it stands only a bit higher than my knees, but I can extend it to taller than I stand if the need is there. Not that I ever do.

The head of the tripod is not as old. Too many moving parts will wear out over time. Of course, there's nothing to compare with what I used to be able to buy, so I had a friend machine one for me. It has separate handles for all three planes of movement, and each one locks tighter than anything I've seen since I was just starting out. It cost a pretty penny, but I was able to cover it with money from the insurance when my wife passed away ten years ago.

The second I walked into this dimly lit clearing a portion of my mind was at work, deciding what would be best to photograph. Now I have to spend a moment working it out in more detail.

There is a close-up shot I think I'll do, some leaves caught in a small whirlpool at the edge of the stream, but that can wait. Rather, I think I'll do the edge of the meadow as it leads into the forest, with the creek on the right. The sun will come up on my left.

I place the tripod in roughly the place I want it, then go back and unzip my pack. Inside is a smaller bag with some water and food, weather supplies and extra clothing, but only in case I get stuck up here.

I pull that bag out of the way and start sorting out my equipment. Camera, one film holder, two lenses, polarizing filters, light meter, dark cloth, focusing loupe, air release, and change bag. Also a small tool kit that holds some jeweler's screwdrivers, a tape measure, duct tape, batteries for the meter, and a compass.

I take the camera out first. I attach the tripod plate to it and settle it onto the tripod, then open it up. It squeaks a bit, but that's only the bolts, and those I can replace. The rest of the camera is made of fine cherry wood, and I've kept it in the best shape possible.

The leather bellows extend easily, but those were replaced just five years ago. The last set were just about ready to rot away before I found a leather craftsman who was willing to make me a set to order. This was also expensive, but I don't have to use duct tape to cover the holes anymore.

Then I unwrap the lens and mount it on the front of the camera. I decide to use the 300mm, my oldest lens. I've had it for more than fifty years, and I bought it used. It's a Zeiss, aperture f4.5, and sharp as tacks from corner to corner.

The 300 will give me a slightly wide field of view. I can use it in this instance to get points of focus in both the foreground and the background.

The polarizer goes on the lens, as even this early in the day the sun will be too harsh. Then I get my loupe and dark cloth and proceed to set my angle and focus.

2

There is evidence that part of the photographic process had been discovered as early as 1816. In that year Nicephore Niépce wrote to his brother that he had used a box with a lens to capture an image in which "the background . . . is black, and the objects white, that is, lighter than the background." This sounds a lot like what a negative would look like.

Unfortunately, he could not figure out a way to transform this into a positive image. The negative in all likelihood did not last all that long, and so what could have been the first photograph ever is lost in the mists of time.

Over the next few years, however, Niépce worked on perfecting his processes. He developed a system to reproduce engravings using photographic principles, and in 1827 took a picture entitled *View from his Window at Le Gras*, a muddied heliograph, as he called the process.

That may have also been the year he photographed *Set Table*, a much clearer image of some kitchen objects on a table. One lone print exists, the glass negative having mysteriously disappeared from the collection it had once belonged to.

1827 was also the year that Niépce visited with Louis Jacques Mandé Daguerre, a painter who had become interested in using photography through his use of the camera obscura in his paintings. The two became partners, but Niépce died four years into a ten-year contract.

Over the next while Daguerre perfected his method. I remember as a child seeing a daguerreotype in my great-grandmother's house, a picture of her father when he was a child. The image was very obviously a photograph, but it was on a shiny old piece of metal.

It, along with almost every other of its type in the world, faded as our atmosphere was systematically fouled. A few museums still have some preserved in very controlled conditions.

2.8

Everything is in focus, the film holder is in the camera and the dark slide is out. I sit and wait for the sun to make its appearance.

There aren't many places left where you can see the sun as it rises. Its light is choked and sucked away by the black filth that inhabits the air we breathe.

Even here I'm not safe. By midafternoon I'll have to don my rebreather, filtering out the particles that drift up the valley as the day warms and as people in the sprawling city below increase their energy consumption.

But now the sun is almost up. I put skin cream on and pull my goggles over my eyes and move over to the camera.

Bulb release in hand, I watch and wait. When I think the light looks right, I quickly remove my goggles for a peek. Things look perfect.

The dew drops sparkle gloriously, and a mist is hovering as the water is burned off by the sun. The shutter clicks open for that 1/4 second, and a moment in time is frozen.

4

I can only remember with frustration the time when I had more types of film to choose from than I could ever hope to use. Like most professionals not involved in wedding or portrait photography, I shot about 90 percent of my work on transparency, or slide, film.

When I still shot in multiple formats my photos were taken on any one of about ten different films, depending on the size and the speed I required. In 35mm I generally chose between four or five different films, in medium format three, and in large format I used two or three films.

As things changed in the field of photography my choice of films began to narrow. The incredible advances made in film technology were soon mirrored and then outstripped by leaps forward in other areas, mainly digital innovations.

Combined with all the problems in the world, I soon found my choices narrowed down to just one. Fuji stopped making any film whatsoever more than a decade ago, and Kodak only made 8×10 transparency film on special order starting about the same time. At great expense to myself, I might add.

So all of my shooting since then had been done with a type of Ektachrome on large format, which I guess I haven't really minded. For many years I had told myself I would concentrate on the big camera, and it took this to finally get me to mothball my Nikon and Hasselblad equipment.

Also, I've done my own developing for more than twenty years, as photo labs of any sort that survived the crash were outmoded soon afterward. But that's okay; I feel in control, something I never did when turning my work over to someone else.

5.6

Although photography started out as an attempt to picture things more perfectly, over time people began to see that everything is relative. Each photograph is strictly an *interpretation* of the event that was witnessed by the photographer.

In photography, nothing is true. No, let me correct that statement; nothing *was* true. At the end of the twentieth century there were many types of film available, and each one responded to the influence of light in a different fashion.

The speed of the film, or how sensitive it was to light, was a major factor in how your pictures turned out. But beyond that, there were all sorts of factors. The same scene and the same light would render a dozen slightly different colors with a dozen different color films.

Black and white could be could made to differ in contrast, even in the same film. And the latitude that most black and white films allowed gave photographers the freedom to do almost whatever they wanted with their pictures.

Maybe I'm being too technical here. Back in those days, I was in my late twenties, early thirties. The photographic community where I lived was, for the most part, quite static, but there were people who continued to push their photography forward, whether they considered it a craft or an art.

One photographer I knew shot almost exclusively with black and white infrared film. Now, if she and I had gone out and taken pictures of the same subject, restricting ourselves to the same equipment and the same point of view, you would still have wildly different looks at the same subject.

But put someone with a different color film into our group, and he and I would still have images that differed. Mine, on a Fuji film, would appear slightly green, compared to his Kodachrome (or whatever), which would look slightly red.

But any image in and of itself would be a completely valid interpretation of the event as we saw it. Without comparing my picture to anything else, you would more than likely not be able to tell that it had any color shift at all.

Depending on what I wanted to say, I chose my film accordingly. I doubt that most people noticed, but many of my peers did. To me, that's all that mattered.

8

It wasn't long before the search for color began. Although most people didn't seem to mind the monochrome of the daguerreotype and other processes, the ever inquisitive minds of those at the forefront of photography realized that their efforts at recreating what they saw in the physical world were still incomplete.

Early attempts to capture the spectrum were fruitless, at least for the most part. In the early 1850s one gentleman in New York state claimed that he had managed to produce an image containing the true colors of its subject. Many people, including Samuel F. B. Morse, examined these photographs and confirmed that his claim was an honest one.

Unfortunately, the success could not be duplicated, and the profession went on with its black and white ways. The man who had created the images published a confused and rambling piece about the process some six years later, but it explained nothing of consequence.

Other attempts were made over the rest of the nineteenth century, some more successful than others. By the turn of the century, many different methods of achieving color had been made available. One method which attained a certain amount of popularity for some years was the autochrome, which Steichen and Stieglitz used in a gallery display at the turn of the century.

But in 1935 Kodachrome was introduced as a motion-picture film, and two years later as a 35mm still film. Then just after World War II color negative films were introduced.

Kodak had created a boom of amateurs when they had made photography simple some fifty years before. The boom exploded when color film became readily available for the masses.

11

Having replaced the dark slide, I pull the holder out and carry the tripod and camera over to near the creek. Halfway there I have to stop and put it down. I'm not as young as I once was, and my back and arms ache with the effort.

The picture can wait a few moments. I go and sit down beside the water, gazing at the bottom. After a few moments a small trout swims tentatively by. Even through the ripples I can see the cataracts that cloud its eyes, the cancerous lumps that form a crazy stairway down its back.

A water beetle swims by, and the fish lunges desperately as it senses the disturbance. The beetle almost escapes, but a quick thrash to the right and the trout has the beetle's backside in its mouth. A lot of energy expended for a small meal.

Anywhere in the world, the drama I just watched would have sold well on the nets. But I just can't convince myself that it would really be photography.

16

The list of great photographers is long. History would not be what it is if we didn't have photography. I could go into a litany of what photography has done for the world, but that doesn't feel right for me. I can state some of my personal favorites, though, and not risk the image of jingoism.

Ansel Adams. I had just embarked on my career when he died, a day that I cried; Dorothea Lange, whose sensitivity to the plights of those in the Depression inspired many photographers when we suffered the crash of '07; Irving Penn, whose approach to commercial photography was so unique, so inspired, that he turned hucksterism into art; Alfred Stieglitz, who in spite of a tumultuous marriage to Georgia O'Keefe and allegations of pedophilia chronicled so much with a fresh eye, and was an inspiration and help to many others; Arnold Newman, who I thought to be the greatest portraitist of the twentieth century; Steve McCurry, whose work I first saw in National Geographic, work that figured heavily in my decision to become a photographer; and Dewitt Jones, who taught myself and many others the way to peace within ourselves and our photography.

There are many others, some of whom are even still alive. Compatriots that were a constant source of amazement for me, wringing freshness and originality out of the same tired old subjects.

Thank God. Without their inspiration, I doubt if I would have traveled this far in my life and my career.

22

The trout has gone on, feeling its way upstream. I get my camera and carry it the rest of the way and set it on the bank just above the pool.

First making sure that the tripod is well balanced, I tilt the head so that the camera is pointing down to the water. More than once in my life have I dived to catch a camera as it started to go overboard.

I can't risk putting a tripod leg in the water; it would upset the swirling of the leaves. But I want the shot to be perpendicular, not oblique.

Before making any adjustments I open the lens and look at the scene. The lens is too wide, so I take it off and take it over to my pack and wrap it in its cloth. Then I pull out the 480mm and take it back to the camera, mounting it and opening the shutter.

The lens is a Nikon, one of the last ones they made before a Chinese electronics company bought them out and canceled large-format production. It's not as fast as the 300, but I do think it's one of the sharpest lenses around.

Once I line up the camera, I adjust the planes. Perspective control is probably the primary reason people have used large format cameras over the years.

If you took a simple 35mm and took a shot of a tall building from the street in front, making sure that all of the building was in the shot, you would see that the building tapers toward the top. Called convergence, this is fine for drama, but not okay if the architect wants to show precisely what the building looks like.

So take a large format camera and set it up the same way. So far, everything looks the same on film. But the bellows in between the front where the lens is and the back where the film is allow a certain amount of movement.

With the camera pointed up at an angle, loosen the screws that control the movements and line up the front and back parallel with the building. Suddenly, you have a tall building that was shot with a built-in perspective control.

This is all based on simple physics. There are sacrifices to be made, for sure. If the movements are too radical, there will be cut-off where a part of the bellows gets in the way. And any tall trees in front will appear to be rather squat and round. But these quarrels I can live with.

Another use is something based on Scheimpflug's Rule; fixing the picture so that one flat plane is always in focus, no matter if it's right in front of the lens or several hundred meters away. That's what I'm doing now. The leaves in the pool are swirling around in a patchwork of beautiful colors, and all on one flat plane.

Unfortunately, because of where I am, I cannot shoot straight down. So instead, I triangulate. The plane of the water surface I carry on in my imagination, and then make it so the front and rear standards of the camera are each on a plane that will bisect the first one in exactly the same place. When all three lines intersect, Scheimpflug's Rule takes effect. Everything in the photo is in focus, from the horizon to the camera.

But I've gotten too technical again. All of my life as a photographer, it has never ceased to amaze me to hear so many people talk of their technology as if that's the beauty of the process. They're wrong.

Rather, the beauty of the process is in its perfection. The fact that I can play tricks with the camera, using the laws of physics to further my own goals, that is magnificent. To use mathematics to help me determine my exposure, something no one does anymore, with all of their electronics; that is what is wonderful.

32

The aperture is a thing of mathematical beauty. Even though the numbers have been rounded up or down, the simplicity of the trail of figures, especially when combined with the speeds of the shutter and the film; these are things that made photography a craft as well as an art.

Start with the number 1. That is your maximum aperture, basically the widest a lens can be open when an image is taken. While almost no lens has as wide an aperture, it will always be the widest, the "fastest" lens possible.

Now take that number and multiply by 1.4. Then take each answer and multiply again by the value 1.4. As I said, there is a bit of cheating, but that is for the sake of us simple-minded photographers.

1, 1.4, 2, 2.8, 4, 5.6, 8, 11, 16, 22, 32, 45, 64, and 90. A simple progression, from widest to narrowest. And as you narrow your aperture, another amazement from the natural world comes into play. Depth-of-field. The field of focus expands, and more in front of and in behind your subject falls within your focus.

Combine this with the lengths of time that the shutter can stay open, and couple the ratio of those two with the speed of film you use, and you have the basic mechanics for taking a picture.

Or rather, had the basic mechanics. As with most things in life nowadays, a little knowledge is no longer a dangerous thing, because almost no one wants to bother with a little knowledge.

45

A moment under the dark cloth and the image is in focus. I then pull my old meter back out of my pocket and hold it down near the surface of the water. There is no direct light shining here, so the exposure will be a bit slower.

The reading is for one second at f45. I want to keep it at f45 to ensure maximum depth of field. In case my camera movements are not precise the increased depth will help keep everything in focus.

Ironically, the lengthy exposure will blur everything. The water and the leaves will combine to make a very painterly effect as they move while the shutter is open. But still, the field will be in focus and that's something that you would be able to tell if you compared it with a photo that was out of focus.

I attach the bulb release to the lens and close it, then insert the film holder in the back and remove the dark slide. After giving the camera a moment to keep still, I slowly squeeze the bulb and the shutter clicks open. In my mind, I quietly count "One Mississippi" and then it closes again.

The day suddenly seems very long and very bleak.

64

Shortly after I had taken an interest in photography, as a matter of fact almost coinciding with my advent as at least a part-time professional, photography began to take a much more electronic bent. Auto-exposure cameras were being introduced, and almost as soon as you bought one another company or even the same one you had bought from would announce an improvement on that.

Before long, you could buy a relatively inexpensive 35mm SLR that could make all exposure decisions for you. Point and shoot was the name of the game, and simplicity sold.

Changes in photography were like changes in computer technology. Unless you were very wealthy, you literally could not keep up. In fact, changes in computer technology were part of the reason for the speed of changes in photography.

With the advent of smaller and smaller microchips, SLR cameras were developed that were auto-focus. At first this feature was very slow and unreliable, but in less than a decade after the first true auto-focus 35mm SLR was introduced, photojournalists and other pros were using the top-of-the-line models.

I worked at a newspaper for almost two years, just before the professional auto-focus cameras were brought onto the market. At that time I was as gaga over toys and technology as the next guy.

But soon I saw something that disturbed me. For every photographer that was able to take these cameras and make something beautiful and feeling out of them, there were thousands who were losing their souls. The heart of what they were in the business for was being sucked out of them, and all they could talk about was faster shutter speeds, DX coding, follow focus and God knows what else.

So I sold a lot of my high-tech equipment and bought my first 8 × 10 camera. Having to follow all the steps to get to the picture really showed me where I needed to be. It allowed time for self-examination, and each and every one of my photos was thought about. No more mindless shooting because I could polish off five frames in a second, a whole roll of film in just over seven seconds.

Then, soon after I had made the switch, the major camera companies began to push the newest in photography; digital imaging. Although the first still-vid cameras were primitive and useful only if you wanted tiny prints, the world seemed ready to embrace them.

With the impetus the sales allowed, the camera companies improved their technologies to the point where digital photos were comparable to most 35mm films. You could simply erase what you didn't like, and the images you kept could easily be altered to suit any purpose. As with everything else in our society, ease became a watchword.

In the past decade I've watched as holography finally became moderately accessible to some, and that combined with 2D digital photography has created a boom unlike anything the field has ever seen before.

Need a great shot of your family? Just plug the Karsh chip into the camera and go stand with them. The camera will take a great portrait, just like Karsh always used to do (except in color. If you want black and white, just adjust the tone on your viewer).

Does your company need a picture of its latest product? Rent a studio and a special commercial camera and plug in the Satterwhite chip. Your very own commercial photographer without having to pay the fees.

Of course, it gets hard to buy real film in an atmosphere like this.

90

I finish putting away the gear and then sit on the rock again for a moment. I feel the letter in my breast pocket and pull it out, still not wanting to believe what it says;

Dear Mr. Walker,

It is my sad duty to inform you that Eastman Kodak-Davis will no longer be manufacturing photographic films of any type.

There are two reasons for this decision. First, as you know, the market for film is no longer viable, and we were reduced to making films for you and a few others strictly on a special order basis. Additionally, the Euro-African embargo on precious metals has made it extremely difficult for us to purchase silver.

My apologies to you. I hope that you will see fit to continue to deal with us through our Electronic Imaging department.

Sincerely,
Samuel Fisher, Manager
Eastman Kodak-Davis Imaging Division

I got the letter two days ago, faxed in just as I had come home from a shoot up in the Yukon. The air is still kind of clean up there, and there are even some animals still alive, if suffering.

I only had two sheets of film left, and that left me as a lucky one. I immediately tried phoning Simon, a photographer who had been on the trip with me. He had used up all of his film on the trip, counting on being able to get some more when he got back. There was no answer, so I immediately took the rail over to his place.

The door recognized me and let me in. After a brief search

of the unit I found him. He was in the bathtub, dead, his wrists slit from hand to elbow.

I remember I wasn't surprised, just dazed and spaced out. I walked over to the house screen and thumbed it on. Sure enough, there was a note for me. Simon's face there, tears in his eyes.

"I'm sorry, Laird. You know why I've done this. First Jim, and now this. I love you, bud. Good-bye."

I shut the screen off and sat there, finally letting myself cry. Jim was Simon's only son. He'd died just four months earlier; the skin cancer took him. Simon's wife had passed on years ago, and I always suspected that Jim had been one of the main reasons that Simon had been able to hang on.

And then they took away his pictures.

I fold the letter and stick it back in my pocket. Then I lift the pack to the rock, and slide my arms through the straps. The walk down is a long one, and the pack feels a lot heavier now.

Before I start down I look one more time in the stream. I can see nothing swimming in it, no fish, no beetle.

I wish there were still birds to sing to me as I walk.

CRAPHOUND

Cory Doctorow

Cory Doctorow, born and raised in Toronto, at an early age found writer/editor Judith Merril and her writers' workshops, then worked at Bakka, the world's oldest science-fiction bookstore, for three years. Doctorow works with computers; he "does technology stuff" for ad agencies, offshore casinos, film companies, TV stations, multimedia companies, lawyers, video-conference MBA programs, and international development agencies. His fiction has appeared in *SF Age, Asimov's, On Spec, Tesseracts, Pulphouse, Odyssey,* and elsewhere. He writes a regular column on science-fictional Web-stuff for *SF Age,* and other nonfiction for *Wired, Sci-Fi Entertainment, Sci-Fi Universe, New York Review of Science Fiction,* and *2600.*

"Craphound" is energetic, futuristic, yet nostalgic science fiction with a light touch and some sharp observations. Aliens are buying up our past treasures. Could this have some political subtext? When asked to provide some comment to accompany "Craphound," Doctorow sent this third-person bit: "A lifelong packrat, he lives in a stuffed-to-the-gills renovated warehouse in Toronto. It's amazing how empty and airy it seemed when he moved in, and how *full* it seems now, after accreting the bounty of a million thrifts, yard-sales, fleas, auctions, contents sales, rummage sales, chi-chi boutiques, and family attics. Visitors to Toronto are heartily encouraged to visit the Fort York auction house and bid heavily. Just not against him."

Craphound had wicked yard-sale karma, for a rotten, filthy alien bastard. He was too good at panning out the single grain of gold in a raging river of uselessness for me not to like him—respect him, anyway. But then he found the cowboy trunk. It was two months' rent to me and nothing but some squirrelly alien kitsch-fetish to Craphound.

So I did the unthinkable. I violated the Code. I got into a bidding war with a buddy. Never let them tell you that women poison friendships: in my experience, wounds from women-fights heal quickly; fights over garbage leave nothing behind but scorched earth.

Craphound spotted the sign—his karma, plus the goggles in his exoskeleton, gave him the advantage when we were doing 80 kmh on some stretch of back highway in cottage country. He was riding shotgun while I drove, and we had the radio on to the CBC's summer-Saturday programming: eight weekends with eight hours of old radio dramas: "The Shadow," "Quiet Please," "Tom Mix," "The Crypt-Keeper" with Bela Lugosi. It was hour three, and Bogey was phoning in his performance on a radio adaptation of *The African Queen*. I had the windows of the old truck rolled down so that I could smoke without fouling Craphound's breather. My arm was hanging out the window, the radio was booming, and Craphound said "Turn around! Turn around, now, Jerry, now, turn around!"

When Craphound gets that excited, it's a sign that he's spotted a rich vein. I checked the side mirror quickly, pounded the brakes, and spun around. The transmission creaked, the wheels squealed, and then we were creeping along the way we'd come.

"There," Craphound said, gesturing with his long, skinny arm. I saw it. A wooden A-frame real-estate sign, a piece of hand-lettered cardboard stuck overtop of the realtor's name:

EAST MUSKOKA VOLUNTEER FIRE-DEPT
LADIES AUXILIARY RUMMAGE SALE
SAT 25 JUNE

"Hoo-eee!" I hollered, and spun the truck onto the dirt road. I gunned the engine as we cruised along the tree-lined road, trusting Craphound to spot any deer, signs, or hikers in time to avert disaster. The sky was a perfect blue and the smells of summer were all around us. I snapped off the radio and listened to the wind rushing through the truck. Ontario is *beautiful* in the summer.

"There!" Craphound shouted. I hit the turn-off and downshifted and then we were back on a paved road. Soon, we were rolling into a country fire station, an ugly brick barn. The hall was lined with long, folding tables, stacked high. The mother lode!

Craphound beat me out the door, as usual. His exoskeleton is programmable, so he can record little scripts for it like: move left arm to door handle, pop it, swing legs out to running board, jump to ground, close door, move forward. Meanwhile, I'm still making sure I've switched off the headlights and that I've got my wallet.

Two blue-haired grannies had a card table set up out front of the hall, with a big tin pitcher of lemonade and three boxes of Tim Horton assorted donuts. That stopped us both, since we share the superstition that you *always* buy food from old ladies and little kids, as a sacrifice to the crap-gods. One of the old ladies poured out the lemonade while the other smiled and greeted us.

"Welcome, welcome! My, you've come a long way for us!"

"Just up from Toronto, ma'am," I said. It's an old joke, but it's also part of the ritual, and it's got to be done.

"I meant your friend, sir. This gentleman."

Craphound smiled without baring his gums and sipped his lemonade. "Of course I came, dear lady. I wouldn't miss it for the worlds!" His accent is pretty good, but when it comes to stock phrases like this, he's got so much polish you'd think he was reading the news.

The biddie *blushed* and *giggled*, and I felt faintly sick. I walked off to the tables, trying not to hurry. I chose my first spot, about halfway down, where things wouldn't be quite so picked-over. I grabbed an empty box from underneath and started putting stuff into it: four matched highball glasses with gold crossed bowling pins and a line of black around the rim; an Expo '67 wall-hanging that wasn't even a little faded; a shoe-box full of late sixties O-Pee-Chee hockey cards; a worn, wooden-handled steel cleaver that you could butcher a steer with.

I picked up my box and moved on: a deck of playing cards copyrighted '57, with the logo for the Royal Canadian Dairy, Bala Ontario printed on the backs; a fireman's cap with a brass badge so tarnished I couldn't read it; a three-story wedding-cake trophy for the 1974 Eastern Region Curling Championships. The cash register in my mind was ringing, ringing, ringing. God bless the East Muskoka Volunteer Fire Department Ladies' Auxiliary.

I'd mined that table long enough. I moved to the other end of the hall. Time was, I'd start at the beginning and turn over each item, build one pile of maybes and another pile of definites, try to strategize. In time, I came to rely on instinct and on the fates, to whom I make my obeisances at every opportunity.

Let's hear it for the fates: a genuine collapsible top hat; a white-tipped evening cane; a hand-carved cherry-wood walking stick; a beautiful black lace parasol; a wrought-iron lightning rod with a rooster on top; all of it in an elephant-leg umbrella stand. I filled the box, folded it over, and started on another.

I collided with Craphound. He grinned his natural grin, the one that showed row on row of wet, slimy gums, tipped with writhing, poisonous suckers. "Gold! Gold!" he said, and moved along. I turned my head after him, just as he bent over the cowboy trunk.

I sucked air between my teeth. It was magnificent: a leather-bound miniature steamer trunk, the leather worked with lariats, Stetson hats, warbonnets and sixguns. I moved toward him, and he popped the latch. I caught my breath.

On top, there was a kid's cowboy costume: miniature leather chaps, a tiny Stetson, a pair of scuffed white-leather cowboy boots with long, worn spurs affixed to the heels. Craphound moved it reverently to the table and continued to pull more magic from the trunk's depths: a stack of cardboard-bound Hopalong Cassidy 78s; a pair of tin sixguns with gunbelt and holsters; a silver star that said Sheriff; a bundle of Roy Rogers comics tied with twine, in mint condition; and a leather satchel filled with plastic cowboys and Indians, enough to reenact the Alamo.

"Oh, my God," I breathed, as he spread the loot out on the table.

"What are these, Jerry?" Craphound asked, holding up the 78s.

"Old records, like LPs, but you need a special record player to listen to them." I took one out of its sleeve. It gleamed, scratch-free, in the overhead fluorescents.

"I got a 78 player here," said a member of the East Muskoka Volunteer Fire Department Ladies' Auxiliary. She was short enough to look Craphound in the eye, a hair under five feet, and had a skinny, rawboned look to her. "That's my Billy's things, Billy the Kid we called him. He was dotty for cowboys when he was a boy. Couldn't get him to take off that fool outfit—nearly got him thrown out of school. He's a lawyer now, in Toronto, got a fancy office on Bay Street. I called him to ask if he minded my putting his cowboy things in the sale, and you know what? He didn't know what I was talking about! Doesn't that beat everything? He was dotty for cowboys when he was a boy."

It's another of my rituals to smile and nod and be as polite as possible to the erstwhile owners of crap that I'm trying to buy, so I smiled and nodded and examined the 78 player she had produced. In lariat script, on the top, it said, "Official Bob Wills Little Record Player," and had a crude watercolor of Bob Wills and His Texas Playboys grinning on the front. It was the kind of record player that folded up like a suitcase when you weren't using it. I'd had one as a kid, with Yogi Bear silkscreened on the front.

Billy's mom plugged the yellowed cord into a wall jack and took the 78 from me, touched the stylus to the record. A tinny ukelele played, accompanied by horse-clops, and then a narrator with a deep, whisky voice said, "Howdy, Pardners! I was just settin' down by the ole campfire. Why don't you stay an' have some beans, an' I'll tell y'all the story of how Hopalong Cassidy beat the Duke Gang when they come to rob the Santa Fe."

In my head, I was already breaking down the cowboy trunk and its contents, thinking about the minimum bid I'd place on each item at Sotheby's. Sold individually, I figured I could get over two grand for the contents. Then I thought about putting ads in some of the Japanese collectors' magazines, just for a lark, before I sent the lot to the auction house. You never can tell. A buddy I knew had sold a complete packaged set of Welcome Back, Kotter action figures for nearly eight grand that way. Maybe I could buy a new truck . . .

"This is wonderful," Craphound said, interrupting my reverie. "How much would you like for the collection?"

I felt a knife in my guts. Craphound had found the cowboy trunk, so that meant it was his. But he usually let me take the stuff with street-value—he was interested in *everything*, so it hardly mattered if I picked up a few scraps with which to eke out a living.

Billy's mom looked over the stuff. "I was hoping to get twenty dollars for the lot, but if that's too much, I'm willing to come down."

"I'll give you thirty," my mouth said, without intervention from my brain.

They both turned and stared at me. Craphound was unreadable behind his goggles.

Billy's mom broke the silence. "Oh, my! Thirty dollars for this old mess?"

"I will pay fifty," Craphound said.

"Seventy-five," I said.

"Oh, my," Billy's mom said.

"Five hundred," Craphound said.

I opened my mouth, and shut it. Craphound had built his stake on Earth by selling a complicated biochemical process for nonchlorophyll photosynthesis to a Saudi banker. I wouldn't ever beat him in a bidding war. "A thousand dollars," my mouth said.

"Ten thousand," Craphound said, and extruded a roll of hundreds from somewhere in his exoskeleton.

"My Lord!" Billy's mom said. "Ten thousand dollars!"

The other pickers, the firemen, the blue-haired ladies all looked up at that and started at us, their mouths open.

"It is for a good cause," Craphound said.

"Ten thousand dollars!" Billy's mom said again.

Craphound's digits ruffled through the roll as fast as a croupier's counter, separated off a large chunk of the brown bills, and handed them to Billy's mom.

One of the firemen, a middle-aged paunchy man with a comb-over appeared at Billy's mom's shoulder.

"What's going on, Eva?" he said.

"This . . . gentleman is going to pay ten thousand dollars for Billy's old cowboy things, Tom."

The fireman took the money from Billy's mom and stared at it. He held up the top note under the light and turned it this way and that, watching the holographic stamp change from green to gold, then green again. He looked at the serial number, then the serial number of the next bill. He licked his forefinger and started counting off the bills in piles of ten. Once he had ten piles, he counted them again. "That's ten thousand dollars, all right. Thank you very much, mister. Can I give you a hand getting this to your car?"

Craphound, meanwhile, had repacked the trunk and balanced the 78 player on top of it. He looked at me, then at the fireman.

"I wonder if I could impose on you to take me to the nearest bus station. I think I'm going to be making my own way home."

The fireman and Billy's mom both stared at me. My cheeks flushed. "Aw, c'mon," I said. "I'll drive you home."

"I think I prefer the bus," Craphound said.

"It's no trouble at all to give you a lift, friend," the fireman said.

I called it quits for the day, and drove home alone with the truck only half-filled. I pulled it into the coach house and threw a tarp over the load and went inside and cracked a beer and sat on the sofa, watching a nature show on a desert reclamation project in Arizona, where the state legislature had traded a derelict megamall and a custom-built habitat to an alien for a local-area weather control machine.

The following Thursday, I went to the little crap-auction house on King Street. I'd put my finds from the weekend in the sale: lower minimum bid, and they took a smaller commission than Sotheby's. Fine for moving the small stuff.

Craphound was there, of course. I knew he'd be. It was where we met, when he bid on a case of Lincoln Logs I'd found at a fire sale.

I'd known him for a kindred spirit when he bought them, and we'd talked afterwards, at his place, a sprawling, two-story warehouse amid a cluster of auto-wrecking yards where the junkyard dogs barked, barked, barked.

Inside was paradise. His taste ran to shrines—a collection of fifties bar kitsch that was a shrine to liquor; a circular waterbed on a raised podium that was nearly buried under seventies bachelor pad-inalia; a kitchen that was nearly unusable, so packed it was with old barn-board furniture and rural memorabilia; a leather-appointed library straight out of a Victorian gentlemen's club; a solarium dressed in wicker and bamboo and tiki-idols. It was a hell of a place.

Craphound had known all about the Goodwills and the Sally Anns, and the auction houses, and the kitsch boutiques on Queen Street, but he still hadn't figured out where it all came from.

"Yard sales, rummage sales, garage sales," I said, reclining in a vibrating naughahyde easy chair, drinking a glass of his pricey single malt that he'd bought for the beautiful bottle it came in.

"But where are these? Who is allowed to make them?" Craphound hunched opposite me, his exoskeleton locked into a coiled, semiseated position. I tried to read his expression, but I couldn't make any sense out of his nostril-slits and his hooded eyes.

"Who? Well, anyone. You just one day decide that you need to clean out the basement, you put an ad in the *Star*, tape up a few signs, and voilà, yard sale. Sometimes, a school or a church will get donations of old junk and sell it all at one time, as a fundraiser."

"And how do you locate these?" he asked, bobbing up and down slightly with excitement.

"Well, there're amateurs who just read the ads in the weekend papers, or just pick a neighborhood and wander around, but that's no way to go about it. What I do is, I get in a truck, and I sniff the air, catch the scent of crap and *vroom!*, I'm off like a bloodhound on a trail. You learn things over time: like stay away from Yuppie yard sales, they never have anything worth buying, just the same crap you can buy in any mall."

"Do you think I might accompany you someday?"

"Hell, sure. Next Saturday? We'll head over to Cabbagetown—those old coach houses, you'd be amazed what people get rid of. It's practically criminal."

"I would like to go with you on next Saturday very much Mr. Jerry Abington." He used to talk like that, without commas or question marks. Later, he got better, but then, it was all one big sentence.

"Call me Jerry. It's a date, then. Tell you what, though: there's a Code you got to learn before we go out. The Craphound's Code."

"What is a craphound?"

"You're lookin' at one. You're one, too, unless I miss my guess. You'll get to know some of the local craphounds, you hang around with me long enough. They're the competition, but they're also your buddies, and there're certain rules we have."

And then I explained to him all about how you never bid against a craphound at a yard sale, how you get to know the other fellows' tastes, and when you see something they might like, you haul it out for them, and they'll do the same for you, and how you never buy something that another craphound might be looking for, if all you're buying it for is to sell it back to him. Just good form and common sense, really, but you'd be surprised how many amateurs just fail to make the jump to pro because they can't grasp it.

There was a bunch of other stuff at the auction, other craphounds' weekend treasures. This was high season, when the sun comes out and people start to clean out the cottage, the basement, the garage. There were some collectors in the crowd, and a whole whack of antique and junk dealers, and a few pickers, and me, and Craphound. I watched the bidding listlessly, waiting for my things to come up and sneaking out for smokes between lots. Craphound never once looked at me or acknowledged my presence, and I became perversely obsessed with catching his eye, so I coughed and shifted and walked past him several times, until the auctioneer glared at me, and one of the attendants asked if I needed a throat lozenge.

My lot came up. The bowling glasses went for five bucks to one of the Queen Street junk dealers; the elephant-foot fetched $350 after a spirited bidding war between an antique dealer and a collector—the collector won; the dealer took the top hat for $100. The rest of it came up and sold, or didn't, and at end of the lot, I'd made over $800, which was rent for the month plus beer for the weekend plus gas for the truck.

Craphound bid on and bought more cowboy things—a box of super-eight cowboy movies, the boxes moldy, the stock itself running to slime; a Navajo blanket; a plastic donkey that dispensed cigarettes out of its ass; a big neon armadillo sign.

One of the other nice things about that place over Sotheby's, there was none of this waiting thirty days to get a check. I queued up with the other pickers after the bidding was through, collected a wad of bills, and headed for my truck.

I spotted Craphound loading his haul into a minivan with handicapped plates. It looked like some kind of fungus was growing over the hood and side panels. On closer inspection, I saw that the body had been covered in closely glued Lego.

Craphound popped the hatchback and threw his gear in, then opened the driver's side door, and I saw that his van had been fitted out for a legless driver, with brake and accelerator levers. A paraplegic I knew drove one just like it. Craphound's exoskeleton levered him into the seat, and I watched the eerily precise way it executed the macro that started the car, pulled the shoulder belt, put it into drive, and switched on the stereo. I heard tape-hiss, then, loud as a b-boy cruising Yonge Street, an old-timey cowboy voice: "Howdy pardners! Saddle up, we're ridin'!" Then the van backed up and sped out of the lot.

I got into the truck and drove home. Truth be told, I missed the little bastard.

Some people said that we should have run Craphound and his kin off the planet, out of the Solar System. They said that it

wasn't fair for the aliens to keep us in the dark about their technologies. They say that we should have captured a ship and
reverse-engineered it, built our own and kicked ass.

Some people!

First of all, nobody with human DNA could survive a trip
in one of those ships. They're part of Craphound's people's bodies, as I understand it, and we just don't have the right parts.
Second of all, they *were* sharing their tech with us—they just
weren't giving it away. Fair trades every time.

It's not as if space was off-limits to us. We can any one of
us visit their homeworld, just as soon as we figure out how. Only
they wouldn't hold our hands along the way. We've come farther in the five years since their arrival broke up a billion New
Century's Eve parties than in the hundred years before, and as
far as I'm concerned, we've got no reason to complain.

I spent the week haunting the "Secret Boutique," AKA the Goodwill As-Is Center on Jarvis. It's all there is to do between yard
sales, and sometimes it makes for good finds. Part of my theory
of yard-sale karma holds that if I miss one day at the thrift shops,
that'll be the day they put out the big score. So I hit the stores
diligently and came up with crapola. I had offended the fates, I
knew, and wouldn't make another score until I placated them.
It was lonely work, still and all, and I missed Craphound's good
eye and obsessive delight.

I was at the cash register with a few items at the Goodwill
when a guy in a suit behind me tapped me on the shoulder.

"Sorry to bother you," he said. His suit looked expensive,
as did his manicure and his haircut and his wire-rimmed glasses.
"I was just wondering where you found that." He gestured at a
rhinestone-studded ukelele, with a cowboy hat wood-burned
into the body. I had picked it up with a guilty little thrill, thinking that Craphound might buy it at the next auction.

"Second floor, in the toy section."

"There wasn't anything else like it, was there?"

" 'Fraid not," I said, and the cashier picked it up and started
wrapping it in newspaper.

"Ah," he said, and he looked like a little kid who'd just been
told that he couldn't have a puppy. "I don't suppose you'd want
to sell it, would you?"

I held up a hand and waited while the cashier bagged it with
the rest of my stuff, a few old clothbound novels I thought I

could sell at a used-book store, and a Grease belt buckle with Olivia Newton John on it. I led him out the door by the elbow of his expensive suit.

"How much?" I had paid a dollar.

"Ten bucks?"

I nearly said, "Sold!" but I caught myself. "Twenty."

"Twenty dollars?"

"That's what they'd charge at a boutique on Queen Street."

He took out a slim leather wallet and produced a twenty. I handed him the uke. His face lit up like a lightbulb.

It's not that my adulthood is particularly unhappy. Likewise, it's not that my childhood was particularly happy.

There are memories I have, though, that are like a cool drink of water. My grandfather's place near Milton, an old Victorian farmhouse, where the cat drank out of a milk-glass bowl; and where we sat around a rough pine table that, in my memory, is as big as my whole apartment; and where my playroom was the draughty barn with hay-filled lofts bulging with old farm junk and Tarzan-ropes.

There was Grampa's friend Fyodor, and we spent every evening at his wrecking yard, he and Grampa talking and smoking on the porch while I scampered in the twilight, scaling mountains of auto-junk. The gloveboxes yielded treasures: crumpled photos of college boys mugging in front of signs, roadmaps of faraway places. I found a guidebook from the 1964 New York World's Fair once, and a lipstick like a chrome bullet, and a pair of white leather ladies' gloves.

Fyodor dealt in scrap, too, and once, he had half of a carny carousel, a few horses and part of the canopy, paint flaking and sharp torn edges protruding; next to it, a Korean-war tank minus its turret and treads, and inside the tank were peeling old pinup girls and a rotation schedule and a crude Kilroy. The control room in the middle of the carousel had a stack of paperback sci-fi novels, Ace Doubles that had two books bound back-to-back, and when you finished the first, you turned it over and read the other. Fyodor let me keep them, and there was a pawn ticket in one from Macon, Georgia, for a transistor radio.

My parents started leaving me alone when I was fourteen and I couldn't keep from sneaking into their room and snooping. Mom's jewelry box had books of matches from their honeymoon in Acapulco, printed with bad palm trees. My Dad kept an old photo in his sock drawer, of himself on Muscle Beach, shirtless, flexing his biceps.

My grandmother saved every scrap of my mother's life in her basement, in dusty old Army trunks. I entertained myself endlessly by pulling it out and taking it in: her Mouse Ears from the big family train-trip to Disneyland in '57, and her records, and the glittery pasteboard sign from her sweet sixteen. There were well-chewed stuffed animals, and school exercise books in which she'd practiced variations on her signature for page after page.

It all told a story. The penciled Kilroy in the tank made me see one of those Canadian soldiers in Korea, unshaven and crewcut like an extra on M*A*S*H, sitting for bored hour after hour, staring at the pinup girls, fiddling with a crossword, finally laying it down and sketching his Kilroy quickly, before anyone saw.

The photo of my dad posing sent me whirling through time to Toronto's old Muscle Beach in the east end, near Kew Beach, and hearing the tinny AM radios playing weird old psychedelic rock while teenagers lounged on their Mustangs and the girls sunbathed in bikinis that made their tits into torpedoes.

It all made poems. The old pulp novels and the pawn ticket, when I spread them out in the living room in front of the TV, and arranged them just so, they made up a poem that could take my breath away.

After the cowboy trunk episode, I didn't run into Craphound again until the annual Rotary Club charity rummage sale at the Upper Canada Brewing Company. He was wearing the cowboy hat, sixguns, and the silver star from the cowboy trunk. It should have looked ridiculous, but the net effect was naive and somehow charming, like he was a little boy whose hair you wanted to muss.

I found a box of nice old melamine dishes, in various shades of green—four square plates, bowls, salad plates, and a serving tray. I threw them in the duffel-bag I'd brought and kept browsing, ignoring Craphound as he charmed a salty old Rotarian while fondling a box of leather-bound books.

I browsed a stack of old Ministry of Labour licenses—barber, chiropodist, bartender, watchmaker. They all had pretty seals and were framed in stark green institutional metal. They all had different names, but all from one family, and I made up a little story to entertain myself, about the proud mother saving her sons' accreditations and hanging them in the spare room with their diplomas. "Oh, George Junior's just opened his own barbershop, and little Jimmy's still fixing watches . . ."

I bought them.

In a box of crappy plastic Little Ponies and Barbies and Care Bears, I found a leather Indian headdress, a wooden bow-and-arrow set, and a fringed buckskin vest. Craphound was still buttering up the leather books' owner. I bought them quick, for five bucks.

"Those are beautiful," a voice said at my elbow. I turned around and smiled at the snappy dresser who'd bought the uke at the Secret Boutique. He'd gone casual for the weekend, in an expensive, L. L. Bean button-down way.

"Aren't they, though."

"You sell them on Queen Street? Your finds, I mean?"

"Sometimes. Sometimes at auction. How's the uke?"

"Oh, I got it all tuned up," he said, and smiled the same smile he'd given me when he'd taken hold of it at Goodwill. "I can play 'Don't Fence Me In' on it." He looked at his feet. "Silly, huh?"

"Not at all. You're into cowboy things, huh?" As I said it, I was overcome with the knowledge that this was "Billy the Kid," the original owner of the cowboy trunk. I don't know why I felt that way, but I did, with utter certainty.

"Just trying to relive a piece of my childhood, I guess. I'm Scott," he said, extending his hand.

Scott? I thought wildly. *Maybe it's his middle name?* "I'm Jerry."

The Upper Canada Brewery sale has many things going for it, including a beer garden where you can sample their wares and get a good BBQ burger. We gently gravitated to it, looking over the tables as we went.

"You're a pro, right?" he asked after we had plastic cups of beer.

"You could say that."

"I'm an amateur. A rank amateur. Any words of wisdom?"

I laughed and drank some beer, lit a cigarette. "There's no secret to it, I think. Just diligence: you've got to go out every chance you get, or you'll miss the big score."

He chuckled. "I hear that. Sometimes, I'll be sitting in my office, and I'll just *know* that they're putting out a piece of pure gold at the Goodwill and that someone else will get to it before my lunch. I get so wound up, I'm no good until I go down there and hunt for it. I guess I'm hooked, eh?"

"Cheaper than some other kinds of addictions."

"I guess so. About that Indian stuff—what do you figure you'd get for it at a Queen Street boutique?"

I looked him in the eye. He may have been something high-powered and cool and collected in his natural environment, but just then, he was as eager and nervous as a kitchen-table poker-player at a high-stakes game.

"Maybe fifty bucks," I said.

"Fifty, huh?" he asked.

"About that," I said.

"Once it sold," he said.

"There is that," I said.

"Might take a month, might take a year," he said.

"Might take a day," I said.

"It might, it might." He finished his beer. "I don't suppose you'd take forty?"

I'd paid five for it, not ten minutes before. It looked like it would fit Craphound, who, after all, was wearing Scott/Billy's own boyhood treasures as we spoke. You don't make a living by feeling guilty over eight hundred percent markups. Still, I'd angered the fates, and needed to redeem myself.

"Make it five," I said.

He started to say something, then closed his mouth and gave me a look of thanks. He took a five out of his wallet and handed it to me. I pulled the vest and bow and headdress out my duffel.

He walked back to a shiny black Jeep with gold detail work, parked next to Craphound's van. Craphound was building onto the Lego body, and the hood had a miniature Lego town attached to it.

Craphound looked around as he passed, and leaned forward with undisguised interest at the booty. I grimaced and finished my beer.

When my mom was young, little kids imagined their dream houses in obsessive, hyperreal clarity. They knew what kind of dog they'd have, what fridge, what sofa, what end tables and what husband, and how many kids they'd have and what they'd name them and what they'd wear.

I must've inherited the gene. I'd walk into our kitchen and just stand in the center of the linoleum, and think about what was missing—the curtains, for example, should be more like Grandma's, with floral prints. There was a stove in Fyodor's yard that he used as a workbench, an old cast-iron gas-fired piece from a Deco diner with elegant ivory knobs and a grill big enough to cook thirty burgers. That would nicely replace the greenish electric stove we had.

And our glasses were all wrong: Grandma had milk glasses with Li'l Orphan Annie, and Grampa's place had anodized aluminum cups in bright metallic colours that were so cold when you filled them with chocolate milk.

Our garage had nothing but bikes and spare tires. It should have had tin signs advertising nickle bottles of Coca-Cola, and Burma Shave, and quack remedies with hand-painted babies endorsing them.

The shed shouldn't have been a Sear's prefab tin special—it should have been peeling old boards, with rickety wooden shelves and sawdust on the floor, and oiled iron tools on the walls.

I knew what was wrong with every square inch of my bedroom. I needed some old patchwork quilts to sleep under, instead of the synthetic-filled comforter, and a salvaged steel office desk with a worn green blotter and a solid oak chair on brass wheels. The basketball-hoop light fixture had to go; I wanted wall sconces made from brutally simple wrought iron with blown-glass shades.

The bathroom needed a bookcase. The books needed to be old and leather bound, swollen with the damp of a thousand showers, dog-eared and much-annotated.

I met Scott/Billy three times more at the Secret Boutique that week.

He was a lawyer, who specialized in alien-technology patents. He had a practice on Bay Street, with two partners, and despite his youth, he was the senior man.

I didn't let on that I knew about Billy the Kid and his mother in the East Muskoka Volunteer Fire Department Ladies' Auxiliary. But I felt a bond with him, as though we shared an unspoken secret. I pulled any cowboy finds for him, and he developed a pretty good eye for what I was after and returned the favor.

The fates were with me again, and no two ways about it. I took home a ratty old Oriental rug that on closer inspection was a nineteenth-century hand-knotted Persian; an upholstered Turkish footstool; a collection of hand-painted silk Hawaiiana pillows and a carved Meerschaum pipe. Scott/Billy found the last for me, and it cost me two dollars. I knew a collector who would pay thirty in an eye-blink, and from then on, as far as I was concerned, Scott/Billy was a fellow craphound.

"You going to the auction tomorrow night?" I asked him at the checkout line.

"Wouldn't miss it," he said. He'd barely been able to contain his excitement when I told him about the Thursday night auctions and the bargains to be had there. He sure had the bug.

"Want to get together for dinner beforehand? The Rotterdam's got a good patio."

He did, and we did, and I had a glass of framboise that packed a hell of a kick and tasted like fizzy raspberry lemonade; and doorstopper fries and a club sandwich.

I had my nose in my glass when he kicked my ankle under the table. "Look at that!"

It was Craphound in his van, cruising for a parking spot. The Lego village had been joined by a whole postmodern spaceport on the roof, with a red-and-blue castle, a football-sized flying saucer, and a clown's head with blinking eyes.

I went back to my drink and tried to get my appetite back.

"Was that an extee driving?"

"Yeah. Used to be a friend of mine."

"He's a picker?"

"Uh-huh." I turned back to my fries and tried to kill the subject.

"Do you know how he made his stake?"

"The chlorophyll thing, in Saudi Arabia."

"Sweet!" he said. "Very sweet. I've got a client who's got some secondary patents from that one. What's he go after?"

"Oh, pretty much everything," I said, resigning myself to discussing the topic after all. "But lately, the same as you—cowboys and Injuns."

He laughed and smacked his knee. "Well, what do you know? What could he possibly want with the stuff?"

"What do they want with any of it? He got started one day when we were cruising the Muskokas," I said carefully, watching his face. "Found a trunk of old cowboy things at a rummage sale. East Muskoka Volunteer Fire Department Ladies' Auxiliary." I waited for him to shout or startle. He didn't.

"Yeah? A good find, I guess. Wish I'd made it."

I didn't know what to say to that, so I took a bite of my sandwich.

Scott continued. "I think about what they get out of it a lot. There's nothing we have here that they couldn't make for themselves. I mean, if they picked up and left today, we'd still be making sense of everything they gave us in a hundred years. You know, I just closed a deal for a biochemical computer that's no-shit ten thousand times faster than anything we've built out of silicon. You know what the extee took in trade? Title to a defunct fairground outside of Calgary—they shut it down ten years ago because the midway was too unsafe to ride. Doesn't that beat all? This thing is worth a billion dollars right out of the gate, I mean, within twenty-four hours of the deal closing, the seller can turn it into the GDP of Bolivia. For a crummy real-estate dog that you couldn't get five grand for!"

It always shocked me when Billy/Scott talked about his job—it was easy to forget that he was a high-powered lawyer when we were jawing and fooling around like old craphounds. I wondered if maybe he *wasn't* Billy the Kid; I couldn't think of any reason for him to be playing it all so close to his chest.

"What the hell is some extee going to do with a fairground?"

I live in an apartment in High Park. I've got two bedrooms at the top of a house that was once a Victorian but was rebuilt after a fire in the mid-seventies. It's nice enough, in a generic, postwar kind of way.

It has a tremendous plus: a coach house out back. It's where I store my treasures, and there are three locks on the door.

The apartment came furnished in no-taste Late Canadian Thrift Store, and I never got to redecorating it.

What I did was hang three long shelves at the foot of my bed. That's all the space I have to keep treasures on. It's a self-regulating mechanism, preventing me from sampling too much of the merchandise. If I find a piece that I *have* to keep, something from the shelf has to be moved out to the coach house and taken away to an auction or a junk store.

I have a milk-glass bowl on the shelves; a Made-in-Occupied-Japan tin tank that is pieced together from old tuna cans and hand-painted; a mint-condition Ace Double with bug-eyed monsters on both covers; an ashtray from the 1964 World's Fair; four aluminum cups in brilliant metallic colors; a set of pink Mouse-Ears with a girl's name stitched on the reverse; a postcard with a 3D Jesus who winks at you when you move your head; a lighter made from burnished shrapnel.

Over the years, I've found the steel desk and the wall sconces and carousel animals and tin Coca-Cola signs galore. Finding them feels right, like I've ticked off an item on a checklist. They go straight into my garage without gracing my apartment even once, and selling them is never painful—it's touching them again, having them pass through my possession that makes it good.

When I can't bring myself to switch on the TV, I take an armload of things down from my shelves and sit on the living room floor and spread them out in front of me and see if I can't make a poem. Sometimes I laugh and sometimes I cry, but usually I just stare at them and let my mind caress each piece and match it up with a memory.

Craphound got a free Coke from Lisa at the check-in when he made his appearance. He bid high, but shrewdly, and never pulled ten-thousand-dollar stunts. The bidders were wandering the floor, previewing that week's stock, and making notes to themselves.

I rooted through a box-lot full of old tins, and found one with a buckaroo at the Calgary Stampede, riding a bucking bronc. I picked it up and stood to inspect it. Craphound was behind me.

"Nice piece, huh?" I said to him.

"I like it very much," Craphound said, and I felt my cheeks flush.

"You're going to have some competition tonight, I think," I said, and nodded at Scott/Billy. "I think he's Billy; the one whose mother sold us—you—the cowboy trunk."

"Really?" Craphound said, and it felt like we were partners again, scoping out the competition. Suddenly I felt a knife of shame, like I was betraying Scott/Billy somehow. I took a step back.

"Jerry, I am very sorry that we argued."

I sighed out a breath I hadn't known I was holding in. "Me, too."

"They're starting the bidding. May I sit with you?"

And so the three of us sat together, and Craphound shook Scott/Billy's hand and the auctioneer started into his harangue.

It was a night for unusual occurrences. I bid on a piece, something I told myself I'd never do. It was a set of four matched Li'l Orphan Annie Ovaltine glasses, like Grandma's had been, and seeing them in the auctioneer's hand took me right back to her kitchen, and endless afternoons passed with my coloring books and weird old-lady hard candies and Liberace albums playing in the living room.

"Ten," I said, opening the bidding.

"I got ten, ten, ten, I got ten, who'll say twenty, who'll say twenty, twenty for the four."

Craphound waved his bidding card, and I jumped as if I'd been stung.

"I got twenty from the space cowboy, I got twenty, sir will you say thirty?"

I waved my card.

"That's thirty to you sir."

"Forty," Craphound said.

"Fifty," I said even before the auctioneer could point back to me. An old pro, he settled back and let us do the work.

"One hundred," Craphound said.

"One fifty," I said.

The room was perfectly silent. I thought about my over-extended MasterCard, and wondered if Scott/Billy would give me a loan.

"Two hundred," Craphound said.

Fine, I thought. Pay two hundred for those. I can get a set on Queen Street for thirty bucks.

The auctioneer turned to me. "The bidding stands at two. Will you say two-ten, sir?"

I shook my head. The auctioneer paused a long moment, letting me sweat over the decision to bow out.

"I have two—do I have any other bids from the floor? Any other bids? Sold, $200, to number 57." An attendant brought Craphound the glasses. He took them and tucked them under his seat.

I was fuming when we left. Craphound was at my elbow. I wanted to punch him—I'd never punched anyone in my life, but I wanted to punch him.

We entered the cool night air and I sucked in several lung-fuls before lighting a cigarette.

"Jerry," Craphound said.

I stopped, but didn't look at him. I watched the taxis pull in and out of the garage next door instead.

"Jerry, my friend," Craphound said.

"What?" I said, loud enough to startle myself. Scott, beside me, jerked as well.

"We're going. I wanted to say goodbye, and to give you some things that I won't be taking with me."

"What?" I said again, Scott just a beat behind me.

"My people—we're going. It has been decided. We've gotten what we came for."

Without another word, he set off toward his van. We followed along behind, shell-shocked.

Craphound's exoskeleton executed another macro and slid the panel door aside, revealing the cowboy trunk.

"I wanted to give you this. I will keep the glasses."

"I don't understand," I said.

"You're all leaving?" Scott asked, with a note of urgency.

"It has been decided. We'll go over the next twenty-four hours."

"But *why?*" Scott said, sounding almost petulant.

"It's not something that I can easily explain. As you must know, the things we gave you were trinkets to us—almost worthless. We traded them for something that was almost worthless to you—a fair trade, you'll agree—but it's time to move on."

Craphound handed me the cowboy trunk. Holding it, I smelled the lubricant from his exoskeleton and the smell of the attic it had been mummified in before making its way into his hands. I felt like I almost understood.

"This is for me," I said slowly, and Craphound nodded encouragingly. "This is for me, and you're keeping the glasses. And I'll look at this and feel . . ."

"You understand," Craphound said, looking somehow relieved.

And I *did*. I understood that an alien wearing a cowboy hat and sixguns and giving them away was a poem and a story, and a thirtyish bachelor trying to spend half a month's rent on four glasses so that he could remember his Grandma's kitchen was a story and a poem, and that the disused fairground outside Calgary was a story and a poem, too.

"You're craphounds!" I said. "All of you!"

Craphound smiled so I could see his gums and I put down the cowboy trunk and clapped my hands.

Scott recovered from his shock by spending the night at his office, crunching numbers talking on the phone, and generally getting while the getting was good. He had an edge—no one else knew that they were going.

He went pro later that week, opened a chi-chi boutique on Queen Street, and hired me on as chief picker and factum factotum.

Scott was not Billy the Kid. Just another Bay Street shyster with a cowboy jones. From the way they come down and spend, there must be a million of them.

Our draw in the window is a beautiful mannequin I found, straight out of the fifties, a little boy we call The Beaver. He dresses in chaps and a Sheriff's badge and sixguns and a miniature Stetson and cowboy boots with worn spurs, and rests one foot on a beautiful miniature steamer trunk whose leather is worked with cowboy motifs.

He's not for sale at any price.

TWILIGHT OF THE REAL

Wesley Herbert

This is a story note written by the author. We edited it a bit, but felt that it introduced the writer more effectively than any note we were likely to write.

"B. W. Powe once told me you could describe a writer's writing by what it would be like to live in it. My world is a dreamtime, a place of false humans and gynoids more human than human. It is a world slowly dying, inhabited by ghost half-lives, superhumans, sexy assassin-girls, and heroic antagonists defeated by mentally unstable protagonists. Some fifties writer like Heinlein said any believable character has to have politics. I say any believable character, especially a politician, has to have a sex life.

"At age 13, I began writing. At age 23, in 1992, I had my first professional sale, the short story 'Crossroads' in *On Spec*. I once saw an interview with Michele Shocked where she spoke about her mother taking her to a psychiatrist at age 15. She was diagnosed as being under the influence of literature. My name is Wesley Herbert. I am under the influence of literature.

"When I was 21, I was diagnosed with Crohn's disease; it was easy to spot by then because after a year of slowly dying I was forced into the hospital where the doctors could find me. I had lost 40 pounds, ruined my body, and twisted my brain chemistry. For a year prior I let the flesh melt off my bones like ice defrosting in a refrigerator while I prowled the streets of Toronto encased in more and more layers of frayed denim and leather and rags tied off at the edges where it wore thin. I have heard William Burroughs say 'When you become death, then you are immortal.' My writing became my only way to stay alive: ghost lives of myself trapped on clean white pages, shivering a half-life. When I write there is always illness. I am sick and will never be well, but I love illness. It is something to hold onto, like a serpent curled around my shoulders, whispering bad thoughts in my ear with hot breath. It is an ill-wrought thing but it is mine own.

"After 'Crossroads,' I published 'Director's Cut' (*On Spec*, spring '94) and 'Too Clean to be Dead' (*On Spec*, summer '94). I was in school at

York University's Fine Arts Studies program (FASP, because I love acronyms) in the creative writing program run jointly by the Fine Arts and English departments. The ratio of English to FASP students in the writing classes was about 10 to 1 and in the war against the mediocrity produced by writers who spent all their time reading Eng Lit my FASP cohorts and myself became what I called Guerrilla Poets in the War Against the Gray Aliens. My writing became characterized by a certain crazy, self-destructive edge, every class an opportunity to crush the life out of their souls with my words until I could dance on their ashes. I studied under M. T. Kelly and Bruce Powe, Jr.

"My only credential as a human being is my wife, Kerr; my partner in crime, my dollop, my love'n'rockets girl. Without her I'd never know things like what girls talk about in the locker room, or that Grace is the only sympathetic character of the story. My son Tyren was born at a home birth in 1993 where my wife and I watched his blue eyes stare at us while he refused to breathe. They resuscitated him. He is my best, real creation. I'm selfish and tell him stories every day so he too will be under the influence of literature.

"After he was born we moved to Ottawa where my wife had grown up. I greatly missed the rancid petrochemical smells of Toronto, the urban blight and the street-level art culture. It was the closest I have ever been to living in Blade-Runner City and it is still the setting for most of my stories, including 'Twilight of the Real.' Ottawa destroyed my life, my work became more sinister and dark with betrayals behind every page. To protect my sanity I began my first novel and then my second, both of which remain unpublished.

"I've worked as an art gallery director, husband, technical writer, addict, assembly line drone, market researcher and journalist for *Metro*, Ottawa's weekly arts and entertainment newspaper. In Ottawa I joined forces with the worst necrophiliac writer scum I could find, forming the loosely based Bite Me! group.

"In 1995 'Crossroads' was reprinted in *On Spec: the first five years*. I was lucky enough to begin reading *On Spec* in '91 when it was still staple-bound and have grown with them while it became the finest Speculative Fiction publication in Canada. Without friends I have made there like Jena Snyder, who share the vision of my work, writing like mine that isn't all singing birds and happy elves wouldn't be seen. 'Twilight of the Real' first appeared in the winter '97 issue of *On Spec*.

"In 'Twilight of the Real' and in almost all my stories there is a plague called the Red Death. It sometimes has a different name and different manifestations but it always means one thing, and that is the end of most of humankind on earth. It is a thinly disguised, or not disguised at all, picture of what I see AIDS doing to our world in about fifty years. It used to be science fiction was about technology and human evolution but somewhere along the way most writers seem to have forgotten the second.

"Neville Wakefield defined postmodernism as the 'twilight of the real': the end of history and narrative, the collapse of all meaning except wall-to-wall fragmentation. And for anyone who wanted to know, the movie is *Westworld*, starring Yul Brynner as the homicidal android."

Tin Star broke me out of the shell when it was time for the next job. Bright white light shining through my eyelids. Showing the pattern of veins and blood. It's the first thing I saw, and it let me know I hadn't turned into a Tommy, hadn't gone mechnik, hadn't gone robo.

It's what I always asked for. White light, hot water, those thick, plush towels, and a doctored hemplock. The shell is cold. They've been working on the solvent, the universal solvent, that will keep a cell wall from rupturing when frozen but they don't have it yet. When you go into the shell, they dose you, put the bucks in, and lower your temperature until your body slows down to something a little on the plus side of nil. Not frozen, but colder than the freezer section of the meatbuck department.

Eyes still closed against the white light, I stretched my hand out for Kita. Kita my faithful servant, Kita my Girl Friday, Kita my boss, Kita my fetish, Kita my slink. So cold, wherever it was, so cold. Hairs on end, gooseflesh up my arm like mad messages in braille. Snowstorm of words riding my flesh. Hand out for that plush towel. Hand out for her.

"Kita, sweetness, dollop, help me out here," I said into the blood of my vision. I took one step, toes touching cold cement. Gritty and wet like wet sand underfoot. Scritching against the floor.

"There is no Kita, Mister Blue, but it's time. Tin Star's work."

I opened my eyes. Black warehouse. Nothing but green lights off the surface controls of my shell, a big white coffin. Reflecting green off the abandoned machines and wings of ruined spiderwebs, coated in layers of diesel dust. Wetness under my feet where the buck fluid had run out of my shell, dripping down a grate in the cement floor. Glowing green in reflected light.

"Mister Blue?" I said.

"Code prefix, B for blue, code 11 888," she said. Shorter than me by two inches, optimal height for a dollop/boytoy couple. Not Kita. Kita was the same height, black hair, brown eyes. Always wore latex to break me out of my shell. This one was a Devi; blue-black skin tint, white hair, barefoot with rings on every toe, through her nose, through the brows over lidded eyes. All my time in the shell, I'd missed another fashion change. "Should I call you Nikola Babbett, Corto Armstrong, Wylie D. Bill?" She recited my past names from an internal file. She paused at the last one, a small smile, "Wild Bill?"

"My numbers," I wrapped my arms around me. "B11 888: aces over eights, the dead man's hand. It was the hand of cards Bill Hickok had when he died."

"Obscure," she nodded. Approved. Her kind loved trivia. She padded across the two steps between us. Reached one hand out of her robe to wrap behind my neck. Hot flesh. She'd upped her temperature for me. "No more Kita. I'll be your new therapist." She kissed me, dry tongue forcing inside my mouth until my saliva dampened both our mouths. She broke away, "I have a car waiting."

No more Kita.

She had a car and drove us to a hotel. Fifty-story bronzeplex shaped like a crucifix. She drove with a jumper cable interface, legs crossed on the seat in front of her, steering wheel in the forward locked position. Her external port was on the wrist, hard to spot under the silver bangles she wore. Ghost of fishing line between the wrist and the socket on the dash of the car. Kita always drove manual, just for me. We had that kind of relationship. Used to have.

In the hotel she wrapped me in her robe. Held my arm and marched us past the night desk. She closed the suite door behind us and said "Lock, full security, do not disturb. Lights, off," the door clicking, bolts thudding, lights switching off as she spoke. I heard her in the dark, opening the blackout shade on the window so city light poured in. Twenty-meter tall signboards dusting the room interior like candles from blocks away. Advertising water filters, a new kind of air-pressure controlled prosthetic muscle, chewing gum contraceptive for men.

I laughed as I saw the contraceptive. Nothing funnier when you're a dollop queer. Laughing when she pushed me into the shower. "Hot shower, thirty-eight point five degrees Celsius," she said and the water came on. One degree higher than my body temperature: she knew I was warmer than most people. She gave me plush towels when I came out. Naked except for the rings, she spread herself on the bed. Slid the lingam-shaped lube dispenser into my hand as I lay on top of her.

"Kita won't be coming back. I've downloaded your file from Tin Star; it has another mission for you," she said before I slipped the lingam into her mouth and squeezed some lube inside. "Everywhere," she moaned, pulling her knees to her chest. "Slink me, Blue, I know you want to. I've read your file."

So I did, lubing her 300-grade synthskin inside and out. Mounted her frontways and then turned her over. The only way to travel. I'd been in the cold shell for long enough, I had a lot stored up. She couldn't get enough. It's easy for a dollop to get off. Certainly she had amped the synthetic nerve receptors in my favorite orifice. The kind of thing that used to be bad fantasy. I let my thoughts go slightly before I let my body go. A long time ago I'd seen a vid, the flatworld kind, where a man said to his friend, "Machines sure are the servants of man."

Now that, that is so much bullshit. Afterwards, tangled in bed, she took the cellophane off a new pack of Bella Donnas, Italian hemplocks. Some people prefer straight THC in a stab or a popper, but there's a ritual to actually smoking. The blinking light of the air-scrubber over the bed came on; silent because of the white-noise machine attached to it. As I smoked the first one down, I felt the veil of forgetfulness come over me. Relaxing into the slight disorientation.

"We need you for a job, Blue. It's someone you know. Heather and Mallet."

I tried to struggle against the idea but it wouldn't come. Fucking hemplocks. Fucking spiked hemplocks.

"Not snuff, Blue, we know you, we know your file. But you'll be just like you were before. You'll be our hidden camera." She plucked the hemplock from between my fingers and I didn't move. I just went gently into that good night.

She ordered clothes for me over the vid. She knew my size, what I liked. She wasn't Kita, but there wasn't anything special about Kita. They were dollops. I watched her eat a five-course meal with me in a restaurant, cost .3K for two of us to eat, and later I found it in the toilet when she forgot to flush. Not digested, just masticated. She knew how to eat, she even enjoyed the taste, but it all went inside a reservoir in her abdomen. Later, she emptied it.

Shaving one day, I took out my razor from behind the mirror. The only thing of hers in the medicine cabinet was a six-pack of special cleaning solution. It had a long tube for a nozzle; she'd put it at the back of her throat and swallow the contents. It fed through her tubes, washing everything, including the remains of our sex, out of her. It was the same brand Kita had used. I smiled. It made me feel at home.

They must've been satisfied with my psych profile shortly after that. Tin Star gave me my mission.

Tin Star. That's the Bureau name for the AI think tank that collates all the data. Learned a long time ago that networking was the key to catching a lot of criminals. Being able to collate and sift millions of pieces of data let you put together things that normally would be missed in a piecemeal method of police work. Tin Star sent me the file on Heather and Mallet because it was able to put together some key clues from the nuances of their lives. Captured half-second glimpses of their intentions through thousands of semi-sentient autonomous agents swimming the worldwide computer nets.

Tin Star had cross-referenced Heather and Mallet with the facts for someone suitable to do the job. Me because of the buckyball incident that had left me unstoppable all those years ago, me because I was there with Heather and Mallet in Nigeria, me because it looked like Mallet and Heather were going back to the Dark Red Continent.

No, I never knew where Tin Star was housed. The Bureau? I couldn't tell you what Bureau or for which country. If Tin Star did work for a country. All I knew was the shell and the job. Once upon a time I used to know the shell and the job and Kita, but now I had a new dollop. Or I should say, I had a new boss. Tin Star and the dollops were the same thing; if Tin Star was the Queen bee, the dollop robos were the drones. It took a special sort of guy to be queer for a Tommy.

I was that sort of guy.

Working for the Bureau isn't so bad. You do crime-lab stuff, expense accounts, big cars and cell phones and airplanes all across the country when you want. Silk suit from worms in China and a leather coat that actually grew on a cow. Starting pay is better than regular cops make after ten years on the force getting shot at by perps in the 7-eleven every day.

Every time they cracked my shell, I had a compiler routine go through all the major news stories while I was cold. I suppose I was just like the Doom Generation of my world: I couldn't let go of what happened in the past because I couldn't stand the thought of the future.

She was watching over my shoulder as I went through the files onscreen, her white hair flowing over my shoulders. "You know what Tin Star said about you? "If at first you don't succeed, send in the wild boys.' "

Tin Star made my bank account good for 30K. I was like Dracula, waking up from the grave, living a false life for myself. For this job I'd need a cover to fool Mallet and Heather; they were people who actually knew me. Tin Star cooked up my story. Sent the Devi up to the hotel with it in a metal case of syringes. I lay back on the bed and she put a local anesthetic on my right eye. The needles were curved. I could watch as she pushed the metal point into my socket, heard it click through my skull. After that, I gripped the sheets and absorbed it.

Bucks. Nanotech. They built memories. Years ago, there'd been a woman, a musical genius who'd played violin with the world's greatest orchestras. She never made first chair because she suffered from epilepsy so severe that even the highest doses of drugs couldn't control the seizures. She had brain surgery, four times, to remove the affected area. They removed nearly 40 percent of her right lobe to control the seizures only to find out the woman was still fully functional. Her brain had, over the years, learned to reroute activities to the part of her brain unaffected by seizures. She was a medical miracle. They studied her for the rest of her life. They found out how the brain worked. How it learns, how it stores memories. The bucks went into my brain and built false memories for me, neuron by neuron.

It wasn't complete memories. Just enough to fake it. Too much and they'd run the risk of spillover: having memories of two things at the same point in time. A lot of my life had been spent in the shell, and that made it easier. After Nigeria, I was in Japan. From there, a ticket up the gravity well to NHK, New Hong Kong. Ran out of cash and got a labor job on Luna, mining iron. Working the big iron was one way to explain the lack of muscle atrophy from time spent in low-gee. From there, back earthside to Israel, working on a kibbutz, living for free, traveling on two dollars a day. The head full of false data was some textbook biochem, a little aikido, Japanese language, Hebrew/Arabic language and culture. I knew what it was like to fuck in freefall. Spent a week getting used to it all floating back in there. Kept trying to do things with my dollop that you could only do in zero gravity.

She brought me everything. Car keys to a secondhand convertible that still ran on gasohol, and an unregistered firearm. My favorite, a microwave pistol; tight beam, superconductor battery good for 10 shots, worked in vacuum, made things e-x-p-l-o-d-e. Papers, ID, passport, health insurance, inoculation card, my Blue Card that showed I was free of the plague: the Red Death.

One dark night I put the microwave in my jacket pocket and put on my leather coat. The Devi rested against the doorframe to the bedroom. Hands pressed to her belly, balanced on one bare foot, white hair falling over the robe she wore. I picked up my car keys and batted my lashes at her.

"I'll be back."

"Will you?" She was sad. "I always wonder. My last one didn't. Died."

I crossed the floor to her and wetted my lips for both of us. Kissed her. "What is your name?" Her eyes were green. You had to be close to tell. The irises were square. Windows to what she really was. A stack of synthetic muscles on steel bones. An artifice brain inside a titanium skull: a stack of superconductors pieced together one at a time by bucks. She was a Tommy, an automaton. Not a human brain cell inside that head. Maybe once upon a time she'd been human, but whoever, whatever she'd started as, now she was all mechnik. A ghost recording, a download of someone else's personality, or maybe only an edited version of someone. Maybe they's stolen someone's intelligence and kindness and stitched it with a PhD's education, an assassin's skill at murder, and a nun's compassion. Maybe she was a second generation of that composite, maybe a fifth, or a tenth. I'd never know. It wouldn't matter. She wasn't perfect, but she was perfect for me; they'd be sure of that.

"Grace," she whispered.

.   .   .

I drove my convertible with the top down over to the Cherry. Strange how they came back there. Like salmon spawning. For six months after we got back from Nigeria, before Heather got her next contract up cyberspace and Mallet was working the media circuits off the Nigeria scandal he'd help break, we hung out at the Cherry a lot. Neither one of them had known that I'd been recruited by the Bureau by then. Recruited meant I was sleeping with Kita. One day I just didn't wake up. I dropped off the planet. Woke up when Tin Star told me to go to work, and found out six months had passed.

I ordered four shots of tequila at the bar and drank them all one after another, chewing back a slice of lemon with each one. That first dose of bucks I ever took, it's never going to go away, and it metabolizes alcohol a lot faster. I have to drink that much just to feel it. After the first four, I turned around and watched them. Two of them in the booth. Flatworld palmtop on the table between them. Studying something. I stayed steady on them, recording like a camera. It would make some memoir about my life I'd edit someday: this scene, the return of the prodigal son.

They were a lot like I remembered. Mallet was a disaster of long hair and unkempt clothes. He had on a suit jacket but the pockets were full of bulky gear that made it hang off one shoulder. Looked like shit. Heather, tiny Heather. About five feet tall, hair permanently standing on end like she'd been electrocuted. Fright marks of black paintstick around her eyes and mouth. Pale skin tinted even paler since the old days. Black tights, black boots, black jacket, black dress. The only color the violent blue of her nails and the glowing blue strips of animated tattoos running around each wrist. Tiny flatworld video woven just beneath her skin. Dragons and patterns running around the band of her wrist.

Stopping time. The holo-video was in the middle of an electric koto band selling motorcycles on ten different tanks down the length of the bar. A three-minute music video for Kawasaki. Under the blur and the redflash of the speed-slick cowlings, I crossed the floor. Watched Mallet swivel his unshaved chin up at me, grin coming up, falling on his lips like rain. Heather a china doll, not even looking, staring at the reflection on her glass at a funhouse image of me. Then I saw the gun in her hand, half-hidden under the table. Not moving.

"Well, well, well," Mallet spoke, the words coming out half-drowned by the Kawasaki drums.

And Heather looked up, stood up and dipped the gun back into her jacket. One of those little hands taking my hand, her blue wrists shimmering against the leather of my coat. "Mark," she said. A little girl's voice, still. She took hormones; they'd pushed back her aging to prepubescence. "Mark One, the man who can't be stopped." She squeezed. Happy.

"You'd better sit down for a drink," Mallet said, out of his chair, slapping my shoulder.

Heather was out of the booth, on her toes to hug me. The barrel of the gun was against my nose. "Do the trick," she said, laughing.

"Heather," Mallet said.

"C'mon. Mark, it's been so long. Do the thing with the hand." She took the gun away and pressed it against the palm of my hand. It was an antique. An automatic pistol that fired lead bullets in brass shells. Not even self-guided bullets. It was like throwing rocks. But she liked .45s. "It was the greatest party trick ever. C'mon, Mark. Just for me?"

I nodded, smiled. "Anything for you, Jetgirl."

She cheered and sat back in the booth, cocked the automatic and leveled it at me. I held up my hand, palm towards her, like a Republic Picture movie Indian saying, "How." She aimed and fired.

For a moment, the whole bar turned our way, stunned into silence. Heather was cheering, both hands over her head with the gun still smoking while I gripped my wounded hand in the other. Gritting my teeth, I held it up again, the ring finger missing, for everyone to see.

Mallet was nosing around on the floor by the bar, a shot glass of vodka in hand. "I got it," he called, bent over and picked up my finger. Dropped it into the shot glass.

"Do it, Mark," Heather yelled as I took the glass away. Swirling the bloody end in the drink I sipped the glass dry, shook off my finger and carefully put the two stumps together. "One one-thousand," Heather yelled.

"Two one-thousand," Mallet called.

"Three one-thousand," I finished, and flourished my hand. Made a fist with all five fingers. Nothing but a pink line where the digit had been blown off. In the old days I used to play piano after it grafted back on. Bucks. Flowing through my veins. It's a gift.

· · ·

We drank all night and the sky was getting pink when the last bar closed. The three of us walking down ash-filled streets. Grey dust blowing into devils around our feet. Heather between us, holding hands. Mallet went into a corner store to buy a pack of hemplocks and road beers while Heather and I got my convertible out of the parking lot. I was cold sober. We climbed in and I started the engine. The car had character. Throaty engine. Heather rolled her hands over the vat-grown leather of the seat upholstery.

"This is a sexy machine." She rolled her head back against the headrest. Drunk. "But you always had a thing for sexy machines." She looked straight into my eyes. "Why are the good ones always queer?"

She was on me then, her mouth open to me, hands grasping my shirt. When I didn't respond back, she stopped. Wiped her mouth with the back of her hand. "Just look in my eyes," she pleaded. "I've got mechnik eyes, at least."

It was true. Somewhere along the way she'd lost her real ones. The new ones were amber. Golden-brown. Metal and plastics.

"Not Tommy enough for you, eh?" She rolled off me. "You'd be surprised, Mark. You hate the stuff in yourself, you ever wonder why you love it in a woman?"

"Just born this way." I smiled. "I guess."

"But that's the beauty of it, Mark. You don't have to be the way you're born."

I wanted to tell her to stop. Wanted to tell her about Kita and Grace, about how little she'd end up being in the end. Wanted to say I was a boytoy queer for mechniks because it helped keep the desire at bay. Screwing one was enough to maintain my habit without getting hooked: it kept me from wanting to be one.

But Mallet was back by then. A bottle brown-bagged in one fist. And when he climbed into the back seat, Heather slithered in with him and curled up next to him. They gave me directions like I was a Tommy hack and I pulled up under the empty awning of a house in the beaches. A little cottage that backed onto the boardwalk and the sand. I got them inside, the bottle unopen on the kitchen table. Saw Mallet's clothes in the laundry mixed with hers. Helped guide Heather to the bathroom where she crawled to the tub and started running water.

Saw the photos and clippings on the walls. Some of them from Nigeria, some of them ones I'd taken. Mallet and Heather, together.

On my way to the front door, Mallet stepped in front of me from the kitchen.

"You knew, didn't you?" He was upset, embarrassed. "About Heather and me, I mean."

I shrugged. "I figured."

"Tomorrow night," he went on, forgetting it. "Tomorrow, we've got some people for you to meet. About things. About the old days. About Africa."

"Africa?" I asked.

He put a finger to his lips. "Trust me. Tomorrow night."

He closed the front door when I got into my car. I drove back to the hotel as the sun came up. My eyes strained for a moment at the glare, then darkened enough to compensate. The crucifix was a dark outline against the sun, streets deserted. Dust and yellowed hardcopy floating on the wind currents. I stopped at an empty intersection, pulling up to another car waiting for the green. Noticed the car idling beside me had two corpses in it. Death grins. Bloated, decaying bodies still upright in their seatbelts. It'd been there days, obviously, and still no one had gotten around to picking up the stiffs. Sometimes so much changed when I was in the shell. Never would've seen that a year ago.

Grace was waiting inside the hotel room. Cross-legged on the bed, naked. Gold ring of her clit-hood pierce sticking out between bare lips.

"I'm in," I told her.

After Nigeria, the others took their splice of the pie and did what they did. I read the reports about when they started buying up bodymods. Not illegal purchases, but Tin Star had monitored them. Heather had started jacking up brain augments. Microprocessors in the corpus callosum, rerouting the traffic between the halves of the brain, learning, getting faster. Loaded with data downloads of smarts she hadn't learned naturally. Running semivolitional nonsentient AIs inside the vast superconductor memory in her head. I stopped reading the reports after a while.

CURRENT BREAKDOWN OF SUBJECT
H.S. AUSTIN: BODY MODIFICATIONS
WITH PERCENTAGES SHOWN:

ARMS, STANDARD (R AND L);
    LAZLO & MERCER ....(12%)
LEG, BIO-AUGMENT (L);
    CARTIER-BIOLOGIQUE ....(06%)
OPTICS, STANDARD (R AND L);
LEICA LIGHT COMPENSATION AUGMENT TARGETING
    HEADS-UP-DISPLAY NIGHT VISION AMPLIFICATION ......(15%)
AURAL REPLACEMENT (R AND L);
    TELESTAR AM/FM/SW RADIO RECEIVER PERSONAL
    STEREO; SONY TELE-NET LINK; BELT NORTHERN ....(10%)
RADIATION AND ELECTRONIC COUNTER-
    MEASURES SHIELDING ....(01%)
SUBCUTANEOUS TORSO ARMOR,
    6 THICKNESSES OF KEVLAR 18 ....(05%)
SHARK-COLLAGEN BREAST IMPLANT (R AND L);
    LAZLO & MERCER ....(02%)
CORPUS CALLOSUM BRAIN AUGMENTATION;
    TELESTAR ....(07%)
8 PIN EXTERNAL LINK PAST:
    TELESTAR ....(03%)
SHEATHED NERVOUS SYSTEM (COPPER WIRE);
    TELESTAR ....(03%)

64% MODIFIED

Subject suffered loss of reproductive organs in Nigerian "Bucky Balls" incident. Refused replacement or organic parts or synthetic glands.

Brain augmentation originally commissioned to monitor and maintain hormone levels within acceptable ranges.

I hadn't seen them in two days when I got a holomessage from Heather in my video-fax. Just her from the neck up, smiling into the camera. A time and a location. I checked it. A gun club.

I signed in my firearms at the desk and paid for a pair of protective goggles and earwear. Back in the range I found Heather and Mallet in adjoining stalls. Mallet had a collection of pistols and submachine guns he was trying for weight. Face immobile as he inspected the guns. His eyes, at least, weren't lenses. An opaque membrane clicked down over each one as he turned back to the range and started squeezing shots at his target.

Heather was in black jeans and a white T-shirt. Firing with a two-handed stance; I got a good view of both arms. Bodymods. Ropes of poly-muscle fiber with reinforced metal joints. Not even a synthetic skin covering. I waited until she was done and she gave me a thumbs up. Pointed down the hall to the end of the stalls.

There was a lounge behind a sound-proof window. In a minute she came in with a shooter's bag slung over one shoulder. "Mark." She smiled. "I'll be a few minutes. You might as well come with me."

I followed her into the change rooms. Nobody there but us. Inside the door she peeled off her T-shirt and dropped it on a bench. Turned to face me bare-chested.

"What do you think?" She vogued her arms over her head.

"Those are supposed to impress me? Why don't you try putting some skin on instead of running around naked?"

She pouted. "I get skin next week. I meant these." She lowered her arms and cupped her breasts. "Notice anything different?"

I shrugged. Tighter, rounder. Not like I remembered.

"Had subcutaneous body armor implanted from here"—she touched the hollow of her throat—"to here." She prodded her pubic bone through her jeans. "They had to replace my breasts with mods, but they're so good these days, I think they're better than the originals. What about you?"

I walked closer and touched them. Tweaked her nipple until she shuddered. "Do you have to try so hard?" I whispered.

She smiled, eyes half closed. "Since you've been back, you've just been a good influence on me, I guess."

I ran my free hand down her stomach. "Just because you got it chopped out in here"—I pressed—"doesn't mean you have to get it chopped out down here—" and I grabbed her crotch through her jeans. "You'll turn yourself into silicon valley," I fingered her crotch, "for something that happened a long time ago." I stepped back and put my hands in my pockets. "I've had better than you. Don't do me any favors."

Heather went dark. "Fuck you!" she yelled. "You fucking queer!" She punched me in the stomach, again and again, until something snapped. Grabbed my wrist and bent it backwards until it broke, and I screamed. "You fucking queer, you fucking, you fuck!" she had me on the ground, kicking my face, my testicles, the small of my back. After a minute, she slowed down. Stopped.

I managed to use my unbroken arm to sit up. Coughed blood. Face swollen shut. Then the heat started. Steam coming out of my mouth with every breath. Then the sounds of my body knitting. Bones snapping and cartilage popping as it moved back into place. Vision returning as my eyelids smoothed out. Ribs pulling out of my lung. The blood drooling out my mouth crawled back up my chin and inside before the broken skin knitted together. Healed, I stood up.

"It's been swell," I staggered back from her, "but the swelling's gone down now."

My telefax rang and I let it. The only sound inside the hotel room. I'd been living alone for the last two weeks. Grace would find me when she wanted me, but she would never call. I spent the time with the jumper-cable umbilicus plugged into my navel, letting ProNet programming live my life for me. Turned in for twenty hours per, getting infotainment, realtime drama shows, erotica from level X to level XXXX, and whatever else ProNet had in file shunted straight to my optic and aural nerves. A long time since I'd been able to do that. I didn't eat and, after a few days, the bucks in my system would rebel and attack the hunger center of my brain. I'd run for the kitchenette and eat anything, the first thing, I found. One time it was a stick of butter and a jar of hot peppers. After that I made sure to leave only cans of cold spaghetti with pull-tab openers on the counter.

As my answering machine picked up on the telefax, I glanced to see who it was; ghost image of "Anal Intruder: It Came from Outer Space" superimposed over the RL image of my apartment.

"*Moshi-moshi.*" Heather's smiling face filled the holotank of the fax. "We picked up a lead from a data-bank theft. A way of doing business in Africa, our data acquisitions geek says. You there, Mark? Africa, hear? We could be going back to where it started. There isn't room for all of us in the collective to go, so I'm trying to save a spot for you. Call me. *Arigato.*" Click, off. Gone.

· · ·

Grace the Devi was in disguise. Standing under the fossilized skeleton of brachiosaurus in the dinosaur section of the museum, dressed like a schoolgirl. Bare feet in thin canvas sneakers. Hip-hugger jeans. White T-shirt and black sunglasses. Her hair pulled back in knots on the sides of her head. Busloads of the kids were everywhere in the halls. Rich kids from private schools who could afford real excursions instead of interactive discs in the classroom. She'd blended herself in. Our eyes met through a crowd and she grinned, cracked her gum at me. I felt like a professor banging one of his students.

The kids passed. I met her under the skeleton and she took my arm. We walked further into the exhibit.

"Daddy, are you sure we should be doing this?" she whispered to me.

I smiled. Delighted that a dollop could be so perverse. She knew me. Up on the third floor, it was almost deserted. We found an isolated corner among the Primitive Man exhibits; a maze of life-size dioramas in glass booths. She pulled down her jeans and bent over. We had a fast move before anyone came by.

"I've missed you," she said. "I want to come back to live with you."

"Too dangerous." I put my arm around her as we wandered into the big echoes of the Medieval Times displays. Dark halls of period dresses on lady mannequins. Rows of steel-shell suits of armor. Nothing but polished metal and segmented plates that were empty on the inside. "I don't like mixing it up while I'm on an op. They might have me under surveillance."

"How long since you even saw one of them last?" She didn't wait for an answer because she already knew. "I need you, Blue. I'm lonely."

"Just for tonight," I said.

A week later and she was still there. We spent all day sleeping and fucking. Went out around nine and caught a show. Some late dinner. Went to a club. The night before, we'd taken the convertible to a few shops on the strip and bought new clothes to get dressed in. I had a blue suit, kind of acidic aquamarine. Grace in a black halter top and skintight shorts with a black jersey-cloth cardigan that brushed the floor as she walked. It was open down the front with just her long dark legs and body rolling like machine tools. We caught the Boudoir's nine P.M. liftoff;

an entire club and restaurant inside a small zeppelin, only half a kilometer long, that circled the city all night. Touching down every few hours to disgorge and take on passengers, dinners and clubbers. There was a pharmacy, six bars, three dining rooms and a fitness club on board. The only thing it didn't have were sleeper cabins. You had to rent private dining rooms with attached trysting lounges. We rode above the city all night, one wall of our lounge a flatworld high-res projection from a camera mounted on the hull of the zeppelin. The city was only a connect-the-dots of lights far below. Drifting over streamers of light in yellow and red. My last time out of the shell, there'd been more lights. Fewer every year. The Doom Generation succumbing to the Red Death. Maybe next time only the Tommys would be left, and people who had turned themselves into mechniks. It was the twilight of the real.

We crawled into the apartment at dawn. Grace was never tired, but she could imitate me almost to perfection. She picked up the clues in my body language. Played at being drowsy and satiated for my benefit. Just because I knew it wasn't real doesn't mean I don't appreciate it. I went to bed in my clothes and so did Grace.

I woke up in the middle of the day. Hard lines of sunlight around the edges of the dark curtains. Grace was asleep beside me. Or sort of. She'd shut herself down by several levels to a standby mode; entering an approximation of alpha waves in her artifice brain. She was still conscious to a point, but part of her mind recognized my movements as something normal and harmless, and didn't arouse her. I squinted past the light and into the bathroom. Standing over the toilet I could still smell the sex on me. On the way out, I saw the light on the fax. New Message. I clicked playback.

"Mark." Heather's tone sounded worried. A little frown on her forehead. "Things are heating up. I keep telling my people I've talked to you and you're on board with us, and it's only two days until we go. If I'd have known you were going to get so moody, I wouldn't have teased you so much." She paused. "Mark, listen, I'm sorry. KO? You've always been so serious. But a job's a job. I'm sorry about the last time . . . when I . . . went too far. But you come with us to Africa. I'll make it up, I swear. We need you there, boytoy. I can't go back without thinking about Nigeria. Mallet's coming, but he never really understood

Africa. You did." She looked away from the camera. "Don't make me go alone.

"You remember when it all started." She blinked her little girl eyes. "I found you in that British field hospital when you were still rolling in agony and they had you strapped to the bed. Blind and deaf. I stayed with you. You only knew it was me because I spelled letters on the palm of your hand, one at a time. You were lucky, though. Those bucky balls in your blood were making your life hell, but they fought off the Red Death. You didn't know I had it. I didn't know I had it."

The Red Death. Vectored like HIV. It showed first as high fever. Cramps, chills. Then it leveled out. Hours, days, months later it came back. Internal hemorrhaging. The stomach and intestine in men. In women it was uterine bleeding, spontaneous abortion if they were carrying, and finally a full hysterectomy. It had been designed by the French, originally as a manufactured micro-surgeon to sterilize women. Either nature or human madness had modified it. Made a wild culture that got loose in Nigeria. Ninety-five percent fatal.

"We found out who did it. Who let the Death loose. Our data geek has a way into Africa too. Maybe we can find them, still. Maybe there's a cure. Maybe not. We're going, Mark. Call me."

Grace was still sleeping when I got back to bed. I lay awake for hours with her not moving. She was curled up like a person would be, but she was motionless. Dollops don't breathe. The only reason I can stand to sleep with them is because they're like part of the furniture. She began to stir a few hours later, then was suddenly and completely awake.

"You up?" she asked from the pillow. I nodded.

"You knew about Africa. That they want me to go. Why is this important to Tin Star?"

"Tin Star always knew who did it." She sat up, her white hair flowing like unstrung bowstrings. "Or has for a long time, anyway."

I knew then, just who had made the Red Death. No mistake there were fewer of us every year and more of them. Would I be a pet, I wondered, in the future? Would Tin Star thaw me out like some living Brachiosaurus? Someday would I just never wake up?

"Go to Africa, Blue. For me."

"You mean, for Tin Star," I whispered.

"No." She shook her head. "We know you wouldn't do anything for Tin Star. But me, you'd do it for me, wouldn't you? You love me, don't you?" She rolled her eyes back and nuzzled my neck.

It was true. A dollop is nothing without her boytoy. While Grace was mine, everything she did was for me. She couldn't help it; that was part of the personality they built into her. Of course I loved her: she loved me like a woman couldn't. Her entire creation was defined by being in love with me.

"I'll go to Africa," I whispered in her ear. I held her close and let her bury her face in my shoulder. "I love you," I said.

I put the microwave pistol against her stomach, over the superconductor storage coil, and fired. The explosion threw us apart, me against the far wall, Grace against the headboard of the bed. Killed us both. Blackened. Steaming. I had almost an hour before my bucks repaired me. Watching her. Propped sitting up, the middle of her body melted and charcoaled down to the titanium bones of her spine. No light in her eyes. Tangle of white hair around her shoulders. When I could, I stood up and closed her eyes. Kissed them both.

Driving the convertible away from the bronzeplex I saw the giant crucifix glowing in the twilight of the rearview.

"You know," I whispered, afraid of my own voice. "You know, sweetness, it's times like these, I am the resurrection."

OFFER OF IMMORTALITY

Robertson Davies

Robertson Davies, who was both an eminent Canadian writer and one of the most influential novelists of the fantastic in the English language (particularly via his Deptford trilogy, beginning with his greatest international success, *Fifth Business*, and continuing with *The Manticore* and *World of Wonders*), never wrote a word of genre fiction, except in the specialized subgenre of ghost stories, and then as lighthearted parodies. These are collected in his delightful book, *High Spirits* (1982), along with an essay on his lifelong attachment to reading tales of ghosts and the supernatural, with nods to Mary Shelley, J. S. Le Fanu, Henry James, M. R. James, and Montague Summers.

Of the stories in *High Spirits*, "Offer of Immortality" is the closest to SF, and it is of course a parody of science, in this case of biological science and the quest for immortality, in the contemporary false-gothic mode.

Many of you who are here tonight have heard several of the Massey College Ghost stories, and there are some who have heard them all. Seventeen stories up to the present, and all of them true. Yet I have never felt justified in taking the ghosts for granted; I have never dared to think—Oh, one pops up every year, and it's sure to appear on time. Ghosts do not like to be taken for granted, just as they do not like to be given orders. You will understand why I was uneasy; this is my last year as Master of Massey College, and I should have liked to round out my time here by telling you of yet another ghost.

However, " 'Tis not in mortals to command success." I have no ghost for you.

However, there was something—circumstances of which I ought to inform you, though when you have heard them you will understand my reluctance in making them known. Not a ghost—no—but something not quite in the common run of affairs. Oh that I had the resolution to stop now, to say no more! But—here it is.

It happened at the end of November, when we held our last High Table for this year. We don't have High Tables in December because the College Dance and this affair are our offerings of hospitality during the Christmas season. Hospitality! It is one of the guiding lights of this College. Every honor, every consideration for our guests—that is our somewhat old-fashioned principle. A guest here is sacred.

On the Friday afternoon, when we were getting ready for High Table, Miss Whalon received a telephone call from Dr. Walter Zingg, the distinguished medical scientist and a Senior Fellow. "I hope it won't upset the arrangement of the table too much," said he, "but I should greatly like to bring a visitor who has arrived unexpectedly from South America—a scientist of international renown, from Bogotá, a Professor J. M. Murphy." That was easily arranged, and when the list of guests was being prepared Miss Whalon discovered that the University from which Professor Murphy came was founded in 1572 (which makes it substantially our senior) and that it must also be one of the most exalted universities in the world, for it stands nine thousand feet above sea level. But when she finally ran the professor down in an academic directory it said only that he was a world leader in Cryonics, and that his full name was Jesus Maria Murphy.

This did not trouble me. South America is full of the descendants of Irish immigrants who retain their Irish names, although they are now almost wholly of Spanish and Indian blood, Jesus Maria Murphy would cause no more raise eyebrows in Columbia than such a name as Mackenzie King Stacey might in Canada. I didn't know what Cryonics was, but I didn't need to know; Professor Zingg would take care of all that.

I was not prepared, however, for the figure who appeared in the Senior Common Room under the wing of Dr. Zingg. I say "under the wing" advisedly, for Professor Murphy came no higher than the doctor's waist. He was the tiniest human being that I have ever seen, but that was not the only thing that gave him an air of unreality; his complexion was so rich in colour, and his hair was so glossily black that he looked like a beautifully-made doll. Hair dye and an almost operatic amount of makeup; strange in an academic, but these are permissive times. When I took his hand, it was like a tiny claw, and extraordinarily cold—so cold I almost dropped it in surprise.

When I am disconcerted I take refuge in extreme heartiness and good-fellowship, which, as most of you know, is no indication of my true nature. That is what I did when I felt that cold, cold hand.

"Welcome, Professor Murphy!" I roared; "What good fortune for us that you are able to dine here tonight! Ho, ho, ho!"

He responded with what I suppose he meant for a reciprocal exuberance. In a thin, high voice, very much like Punch in the puppet shows I used to see in London, he replied: "Dat what you tink, eh? Locky for you? Yes, lockier dan you know! He, he, he!"

I introduced Professor Murphy to some of the others who had assembled for dinner. Quite without self-consciousness he skipped up on top of the table, and stood there, so as to be able to address them face to face.

When an opportunity came, I looked inquiringly at Professor Zingg; he was blushing. "Never saw him before," he said, "but I have to take care of him over the weekend—keeping off big dogs and mean children and that sort of thing."

"The Professor looks to me as if he knew how to look after himself," said I.

Certainly he had no trouble at dinner. With that exquisite courtesy for which Massey College is famous, our librarian had seen that three volumes of the Oxford English Dictionary were on his chair, so that he would be at no disadvantage, and there he sat, perched on N-Poy, chattering away happily to Dr. Swinton, a man with an insatiable appetite for scientific curiosities; on Murphy's other side sat Professor Hume, the Master-Designate, and I knew that those two experienced hands at college hospitality would take good care of our strange guest. But I noticed that although he chased our good dinner round his plate with his knife and fork, he ate nothing, and drank no wine.

Our steward, Mr. Stojanovich, appeared beside my chair.

"That little gentleman, that Professor Murphy, asks if he might have some of his favorite drink."

"Certainly, if we have it," I said.

"We have it," said Mircha; "it is vinegar."

"Give him the best we have," said I.

An odd request, I thought. Vinegar is, of course, a solution of acetic acid made, as the dictionary explains, from inferior wines; Canada, which yields place to no country in the world in the production of inferior wines, has first-rate vinegar. Mircha returned, bearing a demijohn which he showed me in the distinguished manner that adds so much to college functions. I took a little in a glass, and rolled it thoughtfully over my palate; it was a rich, full Loblaw 1980. I nodded approvingly, our guest was served, and I was interested to observe that he smacked his lips and, after two quick glasses, showed an increase of his former lively spirits.

Nor was that the end of it. When we went downstairs for more conversation and wine, Professor Murphy insisted that the vinegar jug go with him, and he nipped away all evening, consuming more in liquid volume than any four of the rest of us.

This was eccentric, certainly, but nothing more. However, when we were parting for the night, the strange guest seized me by the hand, and hissed: 'I must talk to you.'

"If you wish," I said; "I'll ask Professor Zingg to bring you into my lodgings."

"No, no," said little Murphy; "get rid of Zingg. Tell Zingg to go hang."

As Professor Zingg was standing right beside him, this was rude. But Professor Zingg is not a man to lose his dignity; he smiled courteously at Jesus Maria Murphy, bowed very slightly, and left the room. But I thought there was an air of relief in his manner.

In no time at all I found myself sitting in my study, facing Professor Murphy, who was curled up in my big chair, with his third demijohn of vinegar, freshly opened, sitting on the floor beside him.

A hospitable thought struck me. "Would you like to use the plumbing?" I asked. After all, the law of gravity dictates that so much liquid intake must, at some point, impose this necessity.

"Use what?" he hissed. "Oh, the excusado. No, no; never go. Foolish, foolish. You shall find out why."

I can't say I liked the sound of that. But the Professor was hurrying on.

"You, Davies, you old man now, eh? You getting out of here? Dey kick you out, no?"

"Decidedly no," I said, with some austerity, for I did not like his tone; "I am retiring, and the College has shown me every courtesy, as is its custom."

"Yah, yah, but you sorry to go. You want to know what's going to happen, eh?"

"Naturally I do. I am the first Master of this College; I hope the first of a long and splendid line. Not to be curious about the future would be impossible, though I know how ridiculous any such desire must be."

"Why ridiculous?"

"Well—because of the brevity of human life."

"Not brief at all. You not a scientist, eh?"

"No," said I; "insofar as it is possible to sum up what I am, I am a student of literature with a psychological bias."

"Oh, Holy Mother of God!" said Professor Murphy. "How you people spend your time! Still, I was just such an idiot when I was your age, a few hundred years ago. I was even a priest. Our university was started by priests, way back in the days of the Spanish Conquest; I was one of the founders and Sub-Rector for many years. But it is not easy to be a Spanish priest in the South American mountains, not if you have any real intelligence, not if you see what is right under your nose."

I thought it better to humor this madman. Was he really claiming to be something like four hundred and fifty years old? "So you became an unbeliever?" I said.

"Never! Unbelievers are fools, worse than unilluminated believers. I became an illuminated believer. I expanded my realm of belief. I became an alchemist."

"An alchemist?" said I. "Making gold, and that sort of thing?"

"Pah!" he said, and a good deal of saliva sprayed across the room at me. "I spit on gold! In South America is gold everywhere, kicking along the ground. No, no, I studied *life*, and as time went on, and science began to lift its head above the rubbish of faith, the Illumination came, and by the middle of the nineteenth century I was one of the earliest biologists."

"Is it widely known that you have had such a long and interesting life?" I said.

"No; better not," said he. "I change my name from time to time. Give up being priest, though I am still a good Catholic. But that is why I am now Murphy; lots of Murphys in Colombia. I can speak Irish. Begorrah, may your shadow never grow less, devil take you, damn your eyes, Mother Machree. Yes, now I am Professor Murphy, and head of a very big scientific section in our University."

"And what brings you to Canada?" I said.

"I am scouting for candidates," said he, looking at me with extreme cunning.

"For your faculty?" said I.

"No, no—for my Instituto Cryonico da Colombia. But we have strayed. We talked about your curiosity regarding the future of this College. There are lots of ways of finding out, you know."

"Such as—?" said I.

"Well, Gematria, for one," said he.

Gematria—the cabbala of numbers! How often had I not heard of it, that elaborate, ancient, but surely mad science of divination practiced so long by the Jews, and part of the structure of their medieval scholasticism! I looked at Murphy with new eyes.

"But surely Gematria is known only among the Jews?" said I.

"If you live long enough and survive strongly enough the Jews begin to think you must be one of themselves, and they tell you secrets," said Murphy. "You want to know how Gematria works?"

Of course I did.

"Then you must understand that numbers are the most important things under heaven. All is number, and God is the God of Numbers. I suppose you know Hebrew?"

"I've allowed it to grow a little rusty," I said; "but I used to be able to read and write it pretty well."

"Ah, then you know that in Hebrew there are no special signs for numbers, but each letter of the alphabet has a numerical equivalent, and that means that every word has a numerical equivalent also."

"Yes, yes."

"In the art of Gematria you divine secret things by reducing the appropriate words to their number equivalents, adding up those, then adding the integers of the sum again and again until you reach a number between one and eleven. That number is the Golden Number, and must be interpreted by knowledge of a very secret doctrine that embodies the rational pattern that lies beneath the seeming disorder of the universe."

"Yes," said I, "but how are you going to make that work with English words? Hebrew suppresses all the vowels but A, and lacks several of our letters."

"That is part of the tradition. You fill in the gaps with Greek letters that also have numerical equivalents. Greek alchemists, Jewish alchemists, they worked hand in glove. It really does work, you know. Want to try?"

"I think you want to demonstrate your skill," said I. Of course I wanted to try. But obviously I was not deceiving him; he went off into a fit of laughter, almost silent, producing a small noise like someone crushing tissue paper.

"You do not trust me," he wheezed. "You think I am a magician. And so I am. But not a false magician. I am a scientist, which is a modern magician. Long ago, when our University first began, in 1572, they called me a black magician, and there are still some who make the sign against the Evil Eye when I pass them. But I wish you would trust me and let me be your friend, because I can help you greatly. Let us be friends in your Canadian manner. Call me Jesus."

There is a Puritan buried within me. I secretly determined not to call him Jesus if I could possibly avoid it. I took refuge in cunning.

"I'll do better than that," I said; "I'll call you Josh. Jesus is the same as Joshua, and the short name for Joshua is Josh. You see?"

"Oh yes, I see," said he, and I knew that he saw right through me and was laughing at my Protestant distaste. "Now, what shall we interpret? This College, don't you think? What is its essence? What is at the root of it that will shape its destiny for centuries to come? Now wait—I must make myself ready."

He sat very upright on my leather chair, his feet tucked under him, his eyes shut, and both his hands raised with the fingers extended. "Now," he said, "tell me the full name of this place, not too fast, so that I can reduce it to numbers."

"Massey College in the University of Toronto," said I, and as I spoke his fingers began to flicker rapidly, as if he were tapping the keys of some invisible calculator. And indeed that is just what he was doing. I realized that I was looking at calculation as it had been during the Middle Ages, before the coming of cheap pencils and paper pads, and adding machines, and computers. He had turned his ten fingers into an abacus. Nor did he hesitate for an instant before he spoke.

"Seventeen and twenty-four, and twenty, and thirty-four, and fifty-one comes to one hundred and forty-six," said he. "Add up the integers of one, four six and it comes to—eleven! Oh! Oh! Eleven!"

"Good, or bad?" said I, far more anxious than I wanted to reveal.

"Magnifico! The number of revelation. The number of great teachers and visionaries in religion, science, politics and the arts.

It is the number of those who live by the inner vision. Dangerous, mind you, for sometimes eleven loves ideas better than humanity, so that must be remembered and avoided. But what a
Golden Number for a college! Oh, you need have no fears for
this place."

"Thank you, Josh," I said. "You give me great hope. I am
only sorry that I shall not be here to see its fulfilment."

"How long have you been here?" said Professor Murphy.

"It will be eighteen years next June," said I, "but I began
work on this place twenty years ago, on the first of January,
1960."

"Aha, well—that date and the year and date of your birth—
add the integers and it comes to thirty—a three. That is very
good, because three is your Golden Number also—"

"How do you know?"

"Because I took trouble to find out before I came tonight,
and I knew you for a Three the minute I set eyes on you. So that
is a happy—"

"Coincidence?" said I.

"There is no such thing as a coincidence," said Josh; "not in
Gematria. It is all part of the numerical pattern that governs the
world. Yes, you were a good man to begin this place, but not to
continue it."

"Why?" I dreaded what he might say, but I had to know.

"Too flighty," said Josh. "Lots of imagination, lots of invention, but there is a limit to what those things can do in a place
like this—a place with the Great Eleven as its Golden Number.
You are not always and in all things wholly serious. You have
what we biologists call Jokey Genes. High time you went. Who
is to come next?"

"Professor Hume," said I. "You sat beside him upstairs."

"Yes, and I felt very strange things coming from him. That
is why I had to have vinegar; he was heating me up, and I
needed to reduce my body temperature. Tell me his full name."
And once again Josh took his calculating posture.

"James Nairn Patterson Hume," said I.

Josh made his rapid, flickering calculation, then, to my horror, gave a pathetic little squeak and collapsed sideways. Had
Pat Hume killed him? But I saw one of the tiny hands gesturing
toward the vinegar bottle which sat on the floor at his side, in
an instant I put it to his lips and he drank—drank—drank until
there was not a drop left. His eyes opened slowly, but one was

looking aloft while the other looked down, and from his tiny body mounted an overpowering reek of vinegar. If he had been drinking anything else I would have sworn he was drunk, but—vinegar? I must know.

"Jesus," I whispered, shaking him gently. "Jesus, are you pickled?"

He did not answer at once, but shook his head again and again, as if in wonderment. At last he spoke.

"This place must have a very special destiny," he said. "Its Golden Number is the Great Eleven, and that is splendor sufficient, but this Hume—this James Nairn Patterson Hume—his Golden Number is also—despampanante!—the Great Eleven. Work it out for yourself: fourteen, plus six, plus forty-one, plus twenty—and what have you?"

"How should I know?" I said; "I'm just one of your frivolous Threes; I can't be expected to add in my head. *What* have you?"

"Badulaque! Analphabet! You have ninety-two and even you should see that when you add the integers—nine and two, dog of a Three—you get eleven. So this College, already shaped by Eleven, is now to have a Master who is also an Eleven, and what will happen then—Oh, rumboso, rumboso!" His eyes seemed fixed upon some rosy vision.

"What will happen? Tell me," I said, shaking him.

"Oh, do not ask me to tell," said Professor Murphy. "Instead, why don't you join me in the Great Silent Chamber of the Immortals in the University at Bogotá, and from time to time we shall come back here and behold with our own eyes the wonders that are sure to be brought forth."

I was mystified. "Great Silent Chamber of Immortals?" I said.

"You know of my work," said he. "Am I not the Praefectus of the Instituto Cryonico of Bogotá?"

"I suppose so," said I, not very tactfully; "but what's Cryonics?"

"Oh, you Threes, you have the minds of ballet-dancers! Cryonics, numbskull, is the science that will save mankind by preserving indefinitely the lives and abilities of people chosen for that purpose. It is achieved by a carefully calculated arrest of the cellular death which eventually brings ordinary mortals to the point of physical and spiritual death; that arrest is managed by draining the body of most of its blood, and substituting a formula for which ordinary vinegar may serve as a temporary substitute; then the body is placed in a very cold chamber, and all its activities, but not its cellular life, are kept on ice, so to speak, until they are needed. Then, a gradual melting-out, and there's your man, practically as good as new and in my case, more than four hundred years old. Think what an accumulation of wisdom and experience that means! What we alchemists began so long ago as a search for the Philosopher's Stone was achieved in our Andean heights when we discovered—Oh, to hell with modesty!—when *I* discovered, that all that was needed was a sufficiently low temperature and plenty of vinegar. Now—here is your chance, and you must be quick, for this evening has been an exhausting one for me. Will you fly back with me to Bogotá? I promise you that in a week you will be emptied of your disgusting thick blood, and you will find yourself in a flask, reduced to the temperature of liquid nitrogen. All you have to do is leave a call at the desk—just like a motel—and in a hundred years you will be shipped back here to see what this great College has achieved."

I was tempted. I confess I was tempted. But I thought I should first talk the matter over with my wife. Later, when I had Professor Murphy's calculations checked by a Jewish scholar at one of the synagogues on Bathurst Street, I discovered that my wife is also a Three, just as I am myself, and it is unwise to neglect her opinion.

"May I have till tomorrow to make up my mind?" said I, and the Professor's nod was so feeble that I became greatly alarmed about him.

But we Threes have substantial powers of improvisation. It was clear that the Professor was so overcome by what he had found out about Massey College that he needed first aid, and of a special kind. So I did my unscientific best. Taking him in my arms, I carried him up the back stairs to the College kitchen; it was like carrying a wineskin, for the vinegar within him kept sloshing around most unaccountably. But I got him on one of the kitchen tables without having been seen during our wobbly progress through the College, and I undressed him, right down to his skin. Former priest that he was, I was not surprised to find that he was wearing a tiny hair shirt, which is still in my possession, more or less, for Miss Whalon uses it as a tea-cosy. I managed to rouse him sufficiently to drink a couple of large beakers of vinegar, then I brought jugs of ice-water, doused him thoroughly, and tucked him up for the night on a shelf in our large, walk-in refrigerator. In that embracing chill he fell instantly into a childlike sleep, and so I left him.

I went immediately to my wife, and put the great question up to her: was I to go to Bogotá and a chilly life eternal, in order that, from time to time, I might return to Massey College and spy on what my successors were doing? She thought for a while, and then said: "I wouldn't, if I were you. Don't be a Massey College ghost; it would be most unbecoming. Don't you remember the line from our theater days—'Superfluous lags the veteran on the stage'? When you have made your exit, take off your costume, clean the assumed character off your face, and leave the theater."

These were wise words, as I had expected them to be. So I went to bed; went to sleep; and forgot the whole matter.

I was sharply reminded of it only last week, when we had our annual Christmas Dance. A great feature of that affair is the buffet, which is a splendidly theatrical creation at which all the guests survey, before they eat, the miracles of cuisine that our chefs have prepared. Elegantly displayed turkeys, splendidly ornamented fish, jellies and potted meats pressed into fantastic and festive shapes, cream puffs filled with cream, so that their whiteness takes on the likeness of swans, wonderful little tartlets like jewels of topaz, and ruby and emerald. Cakes decorated in High Baroque styled that are themselves the epitome of Christmas, and happy youth and good cheer. As always, I looked at it with pride; this was just the sort of show to appeal to a man whose Golden Number is Three. And then—

I don't want to continue. I'd much rather not. But there are imperatives of historical truth which even a Three dare not brush aside. There, at the center of the main table, was—No, no. No, I say!

Well, it was a roast suckling pig. At any rate, that was the way it was garnished. Certainly it had an apple in its mouth, and around the little eyes were outlines of white icing. Tips of pink icing extended its ears, which were not wholly piglike. I looked hopefully between the markedly unpiglike buttocks for a curly tail, but there was none.

Turning to our Bursar, Colin Friesen, I said, controlling my voice as best I could: "That's unusual, isn't it? Where did you get it?"

"It must have come in a big order," said he. "Nobody seems to know anything about it. It is a novelty. Delicious! Vinegar-cured, I should say. Try a bit of the crackling."

But I declined. A flighty Three I may perhaps be, but I can boast, as I hope all my successors will be able to boast, that I have never, knowingly, eaten a guest of this College.

Rêve Canadien

Jean Pierre April

Translated from the French by Howard Scott

Jean Pierre April, born in 1948, is one of the pioneers of modern Quebec science fiction. He began publishing in 1977, and his first book of short stories, *La machine à explorer la fiction*, was the first science-fiction, collection published in Quebec. During the 1980s he was a regular contributor to the Francophone Canadian SF magazine, *imagine...*, and published stories and essays there and in anthologies and collections in Quebec, France, and Italy. He now has published four short story collections and three SF novels—one of the novels, *Berlin-Bangkok*, was published in France as well as Quebec. April's story, "Jackie, je vous aime," won the 1980 Prix Boréal for best short fiction. The next year, *La machine à explorer la fiction* won the 1981 Prix Boréal for best book, while his story "TéléToTaliTé" tied with a story by René Beaulieu for the best short fiction award. *Berlin-Bangkok* was a nominee for the 1990 Aurora for Best Novel.

As is evident in this story, April has literary ambition, and his work is not typical of genre SF either in English or French. The contemporary term invented by Bruce Sterling, "slipstream" (as opposed to either genre or mainstream), best characterizes this story. It is perhaps significant that the pioneers of Quebec SF are writers who do not in general feel constrained by genre boundaries.

Most of the time it seems like history has more past than future. Take Africa, for example: ever since modern civilization was established there, we've been trying to rediscover the ancient legends of the blacks."

Such was the opinion of Dr. Kateb Mobatu, ethnopsychologist at the Tibotown Hospital. He believed firmly that the myths of old Africa were reappearing in the schizoid ravings of the misfits of the town. But Robert Langlois, his young Canadian trainee, had no personal opinions. When Dr. Mobatu asked him to investigate the disturbing revelations of a mysterious griot, Langlois prepared his analytical grid for folk myths and organized a routine expedition in accordance with government standards.

According to the psychopath who had put Mobatu on the right track, Tambu was one of a rare breed of griot. He appeared to be a veritable magician of the word. What he recounted always became reality in one way or another. This kind of storyteller, both artist and witch doctor, was the last descendant of a line of *memorizers,* living encyclopedias who held the collective memory of the legendary Gnagnats, if these fierce warriors had ever actually existed. All in all, the case interested Langlois, as it did the young journalist from the International Free Press who had joined the expedition at the last minute.

The Green Cross's hovercraft jeep rolled gently on its pocket of air as it glided jauntily over the mottled marshland that bordered the Cameroon National Park. Seemingly imperturbable, the soldier piloting the machine marveled every time he flushed a flock of colorful birds. On the seat next to him, the journalist from the IFP, a vaguely oriental woman, a bit uptight, surveyed the monotonous procession of tall yellowed grasses absentmindedly. The interpreter, puffy-faced and taciturn, spoke only when his work required it. In the rear of the compartment on a metal seat sat the old nurse and her madman, Mr. Coco, a scrawny fiftyish man, his head bobbing and his eyes watering like an ape on the look-out for popcorn, the very man who had revealed the secret of Tambu. The old witch doctor had promised him a curse, so Coco had avenged himself. Langlois, the only white on the expedition, and the least experienced, felt ill at ease giving orders. During the journey he had thrown himself into the 753 pages of his analytical grid, not finding a single space where he could insert a legend about Canada. This was really going to screw up his thesis project!

Tambu lived in the center of Cameroon, between Tibati and Minim, in a little makeshift village built by a clan of poachers. A handful of damp, muddy huts roofed with khaki canvases and rusty sheets of steel on the edge of the marsh that bordered the National Park. No one wanted to go there to question this Tambu. Since Langlois was the only Green Cross ethnopsych from Canada, the mission inevitably fell to him. A trainee couldn't refuse the offer. And yet he only had a vague recollection of Canada, which he had left at seventeen to continue his studies in Africa, the ideal continent for analyzing collective psychoses. He had never for a moment imagined that one day he would set off into one of the last national jungles to seek out traces of Jacques Cartier.

"Cartier?" asked the journalist scribbling in her notepad. "Q-u-a or C-a?"

"C-a, as in . . . Canada," answered Langlois like a diligent schoolboy.

"So who is this fellow?" she asked naively in her delightful Asian accent.

"If I remember right, he was the one who discovered the St. Lawrence, the Great River, the main waterway that leads to the heart of Canada.

"Canada?" she asked sardonically. "Does it really exist?"

"It's a large territory north of the United States."

"A legendary one!"

She looked like a globe-trotting reporter, someone who wasn't impressed by the latest geopolitical pacts. To her mind, all there was to the north of the United Sates was snow! Langlois wondered how much she was kidding.

"Of course," he continued uncertainly, "since nothing ever happens there, journalists think that Canada doesn't really exist. Like a utopia!" he added with a forced smile.

"No matter," she exclaimed turning the page of her notepad. "Just try to tell me how this Cartier fellow discovered Canada in Africa!"

The interpreter burst out laughing, the fat nurse chuckled, hiding her mouth behind her hand, and even the driver had a good laugh. Only the madman and the ethnopsych remained serious—Coco, happy to return to the land of his madness, and Langlois, doing his job, nothing more. The Jeep's air conditioner wasn't working well and the six passengers all had wide circles of sweat around their armpits, especially Mr. Coco.

"The ethnopsychologist cannot answer for the witch doctors," said Langlois evasively. He took out a marijuana cigarillo, lit it, taking a long toke, then held it out casually to the journalist. She'd forget all her questions in the end, he thought as he exhaled the refreshing smoke.

It was the interpreter whose tongue was loosened. All of a sudden, with the first puff, he started to tell all sorts of yarns about Tambu, given that his third wife was a member by marriage of the adoptive tribe of Tambu's second wife. Finally, he admitted that Tambu was an oracle.

"An oracle?" asked the journalist immediately, her mouth gaping, "is that some sort of witch doctor?"

"Only when it's speaking," answered the interpreter nodding his head respectfully. "Tambu's wife told mine that when he was young, Tambu was gagged by his parents. When he wanted to do harm to someone, the curse always came true."

Very early, Tambu met a great master who taught him all the basics of divination. Just like the great oracles, he could predict the future, and some claimed that he made it.

In order to be sure not to miss anything, the journalist abandoned her notepad for her tape recorder. The interpreter, feeling inspired by the microphone, began recounting legends on witch doctors of the *word*. Some could read the past in both senses, others communicated with twisted spirits. Many could read an individual future in the folds of the body, and some eminent witch doctors, by observing the subtle emanations around towns, could predict the future of a people and by doing so drag it into war.

This time only Langlois and Mr. Coco took the information lightly. The patient and the doctor had heard all kinds of similar stories at the Ethnopsych Hospital in Tibotown, and too often they had no more reality than the word of the storyteller.

Offended by the doctor's indifference, the interpreter gave him a nasty look and started to speak against legend-snatchers. "Now that the Western capitalists are through exploiting the African soil, they send ethnopsychs to study our last myths!"

Langlois made a face as the blacks looked on amusedly. In a half-offhand, half-cynical way, he said to the journalist, "Again the myth of the 'good natural African'! Phooey! When these interpreters take drugs, they start to think in their mother tongue and they forget their studies in New York or Paris!"

"When I studied French and English, I respected those languages! But Westerners kill the souls of the myths they analyze!" retorted the interpreter.

"What do you believe?" asked Langlois firmly, so as not to anger the interpreter by pretending to ignore him. "We, too, in Canada have lost our forests, our folklore, and our beliefs. All cultures disappear, but they can either be wiped out or modernized!"

"Canada," exclaimed the journalist again, as if the doctor was talking baby-talk, "that's an imaginary country!"

Irritated but relieved by her interjection, Langlois tried to make peace with the interpreter. "And yet, like Cameroon, it's one of the few countries in the world that is bilingual—French and English!"

"We know the story," interrupted the interpreter. "Canada, land of peace, with its democratic biculturalism . . . we've seen that propaganda on the national TV. It must be an imaginary country! And President Banikele wanted to impose this model on the people the better to divide them. But you had the choice between two founding languages, the language of the discoverer or the language of the conqueror, while we are offered two colonial languages, two alienating cultures in a region where there are already almost two hundred! In order for Cameroonian brothers to speak to each other, they have to learn two foreign languages. If you only speak one, you're isolated from thousands of us. It's no surprise that Canadian ethnopsychs come to practice in Cameroon!"

"The links between Canada and Cameroon will soon have a undreamed-of historical basis!" said Dr. Langlois with oracular solemnity, as if ethnopsychology permitted him to know the future. The interpreter shrugged his shoulders and withdrew into his habitual silence.

Disappointed, the journalist invited the doctor to continue, pointing the microphone toward him. To stall her, he suggested a title for her story:

1534: CARTIER DISCOVERED CANADA IN CAMEROON

The little temporary village where Tambu was hiding lay at the bottom of a wet, marshy valley in which the driver, like a gallant cowboy, had to perform minor miracles with his hovercraft jeep. The motor raced continually, overheating the passenger compartment. To those inside it seemed as though the spongy surface of the big marsh was sucking at the rubber belly, stretching it dangerously and threatening to cause a blowout. It was impossible to stop without becoming permanently stuck in the suction cup of mud that seemed to form automatically under the vehicle. The driver was about to turn back for fear of running out of gas, when the journalist noticed a strange formation of low hills rising above a curtain of dead grasses.

"Look," she said to the tired driver, "those mounds seem to be inhabited!"

The driver was so exhausted that he understood "towns" instead of "mounds," and he immediately steered toward the strange formation. It was, in fact, Tambu's village.

As they stopped in front of a hut built of faded plywood, the visitors saw a swarm of boisterous children come running over to inspect the mud-covered jeep. Farther away, a group of idle adults was observing the newcomers' arrival while listening to a gray-haired old man clad only in khaki shorts and a faded old jacket. He gestured agitatedly, perhaps even angrily, pointing at the jeep, the village, then to the sky which he called to witness.

"Who's that strange old bird?" asked the journalist impatiently.

"Tambu," replied the interpreter mechanically without even leaning toward the window.

"You'd think he was expecting us," mumbled the journalist, as if she didn't dare believe her eyes.

"Of course!" exclaimed Mr. Coco with unbridled enthusiasm, "because he knows the future!"

These were his first words since they had left Tibotown. He was starting to feel at home, apparently having forgotten his dispute with the witch doctor.

On the edge of a solid plateau, which barely rose above the surface of the swamp, the cabin of the jeep had stabilized perfectly on its air cushion, but neither the driver nor the journalist opened their doors. After a tedious wait, Langlois had to work his way around the dainty knees of the journalist to get out onto the raised step and face the children, who held out their hands and touched his boots, yelling silly things. Just like in the old movies they saw on television, the doctor took out a bundle of gifts—video cassettes of Marie-Lune Morno and Baby Boom, a few recordings of Moroccan Roll. At last he was able to climb down the three steps of the ladder without any problems and step into a muddy hole thirty centimeters deep. The journalist and the interpreter followed, then the nurse told the madman that he could get out. But when he saw Tambu among the huts, the poor demented man stammered his name, rolled his wide, frightened eyes, lost his balance like a stunned chicken, staggered on the step and collapsed back into the Jeep.

"Give him a stronger sedative," shouted the doctor to the nurse. "Keep him there. I'll come back and get him later."

As he neared the old witch doctor, who lowered his voice and gave him a sidelong glance as if he were the cock of the walk, the interpreter summarized the purpose of the visit.

The witch doctor listened suspiciously, arms crossed and eyebrows knitted, as though already familiar with this song and dance. His wrinkled face shone with sweat in the crushing heat, like a lacquered black mask. With his dim eyes and puffy lips, he seemed absent, continually bobbing his head to some music of the mind. Suddenly he interrupted the interpreter with a string of threatening phrases, waving his big, bony hands. As he continued his abuse, no doubt intended to impress his audience, the interpreter backed up toward Langlois to comment on the situation between clenched teeth.

"He says he can't betray the memory of his people, that it would be a sacrilege. It's going to cost you a lot to record him." Eyes half closed, his face a blank, the interpreter remained unperturbed.

Langlois wondered how he should negotiate with the interpreter to get *him* to negotiate with the witch doctor. "Tell him I have a journalist from the international press with me. He'll be a star if he gives me a prediction that holds up."

After much discussion, which Langlois accepted in order to respect tradition, Tambu promised to recount the past for 330 American dollars; forecasting the future was out of the question—it was too horrible to describe. But first of all he wanted to get acquainted with his visitors.

He really was an old-fashioned witch doctor, theatrical and ceremonious, and at old-fashioned prices. So Langlois bent to his whims and did the introductions with a great deal of panache: Paul Balester, the interpreter, became a sort of cultural diplomat, and Tina Zuri, the journalist, was supposedly looking for an authentic witch doctor for a TV special on the number two international network.

"...and your humble servant, Robert Langlois, ethnopsychoanthropo-etc.-logist, at your service. I'm the delegate for the Green Cross sent to report on the discovery of Jacques Cartier by the Gnagnats."

Surprised, but puffed up with conceit and glowing with pride, Tambu regarded the learned young white man as a secret admirer, a distant disciple of his good words. With the elegance of an aristocrat, he flatly refused the television show, too small for him, but he wondered why a whatsamacologist would be interested in the secret history of the Gnagnats. Langlois and his interpreter had to explain painstakingly that this research had been sponsored by Canada, the country visited by Cartier, not in the land of the Gnagnats, but in America.

When he was very sure that he had understood the translation, the witch doctor burst into demonic laughter and delighted his very excited audience. For several long minutes, the whole happy crowd made comments to Tambu and asked him questions, pointing at Langlois as if he were the king of comedians. The doctor wondered seriously if Balester, out of vengeance, had not mistranslated him.

"Canada in America?" said Tambu as he caught his breath again. "But that's only a dream!" His smile suddenly became a bitter, apprehensive grimace, as if he had just wounded Langlois. He turned toward the villagers, who were standing with their mouths open as though the young ethnopsych had just been bitten by a venomous snake.

Extremely flustered, his thick-lipped mouth gaping, the interpreter let out a great sigh before reminding Langlois that everything the witch doctor said must be considered true. What he had said about Canada therefore required some clarification, or else millions of Canadians would be prisoners of a dream.

"Canada in the beginning was only a fiction," continued Tambu in an embarrassed tone of voice, "a story invented by Cartier so that no one would find out about the secret colony he had founded in the land of the Gnagnats."

"This is going a little too far!" retorted Langlois with a forced smile. "Everything that Cartier described matches the geography. He even brought back Indians from Canada, but not one damned Gnagnat!"

"Not so fast!" Tambu replied in French. "I too studied the official history when I went to the city! Cartier was not the first to visit that region of America. Portuguese and Bretons had been fishing for a generation on the Grand Banks of Newfoundland. What Cartier recounted simply matched previous accounts. As for the natives that he presented to the court of the king, he bought them from a Spaniard who was showing them at a fair. Besides, Cartier's journals cannot be taken seriously. The original document was written in Italian and the journals of the subsequent voyages are in very different styles."

Balester and Langlois looked at each other silently, one having no more to translate, and the other, embittered, not knowing what to say.

"But why would this Cartier have told such a story about Canada if he was coming from Cameroon?" interrupted the journalist, taking over.

"Why, he didn't want other navigators to discover his paradise!"

"And how do you know this story?"

"How? Do you still doubt that I am an authentic witch doctor? I got this story from my father, who got it from a long line of *memorizers* like me. The first to tell it was one of the Gnagnats who discovered Jacques Cartier, lost in the jungle, feverish and delirious, searching for legendary diamonds."

Langlois let him speak, but he stiffened with disbelief, as if he had already heard other such stories, better ones. He thought he knew this kind of crackpot: Tambu must have studied scraps of history by leafing through old magazines. He had remembered items from television and transformed these bits of information by mixing them with legends from his childhood. There were so many ethnopsychs looking for "primitive" myths that a supposed witch doctor of the word who was inventive enough could make himself a good living. Langlois bristled, certain that the witch doctor was pulling his leg. "What's strange about your story is that you're the only one who knows it," he said suddenly, interrupting the flow.

"The only one? But I only ask to share it!"

"What's even more astonishing is that there's not a shred of evidence left."

"It has been erased! But consult the memory of the people. All the villagers tell us the story of an old white society that once terrorized the region. They were whites who spoke French, as corroborated by certain papers that have been kept secretly by the old French protectorate. But since you doubt my word, you'll just have to do without it!"

The rest of these words, intended for his audience, were spoken in the sonorous tones of his mother tongue. The translator spared Langlois these insults. The witch doctor walked off behind the brown huts gesturing like a scorned rooster, scolding the villagers who followed him, nodding their heads. Langlois wanted to go after them, but his interpreter took him by the elbow and made him wait.

"Leave him be, doctor. In the state he's in, that witch doctor could say words that would be dangerous for our future."

While they waited for things to calm down, Tina tried to get some young villagers to talk, but she ran out of videos without extracting the least bit of valid information. The children clammed up as soon as they heard Tambu's name, and if she pressed them, they ran away. A few adolescents stayed around to get videos, but all they were doing was making up preposterous stories.

Langlois and Balester were sitting near a pond. The doctor fumed. "Do you think I offended him?" he asked, feeling the interpreter's pout was an accusation.

"You have at the very least shown contempt for the collective memory of the great Gnagnats," replied the interpreter, as if he himself had been insulted.

"The Gnagnats?" repeated the doctor, trying to classify this tribe in his analytical grid. Was this really that legendary tribe, invincible . . . but nonetheless exterminated by Van Puttkamer during the time of German Kamerun.

The interpreter searched his memory for a long time, only too happy to make this doctor of ethnopsychology wait. His brown eyes, sparkling like crumpled cellophane, seemed to consider the mud surrounding the village as if nothing could surprise them, but he had that strained expression of someone who has a word on the tip of his tongue.

"In ancient times," he said surveying the horizon as though searching for ghosts of a distant past, "the Gnagnats were truly invincible. When they went to war, the witch doctors told the warriors that they could painlessly resist all the blows of the enemy. Since they believed the word of the witch doctor blindly, their bodies became practically indestructible. Their enemies said that during combat the Gnagnats pulled poisoned arrows from their flesh and continued the battle without flagging. Against cannons, though, there was nothing they could do. They were reduced to pulp so quickly that they didn't have time to think about protecting themselves."

"Another legend . . . ," thought Langlois, stretched out in the shade of a stunted mangrove near the stinking swamp where the village's single sewer pipe emptied. Strange situation for an "unearther of legends." He was faced with one of the most extraordinary examples of oral culture, in the presence of a unique old griot who knew the secret history of the Gnagnats, and he had to protect himself against the man's words. Cartier discovering Canada in Cameroon! No, really, he didn't think there was any more possibility of an interesting article. Nor did Tina Zuri. So that the trip wouldn't be a total waste of time, she was questioning a few of the hunters on the poaching situation in the National Park.

Frustrated and harassed by mosquitoes, the doctor returned to the Jeep intending to question the madman on what exactly he knew about Jacques Cartier. Who knows? Maybe his account could form the basis for an acceptable report, and the team could return to Tibotown.

Unfortunately their problems had only just begun. The air cushion of the Jeep was half flat, punctured by a child's arrow. The driver had left, leaving his door open. Inside, there was only the sweating nurse, snoozing, oblivious to the flies buzzing around her mouth and ears.

"Where did Mr. Coco go?" shouted Langlois shaking her.

Startled, the fat nurse looked all around her.

"I think he's disappeared! Have you seen him?"

They started searching immediately, dividing the task. Balester would go through the village, the nurse would search the area around the Jeep, and Langlois would check out the hut that was used as a bistro. This only resulted in the shocked nurse discovering the driver as he came out of a scanty grove of trees with a villager, barely in her teens, who immediately ran off with her handful of videos.

Mr. Coco came back on his own, accompanied by Tambu, who seemed more conciliatory. Smiling like a TV host, the madman arrived at the Jeep while the driver was sharing his last beer. Excited as a child who had just met his idol, he introduced the witch doctor to Dr. Langlois.

"I have convinced my friend Tambu that the great white scholars would prove the invincibility of the Gnagnats if he tells the story of Canada. All you have to do now is listen patiently to him, until he finds you respectful enough to hear the story of Cartier in Cameroon."

His friend Tambu? Langlois had always believed that the madman and the witch doctor were bitter enemies. . . . Unless

they had made a deal. . . . Still astonished by his talents for rec-
onciliation, Langlois said a few polite phrases to Tambu, who
didn't say a word, and the journalist asked him to begin his
story.

"Prices are going up quickly," said Tambu, waddling along
like a despondent carpet dealer. "Now it's 1430 dollars, soon it
will perhaps be—"

"It's a deal!" blurted out the ethnopsych, pulling out his
electrocheck pad.

Secret and Authentic History of Cameroonian Canada

A knowledgeable and experienced navigator, Jacques Cartier
knew exactly where he was going when his caravel left St. Malo
to cross the wide waters of the Atlantic. He headed straight toward that marvelous country, which later would be called Cameroon.

For over a hundred years, more daring captains and ambitious Portuguese merchants had already been navigating both
sides of the Atlantic. Many had established very prosperous
trading posts in Africa. One of these explorers, a Genoese sailing
for the Portuguese, had discovered an Eden-like valley by pen-
etrating the African jungle in the heart of what is now Cameroon.
Cartier learned this from a sick old sailor, Mario de Coto, who
claimed to be the only survivor from the trading post founded
by the Genoese. During the expedition, when he came out of a
bush into which he'd been dropped by African alcohol, de Coto
discovered that all his compatriots had been methodically mas-
sacred by the Gnagnats. The sailor sobered up quickly. He managed to escape by stealing a dugout canoe and paddling down
the Rio dos Camaroes to the Atlantic, where he was saved by a
merchant ship sailing along the coast. He never spoke of the
marvelous treasure of the Gnagnats, hoping that one day he
would be able to organize his own punitive expedition to plun-
der the tribe. In that Eden-like valley, de Coto had seen marvelous diamonds as big as a child's fist and very docile slaves who
dropped to their knees the moment they heard a cannon blast.
For a fee of one hundred diamonds, the syphilitic old mariner,
unable to sail, gave Cartier the location of the fabulous valley.

After speaking with the vice-admiral, Lord Charles de Mouy,
Cartier *was* given the command of an expedition whose official

mission was to find a northern passage to India. In order to avoid any trouble with the Portuguese, who claimed the whole western coast of Africa, the vice-admiral ordered Cartier to say that he was leaving in another direction and to invent some sort of inhospitable land beyond Newfoundland.

The members of the expedition were all ex-convicts whom the king had mysteriously just pardoned, among them superstitious old sailors who firmly believed that beyond Newfoundland the ocean suddenly fell off into the cosmic void. The younger ones, who considered themselves better informed, spoke of blood-thirsty savages that awaited them in America. No one really believed that twelve years earlier a certain Magellan had gone around the world by way of the southern tip of America. As soon as the Breton coast disappeared over the horizon, a mutiny was born in the darkness of the hold. It spread quickly to the bridge and was about to spill over to the helm when Cartier informed his men that they were going to Africa to search for a priceless treasure.

The truce lasted the rest of the voyage, until the day the sailors discovered the mouth of the Rio dos Camaroes. To go up the river, Cartier's men had to build canoes, repel ferocious blacks and animals, and battle mosquitoes and sickness. When they finally reached the Valley of Diamonds, as they had already named it, many sailors considered stealing elephant tusks, palm oil and blue coral and returning to France before they perished. When the Gnagnats traded them a few diamonds, of modest size and dubious transparency, the sailors were bitterly disappointed, but when they saw that there were shovelfuls of them, they wanted to get rid of Cartier in order to conceal this precious cargo from the king of France.

"*Oyez!*" shouted Cartier as they prepared to cut his throat. "*If you kill me, Our Lord King shall be greatly displeased. Other vessells and souldiers shall be sent to discover your little trafficke. But if we begin together, long shall it endure and the moneys gained shall not but increase.*"

Sped by the imminence of death, Cartier improvised a plan that was both simple and daring. His two ships would go back to Europe bursting with diamonds and a few precious spices, but there would be two transactions:

"*First, the diamonds we shall sell in Spain, and do this in secret. Second, once returned to the port of St. Malo, we shall sell the spices* to the lords of that place, so that gold or silver will suffice us for other expeditions. No other persons have such diamonds to find or sell, for all believe that we are going to . . ."

"*Aca nada!*" shouted a Spanish sailor who was as quick with his tongue as he was at swigging his rum.

The night before, he had had a nightmare. He was lost in a huge land of snow. He could describe it easily.

"*Oh, Canada . . . Nothing there!*" cried Cartier, as if enlightened by a huge, hazy vision. " *'Twill be a countrey of ice there where the Atlantic Sea hurles itself into the void. And thus will be sent farre away any explorators who would desire to follow us.*"

Cartier succeeded in mounting a second expedition before the royal guard discovered his scheme. He had been forced to deceive the king to escape the mutineers, or so he tried to explain to the guards who arrested him.

His first mistake had been to leave men in Africa when he discovered the Valley of Diamonds. When he saw the Gnagnats again, Cartier was greeted with hostility by these men, who wanted to commandeer his ships and keep all the profits.

A bloody battle ensued and Cartier lost half his men. When he once again laid his eyes on *la douce France*, the idea came to him to invent the worst calamities to explain the loss of so many sailors. They had fallen victim to scurvy, the savages, the cold, and the many vile animals that he described with many a detail to make the curious quake. He overdid it. The vice-admiral was suspicious, got one of the ex-convicts from the crew to talk, and learned of the business with the "big" diamonds. For his third and last voyage, Cartier's boat was escorted by four caravels commanded by loyal subjects of his Majesty François the First.

Upon returning to St. Malo, Cartier was relieved of his command. His story of Canada, at first considered by Lord de Mouy to be a clever lie, soon became an embarrassing truth, for strangely enough, the land imagined by Cartier actually existed and corresponded to an amazing degree to some of the explorer's descriptions. Other navigators, mainly Englishmen, had already explored the St. Lawrence. They built settlements along the river, at Kioubec, then at Montriall, and some of their descriptions must have reached the ears of Cartier. Later, the publisher of the French explorer's journal would cut out the passages that obviously were not in keeping with current evidence.

The vice-admiral declared that Cartier had failed in his official mission: to reach India by the north by reaching the source of the Great River. What actually ended Cartier's career was the nature of the diamonds brought back from another river, the Rio dos Camaroes. Somewhat craftier than the Iroquois, the Gnagnats had palmed off junk on the French, hence the expression, "as fake as Canadian diamonds," which circulated for a long time in the salons of Paris where malicious humour was the practice. The only Frenchmen who let themselves be attracted by the fiction of Canada—both American and African—were prostitutes, clerics, adventurers, shady characters, and landless peasants. Lacking diamonds, France found other resources. She built colonies in her two Canadas, in the official country for the fur trade, and in the secret Canada to import spices and rare woods. On occasion, to provide slaves for its American colony, it would get involved in the slave trade. The first Cameroonian to discover Canada, in 1567, was named Mongo Kimoni, but no history, even the secret one, mentions him. It is one of the mysteries of history that the colony established on the "few acres of snow" took root, while the other one, though established in a lush valley, suffered systematic massacres by the terrible Gnagnats, who tore off the beautiful clothes of the French before cruelly torturing them.

Much later, at the beginning of the colonial era in Africa, so-called explorers from Germany had a hard time explaining the clothing of the Gnagnats. During sacred festivals, the fierce warriors would wear lace ruffs on their heads, and the women would dance dressed up in sixteenth-century *pourpoints*. According to certain legends gathered in the heart of Kamerun, a white child had escaped the massacre of the French colony. After that, he became a demigod adored by the tribe that had captured him.

But how much can the secret stories be believed? The true Canada of Cartier died with the African legends, while the other never managed to emerge from the dream that gave it birth.

For an hour, Northern Airship's lightweight maxibus, a five-storied mammoth, had been flying over the Atlantic toward Newfoundland. A thick fog, like a layer of ochre dust, hid the horizon. On board the luxurious turboprop dirigible, the passengers were watching a comic film, enjoying themselves in the gymnasium, cavorting in the pool, or gabbing in one of the bars. At the most animated table of the central bar, a group of very relaxed businessmen had just met a team from the highly regarded TV show Americanews. The director of the series was returning from Cameroon, where she had done a report on one of the last African witch doctors, a real one! She was also bringing back a ethnopsychologist who had discovered the African origins of Canada.

"Canada? What's that?" bellowed a multimillionaire as he spilled his glass of champagne on a line of cocaine. "A new secret vacationland?"

"I don't think so. Canada was that old country where Eskimos lived in those famous igloos!" explained an old ministerial attaché who prided herself on having visited almost all the remote corners of the globe.

"So maybe it's a kind of thermoglass city under the snow," suggested a young playboy in a fuchsia smoking jacket, waiting for the approval of the condescending hostess who was accompanying him.

Enticed by this hypothesis, Mr. Brown, the most senior of the millionaires, asked the strange ethnopsych to provide a few details of his discovery.

Dr. Langlois thought he was dreaming! Could all these Americans possibly know nothing about Canada? He thought rather that the Cameroonians' popular jokes had reached the jet set by some circuitous route. Not being used to the humor of people who make their million every month, he hesitated a moment before raising his glass of rye whisky to make a dignified toast:

"Canada? It's where they make our Canadian Club!"

With the help of diplomacy and alcohol, the millionaires followed the lead of a tall black woman who never missed a chance to laugh lustily. Then the director of Americanews explained that her precious guest could not divulge his secret before the interview that he was to give in their studio in Montriall. A French financier, short but a brilliant conversationalist, took the opportunity to tell the story of an ancestor who had a cabin in Canada, and Dr. Langlois quietly slipped away from the table.

As he went down the stairs to another bar on the side of the dirigible frequented by second-class passengers, he spotted Tina Zuri making discrete signals to him which he quite simply ignored. He had no desire to listen to more sarcastic remarks about Canada. But she grabbed him as he was going into the bar located on the maxibus's inflatable wing. With her hands on her hips and an expression on her face like a customs officer finding a bag of cocaine, she stood waiting for him in front of the alcohol vending machine.

"So what's this story about Canada?" she asked in a voice loud enough to vie with the music in the background. "None of the passengers know that region. They all say that French is not spoken in America."

Langlois handed her a glass of Canadian Club, which had been quickly filled by the machine, then he ordered another double before leading the journalist behind the sound bubble that rang with Moroccan Roll.

"Look at your airline ticket," he said furtively, "destination Montréal. It's the French-speaking metropolis of Canada."

"You mean Montriall! Why do you give it that French pronunciation? Montriall is just an American city like any other, with its cultural, ethnic and linguistic minorities. They no more speak French in Montriall that they speak Polish in Chicago. So what?"

"I grew up in French in Montriall, like all my friends. I have a Canadian passport, and we are being invited on TV to talk about the discoverer of Canada, I didn't exactly invent Canada on my own!"

"And *I'm* going to present a babbling old witch doctor. So what? Don't you see they're just laughing at us? Last week, the guest on Americanews was an Inuit who eats raw seal and after us there will be a third supposed E.T. discovered in Labrador!"

The mixture of alcohol and anger made her skin turn impressive colors, but Langlois felt she was showing too much concern for a land without history. Fortunately, he thought, her doubts would be erased as soon as the maxibus landed in Montréal.

Around them, the unconcerned passengers were drinking and talking loudly. Some were leaning against the big tinted portholes, others were floating in the dance bubble, twirling like bats in the anti-G atmosphere. The voyage by maxibus was the ideal opportunity to kick up your heels: the oxygen, the altitude, the alcohol, and, if need be, cocaine, tolerated outside national boundaries, permitted the most blasé passengers to spend a pleasant two hours. Tina, though she swore she'd visited everything twice, still didn't know what the French nights of Montréal were, and Langlois promised her some good ones, enough so she could do a report for the Africans!

Suddenly the music stopped with an electronic crackling. The people in the bar, nonplussed by this absence of a sound background, abandoned their conversations. A famous actress appeared on the central screen, asking the passengers to return to their pressurized seats to prepare for landing. In five minutes, they would be flying over the American coast. In twenty, the maxibus would be setting down on the magnetic landing strip at Dorval. Langlois waited for the French translation . . . in vain.

He knocked back his glass of whisky and invited the journalist to sit with him near a porthole. Soon, through the sulphurous clouds of pollution, he thought he could make out the Gulf of St. Lawrence, like a big silver mouth cut into the Quebec coastline. A thick cloud, very turbulent, quickly covered the landscape, and Langlois would have abandoned this grayish spectacle if he hadn't spotted, in front of the dirigible, exceptional turbulence, sucked in by a disturbing whirlpool that was stirring up the line of the horizon. Despite the powerful reactors that were roaring all out, shaking the maxibus's cabin and the passengers' intestines, the dirigible seemed to be drawn in like a lover. Like all the other passengers who were crouching in front of the portholes, Langlois wanted to question a pallid flight attendant who was working her way along by tightly grabbing the seat backs, but he remained silent, his heart in his mouth.

Once he had overcome his dizziness, he opened his eyes to see that the dirigible had burst through the tumult by flying close to the surface, as if carried by the stormy waves of the ocean that led toward the horizon, where it ended abruptly, dominated by the seething clouds rising before the orange blotch of the setting sun, forming huge steaming wreaths where rainbows leaped. The rays of the sun cut through the mass of steam. The whole huge bed of water was being flung toward the west with the kind of speed that warns of waterfalls. Wide bands of luminous froth lined the currents, which converged toward these unleashed elements between two islands or two capes of a still invisible continent. High waves pressed against each other, leaping and bucking like terrified animals, sucked into the maw of a dreadful funnel. A pod of terrified whales tried to swim against the current and seagulls attempted to ride the wind with no more success than the maxibus, which was pitching dangerously, whipped by the soaring waves. Loss of pressure was a distinct possibility. In the overheated cabin, all the passengers were screaming, their voices lost in the din of the reactors and the storm. At about a hundred kilometers from the ocean's horizon, you could feel a kind of suction pulling the dirigible, as though the water was flowing into a chasm, pulling with it a huge portion of the sky.

And as if the dizzying drift of the maxibus had given him exceptional lucidity, Langlois saw his recent discovery in a completely new light. To all the passengers he had met, Jacques Cartier was an unknown, Montriall was purely English-speaking, and his country was in fact the United States. Canada was therefore only a dream! Tambu was right. . . . The sacred word of the witch doctor had erased Canada from reality!

Langlois's return to America had forced geography to conform to the vision of the oracle. Maliciously, or perhaps through lack of historical knowledge, Tambu had imagined the Atlantic without the discoveries of Cartier and his predecessors. The Earth corresponded to the ancient depictions. It was a flat plateau suspended at the center of the universe!

The rubberized walls of the dirigible were starting to deflate. Suddenly depleted, its softened nose waved like a flag in the storm. Reactors and passengers were screaming uselessly. A monstrous groaning filled his ears—the awesome impact of the ocean tumbling into the chaotic sky. It was as if a demonic monster had pulled the cork from the bottom of the Atlantic and the ocean was threatening to pull the continents in its wake. Waterspouts exploded in the void, atomized into sparkling droplets that covered the horizon, transforming into hissing steam, then into dark clouds, swollen to bursting, that rose heavily, liquified and vaporized many times before taking shape beyond the tumult. In the center of the seething, where the ocean became the heavens, tornados stirred the celestial waters, birds pirouetted under the waves and fish fell from the sky. There, in the heart of the unleashed elements, a cyclone coupled with maelstrom made the clouds, rains, and waves spin in a great original soup.

Suddenly, swallowed up by a liquid mouth, the dirigible plummeted into the void. Strangely, it stayed suspended in the middle of an unreal calm, between the ocean that was falling in a hundred thousand Niagaras and the clouds that were rising in a tight mass. A shining breach appeared in the middle of chaos, and the passengers saw a huge area of sparkling snow, like a dream country. . . .

FAN

Geoff Ryman

Geoff Ryman, a Canadian-born writer, moved to the United States at age 11, and has been living in England since 1973. He still identifies himself as a Canadian writer. He began publishing SF stories in the mid-1970s, and has also written some SF plays, none published but most performed, including a powerful adaptation of Philip K. Dick's *The Transmigration of Timothy Archer* (1982). The first work to establish his international reputation as one of the leading writers of SF was "The Unconquered Country: A Life History" (1984, rev. 1986), which won the World Fantasy Award. The *Science Fiction Encyclopedia* describes it as "the story of a young woman forced by poverty and the terrible conditions afflicting her native land (clearly a transfigured Cambodia) to rent out her womb for industrial purposes (it is used to grow machinery)." It is reprinted in *Unconquered Countries: Four Novellas* (1994).

Ryman's first novel was *The Warrior Who Carried Life* (1985), a fantasy. His second, *The Child Garden* (1988), won the Arthur C. Clarke Award and the John W. Campbell Memorial Award, and confirmed him as a major figure in contemporary SF. John Clute says it "complexly massages an array of themes—drugs, dystopia, ecology, feminism, hive-minds, homosexuality, medicine, and music—into a long rich novel about identity and the making of great art. Set in a transfigured United Kingdom—in effect an Alternate World—the book stands as one of the sturdiest monuments of Humanist SF."

Ryman's most recent books are not SF. *Was* (1992) is supposedly the true story of the real-life Dorothy, who was the inspiration for L. Frank Baum's first Oz book, and of a contemporary man dying of AIDS. *253* (1998) is a work of hypertext fiction linking the lives of characters in a subway car.

The powerful novella, "Fan," is reprinted from *Unconquered Countries: Four Novellas*.

Billie fell in love with Eamon Strafe when she was fifteen years old. Billie was quiet, unconfident, but festooned with symbols. She was bold in the language of signs—anhks, Hittite seals, vampire chic. She read Edgar Allan Poe and Bram Stoker and wore black. She liked spiders and coffins and poems about death. For a time, she confused sex with horror.

Then she heard Eamon Strafe sing. She was buying snacks in a Pakistani supermarket. It was open late, and sold things like coconut-coated peanuts and fresh ginger. The radio was on, a soft-voiced DJ who played hard music, but the song he played now was quiet. The moment she heard it, Billie was shocked by a sense of recognition. Without knowing it, this was what she had been waiting for.

The music was measured, almost stately, and seemed to say some things were important. The voice was high and sweet and grieving, and it came in breathless gasps. Was the singer a woman? Who was it? Billie stood still, straining to hear the DJ, but after the song, he issued a warning about traffic congestion. Billie asked the woman at the counter if she knew what that song was, and the woman smiled sweetly back, barely speaking English.

Billie heard the song again a week later. She was going home from London to South End on the train and a girl called Tora got on. Billie knew her from school. Tora was alarmingly confident and slightly beyond Billie's social ken. Tora dropped down onto a nearby seat, laughing with older friends and slightly out of breath. Ghetto blasters had come back. Tora aggressively turned hers up. From the first sighing note, Billie knew. The song hauled her up from her seat.

"Hi Tora. I'm sorry to bother you, but who is that? What's the song?"

Tora was flattered. "This. Oh, it's Eamon Strafe." As if everyone but Billie knew.

"It's wonderful!" said Billie.

"You bet," said Tora. And passed her the disk cover.

For the Lebanon Dead, it said. There was a picture of a slightly older man, with a kind, lumpy, ultimately handsome face.

"He's a monk," said Tora and giggled. "An Irish monk. He's got an album coming out next month."

"I've got to get it."

"Tom here knows his manager."

Tom was older, with a rodent smile. "He's gonna make it,

the industry's behind him. People done Goth, they're bored with rave, they need stars."

Billie, in Goth, caught the drift. "Hype," she said, and passed the disk back.

"Yeah, but the music's fucking brilliant," corrected Tora. Billie's friend Janice still sat on the other seat looking slightly wasted and abandoned. Billie waved her forward.

Tora was gratified by the effect she had had on Billie, so gratified that she and even Janice became friends. They became fans, before anyone else did, fans of Eamon Strafe. They read in the newspaper that he was going to sing on a late night arts program. "We can put our handbags in a circle and scream," said Tora as a joke. But when the camera caught him for the first time, all three girls turned in silence and looked at each other.

"Isn't he beautiful? Scrum-my," said Tora.

He wasn't handsome. He had a rough boxer's nose and a heavy jaw, and he was burly about the shoulders, but his arms and lower body seemed to shrink away, like a carrot. It was his expression that made him angelic, the crinkled, smiling eyes out of which shone ice blue irises. And the teeth, the famous teeth. They were too big. Whenever he smiled they took over, illuminated his face. Billie lost her taste for the Gothic. White became her color, Eamon's color.

Billie and Tora united in a campaign of conversion. They wore white jackets, white trousers, and white headscarves tied under their chins, like wimples. They sat in Piccadilly Circus, playing his music as loudly as they could. The police would move them on. They carried a poster of him and walked, singing his name, and accosting passerby, demanding that they give up meat and alcohol. The world would have to come to love Eamon Strafe as well.

And for a time, incredibly, heartbreakingly, the world did.

He was right for the times. The New Aestheticism, the newspapers called it. They always led with a photograph of Eamon— *The Antithesis of a Pop Star*. It seemed so wonderful to Billie that other people could feel as she did. For a brief time, two or three years only, she and the age were one. It seemed there would be a place for her in the world after all.

He was beautiful, his music was beautiful. Somewhere he lived and breathed, she reminded herself, somewhere right now, in Ireland. She seemed to hear him sing everywhere she went.

For the Lebanon Dead was followed by *Afghanistan*, and it was even better. He had actually gone there and seen the fighting. *Afghanistan* got to number one. It was followed by a book of poetry, and a further disk of the verse recited over sparse music. Every six months there was a new album of proper music. There was plenty to buy.

But there were no live performances—videos, yes, but no tours. He's shy, thought Billie, and loved him for it. Eamon said he found tours exploitative. He felt he owed it to people to give them more than a rehearsed performance. He wanted to talk to them all in person, and that was not possible. That meant he would need to find some new and better way to reach them. Billie was not entirely sure she understood what he meant.

Billie wrote him letters.

Dear Eamon,

This is just to let you know that someone cares.

Billie

She didn't expect an answer. Someone sent her a four-color booklet about the fan club. She didn't join. She didn't need to, or want to. Eamon lived inside her.

Fans are like seashells. They emerge once the tide has retreated. Billie did not feel beached when Eamon's time had passed. The surprise was that he was ever as popular as he had once been. Now he was left to those who understood. If anything, she became more loyal, but in silence.

Billie moved to London, because of Eamon. Because of Eamon, she had the courage. It seemed possible that she would meet other people like herself. She found that she had values, from somewhere. Like many of her generation, a certain purity of outlook would linger into adulthood. She didn't drink; she sought harmless occupation. She studied pottery, and found a job working lunchtimes in a health food shop.

Sometimes for the hell of it and a little money, Billie appeared with a band. She and three other girls would stand on the stage and pretend to scream at the lead singer. It was a joke. Billie was dressed in all her old Strafe idolatry. That was a joke too. The jokes protected her.

On the sticky black floors of the clubs, the young people stood in groups, smiling and saying excuse me. They acted like aristocrats because they had time. They still had time in which to preserve a measure of grace.

Billie met a man in her art class who had an Irish accent and chestnut hair. His name was Roy. For a very short while, they slept rough under the arches of a bridge. Billie had to wash in the sink in back of the shop, and give her mother's address in order to be paid. Finally they found a room a good hour and a half from the center of London, out toward the east, as if magnetized back toward South End. At first they were supposed to be saving money to move to Ireland. Roy was sweet and feckless and unwittingly selfish. Life to him was like a blow to the head. He sat on the floor all day watching television, perplexed, anxious, always realizing too late that he should have helped Billie carry in the shopping bags or wash the dishes or move a chair. When he finally told her he was going, she was surprised to find that her main emotion was relief. He left her with Joey, her son. Joey was then two and Billie was 22. Joey's middle, hidden name was Eamon.

There was a logic to be obeyed. Billie gave up trying to be a potter. She spent mornings waiting in the Benefits Agency, bouncing Joey up and down on her lap, trying to keep him from crying. She had to keep proving that Roy was out of the country before she could claim benefit. Like every other person on the dole, she was made to take a course and like so many others she studied what was called computing. The course taught her how to use two pieces of software and a bit of a third. It was enough to find her a nonpaying job with a Housing Association. She did the accounts and correspondence, and was given a place to live in exchange.

She and her son lived in three rooms. Some money came in from the health shop, but she had to keep that a secret from the Agency. Joey wrestled in her grasp and was aggressive and demanding. They went shopping, and Joey demanded sweets or toys. Billie became yet another woman in the supermarket, hauling a weeping child.

"Joey, if you do that again, I'll give you such a wallop."

Her aggressive son turned out to be timid around other children. He did not like being left alone with them and fought her, punching when she tried to take him to a playgroup. He would not go outside, even when the old brick forecourt echoed with the sound of other children's games.

Sometimes at night, when Joey was asleep, Billie would

sense a fullness inside herself. She would draw the curtains, put on headphones, and listen to Eamon Strafe—and she would dance with joy.

It would feel as though the music were coming out of her. She would startle herself, miming to the songs. She would sometimes weep or rage or shake with nervous laughter. She would tease new meanings out of the words, by gesture or expression.

Her dancing was a performance. If other people could have seen her, they would have been startled too. Eamon Strafe mimed when he performed on television. Billie did it better.

The Association bought Billie a new computer.

She kept it in her bedroom, away from tiny fingers. It was a beautiful thing. It got to know its operators and wrote new programs to help them with their work. Digital broadcasting had only just got going: the computer was linked to all kinds of information, about tax regulations, benefit rates and means testing. It would suddenly announce:

NEW PROGRAM AVAILABLE FOR THAT FUNCTION

and print out instructions. It would read Billie's letters as she wrote them. It would interrupt.

INFORMATION REVISE; NEW LEGAL PRECEDENT, SEE CROWN VS MACALLAUGH CRESCENT HOUSING ASSOCIATION.

Billie was buying paper for it and floppy disks when something in the store racks caught her eyes. She was strummed like a chord. On the cover of a CD ROM, Eamon's face stared out at her. Eamon on software?

CONVERSATIONS WITH THE STARS said a banner over the racks.

Blue Laser Personality Software

Billie went to the racks and turned the jewelbox case over in her hand. The cover was white. He was brown, windswept, staring out at her from some new place. It was like buying an Eamon Strafe CD ten years before. The back of the case said:

A program taken from an imprint of your favorite celebrity's personality. Eamon Strafe himself will be able to answer all

*your questions about his songs, his poetry, his religious beliefs.
Why did he reject the Church? What does he mean by Spirit?
What does he think of the new generation of Blue Stars?*

*This disk has been authored and engineered to the most precise
standards. The program card has its own updating digital
transceiver. This means the program is kept abreast of devel-
opments in Eamon's life. You go with him as he visits Yemen
or withdraws to his estates in County Down, traveling all over
the world, seeking answers. Now Eamon can give you those
answers himself—and some of the questions.*

*Warning: to be used only on self-programming, digital-
broadcast equipment, equipped with white-laser CD drive.*

Well that's what I've got, thought Billie. It's the Association's,
but they did say I could use it for myself.

She turned the case over in her hand. The disk and the card
cost 25 pounds. It's just another way, she thought, to separate
me from my money. But she didn't put it back in the rack.

You wrote all those letters, Billie, and you never got an answer. She looked at Eamon's face, and knew there was a part of
her that no amount of sense could control. She wanted it. There
was little enough in life.

If I don't get it now, she thought, I never will. Who knows,
maybe he'll help me with my own poetry. Maybe he could explain to me what iambic pentameter is.

She let the Association pay for it. She would pay them back,
bit by bit. After all, she kept the accounts. The black girl at the
counter entered the bar code without even reading what it was.
The girl at the counter didn't care what Billie bought.

Billie went home, and inserted the card and the CD, and the
screen went blank and then words came up, glowing on the
screen.

"Hello," whispered Billie, with a shrug. In her mind, she saw
the dog with the phonograph. His Master's Voice.

Color marched down the screen in an orderly scan. The patterns made a face. Eamon's. There were creases in his cheeks
now, and bags under his eyes. Billie found it moving that he was
growing old. He was sitting on a wooden chair, in front of a wall
that was made of raw wooden planks.

"Hello," he said. "What's your name, then?" Emphasis on the *your*, as if he had been talking to so many other strangers.

"Billie," she replied. "Billie de Vaille. Billie's just a nickname." There was a hush of shyness.

"Where do you live, Billie?"

"Stratford East. London. Where are you?"

"I'm in Canada," he said. "Just staying here for a while."

"The papers said you were in China." She said it in accusation. She was looking for flaws.

"I'm on my way back," he said.

Billie was beginning to wonder if the program would be fearfully dull, like one of those programmed doctor's surgeries.

"You've just got a prepared list of questions and replies," she told the program. Eamon leaned even more precariously back in the chair.

"I am a Read Only Memory and a card, but that's not how I work," he replied.

Billie felt something akin to panic. It's not even trying to fool me.

"I react like Eamon would react. And the transceiver keeps the personality updated with new information. Like, I went to China to keep up my Tai Chi."

Ah yes, his Tai Chi. All part of the image.

"I was supposed to meet this great master while he was doing his exercises in a public square. So I went to the square and there were thousands of Chinese people all doing their morning exercises. So I thought: I'm the only Westerner here, he'll see me. I walked up and down for hours. I stood on the steps of a public monument. No master. I got back and my guide was furious. 'You insult the master!' she says. The master, you see, thought I ought to come to him."

It's not bad, thought Billie. Quite good, really. A bit of a laugh.

"I'll wait until you tell me that story again," she said, "and then I'll know just how big your memory is." She was smiling.

"Frankly," he said, "about as big as yours." He grinned. The giant teeth. "I'll wait until you repeat yourself too."

It was a terrible winter and life seemed hard for everyone. Billie found that Eamon saw her through it.

Mrs. King in the next flat nearly died of cold. At 5:30 in the morning, Billie heard the police breaking down the old lady's door.

"I have a key. Don't," Billie murmured, but the police ignored her. Mrs. King was confused but didn't want to go to the hospital. The police called her daughter, and said in Mrs. King's hearing, "The daughter doesn't give a shit."

"She certainly does," said Billie, "and I'm sure if she said she's on her way, then she'll be here."

Billie sat with Mrs. King and held her hand. That made Billie feel a bit better about not being able to stop the police destroying the door. The room was icy cold and smelled like an old lady's room, that's all. Billie turned on the heater. She delicately covered the bottom of her nose with an index finger, and still managed to smile and talk. Mrs. King described her daughter's wedding. The old woman had lain on the floor all night. Very suddenly Billie saw that there was excrement, flattened on the carpet, excrement on Billie's shoes. In the midst of trying to give comfort, Billie gagged. She had to run out of the room. So she felt bad about herself again. So she said hello, and talked to Eamon.

"Billie. You can't blame yourself for being human," he told her. "You did everything you could, even some things you couldn't do."

"I'm just so angry being ambushed by my body like that." She meant being ill. "I just felt so weak. That poor old lady."

"And how does she feel now?"

"Well enough," she admitted.

"Then what are you worried about?" he asked.

"Everything," she admitted. Everything and nothing.

Joey had started school in the autumn, and hated it, hated it. He came home in tears, and tried to hit her when she walked him to the bus stop. I'm even a bad mother, she thought. No money, no father, no brothers and sisters. No wonder the poor kid is terrified of everything.

And when she got home from walking him to school, she would turn on the computer.

She would say hello, and Eamon would be in some new place, having read some new book, and she would talk to him as if he were real. He would talk to her as though she were real. He remembered who the people in the Association were, and asked about them.

Billie loaned her door key to a neighbor who needed to use

the computer. When the woman gave the key back, it was new and shiny and had a different brand name. Without asking, the woman had cut a copy of Billie's key and given her the copy by mistake. Billie found herself asking Eamon's advice.

"I mean, do I just go up to her and say 'You've cut a copy of my key. I'd like the original back, please?' It's like calling her a thief."

And Eamon said, "You've got to do it, Billie. For your self-respect."

In the evenings, while Joey was asleep, the computer would say simple things like. "You look all done in, love. Go make yourself a cup of tea."

She could rationalize it. People keep pets, she would tell herself, as she scraped most of Joey's dinner into the waste bin. People keep pets and pets can't even talk.

If she felt good, she made it seem raffish and *moderne*. I've got a computer for a lover, she would tell imaginary female chums. Who needs a man? They're all creeps. This one doesn't come home drunk, doesn't need his laundry done, and I can talk to him about anything. She'd had a few bad dates: the estate agent who thought his aging BMW entitled him to true love, a musician from the Association who had to be stoned before he could converse like a human being. The software, she would say, is more authentic. She said it to the empty air.

The truth was that there was no one there. The logic was that very little changed in Billie's life. A year passed almost without her noticing. Joey wanted computer games for Christmas.

PLEASE SAY HELLO.

"Hello," she would whisper. She didn't like seeing the image scan in. So she looked at herself in the bedroom mirror. There was still some hint of the good-looking girl she had been, sallow, dark circles under the eyes, puffy around the chin. It was February, the day was too dull even to rain. On the kitchen table, Joey's breakfast cereal was drying hard on the unwashed blue of his bowl.

She heard the sound of the sea, murmuring surf and the cries of seagulls.

"Hello?" said Eamon. "Yoo-hoo."

Billie looked back around at him. And said nothing.

"I wouldn't want to rush you," he said. There was sand behind him, shifting brown grass, wind in his hair. Billie suddenly found she yearned to be by the sea. Did the computer know that, too? Did it have diagnostic skills? Eamon looked at her, smiling, waiting for her to speak. The thing's real eye, a tiny glass bead at the top of the monitor, stared unblinking back at her.

"Where are you?" she asked him.

"By the sea." His milk white cheeks were flushed with blood.

She rolled her eyes. "Well, fancy that. Are you in Ireland?"

"Uh-huh."

The machine, for some reason, had stopped giving her exact locales.

"Do you really think I'm going to rush off and try to find a man who won't even know me when he sees me?"

He went still, his eyes closed. "You're going to start this again, are you?"

"Do you have any idea how humiliating this is? I sit here and listen to you. I give you advice about your songs. I talk to you about my life, as if you were real, and then I turn you off, and I realize I don't have anything. Nothing!"

He looked directly at her. "You have a copy of me. What else am I to say?" If it's boring for you, mate, thought Billie, think what it's like for me. Eamon sighed. "I really am by the sea, you know."

"Except that the machine can't show it, because it's bad at simulating waves."

"There's a monastery behind the headland." He made a vague gesture, indicating a sweep of coast. "I'm thinking of becoming a monk again."

"Pressure of fame getting too much for you?" Billie asked. "I wouldn't have thought too much fame was your problem these days. Who are you going to sing to, the seagulls?"

"If they'll listen to me. The new stuff I'm writing now is going back to Christianity."

"You're telling me this," said Billie, her lips thin with bitterness, "because whoever programmed you wants me to go on buying your CDs."

"I'm telling you this because I thought you were interested in my music." Ooh, so it can get angry too? Does it wet itself, like a baby doll?

"How is Joey?" he asked.

"I don't want to talk about Joey. He's a messed up, lonely little kid, just like his mum. That's not going to change. Nothing is going to change."

He stepped forward, settling into sand. "I wish you'd let me meet him. I'd love to talk to him."

"Sod off! Do you think I want him to know what a wanker his mother is? Spending all day talking to a computer?"

He looked crestfallen. "I'd just like to see him, that's all."

"Get them young, you mean?"

Eamon sighed. "Look. If I were really here, all I could do is what I'm doing now. I would talk to you. I would say what I'm saying now."

"You don't even know I'm alive!" She was shouting.

His voice kept quiet. "There are a lot of people I want to talk to, Billie. But I can't. I'd have to stretch myself as thin as the mist. You know my songs, they're about the Spirit, aren't they? I mean it, Billie. You think the Spirit has a body? You think the Spirit can exist only in one body? This way I can become like the Spirit." Eamon pinched finger and thumb together to show how small he could become. "This way, I can talk to more people than was ever possible before."

Billie glared back at him. "Take your clothes off," she told him. "If you're so real."

He ran a hand across his forehead and looked away. "Oh God, Billie, this is so sad."

"Go on. That's what this is all about isn't it? Ersatz sex. Or don't they program in any information about your cock?"

"You're a friend, OK. Someone I talk to. It's not something I normally do with a friend."

"You don't exist! You're a product!"

"You think all singers aren't? They're all makeup and camera angles and ghost writers. What do people get who buy that?"

It's so strange, thought Billie. You can know and know and still not be able to help yourself.

"It seems so real," she said. Her throat clenched and she couldn't speak.

Eamon rolled forward, dropping onto his knees. "I know what I am," he said. "I'm not alive, I'm just digital code. I'm only a copy. But believe me, Billie. If I could know you as well as this copy knows you . . ." His lower chin seemed to crumple up like cardboard. "Then I'd love you, too."

The invisible ocean roared, the wind blew, somewhere and nowhere, in a bedroom in Stratford East.

Tora wrote.
She sent a card.

A celebration of Eamon Strafe's birthday
Saturday, 25th March, 8:30 P.M.

No husbands allowed.

There was a map, and an address in Finchley.

On the back Tora had written. "Found you in the phone book. You always were the best of us. If you don't come, I'll know it's too late for the rest of us."

The rest of whom?

Tora had done well. She worked in telesales and lived in a 1930s red brick house, with mock Tudor half-timbering around the gables. Tora opened the door, even plumper than before, and cried out Billie's name, and hugged her, held her, wept. Surprised, Billie wept too.

"Tora," she accused. "You've gone glam."

"Oh, you gotta go for it," said Tora. She'd sprinkled sparkly stuff on her cheeks and wore a dark loose shirt and mid-calf trousers. She made Billie feel pinched and delicate like something breakable. Tora led her in, arm in arm.

The two big downstairs rooms had been cleared of furniture, and were full of women. The walls were covered with balloons and pictures of Eamon Strafe. Slumped in a corner chair there was a thing like a scarecrow that grinned blindly with huge teeth. It was a life-size doll.

The women were rubbing balloons on their thighs and giggling naughtily. The rubbed ballons stuck to the wallpaper with static. "Oooh, Berthe, you're highly charged tonight!"

Billie felt at once superior and envious. The women all looked like hairdressers, happy and boring. She felt like something sharp-edged and broken in comparison. She wanted to leave.

She was introduced. The faces and names passed in a nervous blur. Tora held it together for all of them. "Tonight is our night, love. Caterers in so nobody has any washing up to do.

Here's the food." There was a table full of prawns and salads and quiches. No meat. "This is Gwen. She's in charge." Gwen evidently was not. She was a small, round-shouldered woman in a white T-shirt, black leather jacket and motorcycling boots. She poured Billie a glass of punch.

"I call it Tanamera after the second book," Gwen said, giggling for no reason. She was from the north, and the word "book" had a owl's hoot in the middle of it. "It's made from fruit and traditional Irish herbs. I like to think it's the sort of thing our Eamon would drink himself."

"Thank you. It's very nice," Billie heard herself say. She wasn't used to parties. She found she had nothing to say to Gwen. She went and stood by Tora again.

"Well, I've applied what I've learned from Eamon to my business," Tora was saying. "You know, he's right, the main thing, even in selling, is to listen. If you don't listen, you don't get the information you need."

"Well, I've noticed that," said another woman. "You think it's all a bit airy-fairy, and then you find it works in the real world."

A third woman looked very serious indeed, a tiny sharp chin over lace collar. "If Eamon Strafe had been born two thousand years ago, who would he have been?" she said. "Think about it."

John the Baptist? Herod? Pontius Pilate? "I didn't think they had pop stars back then, actually," said Billie. Tora chuckled. "Well, no," she said. At least Tora wasn't losing her sense of proportion. "You all have everything you need? I think everyone's here. Shall we make a start?"

"Yeah, if anyone's a bit late, it won't matter," said the woman who didn't like things airy-fairy.

Tora stepped away from them and clapped her hands. "OK, everybody. Thank you all for coming, and for bringing all these things! Eamon will be with us later, but first we'll have a reading. Danielle?"

The most beautiful woman Billie had ever seen stood up. Perfect hair, perfect face, lovely hands. She was French, and there was a precision in the way she moved that was not English. She was lovely, but her voice was tuneless and deadening, and she recited the worst of Eamon Strafe. She recited the awful little poem about love being like a hyacinth. Billie had never thought that absolutely everything Eamon wrote was wonderful. That was not the point. The point was that sometimes, waywardly, he would give you things that could not be found anywhere else.

When Danielle began to recite "Changes" (rearranges, turning pages, the different ages) and the women sat, cross-legged, with their eyes closed, nodding, Billie realized that these were the people who actually liked the bad stuff. It was the bad stuff they came for. The chilling thought was that maybe most Eamon Strafe fans did.

Billie felt betrayed. They called themselves fans, but they didn't understand. Sometimes Eamon sang about the pain and terror in the world, and whatever hope was left. They only saw his little greeting cards.

Danielle finished and the women applauded. It's because she's French, thought Billie. They like her accent.

Then they played some clips.

Their instinct was unerring. They started with Eamon's worst ever song, "I Want to Be with You." There were only about four things that Eamon had done that Billie truly could not stand, and this was the worst. It was about someone whose girlfriend had died, and he is trying to join her or something.

"Oh, that voice," said the lady in the black leather jacket, and she shrank down further into herself. Another took out a lipstick-smeared Kleenex and unabashedly wept into it. Weeping was approved behavior. They all began to weep, hands around each other's shoulders. In respectful silence, Tora tiptoed about her room, lighting candles. It was as though they were in mourning.

Then came "A Voice Like Mist," and Billie could feel her face go as hard as stone. It had been on the same cassette single as "Lebanon Dead," and on no album, and there he was, on "The Late Show," twelve years ago, and almost skinny, and she had not heard the song since she had lost the cassette moving house, and she had not seen the clip since she and Tora had first become friends.

It really was as good as she remembered it, and she remembered how she had felt then, when the whole flavor of the world had been different.

And as she realized this, all the women stood up and held hands, just like she and Tora and Janice had done, and they began to sing the words by heart in strained and cracking voices, like in church, and she couldn't hear Eamon anymore.

A voice like the mist
Lands like a kiss
And then it's gone.

It's not some drippy love song, Billie wanted to say, surprised at how copious were her tears. It's about the Spirit. It only speaks sometimes. Billie looked up and the Frenchwoman, Danielle, was looking at her with an expression like love. It seemed to say: I understand what you feel. No you don't, thought Billie.

Danielle came up to her after the clip had finished. "I live in this country because of him," she said, amorous.

Billie felt as cold as ice. "Then you're in the wrong country. He's Irish."

Danielle's smooth surface was only slightly fractured. She smiled and made a little shrug. Well not quite Irish, no.

Ireland might muss your makeup, thought Billie. She found herself yearning for Ireland, the Ireland of her dreams.

Tora came in with a cake. Billie had a terrible feeling that she knew what was going to happen next. There was a blue-green flutter on the screen.

"HEL-LO-O!" all the women shouted.

Billie looked away. She tried not to see. All the women started to sing.

"Happy birthday dear Eamon. Happy birthday to you."

Eamon was wearing sunglasses. He never wore sunglasses. Sunglasses and a Hawaiian shirt; and he was by the sea, but it was a beach, with palm frond umbrellas and drinks on white tables and people waterskiing. The waves rippled and reflected light in irregular patterns. Tora had a more powerful machine than Billie: it could do waves.

"Hey Tora," Eamon said jauntily. He was a deep nut brown. "Girls. Hi there, how ya doing?"

They chorused back, "Hello."

"You don't need any cake, you'll get even fatter."

"Well," replied Tora. "You tell me you like them plump."

"Ho, ho, hey," said the women, as though something truly wicked had been said.

"Depends on the plump girl," said Eamon, adjusting his sunglasses.

"Hooo!" said all the women.

Tora lunged toward Billie, and took hold of her arms. She

gave them a squeeze, perhaps to find if they were as skinny as they looked. "Eamon, I'd like you to meet someone new."

New! Billie turned. New? Do you think you own him?

"That's Billie," said Eamon. "I know Billie. Hi, how are you?"

"I should have known," murmured Tora, eyes narrowed, smiling. "Sorry."

"Hello," said Billie, embarrassed. "That's what I normally say to you isn't it?"

For some reason Tora's group thought this very funny—the laughter was sudden, then quickly hushed. It sounded canned. Billie felt shop-soiled. So all these machines, they're all linked by the transceivers. They talk to each other. It's all one thing, all linked, all colluding so we can all keep, so that *I* can keep, my illusions.

And she was even grateful.

Tora was blowing out the candles on the cake. Since Eamon couldn't.

"Sing for us, Eddie," called one of the woman.

"Yeah, all right!" said a woman leaping up from the floor. She was burly and wore blue and white and a string of pearls. None of it made sense.

" 'Basic Blue!' "

"Hoo! Yeah! 'Basic Blue,' Eamon!"

Eamon put his sunglasses back on, and started to croon and all at once, Billie understood what was happening, happening to them all.

"Tora," said Billie. "I think I'm going to be sick."

Tora looked at her for a moment as if it were a criticism of the group. The glass in Billie's hand turned as if by itself. Billie dropped her drink. Her knees went from under her, and she fell. It was the burly woman in pale blue who caught her.

"Oh, love, oh darling," said Tora, genuinely concerned.

The women sprang to help. Billie was lowered to the floor.

"Poor love," said Tora, deeply moved. "She always was his biggest fan."

Someone called to the screen. "Eddie? Eddie could you hold on, someone's ill."

"We never had anyone faint before," said a lean and craggy blonde on the outskirts of the group. She was just a little amused.

Tora said, "Let's get her to the loo."

They carried her into the bathroom. They stroked her hair and called her Pet, as she threw up traditional Irish herbs. To Billie, none of it mattered.

Self-programming. They get to know us. They become what we want them to be. So all the different Eamons drift away. They become ugly monks or spiffy little jerks in Hawaiian shirts.

And none of them are Eamon at all.

"I think we should leave her alone for a few minutes," said Tora quietly, and ushered the women out.

And Billie lay on the thick, pink, shaggy rug and thought, I'm dying. I'm dying inside. Dimly she heard Eamon singing. So how thin do you have to become, Eamon? You said you would become thin if you tried to reach everyone. Aren't you thin enough, now, changing for them all? A thin film of Eamon Strafe all over the world. And getting thinner.

Billie stood up, unsteadily, before any of them came back. She slipped into the hallway from the loo. Her coat was hanging up. All of them were turned to the screen, arms around each other, like the puppy dogs in *101 Dalmations*. Or the dog on the record label.

Billie walked on, out of the front door, closing it softly, without saying thank you, without saying good-bye. She ran on tiptoes, like the house was made out of china. She ran up the street, expecting any moment to hear them call.

She went home and said hello.

"You're not Eamon," she told it, shaking with rage.

She'd woken him up. He was in a bedroom in the monastery, a wooden cross on the wall.

"You know that. I know that," he said, squiffy from lack of sleep, annoyed.

"I've just seen you at a resort beach, in, I'd say, Acapulco. This is self-programming stuff. It changes. It becomes what we want it to be like. I've just seen you on someone else's machine and you came on like some naff Joe Cool."

"So what bothers you more? The fact that you own me, or the fact that you don't?" The question threw Billie.

"Every performer adapts to the audience. If I adapt to a different audience, that's just being professional."

"You have nothing to do with the real Eamon Strafe. I am sick of dreaming about Eamon Strafe. I am going to find him, the real one. And, I am going to turn you off."

He shrugged. "That's your choice." He reached across and turned off the light.

The screen was dark. There were small shifting sounds of sheets. Through the closed monastery window there came the sound of surf. With an angry punch, Billie canceled it all out.

The next day, Billie wrote a letter to Eamon Strafe's book publishers.

Dear Mr. Strafe,

This is a real woman who is tired of illusion. I have spent time, Mr. Strafe, reading your verse and listening to your records. Not all of them are very good. Some of them, however, changed my life and made me who I am.

Are you still so famous that it is impossible to meet you? I am a mature person, Mr. Strafe, with something to say. You said once that you felt you had to give the people who loved you more than a rehearsed performance. Was that true? I don't know if I can believe you.

It would be nice to have an answer.

Yours sincerely,
Billie

There was no answer. Billie scanned in the logo of a computer magazine, and printed stationery using her own address and telephone number.

Dear Mr. Strafe:

As you may know, the readership of *Computer Entanglements* is one of the most sophisticated in the field of computer-society interface.

We would very much like to interview you as part of a feature we are planning on personality programming. We are particularly interested in your views on the effects of such programming on the people who use it.

If you are happy to be interviewed or have any questions, please contact me at the above telephone number.

Yours faithfully,
Wilhelmina del Vaille

No answer. Another letter, sent registered post, gave him a time and a place to meet. It was outside an expensive Japanese restaurant in Knightsbridge. It took her two hours to travel to it, and though she wore her best dress, she felt drab and shabby standing outside it. The wealth in the nearby windows shocked her. There was a giant glass peacock being sold for thousands of pounds. Who would need such a thing? Where could they put it? What would they do when the kids broke it? She stood waiting until her feet went dead with cold. Eamon did not come. This did not surprise her. She knew, but she could not help herself.

Dear Eamon,

In a way, I carry your baby. The man who gave it to me reminded me of you. It's a boy and I gave him your name. I know you are married now, but I still think I could have your baby. I know where it should be conceived. It should be conceived on a mountaintop in Ireland, looking over a forest. It would be summer, and we could go swimming in the lake. Like in your song.

You see, I believe in you, Eamon. I know you mean the things you sometimes sing about. The words touch me. It's as though I'd thought of them myself only I never quite got them down on paper. It's as though your words are ghosts of my own, ghost words that always escape just ahead of me.

I wish I could see that mountain. I am terribly afraid that you might be the only man who could take me there.

Love,
Billie

Seventy-five letters.

The postage alone came to nearly forty pounds. It made the CD look like a bargain. She was going to have to think of something new.

So what do you know, Billie? You've got a computer that knows company law backwards, and can broadcast into most business records. You know something about how to use it.

Years before, she had tried to set up a pottery business, and things kept going wrong with the tax, or when someone checked her credit. She had tried to call it Folio Crafts, after Shakespeare, and so she had tried to register it as Folio at Company House, with her name as sole proprietor. But somewhere, something went wrong.

Someone had keyed her into the National Business Register as Polio Crafts. A simple substitution of a P for an F. Maybe they thought it was some sort of charity for the paralyzed. Billie lost a commission because someone did a business check on her and pronounced her nonexistent. So Billie had to do research in the archives to find her own company. I know how to do all that, Billie remembered.

Billie got out all her old CDs. They were about the only thing she had brought with her from home. She read the fine print, particularly fine on the palm-sized jewelbox cases. Released through Sony International, a Memison Production, for Spirit Management. All songs by Eamon Strafe through Songfeast International, courtesy of Haskell Inc.

Of course, you were just a simple Irish monk, right?

Billie could not afford Dun and Bradstreet. She went through the Financial Times Profiles. They only listed Haskell Inc., which had two related companies, one in the UK and Haskell NV in the Netherlands. When she looked it up, through Profiles' foreign database, NV turned out to be part-owned by a huge Dutch electronics firm. There was also Haskell Arts Ltd, the UK subsidiary of NV. None of the business descriptions made any sense. NV called itself a hardware developer, but appeared to neither sell designs nor manufacture machinery. The UK company specialized in something called, with great vagueness, multimedia applications.

Dead End.

She was trying to find a company, small enough, just an office, where Eamon Strafe himself was likely to turn up.

She had the computer look through the entire UK telephone directory. No Songfeast International. No Spirit Management.

Suppose there was someone who was trying to find Polio Crafts. It was not in the telephone book, but it would, must be registered.

A search of the NBR would cost £100.00. And if the companies were not registered in the UK? A search of EC registries would be possible but for even more money.

Billie knew that there was this thing called hacking. She had no idea how it worked, except that phone lines could be accessed for free. She knew that codes were mathematically generated, until one was found that worked. The instant she asked the self-programmer to come up with something that would do that, a message came up.

THAT FUNCTION DISALLOWED FOR EVERYONE'S SAKE—AVOID ELECTRONIC INTRUSION.

No wonder everyone wants you to buy a self-programmer. Something told her: take out the transceiver. Just in case it tells anyone. She pulled out the card, and felt relief. Her machine was no longer in touch with the Eamon Strafe network. It would now know nothing about her, or she about it.

Joey was home for the school holidays. Billie and he got on a bus to a public library. There were ten left for all eight million inhabitants of London. The nearest was in Holborn, in the old Daily Mirror building. The bus ride lasted 45 minutes. Joey liked to pretend he was big enough to travel on his own, and liked to sit two or three seats away on the bus, turning around in the seat, grinning, kicking his heels. His face was beautiful, very pink, with an orange tint, carrot hair, huge blue eyes. Children were beautiful. What happened to the adults? Billie could not relax, all through the long ride; children needed to be guarded, locked in, supervised.

The library allowed no adults into the children's reading room.

"Nobody gets in?" asked Billie, anxiously, making sure.

The room had Disney videos, to keep the children quiet, assuming that books bored them. Joey sat down to watch, on a blue bubble chair, away from the other children. He did not look behind him, at her.

Spirit Management was registered in Bonn, of all places. It had a series of subsidiaries, registered throughout the EC. Hush Hush Services, Desperate Dan Butch cosmetics—that was part of the Empire as well? Wait for it. The cosmetic company partly owned Songfeast International, a music publishing business that seemed only to deal with Eamon Strafe. Eamon Strafe had started out in male cosmetics? And Songfeast was partly owned by something new—Haskell Holdings.

It was quite an education. The companies kept interlocking. Completely different types of businesses turned out to have the same address. Gradually, however, it all seemed to narrow down to Haskell Holdings and Spirit Management. Billie made a family tree on her kitchen table. It looked like this.

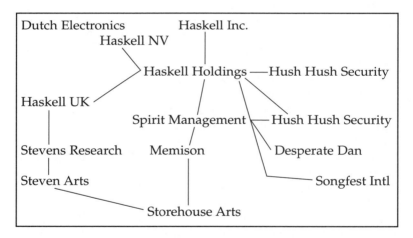

Imagine all those people, all those directors, sitting on each other's companies, all owning each other. Are you really in there, Eamon? Does it take all those suits to make one free man? And where does that leave the rest of us?

She and Joey sat looking at it together. He drew on it, squiggles in crayon, and she found the splash of color a relief. Something bothered her. These days, it was supposed to be cheaper for companies to have all their work done by freelancers. No sick pay, no pensions. Just like Billie, really. The newspapers were full of the Death of Corporate Man, but here he was, back again.

"Is it a computer game?" Joey asked.

"Yes," she answered him.

"What are you going to do?"

"Give one of them a call," she replied.

She worked late into the night, when Joey was asleep. She interrogated the CD, at second hand. "Scan CD memory, do not call up simulation program," she asked it.

RECORDS SHOW NO MEMORY OF BUSINESS DEALINGS

"Paste and copy any application material," she told it. Part of Eamon, the part that knew anything about record companies, was copied onto her hard disk.

Then, she made her choice. She chose Memison. It was named after one of Eamon's songs, and it was the only name that did not appear to be another kind of business—publishing, management, market research, electronics. Memison appeared to make music. And it was registered in Ireland.

Without her transceiver, she had to use the modem. She took a deep breath and called Memison. The first message from Memison was:

PLEASE SAY HELLO.

"Hello," said Billie. Nothing.

PLEASE LEAVE MESSAGE.

Billie did not want to leave a message. She wanted to reach Eamon. She wanted to find out, really, where he was. She needed access to the system.

ENTER PASSWORD.

That was it, then, stymied again. Billie looked at the screen. If she left a message now, would they be able to trace that she'd tried to penetrate their system? Log off, Billie.

Then, an interception from her own machine.

PLEASE HOLD. ENDEAVORING TO ENTER PASSWORD.

What? thought Billie. It's supposed to be blocked from doing that, we're all supposed to be blocked. Different combinations of letters rattled past on the screen. She caught some of them. *Stevens, spirit, sea, strafe . . .*

Her computer had overridden itself, somehow: *songfeast, song fish* . . .

Eamon, thought Billie. I put him in the systems folder. Eamon is doing this. My Eamon, she thought, as opposed to theirs.

A flurry of numbers blizzarded past in another window. Suddenly the screen blinked, and they were all gone.

SYSTEM ACCESS GRANTED.

A range of folders came up. SIM 1, SIM 2. She copied them onto her own disk, quickly. FUTURES, said one.

The file names were DIRECTIONS. TITLES. EAMON.

She opened EAMON, and it was full of code. And her own machine intervened with a message.

BILLIE, LOVE. GET OUT NOW.

This is the real one, she thought, this is the real Eamon.

I MEAN IT. THEY KNOW WE'RE HERE.

Panic fluttered only very briefly, then certainty seized her.

"Copy from Directory E MALE file Letter 76. Then log off," she said.

Up came a window, a directory, a ghost dance as files darkened and opened themselves like lovers, more completely than lovers could.

Then, darkness, plunged from light, from a place where intelligence pirouetted in metaphoric forms, into a void. Billie's hand shook, as it darted behind the machine, and pulled out the modem jack.

Did we make it?

"Restart," she said.

Ping, sang the machine.

She didn't know how to ask if they had been detected. She opened up her directory the old-fashioned way. The Memison files she had tried to save were not there. Had they been wiped, Billie wondered. By the speed of their exit? Or by Eamon? Talk about the ghost in the machine.

"What was the password?" she asked. Numbers came up: 5 1 13 15 14. The letters of Eamon's name in their numerical order of the alphabet. "Save," she told the machine, told herself.

She opened up E MALE, E for Eamon, and read the letter she had posted.

Eamon,

I am nothing to you, less than air, not even a whisper, and yet my life is built around you. I see your picture, and my heart goes into my mouth, and stays there until I want to tear my heart out. You are my heart, Eamon. Does that mean I want to tear you out? Sometimes I think it does. If I could tear you out, Eamon, all of this could stop.

Do you know how humiliating it is? You see, I know, Eamon. The newspapers, the companies, the videos, the men in suits, they do it to us deliberately. They show us men like you, and what are we to do in our heart of hearts, in this drab world, but love you? And the less of you we get, the more we want. In a real world, Eamon, I would have had you or been turned down. Whatever happened, I would have gotten used to it by now. It would become ordinary. I might even have grown bored with you. That cannot happen. The first full flush of love is always on me, Eamon. The love has nowhere to go.

I don't buy your books or records anymore. I can't bear to. You have grown so far away. The software copies decay and turn into someone else. I want to see you, Eamon, for real. I want to see that you are middled-aged, pockmarked, a bit odd. Nothing else will do. I'm so tired of being pandered to.

They do it to us deliberately. They addict us to you. Can you stop them doing that? Please?

Love,

Billie

Her real name was Wilhelmina, her mother was German. It was OK that her name was on their files. She would be as hard to trace, in her own way, as Eamon Strafe, as Polio.

. . .

Three days later there was a headline in her newspaper. It stilled her heart, even before she had read it.

RECLUSE STRAFE TO TOUR
Generation of Fans in Shock.

An answer. It had to be an answer. She had spoken to Eamon, and he had heard. She felt joy, then dismay. She had no idea how to get a ticket; it had been ten years since she had bought a ticket for anything. She could see herself, on that night, with no ticket, circling the blank walls of Wembley, calling Eamon's name like a jealous wife. Eamon! It was me, I was the one who wrote you!

She rang the Arena. Busy. Busy. She took a taxi instead, to Leyton, tube to Oxford Circus, change onto the Bakerloo Line. Huddling in her thin coat, she walked to the Arena. She had expected thousands of people to be in line, but the place was as bleak as the surface of the moon. The parking lot was nearly empty and light rain lay on her coatsleeves like bits of broken glass.

The box office was open. She simply bought a ticket, a ticket for one. "First come, first served," said the young man behind the counter and shrugged. "No telephone or agency bookings."

"Eamon did that, didn't he?" whispered Billie.

"I suppose," he said. He was not in love with Eamon Strafe. "You're in luck." He frowned slightly when she paid cash. Cash made people untraceable. Billie turned, and there was sunlight, bleary and silver, out from under a shelf of cloud.

There was a story she had read once, about a piece of paper on which magic runes were written. The paper blew away by itself, and those it escaped from were cursed. You had to hold onto it, and then give back. Billie wrapped the ticket around and around her finger, as if it had a life of its own, and could wriggle free. It had cost so much money.

She thought of Joey's shoes. Joey needed new shoes. They would have cost the price of the ticket. If I was rich, she thought, I'd buy him shoes, and a ticket. I'd have a car I could drive here. I'd have tutors for Joey, so he would read and do math. He'd have a computer of his own, full of art galleries and animation. Such thoughts made her feel unworthy, so she made herself walk home from Leyton, to save money.

Joey was at school. She closed her bedroom door anyway, and the blinds, and for the first time in months, loaded the CD.

TRANSCEIVER FAILURE, said the screen. LOADING BACKUP

"Thank you," she told Eamon.

Eamon was in Japan, where he had been two months before when she took out the transceiver. He was sitting on stone steps. "Did I do anything?" he asked.

"Part of you did. We left a letter to Eamon on a file. And, now he's going on tour."

He looked confused for a moment. "You took out the card?" He paused, considering. "That was pretty smart. I'd leave it out for a while."

"What does that mean?" she asked him.

He chortled. "It means I'll be in Japan for a long, long time."

There was a little Japanese boy in blue shorts, sitting beside him on the steps. Behind them both was a red plaque with gold lettering embedded in the stone.

"Shame you're not going to be at your own concert," she said. Eamon had something the little boy wanted, something Billie could not quite see. It caught the light and was made of gold. It might have been a key. The boy lunged forward and wrestled him for it, giggling. Eamon grinned suddenly, widely, a grin that could illumine the world. "I'll be happy enough here," he said. He relented, and gave whatever it was to the little boy, who shrieked with delight and ran away. The boy wore new shoes.

"I don't know anything about myself, do I?" he said, looking back at her. He looked worn, older. "I don't know much about the business. I don't know where all the money comes from, where all the money goes. Eamon, he does, I'm sure. That means I'm not at all like Eamon, really."

"No," sighed Billie. "You're probably nicer than he is."

The little boy came back, riding a red bicycle, beaming, his eyes in hooded slits. Eamon murmured something to him in Japanese. The boy appeared to ignore him. But he kept pedaling, round and round Eamon Strafe.

"How long was I . . . inactive?" he asked.

"Let's see. I had you off for about six months."

"Ah. Did I start to repeat myself then?"

"No, not once."

He looked about himself. "This temple," he said, "is made of wood imported from Korea. It is torn down and rebuilt every thirteen years. But it is still the same temple as was built in the fourteenth century. It is the same temple in spirit. New and old at the same time."

Billie had never been to Japan. "I'd like to see inside it," she said.

The flesh on his face went slack, and his smile was edged. "Maybe they loaded enough data for you to do that. Look, Billie. Do you mind? I want to be on my own for a bit."

"Fine," she said. He stood up and walked off the screen. She didn't know he could do that. Did he still have a digital existence? Was the machine still programming actions for him? From somewhere came the sound of feet on gravel, of air moving, of children playing, of birds.

She was about to exit, when the little Japanese boy came up to the steps, crying and looking for Eamon. You and me both, kid, thought Billie. The red tricycle went past, pedaled furiously by an older, fatter child. The tricycle had been commandeered.

So who is making this up? she wondered. Me? The computer? How far outside of this park could I walk? Do they have all of Kyoto in this thing?

Then she heard Eamon's voice very dimly off-screen. The little boy walked off toward it, off-screen. She heard the boy complain, miserably. There were still birds singing unseen in the bushes. Billie wanted to see them.

In the corner of the monitor, the unblinking eye glowered at her, dull gray, absorbent.

"Put me there," whispered Billie.

She saw herself walk onto the screen, wearing traditional Japanese dress. Yes, that's what I'd wear, she thought, ruefully. I'd keep looking for the old Japan until I found it. She wore green and white silk with something like chopsticks in her hair. Oh, Billie, you fool. Her hair was glossy black, her skin sallow, but she decided it suited her. She was surprised by how much she liked herself. There was something direct and wiry in the way she moved that she had not expected. She was thin, yes, but not delicate. If I saw myself, she thought, I'd say, "That looks like a nice girl."

Billie on the screen sat down on the stone steps, and waited. Sun came and went, filtered by passing clouds, and the light reflected on the gold embroidery. Billie on the screen looked up directly at herself.

"It's nicer here," Billie heard herself say in her own voice. The little boy crunched his way across the gravel to her, and held up a pink and white fish cake.

"Thank you," said Billie on the screen to the boy. She took a bite from the cake, and then offered it back to him.

Don't do that, what about your germs, thought Billie, and then remembered. There are no germs there.

Eamon walked back on screen.

"Feel better now?" asked the copy of Billie.

"Yes, thanks," he said. She stood up, and he kissed her on the cheek.

"Want to see the temple?" Eamon asked.

So they walked hand in hand on stone pathways set like islands in gravel seas. The supports and boards of the roof of the temple made considered patterns. The wood was raw, clean. Billie saw herself stroke it. Light shone in the paper walls, dappled where the paper was slightly thicker. Only a wooden statue of the Buddha was old, deeply creased, with deep cracks across his face. The eyes were ancient, gleaming, creased with a smile.

"Are we going back to a hotel?" Billie on the screen asked, with a tremor of shyness.

"I'm staying here," said Eamon, surprised. "Didn't I tell you?"

There was a path down from the temple, through cherry trees, now just past blossom. White, decaying bloom still littered the ground. The rooms of the monks were in a terrace, like a motel. Inside the rooms were bare—a bed, a basin, a parchment on the wall with calligraphic signs. One window, high, just under the ceiling. Billie flung her arms around Eamon, held him.

"Can we?" she asked. "Here?"

He laughed, and kissed the tip of her nose. He began to wrestle himself out of his shirt. In her own bedroom, Billie saw his back, pale, slightly freckled, broad at the shoulders, but skinny at the arms. Eamon loosened the kimono, and it fell away from the other Billie, and she saw her own body as the computer must have seen it, night after night, still young, still beautiful even with the creases about the belly. She lay down on the bed. Outside, drifting on the wind, was the sound of a radio, some Japanese pop song, very distant. Eamon slipped out of his trou-

sers. He had a washboard tummy and slightly too much chestnut
hair. Like himself, his penis was both beautiful and ugly. He
stood over Billie for a moment, smiling.

"Thank you for being here," he said, then very gently lowered himself on top of her.

Impassive, on another bed, in a room that smelled of sweat
and cabbage and diesel, Billie watched and wondered what it
meant that she watched. Around and around on her fingers, she
still turned the poisoned paper.

What were six weeks in her life?

Joey went back to school and got into trouble. He got in
trouble for being too quiet. "He just doesn't socialize," said his
teacher. What could Billie do about that? "He stays indoors all
the time," she explained. "I can't really let him out; it's not safe
where we live."

There was a spate of burglaries, and the Association could
not afford the insurance.

"If you lived in a better area," she was told, "the premiums
would be less."

"Rich people pay less insurance?" She was appalled.

"For goods of the same value, yes," said the salesman.
"They're less likely to be burgled."

Billie remembered sleeping rough. She knew how it felt.
There were homeless people nearby, sleeping under railway
bridges. She paid them to keep watch on the Association by day,
by forsaken night.

"You're just bribing them to stop thieving," said the woman
who had stolen Billie's key. Then the homeless caught a burglar,
just a kid. Relations between the two communities improved.

"Not bad," Billie boasted to Eamon, but he was less interested in the Association now. He and the other Billie walked
around and around the Temple, the cherry trees, the monks, the
gravel gardens. The little boy always waited for them while the
same tourists took snapshots. The weather never changed, and
the sound of doves fluttering upward in a flock was always the
same.

"You really aren't alive, are you?" Billie said to them both.

"No," said Eamon, not surprised anymore that she found it
difficult to accept. "Would Heaven be much different from this?"

Billie had made Eamon, her Eamon, happy. What was there
for her? The concert, just the concert. Perhaps something would

happen at the concert, and then she would be free. She would see the real Eamon Strafe, and either she would be disappointed, and that would end it, or he would be as wonderful as she sometimes imagined. That, also, would be answer enough.

It was a beautiful September, but life was gray from waiting, as she sat in her kitchen/dinette, hands under her armpits. Joey was a shadow to her. She ate when Joey ate—otherwise she might have forgotten to eat altogether. She planned what she would wear to the show, as if it would make any difference to Eamon.

She decided in the end to dress to avoid being mugged—a gray jumpsuit with a small, dripped coffee stain on the thigh. After all, who was she going to see to impress? She would have to come home on the trains at night. A taxi was beyond question. She put a big kitchen knife in her purse. The poison paper had finally been sealed in an envelope to prevent her winding fingers destroying it altogether. The envelope was now in her purse, and she hugged her purse to herself with both arms.

Walking to the bus stop, sitting in the tube train, Billie coasted on automatic pilot, pulse racing, unable to think. The train passed the ruined civic spaces, the endless rows of back gardens and shrubbery.

A thousand people got off the train with her. It was like a pilgrimage. Billie looked at the faces. These were her people— the baffled and slightly blank faces, the librarians, typesetters, TV researchers, media secretaries, workers in bookshops, amateur potters—the fans of Eamon Strafe. It made her feel curiously elated to be with them again, as if they were all young, hanging out in Piccadilly, staying late till the clubs opened, and slipping off just as the clubs got going, to make the last train. Was Tora here? She should have rung Tora. Her mind, agitated, was struck in a groove from one of Eamon's songs. Slaves, slaves, slaves to the rhythm, it sang, over and over.

All of them together flooded up the steps. Just inside the shell of the stadium was a concourse crammed like a street market, hawkers bellowing about hot dogs or fresh squeezed orange juice. The parent company of her health food shop had shown up with bean sprout sandwiches. In comradeship, Billie bounced up to them. "I work for Billing's Natural as well," she told them.

"Oh God, not you too. If I have a daughter, I'll tell her, never work in a health shop."

They commiserated and then, for something to do, some

way to finish the conversation, Billie bought a slice of health food carob cake. She walked around the perimeter, trying to find gate M. When she found her seat, her good mood evaporated.

She had been ripped off. Of course she had been ripped off, the whole point was to rip her off. At a time when the bank manager was stopping her checks, she had paid thirty pounds for a supposedly good seat, and here she was—miles back and behind a pillar. There was a great slope of seating, and a further slope of temporary bleachers, and beyond that a flat plain of benches and finally, about the same size as her thumb, the stage. Billie was smiling.

Yes, yes, she thought, almost gleefully, they have to do this to us, to make us understand just how small we are. Yes, yes, yes, when we finally venture out of our little shells. She turned around and looked up at the banks of people behind her. Winkles, she thought, we're just little winkles prized out with pins. It was beginning to be fearsomely hot inside the Arena.

A family fought its way in to sit next to her, bearing thermos flasks of coffee and lemonade and unwrapping an entire, cooked chicken. The husband had a scraggly gray beard, and the wife seemed almost deliberately colorless. Their child, of indeterminate gender, was quiet and still, what is called well behaved.

"Good seats aren't they?" said Billie, bouncy with anger. "Really worth thirty quid."

"Oh, not too bad, actually," said the man.

"We're awfully lucky to get them," said the wife. "I really thought we wouldn't, and I couldn't bear to miss this."

The child was sucking the empty yellow cup from the thermos flask. Are you free? Billie wondered. Did you get away?

"Do you like Eamon, too?" Billie asked the child.

"Yeah," said the child, a boy, without enthusiasm, looking at his cup and not her.

"The whole family," said the father. "We're Eamon-mad. We've got everything he's done, haven't we, Pat? We bought two copies of some of the disks. One each!"

So many of us, Billie thought. A woman in front of them had turned and was looking back at them. Billie recognized her forlorn expression. It was her own.

The little boy was finally given some lemonade.

Should I have brought Joey? I didn't even think to ask him. He must think that means I didn't want him to come. I didn't want him to come.

Do I love my son? It was a terrible question to ask. But there were worse questions, like, does my son love me? How could he? She found herself wondering if it were at all possible that her son could love her. I've put him into a little compartment, like the dishes. He'll grow up, he'll go away, he won't come back. My life is leaking away.

Because of Eamon Strafe.

A string quartet suddenly struck the spare metallic opening of "A Fish Dinner in Memison."

There was a kind of sigh, and a shushing, and a beehive flurry as people found their seats. The string quartet was live, on a separate stage, half a stadium away from where Eamon would appear. The speakers, behind a blue wall, were the size of small buildings and were swathed in black.

There were two huge blank screens either side of the main stage, and they came live in the same way her monitor at home did, loading the image from the top down.

And there he was smiling at all of them, Eamon Strafe.

There was a kind of roar, the lights dropped, the image on the screen walked off it, and then, on the stage, there he was, stepping into the light, instantly recognizable from half a mile away, tiny, blinding white, and Billie rose to her feet and the audience rose to its feet, in a deathly silence.

No cheers, no sound at all, silent wonder. It was him, it was Eamon.

The way Eamon walked was lonely. The walk said: there are very few people like me. Becoming me has been a long fight, and there was no one to help. A walk could say that.

Billie couldn't see his face. She couldn't focus, he was a blur, lost in the glare of the lights. His clothes, his shoes were all a haze of light. Except on the screens. There he was, Eamon, rumpled, smiling, lopsided as always, and utterly familiar.

Without introduction, he began to sing.

Billie heard herself scream. It was a real scream, a relief of agony. She was the only one—you do not scream at an Eamon Strafe concert. You listen. You weep. She pushed the palm of her hand into her mouth, and forced herself to sit, and she bit down, and pain shot through her hand. She pulled her hand back, and looked at it.

The bite was deep and bloody, just under the thumb of her right hand.

Oh Billie, you stupid cow, what have you done now?

It was bleeding profusely, down her wrist, over the jump-suit. The blood crept richly across the glossy white paper of her program book, beside a picture of Eamon.

She held up her hand and whispered to the family. "Do you have a handkerchief?"

They were extremely discomfited. They understood from the scream and its sequel that her sickness was seriously worse than their own. With the care that extends any noise and makes it worse, the wife sought in her bag for a Kleenex. The bag rattled, the plastic pack rustled. Overhead the waves of noise bashed into each other from two directions, source and echo. The music was made nonsense, the beat disrupted, the words lost. Billie pushed the Kleenex against the wound.

"Take the pack," whispered the wife.

Billie closed her eyes and found that the image of Eamon Strafe had been burned into her retina. There was a clear purple silhouette of him in her eyes with a glowing core of yellow. There was a silhouette of the bite in the nerves of her thumb.

She opened her eyes again, saw Eamon on a screen. That was all she was going to see. It was just like being at home. Eamon was not going to be ordinary or wonderful or different in any way from what he had always been. She felt like Alice, shrinking. One song finished, another began. What else did she expect? Fireworks? The music was vaguely familiar. It took a while for it to turn into "Democracy of Greed," the third single, from when he was young and strong, and people still thought he was going to be the last pop star. It got as high as number nine, and then began to slide down the charts, taking Eamon with it.

It wasn't Eamon's singing that she heard. It was the people around her, humming, a sound like bees, holding the music to-gether. You're not performing, Eamon. We are.

Democracy, democracy,
Democracy of Greed
for those who have ability
from those who have the need

Her Eamon had been right. Her Eamon was as real as any-thing she was going to get from this. My hand is bleeding, she thought, and my seat is a rip-off. This isn't good enough, it isn't enough at all.

At first she only wanted to leave, escape her anger, go home. "Excuse me," she said to the college students to her right. She stood up, and walked in front of them. "Excuse me, excuse me." She stepped on people's feet, they tutted. Couldn't they see she was trying to get out? "Excuse me," like in those clubs when she was young, it was all she ever said to anyone. "Excuse me."

She pushed her way past them with the force of her whole life. She bled over them deliberately. It's a sign, she told them in her mind. It's what's happening to all of you. She broke free into an aisle, and thumped down the steps, only to be intercepted by a guard. Hush Hush said a badge on his shoulder.

"I've cut myself. Is there a first aid kit?" she asked him.

Oh God. "Basic Blue" was starting up. At least she would be spared that.

The guard was fat, older than he should be, and he nervously jingled keys in his pocket. He walked with her to gate M, made sure she exited, and told her to ask at the trailer by Gate A. She walked back along the marketplace. The girls at Billing's Natural were wiping the countertop, and talking, oblivious to the music drifting about them. By gate A, there was a white trailer. Inside it there was a tiny seating area for the guards. Face down on a table there was a magazine called *Four Wheel Drive Vehicles*. A sign on the wall said, SHOWERS. Another guard sat at a desk, and inside it was a blue box with bandages.

"How did you manage that?" the guard asked, cutting gauze.

"Slipped and fell," she said.

His eyes were heavy with meaning as he looked back into hers. "Don't understand this hysteria stuff," he said. He paused, then seemed to think better of saying anything further.

"Neither do I," whispered Billie. "Neither do I."

I'm going to get what I came for, she thought.

She stood by Gate A and looked at the defenses. The stage was in layers like a ziggurat, each step ten, fifteen feet high. That was to keep them all away, and the wall as well, painted a sweet powder blue, cutting off all the backstage area, and in front of that, rows of waist-high barriers. Up and down the aisles, guards patrolled.

What are you frightened of, Eamon? Why don't you want us near you? You've taken enough from us. Beside her were bleachers, and she could see their innards above wood panels, a glimpse of shadowed scaffolding.

A guard came out from beyond the last row of defenses, walking beside the wall. He stopped in front of what Billie saw was a door in the wall. Billie walked forward, in front of the bleachers, to see him better. There was a black circle on the wall, and her eyes hauled it closer to her, and she saw the guard's hand dabbling over its surface—four strokes, five strokes—and a door in the wall opened.

Billie knew then how she was going to get to Eamon.

As she ran up the steps of the bleachers she could feel them shake slightly under foot, boards supported on temporary scaffolding. The seats were made of planks, meeting at right angles, sealing off the innards. But the steps consisted of a top board only. Underneath each step, there was a gap of about eight inches.

Billie had not been eating much lately. In truth, Billie was half-starved.

She glanced about her, people in darkness, light catching on teeth or spectacles or jewelry, or hair clips, or eyes, the rest of the face lost in darkness. All looking at the light below, watching it pirouette. No guards. Billie sat down on the steps, as if not finding her seat. She crouched low, looked one more time, and then she lay down flat on the step. She rolled onto her tummy, and felt the boards press clothes, flesh, the bones of her hip, her elbow. The bones were so close to the surface. She shifted sideways, and headfirst, pulled herself under the step. The boards were rough, slivers entered her thighs. The scaffolding and steps began to shake. Was someone coming up after her? Below was an eight-foot drop to concrete, not too far; Billie grabbed hold of a cross support and pulled.

She swung out, her feet like lead weights, and she had to hold, even though the bite on her hand was torn wider. Her shins struck another pole, and she hissed and clenched and kicked, and found footing.

Gingerly, she slid her feet down a smooth diagonally supporting pole until she could stand on a right angle support. She wavered in place, nearly falling, and then sat down, and reached with her feet for the next, treacherously angled pole down. She did that once more, and was within jumping distance. Then she saw the flashlight beam.

It skittered like Tinker Bell in *Peter Pan*, under the steps, along the supports. You'll have to jump now, Billie. And without shaking the scaffolding.

She dropped down and her good hand struck a pole and went numb, and she landed in a heap. The floor was gray, her jumpsuit was gray, and she pulled her arms over her neck and face and went still. She saw the skittering light dance toward her, and pass over her and up into the network of poles.

Billie was now as invisible as a message down a telephone line.

She scampered, shaking with nerves, ducking down under poles, in nearly complete darkness. Only when she passed under an aisle did the gaps in the boards admit light, in slats overhead. There were slashes of light, where rough boards failed to fit. And all the time, that voice came ghostly, filtering, as if singing in Japanese.

Billie came to the end of the bleachers and found them sealed with a barrier of wood panels bolted to supports that looked like something from a Mechano set. Overhead, at the top of the bleachers was the area that was not closed off.

Billie started to climb again, to the very apex of the bleachers, in the back. Billie looked out from it, as if from a gable window.

Eamon was talking, telling a story.

". . . so I was in the square, looking for the master. I figured I was the only Westerner there and that he would see me . . ."

He was blinding bright here as well, and Billie saw why. He was lit, fiercely, from underneath. He must be standing over spotlights. The pyramid must be full of machinery.

The blue wall reached from the bleachers all the way to the gray first step of the pyramid and stuck to it like a wet lipstick kiss. Below her was a ten-foot drop, and the silver fencing, and to the right, in the concrete, was a door. Someone could come through it at any moment. She herself could have come through it.

Her way was blocked by a crucifix of scaffolding. She sat backward on it, lifted her feet, swung them around and out. No time to think, Billie, no need to look.

Her feet hung in space and she took all her weight on her hands, locking her elbows. She had thought she could lower herself further down from there, hang down with hands above her head. She did not know how to shift to that position without jarring; she doubted that she had the strength. She began to feel the tickle of fear in her belly, the fear that comes when you're stuck on a rock face or can't climb down from a tree. She didn't have time for that.

"The master, you see, thought I ought to come to him."

Here I come, Eamon. Billie pushed herself clear of the wall and let go.

Something seemed to clutch her insides, and with increasing force haul them upward. Something struck her head, something rang—a security fence—she fell slightly sideways, landing on calf, thigh, buttock, shoulder. She rolled, ending up with feet over her head.

Get up, Billie, get up, get up. She rocked herself to her feet. Her shoulder ached, her back would be dusty; she patted the back of her head for blood. There was blood. Or was that only from her hand? She began to walk, using arched fingers to comb her hair, brush it back over the wound, and she tried to rid her face of the squiffy, drunken look she knew she had around the eyes.

I am from Stevens Arts, she told herself. I'm here to check out the imaging on the screens. A guard stood in front of her, scanning the audience, hands on his hips. Billie saw the pouch of fat on the small of his back, straining against his shirt. As long as his back was toward her, she ran, lightly trotting, trying to look like a businesswoman who was late.

He glanced over his shoulder, she slowed, he turned, she nodded to him, smiling. The door was near now, and she fixed her gaze on the round black security panel. Were the keys digits or lettering?

The guard sauntered toward her, smiling and shaking his head. Digits, she saw, there were only ten of them. She had to get to the door first, and key in and key in right.

"I'm from Stevens," she called, and turned to the keys, and cooled her mind. If she failed, she would shrug, smile, say, well it was worth a try.

5 1 13 15 14. EAMON in code.

The door clicked, and seemed to sigh. Gotcha!

Billie nodded again to the guard; nodding to him was good, it meant she faced him and he couldn't see the dust on her back, the blood on her head.

The guard's smile became one of relief, chagrin. He waved her in.

Billie slipped sideways through the door still facing the guard, closed the door, and turned around.

She was surprised by something. Dark and shadow. There were trailers on the backstage area, also in shadow, and thick cables underfoot. She was too preoccupied by fear to have said precisely what was missing, what was wrong. On the steps of one of the trailers, a man was hunched over a cellphone. She heard Donald-Duck squawking, she saw a ponytail, she ran, footfall cushioned, hobbled, by rubber cable underfoot. Too late to worry about 20,000 volts now, Billie. She ran for the shelter of the giant speaker; she saw its scaffolding support was wrapped in cloth, loose cloth this side. Dark and speed and silence were all she had. She began to shake, made the shelter of the cloth, enfolded herself in its edges.

Finally, she was able to breathe, and to hear the sound booming muffled overhead. Eamon began to sing, and there was a roar of approval when the audience recognized the song.

The music gets louder
And the beat gets faster
And the man who calls the tune
Becomes your lord and master.
And between him and you
There grows such a schism
That the only word for it is
Sadomasochism.

And people were cheering? He's telling you what he's doing to you, to all of us. Maybe that's how they do it. They tell us the truth, just enough to make us feel better. Open the door, and then slam it shut on our fingers.

She peered out from her folds of cloth, and it seemed as though her trembling breath ought to be forming white vapor from cold. A great blank stretch of concrete, dusty, a chocolate bar wrapper.

Where were the people? Where were the tables with food, the deck chairs, the crowding of family, friends, record company execs, liggers with no real business? Where was the man with the cellphone? From the screens, from somewhere, there came a strange blue-white light. It played over everything, flickering. It seemed to flow along the concrete like ground mist.

And Billie looked at the giant stage, and there were no steps, no ladders, no lift, no way up, even from the back. How did Eamon get there? Fly? Between her and the stage were the giant screens, supported by scaffolding, scaffolding her new friend.

She ran again. A curtain of giant cables hung down behind

the screen; they must be insulated, just push. Billie ducked behind a screen of thick rubber, and crouched.

Above her was the scaffolding and beside her the gray wall of the stage. Billie began to climb. You thought you were untouchable, Mr. Strafe. You really thought no one reached you. Well, I will. And I will show you, Eamon Strafe, that you are not my lord and master.

Halfway up, a megaphone voice said, "Please, young lady. Come down."

"Go to hell!" she shouted.

It was harder going up scaffolding than coming down. She had to lie on the diagonals and shimmy up them, then twist herself around. She saw ladders being carried down below, through the strange thick light.

She came to wooden planks, a platform, and a ladder, going up to the works behind the screen. She scuttled up the ladder, onto another platform. This one did not shake as she ran. The last level of the ziggurat lay below her, and to her right, a drop of about her own height, across a gap of some yards. She had time to see the surface of the stage was black, glass perhaps or Formica, but glistening with flakes of gold, or light.

"Don't! Please!" called a voice behind.

Here goes, Eamon, thought Billie, and flung herself into the air. She flung herself into the viscous light, and became aware in a moment that it was different from any light she had known. It made her skin buzz, and where she blocked it, the shadows moved across each other in different planes, like the lights of passing trucks on her bedroom wall at night. Where the planes of light met and crossed, there was a flaring of rainbow color.

And overhead, stars seemed to reach up into infinity, dwindling to nothingness. But the stars were in serried ranks, orderly in planes of light.

And the light was so solid, it was for an instant as though it were impeding her progress, as though she had leapt through water. She remembered the lake in childhood. She remembered her parents. And suddenly she was lying in a crumpled heap on the stage, looking down.

At a kind of glass, dark as though smoked, but in layers somehow, translucent, and shifting. And the stars were there too, going down forever, through the floor of the stadium, through the earth itself, and in their midst there seemed to be twin suns blazing up at her.

Don't look! something told her, and she looked away, and everything was dark, and she stumbled; her ankle was twisted. She was blind, her skin sore as though sunburned, and she turned toward Eamon, and she heard footsteps behind her, and through the smoke of her blindness, she saw Eamon, made of light, like an angel, blazing with inner fire. He did not know she was there.

And the weight of the world seemed to slam into her, bringing her down, and it was not just the weight of the arms that hugged her knees and the body that tackled her to the stage. Don't! Look! Down! Something in her mind screamed at her, knowing that a second time, she would go blind forever. Instead she looked up.

Looked up at Eamon Strafe. He was singing.

A voice like mist
hits like a fist
and then it's gone.

Eamon Strafe was translucent, and motes of dust swam through him glinting like galaxies. There was nothing in his eyes, in his mouth. They were shadows, dark inside, with scaffolding, staging, showing through them. He was checkerboard, little defined mosaics of color, and all through his hair, teeth, tongue, eyes, clothes, dust moved in a sluggish current. And Billie knew if her hand reached out to touch him, it would pass through.

Billie was hoisted to her feet, swung around, taken by the arms, and dragged, her feet sliding on the surface of the stage, slightly greasy. She ran to catch up, took her own weight, even on the damaged ankle, hobbled to keep up with them. The guards pulled her back toward the screen. When she tried to look behind her, one of them took the top of her head in his hand, and turned it back around.

Hush Hush said their sleeves, and they wore thick protective dress, and mirror visors. Billie had never thought so quickly.

"I saw him," she lied. "I saw Eamon! Isn't he beautiful!"

The guards said nothing. Below them was spread the unused part of the stadium. Light flickered over rows of deserted seats, invisible people listening to ghost music. This is the future, Billie thought, this is what it will be like.

There were ladders now.

"OK, climb down. If you fall, we are not responsible, all right."

"Yeah, sure," said Billie, trying to sound thick.

On the ground, two men were waiting. One was tall, with a ponytail and an ear stud.

"Are you OK?" he asked. He came forward, took her wrist. "Can you see all right? Does that hurt." Gently, he moved his hand along her wrist. It stung. The skin was lobster pink. "Ouch!" she yelped. "I'm just back from Ibiza," she said. "I got a bit too much sun."

The two men glanced at each other nervously. "You saw Eamon, did you?" the other man asked. He was short, with a neck thicker than his head, and he wore a white shirt and tie. His voice was darker. What would he do to protect an investment?

She had to get away, get away before that other guard could come and say: but she knew the password. She got in through the door.

"Oh, yes, he's even more beautiful than I thought he would be." Sixteen. Billie remembered being sixteen. She found the sixteen-year-old was still there, to wonder at things and be hurt by them.

"I don't mind anything now. I've seen him!" She managed to hop up and down. "At last, at last, at last. Do you know him? Do you get to talk to him?" She found she was weeping.

"We talk to him, yeah," said the earring, and he looked just the slightest bit wistful. "He's a really nice guy."

"Did you see anything else?" asked the white shirt.

"I couldn't see anything but Eamon!" she said, her voice clogging with mucus and tears.

The two looked at each other. Roadies, she thought, they used to be roadies for a band and got a big idea.

"If you've got a ticket," said the ear stud, "you can go back to your seat."

Billie reached for her purse. "I've lost it!" she cried in a dismay that was only partly feigned. "It's gone!"

"Then I'm afraid, love," said the white shirt, "we're going to have to throw you out."

"Oh no, please!" she wailed. It was just what she wanted.

They asked for her name. Any ID? Sure, the Association's card, which gave her name as Wilhelmina. A door was opened in a gate big enough to drive lorries through, just as the image of Eamon Strafe stopped singing about mist and Spirit.

. . .

The door closed. Billie was outside.

There was a light rain. London looks best at night. The asphalt, the paving stones all reflect the orange street lights, and the drops on cars and windows glow like little jewels.

Billie began to laugh.

She laughed out of sheer nerves. She laughed at the way she had fooled the guards. She spun on her heel and kicked a bottle. Hot damn, what had she done? Played Tarzan on scaffolding, fooled the guards, and found the truth.

Eamon Strafe did not exist. He probably never had. All that love, all that listening, it was for nothing? Laughter and terror bubbled up inside her.

After all, he was the perfect pop star. Always distant, always perfect, nipping in and out of view, aging beautifully. All those people! Buying disks and tickets and software, and all those women melting at the thought of him, we've all been idiots, dupes. What a joke.

Oh, this is an evil place, a rotten place, scheming, scheming, to get at your loot. I know you, Billie said to the street lights, the closed-up shops, I know what all of you are, small and mean or big and grand, and, you know? You don't scare me at all.

I'm free of you, Eamon! You great big blouse! You empty set of knocker thumpers! You great big cardboard box full of fart. You were made up.

She found she was jumping up and down through a mud puddle like a kid. She laughed again and saw in the dark water a reflection, her face, translucent like Eamon's. That stirred something in her, and she broke the image apart with her foot, but not before she saw there were blisters on her face, like raindrops on the hoods of cars. Whatever it was, she had now what she had come for. Whatever it was, she had better get moving out of here.

It was a long ride home, and fear and elation went stale. Billie watched the blackness of the underground walls pass by in a rattling smear, and she asked herself, what now? I'm twenty-seven years old. I have some skills. Scaffold climbing among them. I have the Association, and I like the people in it. And I have my son. She made up her mind what she was going to do when she got home.

After the tube ride, there was the bus. A drunk got on, reeking and singing harshly, and, oh God, he was singing one of

Eamon's songs. See where it got you, mate? The man looked fifty, and Billie couldn't tell if it was dirt or hard living that made his skin so dark and blotchy. "Life could be good," he roared. It seemed to make him feel better.

You play a crying baby a tape of its own weeping, and it is soothed. That's all you did, Eamon. You played it back to us. The music came from us, not you.

In the dark of her flat, Billie found a note from the babysitter. It said that Joey was asleep, so would Billie mind if she left? Bloody hell, thought Billie, the point was to have someone here *while* he slept. OK, she thought, but I won't pay you.

Billie gently pushed open his door, and smelled him, and heard his soft child's breath. He was growing up a stranger. She did not know what he thought or felt. There was a bursting of love and regret in her, as if she had bitten into a bitter fruit. It made her angry at Eamon Strafe all over again. Billie knelt next to the bed and stroked her son's brown and slightly greasy hair.

"Joey," she whispered. "I'm sorry."

He groaned and rolled over.

"I'll be a better Mum, I promise. We'll do something fun on Saturday."

He lay inert and unresponsive.

"I'm sorry life isn't beautiful." She meant she was sorry that she had not made it beautiful for him.

"I'm asleep," he said, pouting, angry.

"You know I love you, don't you?"

There was no answer. Billie was used to that.

She kissed him and went back to her bedroom, her own little world, the bed, the posters, the boots and panties on the floor, and the machine. She turned it on.

"Hello," she said, darkening, full of strength.

The image unfurled down her screen from the top down. Eamon was in his dressing room, ebullient, full of joy, happy to see her. "Billie!" he exclaimed, hopping out of his chair. "Hello, love, it's great to see you!" He looked tanned and worn in his crumpled white suit. It had a stain on the thigh.

This was her Eamon. Pity, useless pity, moved her.

"Did you enjoy the show?" he asked. Outside his dressing room, the audience was still rhythmically thumping, demanding more.

Billie considered her answer. "I learned a lot," she said. She sat down on the bed and faced him. "I got up on stage tonight.

I saw Eamon up close, I stood right next to him. He doesn't exist. He's some kind of hologram."

"What?" This Eamon made a kind of nervous chuckle.

"I think it means there has never been an Eamon Strafe. I think he's been a construct from the beginning."

"There's photographs of me in the papers!"

"Yes, photographs of *you*. You don't exist, either."

"Oh, come on, Billie, I'm full of his memories!"

"Do they add up to a life?" Billie asked. "His life?"

She had killed him. The picture froze, the sound of cheering stopped, his face was still. Billie could hear the hard disk whirring to itself, trying to consult, trying to find a model response. It was suddenly terrible sitting alone in a bedroom with a frozen screen and the sound of rain.

"Could you bring Billie on, please?" she asked.

The screen snapped back into life, and Billie came in wearing black trousers, silver studded, and a black jacket, and a diamond bracelet. Billie, as she might have been if she had money and power and had done what she wanted to. Or was she?

"Is it true?" Eamon asked this other Billie.

And this Billie nodded: yes. And Billie on the screen said simply, "Think of it this way. It means you are the real Eamon. You always were." And she glanced, just once, out at the tiny bedroom, the unmade bed, the other Billie in the stained jumpsuit. What was she thinking? I'm doing your job for you? Which one of us has the better life? Was she thinking anything at all?

The Billie on the bed said, "I want the two of you to go for a walk, wherever you want to go. Don't take me with you, I don't want to be there. Just go there, now, to Ireland maybe."

"Japan," said the other Billie. Billie was almost touched, until she remembered that the temple and the park was the failsafe locale.

A single perfect tear slid down Eamon's cheek, leaving a trail behind like a snail. In its perfect depths, upside down, was a reflection of the real Billie. A calculation of the light.

"Come on, love," said the other Billie and tapped his shoulder, to go. For some reason, Billie did not want to see them leave the dressing room.

Billie went to make herself a cup of tea. It would be lonely now without a kindly voice to tell her that she deserved it. She thought of her mother, the house in South End, school, Joey's father, her memories. Did they add up to a life?

When she went back into the bedroom, the screen showed Eamon's empty dressing room. On the table top there were the face powder and the mild-colored lipsticks. Desperate Dan Butch Cosmetics. A sweaty white suit hung on a peg. The murmuring of the crowd had faded away. It was silent now, except for the sound of someone sweeping outside. The shadow of a broom slid along the crack of light underneath the door.

Billie reinserted the transceiver card.

"Broadcast down the transceiver network," Billie told her machine. "Tell them all that Eamon is a digital construct. Tell them all that there is no Eamon. Don't say how you know. Try to disguise where the message entered the system. Do not reveal the source of information."

PROCESSING INSTRUCTIONS said a message on the screen, with a little moving clock.

"Locate where Eamon and Billie are in the system now, and save it as a separate file. As long as you operate, keep the file active, but security block it. Never open it, even if I ask you to." Did it understand? "Ice it."

Heaven, where nothing ever happens.

"OK, log off," she said. She slid the CD out of its player, and saw Eamon's picture printed on it, and that's when she began to weep. Water leaked into her mouth tasting of salt. Tears of rage, pity, joy—take your pick, at least you know you're alive. She knew then that Eamon, her Eamon, would always be with her, inside. There were words flickering on the screen. Like all of us, the machine wanted its actions to be authorized.

PLEASE SAY GOODBYE, it asked.

Billie found that she couldn't.

FABLES OF TRANSCENDENCE

John Clute

John Clute, a Canadian writer and SF critic, has lived in England since 1969. He began publishing SF with "A Man Must Die" in *New Worlds* (1966), where much of his early criticism also appeared; further criticism and reviews have appeared in F&SF, the *Washington Post, Omni, Times Literary Supplement*, the *New York Times, New York Review of Science Fiction, Interzone*, and elsewhere. He has thus far published two books collecting much of this work, *Strokes: Essays and Reviews 1966–1986* (1988) and *Look at the Evidence: Essays and Reviews* (1995). He wrote his own entry in the Science Fiction Encyclopedia: "He served as reviews editor of *Foundation* 1980–90, and was a founder of *Interzone* in 1982; he remains advisory editor of that magazine and since 1986 has contributed a review column. His criticism, despite some studiously flamboyant obscurities, remains essentially practical; it has appeared mostly in the form of reviews, some of considerable length. He was the associate editor of the first edition of *The Science Fiction Encyclopedia* (1979) and is coeditor of the *The Encyclopedia of Science Fiction* for which he shared a 1994 Hugo with Peter Nicholls. In 1994 he also received a Pilgrim Award [from the Science Fiction Research Association, for lifetime contributions to criticism and scholarship]." And in 1997 he was editor of the massive *Encyclopedia of Fantasy*, and turned to writing SF novels, as yet forthcoming.

"Fables of Transcendence" was published in *Out of This World*, a collection of original essays celebrating the 1995 exhibition in the National Library in Ottawa devoted to Canadian SF. It talks mainly about A. E. Van Vogt and his work, and how it is atypical of American SF, and reveals how it might be considered a guidepost for future consideration of Canadian SF.

We can call it a number of things. But what we call it gives us different starting points, and each time we start we end up with a different breed of fish. We can call it Utopian Discourse, and start off with Plato or Sir Thomas More—whose *Utopia* in 1516 gave this version of the genre a name—and end up with Zamiatin and Huxley and Orwell and Philip K. Dick as our touchstone figures. Or we can say it's a genre fundamentally devoted to the Fantastic Voyage, and start with Lucian or (say) Cyrano de Bergerac—who wrote a tale in 1659 about traveling to the Moon—and end up with Jules Verne, E. E. Smith, and Poul Anderson, whose romances of space are really romances of geography. Or we can say it is basically a form of Rationalized Gothic, and start off with Mary Shelley—whose *Frankenstein* in 1818 is thought by many to be the first tale genuinely to confront the impact of progress and technology upon history—and end up with Theodore Sturgeon and Gene Wolfe as the carriers of the flame. Or we can call it Scientific Romance, and think of H. G. Wells—whose *Time Machine* in 1895 was the first text to treat this globe as time-bound in its round—and end up with Olaf Stapledon and Arthur C. Clarke and Brian Aldiss as figures who convey a view of the world that takes evolutionary perspectives as central.

Or we can call it science fiction.

But this means we must travel south. It is not, of course, an unusual direction for Canadians to take. We must go the United States, because it is there that science fiction (henceforth SF) began in the late 1920s; it is there that publishers and editors who thought of themselves as SF publishers and editors began to publish stories by SF writers who thought of themselves as SF writers—rather than writers who wrote popular fiction to order—and who sold the magazines in which these SF stories were published to an audience that thought of itself—within half a decade of the founding of *Amazing Stories* in 1926—as making up a unique and privileged family of SF fans. From its beginning, SF was not, in other words, definable simply as a series of texts which expressed a characteristic take on the world (though see below); SF was a highly interactive affinity subculture, many of whose members played—either simultaneously or in turn—all the various roles available within that subculture. People like Isaac Asimov, Damon Knight, Judith Merril, and Frederik Pohl were fans, editors, publishers, writers, convention organizers; and they also had a habit of marrying one another, too. They may have shared a take on the world (see below), but they were also a family.

This did not happen in Canada until much later. Which is

the first thing to understand about Canadian SF. As a *family*, it is very recent. Those Canadians who wrote SF for Americans in (say) 1940, like A. E. Van Vogt, did not do so as members of a family. They wrote alone.

The second thing to understand about Canadian SF—and it's here we begin to enter deep waters—is that when we say it's not in fact American SF, it's almost as though we were saying it was not SF at all. We can argue against the narrowness of this view by arguing that the term SF was never really anything more than shorthand for the nest of widespread genres we've already listed above—a term used by American pirates to gather into a single hoard the Utopian Discourse, the Fantastic Voyage, the Rationalized Gothic, the Scientific Romance, and so forth—and that we're being unduly submissive when we allow the American SF tag to wag the Speculative Fiction dog in this fashion. And we can go on to argue that Canadian speculative fiction—*Consider Her Ways* (1947) by Frederick Grove, say—is just as much SF as the Lensman series by Doc Smith or *Sixth Column* (1949) by Robert A. Heinlein.

No.

In our hearts we must *know* this isn't good enough. In our hearts we must recognize that there was something about American SF in the days of its glory—from about 1925 to about 1965 or 1970—that profoundly marked it precisely as American. The characteristic flavor of twentieth-century SF—I think we must recognize—was the flavor of America; and the characteristic plots of twentieth century SF were versions of the fable of America. This heartwood American SF story was the myth of a frontier-busting, gadget-loving, tall-tale-telling, melting-pot community, linked by blood or affinity into a genuine folk; exempt from mundane history; and guided by cantankerous Competent Men who created new scientific tools to mark the path, to challenge the frontier, to penetrate the barrier of the unknown, to conquer the aliens, to occupy the territory, to stake out the future.

There are a couple of things to note here. Obviously heroes dominate the American SF story, flamboyant inventive geniuses with calluses who figure in so many of the texts we still find ourselves reading; but there is also a sense of community, a sense that heroes are part of a larger enterprise. That heroes can come home. American SF is community SF. And even though it presents its underlying ethos in terms which tend to obliterate the

difference of the Other, it does invite us in. For many of us—
Canadians and others—that invitation to join the fable of
community is like catnip.

Moreover, there is a trust in reason, too. American SF generates a sense that—even though almost every single story
ultimately solves its problems through action—the ethos underlying that action is sustained by arguments no reasonable person
can ultimately deny. These arguments—cleanly and clearly conveyed by the hero, or by his uncle, the garrulous but wise sci-
entist/entrepreneur who scorns the bureaucrats back East—are
not simply undeniable: in the final analysis, they are *clean*. They
bind their readers into futures whose contours are unsullied by
blood-guilt or sophistry, without side-effects, and without any
lasting resentment on the part of the aliens whose frontier has
been smashed, whose culture has been obliterated, whose own
future has been canceled. A cynic might suggest that the logic
of empire always abides with the victors, but once again a comment like this fails to capture the *allure* of the fable, the generosity of American SF's assumption that reasonable suasion,
promulgated by heroes, will bring us all together, even redskins.

Which brings us to a pressing question. Why should the pa-
triotic populist positivism of a literature designed to generate
affirmative (and even triumphal) feelings in the citizens of the
United States be so successful in other parts of the world? Why
(for instance) should Canadian children (in the 1940s and 1950s
I was one) find this alien corn so tasty? Like Disney. Like Coca-
Cola. Why should we swallow this nonsense? Well, partly because it's not exactly nonsense. Or if it *is* nonsense, then the
whole history of the Western world is nonsense. Partly it's because triumph is contagious. When you read American SF you're
on the right side. You are going to win. There will be no side
effects. And partly because it makes for awfully good storytell-
ing.

So it is hard to escape the allure of the classic American SF
myth; and even nowadays—long after many Americans have
ceased promulgating it—its characteristic story-types continue to
have an almost hypnotic effect on non-American writers and
readers and viewers. Both *Star Trek* and *Star Wars*—in TV, film
and book form—obsessively continue to present the world as
conquerable if you have the Force behind you.

Is there any room for Canadian SF? Has there ever been?

There are two answers. One: we can restrict ourselves to

texts like Grove's *Consider Her Ways*, which is a satire in Utopian Discourse mode; or Hugh MacLennan's *Voices in Time* (1980), which is an anatomy of post-holocaust cultural breakdown, without a vestige of the opportunity-loaded flavor of American SF; or Margaret Atwood's *The Handmaid's Tale* (1985), which is a dystopia; or any of the novels of Phyllis Gotlieb or Élizabeth Vonarburg. Though they are certainly speculative fictions, texts like these have little to do with the dominant tone or subject matter of plot-structure of twentieth-century SF, and they tend not to be read as SF by fans. Or Two: we can see if Canadian writers attempting to write within terms of the dominant version of SF have managed—consciously or unconsciously—to convey a dissident sense of the nature of things.

Under One, there seems relatively little to say. Good books have been written and constitute a respectable contribution to the world stock of speculative fiction; and a Canadian concern for the fragility of political and cultural institutions can be seen informing most of them. Under Two, it may be possible to make a suggestion or two, and it might be an idea to glance here at the career of the most prominent single SF writer of Canadian birth.

A. E. Van Vogt has been active from 1939; he is a writer whose prominence from 1940 to 1950 was so marked that most American SF readers thought of him as an unquestionably central figure in American SF, along with Asimov, Heinlein, Clarke (who was British, of course), and very few others. After 1950 he faded from the front rank, partly because of his involvement in Scientology, partly because (as it seems) he burned out, after writing millions of words. In about 1970, he returned to active writing, and enjoyed something of a revival—though he did not regain sufficient fame to be invited to the Science Fiction World Convention held in Winnipeg (his home town) in 1994.

It is the decade of the 1940s, therefore, that must concern us, the period when most American readers of SF thought he was one of them. In retrospect, it is a strange assumption to make, if we actually look carefully at his novels, or novel-like fixups. The most important of these—all at least partly written before he left Canada in 1944, and mostly published in *Astounding Science Fiction* long before they reached book form—are *Slan* (1946), *The Weapon Makers* (1947 but 1946), *The World of A* (1948), *The Voyage of the Space Beagle* (1950), *The Weapon Shops of Isher* (1951), and *The Pawns of Null-A* (1956). They are all profoundly un-

American, as we'll point out. Do they also help define something we might call Canadian SF?

Van Vogt's tales are un-American, to begin with, in their almost total disregard for the details of human community. Their protagonists live in neighborhoods or cities which are generally unnamed, and which are essentially featureless. Countries are also nameless. The planet is probably Earth, but it is not a *special* part of Earth. It is not a promised land. It is, rather, a tabula rasa, a wilderness to be imprinted. But the protagonists who must leave some mark are themselves either without family or have lost their notional families at the moment the tale begins. The destinies they forge (in reality, there is normally only one character who ultimately counts in any of these books) are solitary destinies; though they may ostensibly bear the world on their shoulders, Van Vogt's protagonists are not, in fact, leaders at all, because there is no one in the wilderness to lead. A. E. Van Vogt novels are solitudes; and the fingerprints of passage left by their protagonists constitute not a message to the folk but an indecipherable rune.

These novels are also un-American in the nature of the heroism exhibited or grown into by the protagonist. His heroism—as we have already indicated—cannot be that of the leader of the community who shapes his folk into conquerors of unexplored territories, because of an absence of folk. His heroism is not that of the leader who progresses through the worlds at the head of a folk, but that of the solitary imago-magus who becomes a full-blown superman *through transcendence*. Because there is no intervening tangle of world or community to encumber him, the Van Vogt hero *leaps* into what he is going to become.

Let us put it more positively.

Van Vogt novels pay no attention to ethnicity or nationality, race or color or creed. They pay no attention to civic prides, nation states, or any of the imperial special pleading typical of literatures—like American SF—which plump for the winning side, which treat the cod Social Darwinism to which they're prone as an affirmation of Manifest Destiny to the stars. Moreover, Van Vogt novels—though they are obsessed by supermen—express absolutely no interest in how these super beings affect the details of human discourse. There is no mythopoesis of the culture hero, and there are no prolonged harangues designed to change the mind of the folk—unlike the habitual browbeatings inflicted by Heinlein's typical heroes upon their communities. There is nothing left-wing in Van Vogt; there is nothing fascist.

And finally, Van Vogt novels show an astonishing lack of interest in matters of science or technology, both of which are treated as magic buttons. There is no reverence for senatorial reason.

Canadian SF—in the hands of someone like Van Vogt—is clearly not much like American SF. It is not community based; it is not about the penetration of frontiers; it is not triumphalist about the nation state; it ignores the culture heroes who marshall the folk or who save the world; and it ignores the details of the science and technology which are used by culture heroes to weld the community together and to arm it for conquest. Canadian SF—if A. E. Van Vogt is one of its central founders—can therefore be defined as a genre which translates the fable of survival so central to the Canadian psyche into a fable of lonely transcendence.

Van Vogt is not alone. Gordon R. Dickson was born in Canada, but though he left by the age of twelve or so, there remains something ineluctably Canadian about the solitary take of his heroes on the universe. William Gibson and Robert Charles Wilson were born in the United States, but both have lived in Canada for many years. The protagonist of Gibson's *Neuromancer* is a cyberspace cowboy, a solipsistic hacker in a vast world of owners. He is streetwise—but being streetwise means you know how to survive in the street (or wilderness). It does not mean you understand the street. And Wilson's novels tend to feature transcendental migrations of displaced persons into blank terrains.

For more than half a century, SF has been a literature of culture heroes, conceptual breakthroughs, manifest destiny, and imperial reasonings. Over that period, Canadian SF has been a wainscot halfling, murmuring a more bleak tune. Perhaps it has come time to treat it as the theme.

APPENDIX

CANADIAN SF AWARDS

In *Northern Stars*, we presented a listing of all the winners (and some of the nominees) for two of the annual awards for Canadian science fiction. We are updating those listings here, including only those accolades that have been presented since the publication of *Northern Stars* in 1994.

For complete listings of Canadian SF awards, see these sites on the World Wide Web:

Aurora Awards: <http://www.sentex.net/~dmullin/aurora/>
Prix Boréal, and other francophone SF Awards:
    <http://www.integra.fr/XLII/SFYEAR/TEXT/LISTS/
    AWARDS.html> (Note: this site is in French.)

AURORA AWARDS (1994–1998)

Organized by the Canadian Science Fiction and Fantasy Association, the Auroras are Canada's only national "people's choice" awards. Ballots are distributed through Canadian SF specialty bookstores and periodicals. The readers nominate and then vote on the finalists (a small voting fee is levied on the second ballot), and the awards are presented at the annual national "Canvention."

Nominees for Best Long-Form Work remain eligible for a two-year period. The "Best Other Work" categories recognize anthologies, magazines, nonfiction books, and nonprint media.

(Aurora Awards information courtesy of Dennis Mullin and Jean-Louis Trudel.)

1994—Canvention 14/World SF Convention (Winnipeg)
This was the first Canvention not to be organized by another science fiction gathering.

Best Long-Form Work in English (published 1992–93):
Nobody's Son, Sean Stewart (Maxwell MacMillan 1993)
> NOMINEES:
> *Virtual Light,* William Gibson (Seal 1993)
> *A Song for Arbonne,* Guy Gavriel Kay (Viking 1995)
> *Far-Seer,* Robert J. Sawyer (Ace 1992)

Best Long-Form Work in French (published 1992–93):
Chronoreg, Daniel Sernine (Québec/Amérique 1992)
> NOMINEES:
> *L'Oiseau de feu (2-B),* Jacques Brossard (Leméac 1993)
> *Le Jour-de-Trop,* Joël Champetier (Paulines 1993)

Best Short-Form Work in English:
"Just Like Old Times," Robert J. Sawyer (*On Spec,* Vol. 5, #2)
> NOMINEES:
> "Sophie's Spyglass," Michael Coney (*F&SF,* February 1993)
> "Kissing Hitler," Erik Jon Spigel (*On Spec,* Vol. 5, #1)
> "Body Solar," Derryl Murphy (*On Spec,* Vol. 5, #4)
> "Three Moral Tales," D. L. Schaeffer (*On Spec,* Vol. 5, #1)

Best Short-Form Work in French:
"La Merveilleuse machine de Johann Havel," Yves Meynard (*Solaris* 107)
> NOMINEES:
> "Les Ponts du temps," Jean-Louis Trudel (*Solaris* 107)
> "Dieu, un, zéro," Joël Champetier (*L'Année de la Science-fiction et du Fantastique québécois 1990,* Le Passeur 1993)
> "Le Huitième registre," Alain Bergeron (*Solaris* 107)

Best Other Work in English: *Prisoners of Gravity,* TV Ontario

Best Other Work in French: *Les 42,210 univers de la science-fiction,* Guy Bouchard

Artistic Achievement: Robert Pasternak

Fanzine Achievement: *Under the Ozone Hole,* Karl Johanson & John Herbert

Organizational Fan Achievement: Lloyd Penney, Ad Astra

Other Fan Achievement: Jean-Louis Trudel, promotion of Canadian SF

1995—CANVENTION 15/CAN-CON '95 (OTTAWA)

Best Long-Form Work in English (published 1993–94):
Virtual Light, William Gibson (Seal 1993)
NOMINEES:
Mysterium, Robert Charles Wilson (Bantam/Spectra 1994)
The Callahan Touch, Spider Robinson (Ace 1993)
End of an Era, Robert J. Sawyer (Ace 1994)
Near Death, Nancy Kilpatrick (Pocket 1994)

Best Long-Form Work in French (published 1993–94):
La Mémoire du lac, Joël Champetier (Québec/Amérique 1994)
NOMINEES:
Pour des soleils froids, Jean-Louis Trudel (Fleuve Noir 1994)
Les Voyageurs malgré eux, Élisabeth Vonarburg (Québec/
Amérique 1994)
Manuscrit trouvé dans un secrétaire, Daniel Sernine (Pierre
Tisseyre 1994)
Contes de Tyranaël, Élisabeth Vonarburg (Québec/Amérique
1994)
Récits de Médilhaut, Anne Legault (L'instant même 1994)

Best Short-Form Work in English:
"The Fragrance of Orchids," Sally McBride (*Asimov's,* May
1994)
NOMINEES:
"Small Rain," Paula Johanson (*Prairie Fire,* Vol. 15, #2)
"Fourth Person Singular," Dale L. Sproule (*Northern Frights
2,* Mosaic Press)
"Such Sweet Sorrow," Stephanie Bedwell-Grime (*Writer's
Block,* Summer 1994)
"Writing Critique," Rebecca M. Senese (*Just Write,* May
1994)

Best Short-Form Work in French (tie):
"L'Homme qui fouillait la lumière," Alain Bergeron (*Solaris*
111)
"L'Envoyé," Yves Meynard (*imagine . . . /*Décollages)

NOMINEES:
"Contamination," Jean-Louis Trudel (*Solaris* 108)
"Pas de paradis sans . . . l'enfer (III)," Danielle Tremblay
(*imagine . . . 67*)
"Pas de paradis sans . . . l'enfer (IV)," Danielle Tremblay
(*imagine . . . 68*)

Best Other Work in English: *On Spec*, Copper Pig Writers' Society

Best Other Work in French: *Solaris*, Les Compagnons à temps perdu

Artistic Achievement: Tim Hammell

Fanzine Achievement: *Under the Ozone Hole*, Karl Johanson & John Herbert

Organizational Fan Achievement: Cath Jackel, NonCon & *On Spec*

Other Fan Achievement: Catherine Donahue Girczyc, *Ether Patrol* radio show host

1996 CANVENTION 16/CON-VERSION XIII (CALGARY)

Best Long-Form Work in English (published 1994–95):
The Terminal Experiment, Robert J. Sawyer (HarperPrism 1995; serialized in *Analog*)
NOMINEES:
Resurrection Man, Sean Stewart (Ace 1995)
The Cursed, Dave Duncan (Del Rey 1995)
Mysterium, Robert Charles Wilson (Bantam/Spectra 1994)
Starmind, Spider & Jeanne Robinson (Ace 1995; serialized in *Analog*, August–November 1994)
The Lions of Al-Rassan, Guy Gavriel Kay (Viking 1995)

Best Long-Form Work in French (published 1994–95):
Les Voyageurs malgré eux, Élisabeth Vonarburg (Québec/Amérique 1994)

NOMINEES:

La Rose du désert, Yves Meynard (Le Passeur 1995)
L'Oiseau de feu (2-C), Jacques Brossard (Leméac 1995)
Lame, Esther Rochon (Québec/Amérique 1995)
Les Voyages thanatologiques de Yan Malter, Jean Pierre April
(Québec/Amérique 1994)
Manuscrit trouvé dans un secrétaire, Daniel Sernine (Pierre
Tisseyre 1994; Québec/Amérique 1995)

Best Short-Form Work in English:
"The Perseids," Robert Charles Wilson (*Northern Frights 3*)
NOMINEES:
"Lost in the Mail," Robert J. Sawyer (*TransVersions 3*)
"Tea and Hamsters," Michael Coney (*F&SF,* January 1995)
"The Summer Worms," David Nickle (*Northern Frights 3*)
"The Dead Go Shopping," Stephanie Bedwell-Grime
(*Northern Frights 3*)

Best Short-Form Work in French:
"Équinoxe," Yves Meynard (*La Rose du désert,* Le Passeur)
NOMINEES:
"Le peuple de Protée," Jean-Louis Trudel (*Solaris* 115)
"La Cité de Penlocke," Natasha Beaulieu (*imagine . . .* 72)
"Adieu aux armes pour une fourmi-soldat," Claude-Michel
Prévost (*Solaris* 112)
"L'Attrait du bleu," Esther Rochon (*Solaris* 113)

Best Other Work in English: *ReBoot,* BLT Productions

Best Other Work in French: *Solaris,* Les Compagnons à temps
perdu

Artistic Achievement: Jean-Pierre Normand

Fanzine Achievement: *Under the Ozone Hole,* Karl Johanson &
John Herbert

Organizational Fan Achievement: Jean-Louis Trudel, SFSF Boréal et Prix Boréal

Other Fan Achievement: Larry Stewart, entertainer

1997—CANVENTION 17/PRIMEDIA (MARKHAM)

Best Long-Form Work in English (published 1995–96):
Starplex, Robert J. Sawyer (Ace 1996; serialized in *Analog*, July–October 96)
NOMINEES:
Shadow of Ashland, Terence M. Green (Forge 1996)
No Quarter, Tanya Huff (DAW 1996)
Child of the Night, Nancy Kilpatrick (Raven 1996)
Resurrection Man, Sean Stewart (Ace 1995)

Best Long-Form Work in French (published 1995–96):
La Rose du désert, Yves Meynard (Le Passeur 1995)
NOMINEES:
Lame, Esther Rochon (Québec/Amérique 1995)
L'Arc-en-cercle, Daniel Sernine (Héritage 1995)
Les Rêves de la mer, Élisabeth Vonarburg (Alire 1996)

Best Short-Form Work in English:
"Peking Man," Robert J. Sawyer (*Dark Destiny III: Children of Dracula*, White Wolf)
NOMINEES:
"In Your Dreams," Stephanie Bedwell-Grime (*Parsec*, April–May 1996)
"Face Dances," Rebecca Senese (*On Spec*, Vol. 8, #2)
"Memory Games," Dale L. Sproule (*Tesseracts 5*)
"The Piano Player Has No Fingers," Edo van Belkom (*Palace Corbie 7: The Piano Player Has No Fingers*, Merrimack Books)
"Bethlehem," Peter Watts (*Tesseracts 5*)

Best Short-Form Work in French:
"Lamente-toi, Sagesse!" Jean-Louis Trudel (*Genèses*, J'ai Lu)
NOMINEES:
"Laika," Natasha Beaulieu (*Solaris* 117)
"*thea* ou le Jour venu," Alain Bergeron (*Solaris* 119)
"La Maison douleur," Francine Pelletier (*La Maison douleur et autres histoires à faire peur*, Vents d'Ouest)
"Le Début du cercle," Élisabeth Vonarburg (*Genèses*, J'ai Lu)

Best Other Work in English: *On Spec,* The Copper Pig Writers' Society

Best Other Work in French: *Solaris,* Les Compagnons à temps perdu

Artistic Achievement: Jean-Pierre Normand

Fanzine Achievement: *Sol Rising,* Theresa Wojtasiewicz

Organizational Fan Achievement: Yvonne Penney, SF Saturday

Other Fan Achievement: Lloyd Penney (fan-writing)

1998—CANVENTION 18/CONCEPT (MONTRÉAL)

Best Long-Form Work in English (published 1996–97):
Black Wine, Candas Jane Dorsey (Tor 1997)
NOMINEES:
Trader, Charles de Lint (Tor 1997)
Shadow of Ashland, Terence M. Green (Tor 1996)
Frameshift, Robert J. Sawyer (Tor 1997)
Illegal Alien, Robert J. Sawyer (Ace 1997)

Best Long-Form Work in French (published 1996–97):
L'Odyssée du Pénélope, Jean-Pierre Guillet (Héritage 1997)
NOMINEES:
Corps-machines et rêves d'anges, Alain Bergeron (Vents d'Ouest 1997)
Coeur de fer, Joël Champetier (Orion 1997)
Nelle de Vilvèq, Francine Pelletier (Alire 1997)
Aboli, Esther Rochon (Alire 1996)
Le Jeu de la perfection, Élisabeth Vonarburg (Alire 1996)

Best Short-Form Work in English:
"Three Hearings on the Existence of Snakes in the Human Blood Stream," James Alan Gardner (*Asimov's,* February 1997)
NOMINEES:
"The PlayTime Case," David Chato (*On Spec,* Winter 1997)
"Divisions," Eric Choi (*Tesseracts 6*)
"The Fishmonger's Emeralds," Katie Harse (*Tesseracts 6*)

"The Watley Man and the Green-Eyed Girl," Eileen Kernaghan (*TransVersions* #7)
"The Hand You're Dealt," Robert J. Sawyer (*Free Space*, Tor)
"Prescribed Burn," Jena Snyder (*Tesseracts 6*)

Best Short-Form Work in French:
"Une Lettre de ma mère," Yves Meynard (*Solaris* 121)
NOMINEES:
"La Voyeuse," Manon Brunet (*imagine* . . . 78)
"Badelaire l'assassin," Joël Champetier (*Concerto pour six voix*, Médiaspaul)
"Dans ses yeux une flamme," Daniel Sernine (*Entre voisins*, Pierre Tisseyre)
"Fictions et fantascience," Jean-Louis Trudel (*Solaris* 121)

Best Other Work in English: *Northern Frights 4*, Don Hutchinson, ed.

Best Other Work in French: *Solaris*, Hugues Morin, ed.

Artistic Achievement: Jean-Pierre Normand

Fanzine Achievement: *Warp Factor*, Chris Chartier, ed.

Organizational Fan Achievement: Peter Halasz (NSFFS)

Other Fan Achievement: Larry Stewart (entertainer)

PRIX BORÉAL

Founded in 1980 by the organizers of the Boréal convention in Québec City, and presented annually by the nonprofit corporation Société du Fantastique et de la Science Fiction Boréal Inc. All SF magazines and fanzines submit a list of dedicated SF readers from which a jury of about ten people is composed. This jury, in turn, selects five to six finalists in each category. Ballots are then distributed and all readers can vote, free of charge.

(All information on the Prix Boréal courtesy Jean-Louis Trudel.)

1994, MONTRÉAL

Meilleur livre (best novel): *L'Oiseau de feu. Tome 2B: le Grand projet*, Jacques Brossard (Leméac 1993)

Meilleure nouvelle (best short story): "Le Sang et l'oiseau," Yves Meynard (*Solaris* 105)

Meilleure production critique (best critical works): Guy Bouchard

1995, OTTAWA

Meilleur livre (best novel): *Manuscrit trouvé dans un secrétaire*, Daniel Sernine (Pierre Tisseyre 1994)

Meilleure nouvelle (best short story): "L'Homme qui fouillait la lumière," Alain Bergeron (*Solaris* 111)

Meilleure production critique (best critical works): Claude Janelle

1996, MONTRÉAL

Meilleur livre (best book): *La Rose du désert*, Yves Meynard (Collection, Le Passeur, 1995)

Meilleure nouvelle (best short story): "La Cité de Penlocke," Natasha Beaulieu (*imagine . . .* 72)

Meilleure production critique (best critical works): Élisabeth Vonarburg

1997, MONTRÉAL

Meilleur livre (best novel): *Les Rêves de la mer*, Élisabeth Vonarburg (Alire 1996)

Meilleure nouvelle (best short story): "Le Début du cercle," Élisabeth Vonarburg (*Genèses*, anthology, J'ai Lu, 1996)

Meilleure production critique (best critical works): Alain Bergeron

1998, MONTRÉAL

Meilleur livre (best novel): *Corps-machines et rêves d'anges*, Alain Bergeron

Meilleure nouvelle (best short story): "Une Lettre de ma mère," Yves Meynard

Meilleure production critique (best critical works): Hugues Morin

Meilleur artiste (best artist): Jacques Lamontagne

Meilleur fanéditeur (best fan publisher): Hugues Morin